Temp  *d.*

"I am no doll." Tempest knew she should turn away but she could not.

"I can see that. You are a woman as other women." His gaze went over the loose blouse that did not fully conceal her upper body. "And yet there is more about you." Now Justin was almost musing. "A quality of mystery that intrigues me. Were I not otherwise committed, it might be different."

"I must go." His idle words stung and hurt. "I must see to Savora."

"See to me instead." With one smooth practiced gesture he swung her toward him, hard against his chest, and his firm mouth closed over hers before she could even begin to struggle.

Other books by Anne Carsley

DEFIANT DESIRE
THIS TRIUMPHANT FIRE
THE GOLDEN SAVAGE

ANNE CARSLEY

TEMPEST

PINNACLE BOOKS   NEW YORK

This is a work of fiction. All the characters and events portrayed in this book are fictional, and any resemblance to real people or incidents is purely coincidental.

TEMPEST

Copyright © 1985 by Anne Carsley

An original Pinnacle Books edition, published for the first time anywhere.

First printing/February 1985

ISBN: 0-523-42232-6

Can. ISBN: 0-523-43218-6

Printed in the United States of America

PINNACLE BOOKS, INC.
1430 Broadway
New York, New York 10018

9   8   7   6   5   4   3   2   1

1

Confrontation

Savannah, Georgia
March 1831

Tempest approached the house warily, looking up at its bulk, white and square in the encircling tangle of uncut bushes and trees. There was no sign of a light and, strain her ears as she might, no sound other than that of the chill spring wind rattling in the branches. The sickle moon glistened low through thin, scudding clouds and caught her eye for a brief moment before she darted toward the tall oak that grew near one wall.

There was no time for hesitation. It was far later than she had intended to stay out and dawn was not far away. She slipped between the low branches and climbed with swift, practiced movements, pausing now and then to listen. Excitement made her heart hammer, and her mouth was dry.

Now she reached the spreading limbs that meshed together just above the window at the third story of the house. Cautiously, she balanced herself and drew one shutter back. White curtains billowed out as she swung over the sill and down. Safe in her own room! Her legs shook in the release of tension, and she leaned against the wall, letting relief have its way.

The sudden flare of light startled Tempest as much as the harsh voice that crackled out at her. "Well, well! Creeping

1

back in after your night's pleasure? Where have you been? Answer me!" The lamp rattled down onto the table and another was lit as Tempest's accuser moved toward her.

It was all Tempest could do not to recoil from the tall woman, gray hair in one long braid, her sharp features made even harsher by the bright lamp she held. The fierce black eyes burned into Tempest's as her mouth twisted with growing rage.

"Aunt Hannah, I can explain. This is not what you think. Please listen to me . . ." Tempest tried to make her voice soft and mollifying, but her own temper was rising.

"Listen to your lies! I'll not waste my time! I know what you've been up to. Acting the slut. How long have you been sneaking out?" She lunged toward Tempest. The hard fingers caught her shoulder and spun her toward the long mirror on one wall. "Look at yourself and see the shame on your face!"

Their faces were reflected back, the wrinkled angry one with the papery skin, sunken cheeks, and jutting bones beside the smooth white one. Tempest wondered if she would look like her aunt when she was old. She stared at herself as if she were a stranger, and in a way, she was. She saw her flaming red hair falling over her shoulders and framing her high-cheekboned face with its small straight nose, arching dark brows, and deep gray eyes. She had not removed the paint she had worn in the play and it accentuated her features, making them glow and entice. Her skin had a shimmer to it and the tiny cleft in her right cheek, a birthmark that most of the Mallorys had, was brushed with color to enhance it. Her chin was rounded and stubborn. Her long legs and slender waist showed to advantage in the old gown she had twisted high in order to climb. The bodice was too tight and her breasts threatened to spill out. She was taller than most girls of nineteen, but that had proved an advantage earlier.

"You are painted like the slut you are!" Her aunt held her remorselessly at the mirror. The familiar litany would start any minute now. The pattern had been set from Tempest's childhood.

Tempest let herself sag a little and dropped her eyes. "I only went walking up by the road to see the strollers and the carriages. I would have been in much earlier, but I saw lights in the house and I was afraid someone would be up. I've done nothing wrong." Should she let her voice shake just a bit?

Plead dizziness? Why had Savora not left the signal for her? What had Aunt Hannah done to her friend and slave?

Too late. Her aunt was shrilling on, and now nothing could prevent her from continuing. "Not many lone women my age would have taken in a penniless orphan. Your father wasted everything away, didn't marry properly. That wretched lawyer friend of his couldn't find anyone else to take you. Anyone would think you'd be grateful, but no! A hardship is all you have ever been."

She paused to catch her breath, and Tempest tried to speak but the tide rolled over her. Aunt Hannah would not stop, could not stop, until the list of her grievances was done.

"Little enough I had, and less now. You had to go scandalize the convent with all your talk about playacting, so they sent you back. Running away from the boarding school in Boston, taking up with improper people, refusing to learn the womanly arts, and you a charity pupil—disgraceful! A sin, that's what it was."

Once this had caused Tempest unbearable pain, but she had learned to endure and think of other things. Aunt Hannah's carping voice faded away. Now her mind went back three weeks and the delight rose once more.

Tempest stood in the grove near the main road leading into the city and watched the newly arrived troupe of players rehearse some of the acts they would perform that night in the tent being raised. Excitement gripped her at the sword fight, the tumbling, a lively dance, and a milling crowd scene, where several saucy girls cavorted before an angry fat man. Two older women carried on an urgent conversation while a younger trilled one high note over and over. A juggler was performing for the travelers who paused to watch, and a young man was raising a banner that spread out in the unseasonably mild wind to announce THE LINWOOD PLAYERS; SHORT ACTS AND PANTOMIMES, MUSIC AND DANCE.

"You could see better if you went closer."

The soft drawling voice made her whirl around in surprise. The young man standing a few feet away was only a year or two older than Tempest, casually dressed in brown, but his olive complexion and heavy-lidded dark eyes and tossing black curls gave him a romantic aura, which was enhanced by the ruffled shirt and long cape he wore.

"I can see quite well. And I really should be going now."
Had she really spoken those prim words? Yes, she had.

He had stepped closer, swirled that cape, made an elegant
leg, and said, "But now that I have seen you, fair one, I can
never content myself until we have spoken together and you
have seen my domain."

She had laughed, unable to resist, and extended her hand in
a lavishly overdone gesture. "May I ask my lord's most worthy
name?"

He touched her fingers and was a boy again. "I am Raoul.
Will you come?"

She had been expected home. Savora was probably searching for her, and she was wearing the old gown she used for
walks or gardening. Nothing but the moment had mattered.

"For a short time only. You may call me Miranda." They
laughed together, and so it had begun.

That first day Raoul had taken her among the troupe, showed
her the folding painted scenery, costumes, paints, played the
elaborate game they had started, and finally confided to her his
dream of becoming a great dramatic actor in one of the New
York theaters. His parents, Austrian immigrants with a passion
for the land, objected and so he had run away. Tempest
revealed little of herself, but he had not found this odd as he
talked constantly of his hopes and ambitions. By the end of the
first week she was meeting him every night, watching the
various acts in the windy tent, and returning his kisses, which
were the first to stir her flesh even as her imagination was
stirred by the performances of the actors. She had been forced
to take Savora into her confidence so as to get in and out of the
house. The slave was cautious but agreeable.

One night, two of the dancers in the crowd scene had a fight
and refused to go on. Almost casually, Tempest offered to stand
in. Raoul spoke to George Linwood, manager of the company,
who, somewhat the worse for drink as he generally was,
laughed and agreed. Tempest, frightened and delighted, had let
her face be painted, put on a low-cut, rather worse for wear
green gown, and moved out with the others. At first she was
stiff and shaky, but Raoul took her hand, leading her in an
impromptu dance that was at first hesitant, then bold. Round
and round they spun until intoxication overtook Tempest and

she could think of nothing except the applause where on previous nights there had been none.

Tempest was allowed to remain in the crowd scene with Raoul at her side even after the dancers returned. Raoul, who was beginning to want more from Tempest than kisses, had urged her to come with the troupe, and she half considered it. The night before last, George Linwood had spoken to her as she came offstage.

Tempest thought she would remember all her life the wind flapping at the walls of the tent, the dimming lanterns, Raoul's blazing eyes, and the chatter of the company around them. The balding little man had a power all his own as he said, "We're leaving in the next couple of days, Miranda. There's no room in the company for you. In nearly every town someone like you comes along and has to be discouraged." Tempest's cheeks blazed, but she had held her head high as he continued. "You're different. There is something about you. A fire, a presence. Passable now, just barely, but in a few years . . ." He shrugged. "Study, learn. Who knows?"

She smiled. "I thank you for your words and this experience. I understand." It was confirmation and accolade, well worth the humiliation of knowing that the entire troupe must have seen part of this encounter time and again. Somehow she would carry out the promise of his words. It was a resolve that made her hold back from Raoul's arms as though she had already passed from him.

"Virgin!" The word exploded into her hearing as her aunt's face was thrust close to hers. "Or shall I get the midwife to examine you?"

Tempest jerked from her reverie and looked in horror into the angry eyes. Aunt Hannah's recollection of Tempest's childhood offenses could go on for hours. What had caused this turnabout? She said carefully. "What are you accusing me of?"

"You have been sneaking out for one reason only. A man! Has he taken you? Of course he has!"

"That is not true! I swear it."

"Even if you are to have a child, you could not be very far along." Aunt Hannah's voice dropped from stridency to a musing note. "I can see that I have been remiss in my duty and have kept you too long with me. You are ripe for marriage. I shall inform your suitor of your consent immediately." She put both hands together and looked at Tempest in triumph. "That is the only answer."

"What are you talking about?" Tempest fought for control; she must not give away the revulsion she felt. "What suitor?"

Instead of answering at once, her aunt picked up one of the hand bells on the table and rang it sharply. Almost at once there was a knock on the door and a tall, middle-aged slave entered. "Wake up that lazy Savora and have her make the pink room ready. You check the lock and prepare to remain on watch outside it. Come back in ten minutes. We shall escort Mistress Tempest there at that time. Hurry and do as you are told!"

The woman nodded and withdrew, her expression incurious. Tempest rounded on Aunt Hannah, who was now smiling as though pleased with herself. The flickering light from the lamps cast shadows up and down the walls while the air in the room seemed heavy and stale with old fury.

"You have asked about your suitor, my dear. Naturally you are curious as to what has been arranged for you." She paused and let her silence draw out. Tempest did not give her the satisfaction of another question, but simply stood facing her. "Mr. Morton Williams of Tidesmar plantation has honored you with a request of marriage to his son and heir. They are wealthy. The match will provide for us all."

"You think to sell me! Is that it? Well, I will not be sold. You cannot force me! Do you think I do not know Eugene Williams is short of wits and his father a known lecher? Would you in all conscience send me into such a situation? I will have none of it." Tempest caught her breath and saw her mirrored reflection, a flame of wrath with drawn brows and clenched fists. It was such a relief to cry out her true feelings. "You have never wanted me here, and that has always been made clear. Very well, let me have the jewelry that I brought here with me. I will sell it and go my way. I can support myself washing, scrubbing, tutoring, or anything else while I study to be an actress! It is all I have ever wanted."

"Nonsense. A young lady does not do such things. You have nothing left, at any rate. I sold those few trinkets to feed us long ago. You have your duty to me in my old age." Aunt Hannah's voice was rising, and her nostrils were faintly blue. "Mr. Williams is eager for a decision as to the wedding date. It is a better marriage than you could ever expect."

"I will not marry Eugene Williams." Tempest grated the words out. She felt suddenly drained. "These are not medieval times. You cannot force me."

There was a slight scratch at the door, and the slave returned. Aunt Hannah motioned for her to approach. Her voice was triumphant as she said, "Agnes, we will take Mistress Tempest to the other room. She has a touch of the brain swelling and must have quiet. Not a word of this to the other slaves, mind you." She waited for the woman's nod, then turned to Tempest. "There are ways and ways to treat you. A few doses of some of my potions will render you calm and compliant. If you persist in this behavior, I, as your guardian, can easily commit you to the local asylum. Think on it."

Tempest knew she spoke the truth. Her aunt was fully capable of carrying out her threats and none would ask whether the action was right. A rebellious young girl had no rights. She, Tempest Mallory, was not regarded as a person. She was a commodity to be sold, a thing to be made useful. Was this how Savora and the other slaves felt?

She let her head droop. "I am so tired. If I could just sleep. Can't we talk about this tomorrow?"

"There is nothing to discuss. You will do as I say." The slave took one arm and Aunt Hannah the other, Tempest swaying slightly against the holds.

Further protest would be useless, Tempest knew. One thing was certain—she could not remain in this house any longer. But she needed time to think of a stratagem by which she could escape.

The room where she was imprisoned was small, sparsely furnished, papered in faded pink. There were no books or papers, and the only lamp had been taken away. She lay down on the sagging bed, fighting the urge to throw herself at the door. Her aunt was murmuring something to the slave just outside, but Tempest could not catch the words. No matter— nothing could be accomplished until daylight. Rest was an urgent necessity.

She took long, deep breaths as she relaxed, trying to will herself to sleep.

There was a soft noise at the door, a faint scrabbling, then silence again. Tempest sat upright, felt in the drawer beside the bed for the stub of candle and lighting materials always placed in the rooms, lit it, and felt much better. She saw that a small piece of paper had been thrust well under the door so that it could not be missed.

When she unfolded it, she noticed that the print was precise and tiny, just as she had taught Savora.

Potion in your food and drinks. Aunt knows about actors. Wedding soon.

Tempest extinguished the candle and felt the walls bend toward her.

2

The Chosen Role

Tempest had reason to be thankful for Savora's warning when Aunt Hannah's personal slave, Agnes, who had been set to keep guard on her, entered the room later with a tray of ham, biscuits, jam, and hot tea—her favorites, which she would ordinarily have devoured. She was starving now and her stomach growled in response.

Agnes eyed her dourly. "I'll just leave this. You eat it all up. Yo' auntie feeling real bad upset." She was fond of her eccentric mistress and clearly blamed Tempest for all the uproar.

Tempest pulled the mug of tea toward her and said, "I hope she is better soon. I ought to go and see her, but I just must rest . . ." She allowed the words to trail away.

"She say you stay here. You will." It was a flat statement.

"Yes. Of course." Tempest lay back on the pillows and pretended to sip at the tea. Under her lashes she watched Agnes stare at her, shake her head, and march out the door, locking it securely behind her.

Seconds later Tempest was up, hiding the food behind the high old chest of drawers, pouring tea and water into the chamber pot. She was very thirsty, but dared not risk even a sip. Aunt Hannah's skill with herbs was too great. Then she dug in the wide compartments of the lower drawer and allowed herself to smile. Nothing in this house was ever thrown away. The rusting keys were still there, just as they had been years ago when she had sought amusement on a rainy day. So was the old black shawl. She caught them up and thrust everything far under the bed, then lay down and pretended sleep while her mind whirled with her scheme.

Agnes checked on her several times in the next dragging hours. Each time the slave's footsteps grew wearier. Surely she would report to her mistress and then rest. Aunt Hannah was given to spells of excitement and exhaustion, alertness and retreat. All required the total attention of Agnes. This would be Tempest's only chance. She had to get to Savora and could only pray that the other girl, who had already helped her so much these past weeks, would do it once again.

After the last check, Tempest tied the shawl over her shoulders and took up the keys to try them in the door. It was a slow, agonizing procedure. Try as she would to be silent, she could not. They scraped and twisted. Her hands were sweaty and her lips bitten before the second to last one finally turned the lock back.

There was no time to spare. Thankful that she had tossed in the bed until it was so rumpled that the first glance would be confusing, Tempest eased the door open and saw that the hall was empty. She fastened the door again and in the next moment was a swift shadow on the stairs.

She had only a vague sense of time, but it must be at least late afternoon. Savora would likely be in the kitchen helping the old cook, who had been born into service here and was now wandering in her wits. She could remember nothing except her one skill. Her niece was like her, but useful for heavy work, and their one male slave would be working in the vegetable patch. Tempest decided to make for the kitchen.

It seemed to take forever. She dared not hurry and knew she must. Each door, every unused room and creaking stair, cried out that she was running away. Often Tempest had thought to do this and had held back, thinking to bring Aunt Hannah to understand her need to go her own way. She should have known better, Tempest told herself sternly. Now she slipped into a narrow dark hall and expelled a silent breath of relief.

One more stairway and she would enter the west wing of the kitchen.

Just then a slim form came swiftly around the corner and Tempest collided with it so that both reeled from the impact. Tempest's first thought was: Agnes! Run! But how and where? In the next moment she was holding Savora's arm and laughing silently in relief. She pulled the other girl with her into the nearest room, a tiny storage area lighted by a slit high in the wall.

"How did you get out? I was going to try to take the key while Agnes slept so that I could come talk to you." Savora was whispering, her black eyes huge in the slanting planes of her face. She was a slim, wiry girl with smooth ebony skin and hair and a grave manner that made her seem older than her twenty years. "You are going, aren't you?"

"If you will help me. Can you just go and listen for anyone coming while I go into the sitting room? I have to take the household money." Tempest had pangs of conscience over that, but the jewelry she had brought with her to this house had been costly, perhaps intended for her dower, but certainly to be kept for her. She would save and pay her aunt back at any rate.

"On one condition." Savora was standing tall now, her voice slightly breathless.

"Condition?" Tempest was puzzled and time was galloping on. She had to hurry. "I don't understand."

"Take me with you!" The normally reticent Savora exuded a power of demand that shook her body. "I have to go. I've thought about it, tried to plan, but they'd have me back in days. Two of us would have a much better chance!"

Tempest remembered the shocked, sick girl she had first known and, in her own loneliness, befriended. Savora had been born in freedom, but stolen away with her mother, sold across the Carolinas, where she saw her mother slain and was herself raped repeatedly before being set aside for breeding purposes. She had sickened and was sold cheaply. Her apathy at that time made her seem dull-witted, but Tempest, in violation of the law of the state, taught her to read and write and they shared much. Later Aunt Hannah discouraged their friendship and they were very careful after that. They seemed mistress and maid, but this irked them both.

Now Tempest said, "Stealing a slave is a terrible offense. What if we are caught?"

"Two are more clever than one, and I have learned to hide just as you have learned to conceal your feelings in these past years. I have to be free or try to be, Tempest. You will not marry into safety because you want freedom to live your own life. I know the risks; how could I not? But I have to try." Her eyes shone as she spoke.

"I'm going to slave country—Jamaica. My friend Morna is not long married and lives there now. Her husband owns a plantation. I lived with her family before coming here and later we went to the same school for a while." Tempest paused. She knew Savora did not really care where they went. She touched the other girl's moist hand. "Of course you must come. We'll make it!"

"You won't be sorry. I swear." Savora sounded near tears.

Tempest drew away from the emotions of the moment. She cracked the door and looked out into the silent hall. "Let's hurry."

The house was calm and silent in the late afternoon peace as Tempest, Savora on watch, crept into the sitting room/den which served Aunt Hannah as both, opened the cluttered desk, and removed the purse, which was filled with bills and silver. "I will repay it." The words rang over and over in her mind, but it did not make her task more palatable. She thrust the money into the bodice of her old dark blue gown. Her shoes were thin but still wearable. Dressed in this way she would seem just another poor woman, one of the many in Savannah who sought to better her lot. What had Morna written? "More people are coming here all the time; I suppose they think to make their fortunes. Robert has trouble with all the missionaries exciting our slaves. You wouldn't believe how many, and lacking in knowledge, too, come over from America and England." Tempest paused. Surely Morna would welcome her for the sake of their friendship. She had written of a formal invitation to be sent to Aunt Hannah. A few months could make little difference in her arrival. So she told herself even as doubt gnawed at her mind. What would Morna be like now?

There was no time for hesitation. Tempest slipped down the stairs like a wraith, stopping only to toss the ancient cloak Agnes used for garden work over her arm, and then moving out the side door, which had been left ajar by Savora just minutes before. If anyone had appeared, Savora would have begun to cough. The silence meant safety.

The air was cool and the sky was gray, but Tempest was heated with excitement as she darted into the shelter of the long unpruned firethorn bushes where Savora waited. She held a battered reticule, a larger cloth bag, and a bonnet and cloak in her arms. When she held the bonnet out to Tempest, who took it thankfully and settled it over her fiery hair, their glances met and they smiled, not daring to speak or congratulate themselves as yet.

"Now we run." Tempest pulled her skirts up and Savora did likewise. Then, for one moment, Tempest looked upward at the house standing unkempt in the surrounding bushes. Here she had been sheltered and here she had grown up. She felt a pang, but smothered it quickly. She whirled and ran toward the road as hard as she could go, Savora just behind.

They kept to the wooded areas, went on barely discernible paths, circled the few houses, alternately running, walking, and stumbling. The one aim was to get as far away from the house as they could before total darkness. They saw very few travelers and those went on horseback without looking around. Tempest thought she knew how the hunted must feel and forced herself to concentrate on the role she must play in the very near future.

In spite of all their efforts, it was full night and a slight drizzle had begun to fall when they came to the main road, which branched out and led into Savannah proper. Public carriages often plied this area; Tempest hoped they would be fortunate enough to find one now. She adjusted the shawl and cloak more closely around her body, made sure the bonnet hid her features, and checked their money, now deep in the reticule that hung over one arm. Savora was also muffled, with her head bent and arms folded. Tempest imagined the burdens of the world, poverty and unending depression, youth gone and loneliness. She allowed her shoulders to slump as her normal proud stance seemed to shrink. Then she and Savora walked as briskly as they dared. Several riders and three closed carriages passed them before Savora called out.

"One's coming. Shall I wave?"

"No, act as if you're helping me." Tempest took Savora's

arm and they turned together as the conveyance, more wagon than carriage, rattled up and stopped as Tempest flapped one arm agitatedly.

She made her voice both demanding and querulous. "Sir, sir, can you take us to the square? We're late now and they'll be going on! Will you and hurry?"

The driver was fat and middle-aged, a cap pulled down over his ears. He surveyed them for a second and addressed Savora. "Where does your mistress want to go, girl? I'm stopping for the night, taking these boxes in." He waved at the covered stacks behind his seat. "Not much room."

"I need to get to my kin over by Washington Square. Can you take us even close?" Tempest let her words run together. "Oh, you think we can't pay. You—get those pennies out. Be quick!"

Savora leaned around her and fumbled in the reticule, then held up a coin so the man could see. He snickered and nodded. "Get in and hold on. You're just lucky I'm going pretty close." Tempest started toward the low bar that was used as a step and caught a whiff of the rum he had been drinking. "Want a sip?"

She sniffed and shuddered. Savora jumped up and began to pull at Tempest. He flicked his whip at the horses, which moved on as he began to laugh. They tumbled together, trying to act upset at his actions. Tempest felt a wave of relief. He seemed drunk enough not to remember them, and if he did so, it would be a vague muffled woman whom he had horrified; few people paid attention to slaves as persons.

Soon he burst into song and urged them to join in. At Tempest's indignant refusal, he grew louder. Under the cover she bent closer to Savora and began to whisper while they rolled on into the well-defined, precisely laid out city, with its individual squares, gardens, and neat houses.

"We'll go down to the wharf and look for a ship called the *Mermaid*, which is to have sailed for Jamaica, where my husband, a Wesleyan missionary, waits. I have been ill, you stayed to tend me, and now it is urgent that I reach him as soon as possible. Naturally, since there is no *Mermaid* and my wits are a bit addled, we must get a ship of some sort. Missionaries are poor, generally always respected, sometimes laughed at. We will bargain as best we can. Anything to get there, and I

know Morna will help until I can pay her back." Tempest
thought wryly that a lot depended on Morna, but she herself
was strong and talented. There must be many things she could
do, and they would be done in freedom.

"Oh, the lassie, she turned over and she kicked another
one . . ." The driver was winding down, his voice cracking
as he took a pull at his bottle. Tempest had a wild desire to
laugh. It caught Savora and they rocked together, hands over
their mouths, while he began to mutter the further exploits of
the lassie.

The half canopy sheltered the driver and the boxes but not
the passengers. The drizzle was sporadic and chilling, but each
turn of the wheels brought them closer to their goal. Tempest
looked out at the now widening streets bordered by tall oaks,
sweet bay, and magnolias interspersed with the vines that
would later flower in a tumbling blaze of color. She came
shopping with Savora or Agnes infrequently and had, on rare
occasions, managed to come into the city alone. Once she had
come to the river, watched the tall ships move along it, and
longed to go with them. Now she would do so in circumstances
she had never imagined.

They moved along the East Road, turned into Houston
Street, and rattled to a halt. The driver turned back to them and
jerked his finger to the right. "I'm going on a few blocks.
Square's yonder. Get out now." His voice blurred thickly with
drunkenness but his palm shaped itself to receive the coins that
Savora had ready. Tempest feared he would complain at the
amount, but he waved them down and began his song again,
not looking back as they stood in the rain.

The sense of urgency gripped Tempest sharply and she
began to feel that pursuit had begun. She and Savora moved
rapidly, oblivious to the cutting wind. They passed the square
and its monument, rounded the small elegant houses, and then
went into another section of cross streets and several alleys,
emerging onto a wider way and down at last to the wharf area
at the great bluff.

It was crowded with ships of all sizes, merchantmen taking
on cargo, others disgorging commodities, sailors and passengers and tradesmen thronging about even this late in the
evening. Onlookers stood about exchanging jokes and laughter

and commenting loudly. The warehouses reared dark against the sky and the red river beyond was peppered with raindrops.

Tempest and Savora approached one tall man who lounged apart, picking his teeth with a straw. She leaned on the black girl, who asked after the *Mermaid* and received the expected response.

"But there has to be!" Tempest's voice was shaky. "It is God's will, you see, and my husband . . ." She broke off and looked away.

Someone guffawed in the little silence that ensued. The tall man shifted uneasily. "This is no place for a woman at night. Look, I tell you what. Go on down until you find the *Corinthian.* Ask for the captain, and say Ed sent you. He might be able to tell you something. Or maybe even take you on if he's in the mood. I know he sails soon for the islands."

"Thank you, sir. We shall pray for you. Bless you!" Tempest was fervent in her gratitude.

The growing audience began to laugh, but a few of the men doffed their hats and murmured civilly. Others peered at Tempest, seeking her face under the old bonnet.

She jerked at Savora's arm. "Come on! We have to try. I must get there. God may move the captain's heart. I pray so!" Was she overdoing it? The urgency she felt was certainly not simulated.

Ed stood aside for them, the rest of the men following suit. They went down the wharf as quickly as they dared and no one followed. Tempest heard someone say, "Too many missionaries! All crazy, if you ask me."

Another voice said, "Careful. You never know."

She smiled to herself in spite of the disquiet that plagued her. Pagans, all of them, and she one herself!

When they came to the small ship with the drooping sails, her bulk seeming to crouch low on the water and belying her proud name, Tempest approached a squat, scowling man who stood watching two sailors carrying a box on board. At her request for the captain, he snapped, "You're talking to him. What do you want?"

She recited the now familiar litany, almost beginning to believe it, while Savora chimed in. His expression grew angrier as they spoke and his brows drew together. The men stopped work and watched. Tempest thought all her life came down to this moment on a dark wharf with the *Corinthian* framed against the sky and danger waiting.

"I don't have much room. What'll you pay?"

She named the lowest figure that seemed feasible and he grinned in derision, his face settling back into the discontented lines. "Not worth one inch of space! I'll not haggle, either. I can take on another two or three for triple that sum and still lose. Charity has no place in the seafaring business. Get on with you!" He turned his back on them.

Tempest heard the strained desperation in her voice and did not care. "Can you not reconsider? I can increase the sum a little, and we both know how to work!"

"Go away. I have no time."

"I am sorry to have bothered you." Anger burned in Tempest, and with affronted pride, she forgot her role, whirling on him with the fire of the Mallorys. "I trust that you will find more affluent passengers!"

Just then there was rush of wheels, an excited voice calling out and horses began to neigh. An ornate carriage drew up on the street just beside the wharf and from it came the cry, "Wait! Wait! This is urgent!"

Tempest met Savora's eyes. It seemed that the pursuit was begun and finished.

3

The Sleeping Lion

The tall man who emerged from the carriage called out. "Ho, Jacky, can we sail at once? There is need and I have gold!" His voice was deep and resonant, a touch rueful.

The captain grinned, exposing several snaggled teeth. "Your lady's husband or lover rides after you, is that it?" His laughter pealed out just as the man's companion leaned forward into view.

Tempest saw the pale oval face and loosely curling blond hair thrust back over ears shimmering with diamonds. She spoke to him in a pleading cascade of words that caused him to shake his head emphatically. Then he kissed her, gestured to the coachman, and the equipage pulled away in one smooth motion.

"That is a strong possibility." The newcomer strode toward them with a firm stride. "Come, man, can we go?"

"I have to take on more cargo, and several more passengers will be arriving for this Jamaica trip. And these . . ." He waved at Tempest and Savora.

His voice trailed off as the man said, "Nonsense, you villain, you know I'll make it worth your while and over that." He came up to the captain and whispered. Both guffawed as they moved closer to the gangplank.

There was a strange familiarity about him to Tempest. He was lithe, long-limbed, and muscular, with skin darkened by the sun. Tawny hair curled around his ears and neck, springing up over his high forehead. She saw his face in profile, the square chin, long straight nose, slashing dark brows meshing into a handsomeness that was almost too perfect. He turned slightly and she noticed the sliver of a scar on one cheekbone, which showed white and stretched toward the carved mouth. In the flickering light she could tell that his eyes were some strange dark color with darts of brilliance. As she watched, he glanced up, felt her scrutiny, and his face grew hard. He was a commanding man, likely a harsh one, and fancied himself a gallant. Where had she encountered such a one?

"You persuade me, Justin! Damn you, the fee'll be high. We go!"

Justin laughed, his head thrown back in a merriment that struck Tempest as false. It was then that she remembered where she had seen him. One evening at the play, during the part in which she and several others strode boldly around the cuckolded husband in an attempt to lure, this Justin had spoken aloud to the dark-haired beauty at his side, laughed extravagantly, raked the company with his eyes, and then departed noisily. Tempest now vividly recalled that mocking gaze and arrogant downward curl of his lips.

Now he was saying, "Why are these draggles standing about, Jacky? Shouldn't you get them on board in a hurry? We don't want your ship to get a worse reputation than it has already!" He laughed again and the strange note was present.

"Yes, let us go below, Captain, since we sail at once." Tempest took the opportunity so blessedly offered and withdrew the purse so that he could see it. She ignored Justin, in his elegant tawny broadcloth so nearly the color of his hair. Her voice went low in singsong as she continued, "God will reward you for taking his missionaries in! Our prayers will rise up for you now and in my husband's congregation!"

Justin sniffed and yawned behind a long-fingered hand blazing with jewels.

Greed appeared in the captain's eyes as he bellowed up at his men. "Ready sail!" He turned back to Tempest. "You are fortunate, madam. My last excellent cabin is yours, but the wench must occupy it with you. There is no other room. You shall pay as soon as we are fully launched."

One of the sailors appeared at his elbow and gestured for them to follow him. Justin and the captain walked swiftly behind, both laughing over what seemed to be a private joke. Tempest leaned on Savora and spoke in a monotone to her of the mythical husband's labors in Jamaica. She felt Justin's eyes piercing her back and prayed that she did not give him opportunity to recognize her. Her gait was slow, her shoulders bent a little, and her speech was slurred. She wanted to laugh aloud at the incredible fortune that was theirs, and her spirits rose with every step.

The excellent cabin was tiny and airless, lit only by the small lantern their guide left with them. A shelf set into the wall and covered with an old blanket was the only bed. Across from that, an empty chest covered with a ragged cloak had been placed. Two hooks at eye level were apparently intended for their clothes. There was nothing else. A thick, stale smell rose up as if soap and water were alien things here.

"Beautiful!" Tempest sank down on the bed, hoping that it was not filled with lice. Savora glanced at her and smiled as she began to unfasten the cloth bag she carried. "I just hope we can both remember all the lies I may have to tell in addition to the ones already told."

Tempest yawned and felt her stomach growl.

Savora pulled out half a loaf of bread and some cheese, handing them to Tempest. Then she shook out the rest of the contents: a comb, two old white shirtwaists, a black skirt shiny with wear, a few chinking coins tied in one corner of it, and another shapeless bonnet. "I brought all I had. We can share if you want to." She was half apologetic when she gestured toward these treasures that would at least enable them to have a change of clothes. "I mean you might not think a slave's things fitting for a lady and all."

Tempest said her thought of an instant ago. "They are treasures and you know it. Savora, don't think slave and lady. We are together and equal, no matter what guise we have to assume until Jamaica. Morna will help you for my sake. She always was gay and spirited. You are my friend, really my only friend except for her, and you know it." She took some of the food and offered some to Savora. "This is another kind of play-acting, the kind I will do to great audiences one day. All right?"

The ship swayed under them, then began to move back and forth. Sailors called out to each other and a woman's strident voice was heard remarking on someone's ancestry. Steps thumped along toward their cabin. There was a beating on the door and Tempest and Savora both turned toward it.

The bearded man who leaned there looked drunk and appeared to have a disposition fully as evil as the captain's. "Came for passage money. Cap'n said you'd know how much and to get it all. Jamaica's a long way off and we stop other places. Got to have everything in order. Cap'n smart that way." He extended a dirty hand and smirked at Tempest, who ducked her head and began to count out the precious horde.

"How long to Jamaica?" She was thankful for the bonnet that hid face and hair. "I'm so anxious to get to my husband, you see."

"You're lucky to be on board, so cheap and all." He gave a cackle. "Weeks, of course. Weeks. But we'll get there." One arm thrust out toward the food in their hands. "And the food's even good. Wouldn't be doing any of them caterwaulin' hymns, though. Cap, he touchy."

"I understand. We will pray for him. And you, too, of course." Tempest hoped she sounded pious enough for him to leave.

He snorted, checked the money, pushed it into his pocket, and backed out. "Sure, lady, sure." The door banged behind him with an emphatic sound.

"You play well at the missionary." Savora had forgotten her gravity and grinned at Tempest.

She reveled in the bounce of the ship but was suddenly acutely aware of her own exhaustion and the pitifully few coins that remained to them. All she could think of was food and bed at the same time. "We do what we have to, Savora." She disposed of her portion in a few quick bites and added, "Shall I take the bed for tonight, or do you want it first?"

"I'll sleep at the door. There's no lock. Keep the bed. We're not in freedom yet." Savora's voice was almost sharp as she swung from one mood to another.

Tempest wanted to talk to her, draw her out, and renew the camaraderie they had felt earlier, but the hard shelf felt as if it were the softest mattress. The world was spinning away as she lay back. Over the fringes of her fading consciousness, she heard Savora singing low in her throat. "Out, out, from old Pharoh! Goin' out, goin' out, and de Lawd he be before us!"

"And a good helping of our own wits doesn't hurt." Tempest meant to speak out loud, but sleep whirled her away.

She surfaced to motion and strangeness. In one movement she sat upright, trying to adjust her eyes to the darkness. Had she had a nightmare so fearful that she could not recall it or had someone tried the door? Savora was curled in a ball more than a foot from it and her head was hidden in her arms. Tempest ran her fingers through her hair, then felt around for the concealing bonnet. She knew that sleep would not come again; now fresh air was a necessity or she might stifle. Always, Tempest roused early in the morning. Likely this was no more than old habit.

A few minutes later, muffled in cloak and bonnet, Tempest made her way through the corridors she dimly recalled from the night before. She had thought then that they must be in the depths of the hold, and judging from the distance and the smells, she was not far wrong. No one was about, and she was grateful for that. She wondered what the other passengers were like and if they had been as churlishly accepted by the captain as she and Savora. What did it matter? They were headed for Jamaica and reunion with Morna.

She pushed open a final door to emerge on the clean-swept deck. A few swift steps took her to the wooden side, where she leaned, breathing in the fresh, cool air. It was so early that the gray morning seemed patched with darkness. A clean line of light lay on the horizon and faint pink showed just above. The *Corinthian* was in the open sea, but land smells and a few whirling gulls reminded her that the Savannah River could not be far distant. The sails were spread before a gusting wind, and the ship appeared to increase her speed as Tempest watched.

She drew in long, hungry breaths, not noticing that the cloak flew open and her gown was molded against her body. The bonnet strings irritated her throat and she pulled them looser. A few strands of hair escaped to be followed by others. She heard footsteps approaching and whirled around so that she would not be seen other than in her guise of drab older woman. As Tempest stuffed her hair back, she pretended to be immersed in the rising dawn, but all her senses were alert.

"Good morning, madam. You are out early. It is very brisk

and fresh, is it not?" The words had a hint of British accent combined with the elision of southern speech, and they emerged with a studied correctness. Tempest recognized the voice from the night before. It was the man called Justin.

She had to turn and face him. Why not? The odds of recognition were slim. Caution must be her watchword. "You startled me." Her voice was low and flat, obviously discouraging.

He stood a few feet from her, swaying with a motion that had nothing to do with that of the ship. His collar was loose and his hair hung in curls over his forehead. She saw that he was younger than she had thought, perhaps thirty. He must tower well over six feet, and his muscles spoke of outdoor work or sport. One hand went to his forehead as he said, "I am Justin St. Trevian. I started out for my cabin, but took a wrong turn." Again the carefully enunciated words. He was very drunk and fighting it.

"Mrs. Hutt." Tempest sharpened her voice. After all, missionaries were against intoxication and those who imbibed. She was certainly safe in showing shock. "If you go through that door just yonder, I believe you'll find your way." She moved back a little and made as if to resume looking at the sea, but watched him out of the corner of her eye. Something about him fascinated her and it was not just the handsome face.

He was beside her in one movement and both hands closed on her arm to send little chills sliding over her body. The first sunlight struck his hair, turning it to tawny gold. He stared down at her with the strangest eyes she had ever seen. They, too, were tawny, with little amber flecks that might be yellow in another light. Their depths were a deeper amber-brown that changed and altered as she watched. Behind them something dangerous waited and assessed. He reminded her of a lion at rest but poised; there was a stalking quality about him that made her think of the hot sun of another country and the great beast, prey at its feet. Something in Tempest sprang to meet this quality and they stared fully at each other. They were alone in the world. Everything else faded before the shaking power which held them confronted.

His mouth quirked as he swayed against her. "Mrs? I didn't catch the last name. That's an ugly bonnet, surely you know that?" His words were more slurred and his eyelids drooped a little. Then practiced fingers were pushing the headgear back and tangling themselves in her hair.

Tempest tried to draw back, but by that time she was captured in his arms, held against his chest while his hungry lips sought hers. Oddly enough, he smelled of sandalwood and rich brandy; she would have thought a night of drinking to leave marks and smoking odors. Then thought left Tempest and she was one driving emotion, one pillar of flame in the dawn. Her arms rose to go around his neck while they fused together. His mouth drew on hers slowly at first and then more powerfully as their tongues met and drew back. His hand went to her breast under the rough gown and found the turgid nipple. One knee was thrust between her legs and she welcomed the pressure against the ache beginning in her mound.

The *Corinthian* lurched suddenly and they were thrown off balance. Justin went against the rail and swayed there. The amber eyes fixed on Tempest and a pulse hammered in his throat. "Let's find my cabin, little pretty. What do you say?"

Tempest knew she could not blame him. She had not recoiled from his embrace, but rather thrown herself into it. He was truly a man for the ladies; those she had seen with him were beautiful and likely in love with him. What more natural than for such a man to seek a shipboard doxy? And what was she who had responded so rapidly to him and yet found Raoul's caresses sweet? Never a doxy, she told herself sternly.

She spoke with the voice of Tempest Mallory, who had always held honor high. The quiet, meek Mrs. Hutt was forgotten. "I say no, sir. You have forgotten yourself. Let this be done between us. Go your way now."

He stared at her, and she saw the beginning sheen of anger in his eyes. "You speak with command?" One hand reached toward her and stopped.

"I do." It took all the effort at her command to fasten the bonnet, turn her back, and walk toward the door that led back to her cabin. As she went, she heard his angry bark of laughter and knew that matters had just begun for Tempest Mallory and Justin St. Trevian.

4

The Kindled Fires

". . . Therefore, now amend your ways and your doings
. . . obey the voice of the Lord and repent, for all are in His
hands."

"Yes, Lord! It all true!"

Tempest and Savora paused for breath and walked silently
together, hands folded, in the portion of the deck closest to
their cabin, which they had appropriated as their own. It was
late afternoon on the fifth day after the ship's departure.

Her sails hung limp in the warm air and the few sailors
worked lethargically at the necessary duties. Two older men,
apparently gamblers, played cards now a short distance from
the girls as they had done every afternoon and argued bitterly
with each other. Far ahead, an older man and woman in rich
clothes stood together, he coughing and she holding his hands.
Tempest wondered now, as earlier, if they sought the warmer
climes for the dread disease of consumption. His lungs
sounded as if they were being torn apart. Thanks to the
captain's orders, resented at first but now appreciated in a way
he never intended, Tempest and Savora remained in virtual
seclusion due to their supposed calling. Savora brought their
food, tended to the meager washing, picked up information,

and helped Tempest in her role of slightly dotty missionary as they quoted Scripture, sang softly, and offered prayers for redemption of all and sundry.

"I vow when we get to Morna and are established, I shall have a red dress the very color of my hair and the neckline must plunge to my stomach. How tired I am of this role that is our safety!" Tempest spoke through pursed lips while Savora nodded gravely. What would she have done without the dark girl? There was no reading matter on board, and the hours would have hung endlessly had they not been able to tell each other stories both real and imagined. Sharing brought them closer, but Tempest had not told her of Justin and their encounter. Savora slept long that first morning and Tempest had composed herself before she roused. She had mentioned Raoul only in passing during that episode also. Some things must be kept secret.

"There's the fine gentlemen again." Savora tilted her head as if to look at the reddening sunset and Tempest followed her gaze, fighting to control her breathing. Why did that rake affect her in this manner?

Justin St. Trevian wore an elegant suit of bottle green, and shining black boots encased his long legs. Rings flashed green fire as he gestured with both hands. The two women who walked with him, both dark and rather plump in thin white dresses, were flirting and giggling in a language that sounded as if it were Italian. They were a good distance away, but he lifted his head, nodded correctly to Tempest and Savora, said something to the women, and the trio burst into gales of laughter. Tempest thought them harlots, and obviously, he was a man who could not be without women. Traitor flesh that had yearned to yield to him! But the memory of that kiss haunted her nights.

Tempest brushed such thoughts aside and began to quote from Ezra in sturdy tones while Savora dropped behind to murmur "Yes'm" and "Praise be" at discreet intervals. In an effort to forget Justin, Tempest concentrated on the information she and Savora had gleaned about the captain and his ship.

The *Corinthian* carried slaves to be tempered in the plantations of Jamaica before being set to work in the Georgia ones; they would thus bring a higher price. It was illegal to bring slaves onto the island and offer them for sale, but many traders did so and flourished. The slaves were housed far below and exercised in the night. Savora had watched them several times and heard the guards talking. In the course of this there had been some mention of diamonds and rare goods in conjunction with Cuba. She and Tempest wondered if the captain, said to be both cruel and mercurial, were engaged in smuggling or even a form of piracy. They whiled away the time in speculation.

The rising breeze stirred the folds of her gown and touched her flushed face under the bonnet. How glad she would be to get rid of that headgear! Would Morna be the same? She recalled her words to Savora in one of their moments of mutual reassurance. "Her father was my father's friend and lawyer. I lived with them after the typhoid killed my family. The plantation in Virginia was sold for debts, and there were no relatives except Great-aunt Hannah." She had told Savora this before, but it helped to share that old hurt once again. "Aunt took me after a year, but Morna, who was two years older, and I remained close. Later we went to the same convent in Charleston before she went to relatives in France. We were in all sorts of mischief; no one loved a good time better than Morna. Lots of times we acted together and I think that is where I really began to want to be a good actress. We were going to run away and try."

Savora had said, "At least you were free to attempt it." Her dark eyes smoldered at the very sound of the word.

Tempest was long used to her moods. "Not so free. Morna's husband was found for her by her father a year or more ago. He is rich, I understand, and older than she. There was no choice. Her father was ill and wanted to see her settled before he died. She wrote me that he sometimes sent money to Aunt Hannah for me. Aunt never mentioned it." That helped to ease the pain of theft. "Anyway, Morna and I wrote several times a year, and I think she is happy. We will be welcome, Savora, and you are to be free."

"I want nothing else except your own happiness." Savora sometimes spoke quaintly in the style of the books from which Tempest had taught her to read, and it added to her charm.

"Mistress! Mistress Hutt! Ma'am?"

Savora's voice pulled Tempest from her reverie with a start. She always called Tempest by the name they had decided upon

and it sometimes took a few seconds to respond. "What is it?"
Irritation burned in her as she longed to be free of masquerade,
for a full bath and fresh light clothes. "What is the matter?"

Savora nodded toward the towering thunderheads in the
south, which had blown up out of nowhere. Black strings of
clouds masked the dropping sun as it gleamed red over the
chopping waves. "Storm coming. Look at the clouds."

Sailors moved briskly about now, lassitude forgotten. The
two plump women stood alone, for Justin and the captain
spoke together, apparently in argument, for the latter's face was
contorted as one fist slammed into the other. The clear side of
Justin's profile was in view and Tempest could see the straight,
compressed lips. Lucifer might have looked so, she thought
fancifully, and felt again the licking excitement of that first
morning.

"No! By God, no! Damn you, I am the master here and
don't you forget it!" Captain Jacky shook his fist in Justin's
face and stamped away. He paused outside one of the doors to
call to one of his men. "Get those passengers inside! Hurry up
with you! You, too, Mr. St. Trevian!"

Justin raised his head and his eyes focused on Tempest. She
knew he could not recognize her and probably did not even
remember the moment they had shared, but she could not look
away. "Lead us not into temptation." The words came
automatically to her lips, but nothing could be further from her
heart. The ship jerked as lightning flickered just overhead and
wind filled the sails. Justin's companions shrieked and ran back
to him, but the power between Tempest and Justin was not
broken until Savora interposed herself. "Let's leave ol' storm,
mistress. You tired."

The storm actually hit several hours later. Savora, who had
memories of traveling on the slave ship with her mother,
seemed all huge eyes as she drew herself into a corner. "It will
be a bad one. I just know it." Then, just as if they were truly
the missionaries they pretended to be, she began to mutter
prayers and snatches of the responses practiced since the
voyage began.

Tempest sat beside her, feeling her own fear grow as the ship
lurched, rolled, and dropped down into the hollows between
the waves. She put the lantern out lest it break and start a fire.
They sat in total darkness while the storm raged. Earlier it had

been possible to doze a little as the *Corinthian* ran ahead, but now there was nothing to do but wait. The cabin was stifling. It was as though they were at the bottom of a sea of fetid air. Despite that, however, Tempest felt chilled, and when she touched Savora for comfort, the girl's skin was cold.

Now and then Tempest heard low wails as if a massive dirge were being conducted and guessed that the slaves were crying their misery. The timbers of the ship cracked and protested against this endless hurling. At times they poised straight down, fell, and were tossed upward. Tempest felt bruised and exhausted, terrified at the thought of death when she had not yet begun to live, and bitterly cheated that everything should end this way. Tears burned at her eyelids, but she was too defiant to shed them.

Savora began to babble and now it was not the Christian God who was the subject of her supplications. This was to an older pantheon and there was a savagery in the tone, a harshness in the unintelligible language, that brought shivers to Tempest's spine.

"Savora, it's going to be all right. Please stop that, and let's talk about what we're going to see and do in Jamaica. Morna told me she and her husband, Robert, have this absolutely beautiful home . . ."

Savora arched upward, gurgled and her eyes rolled back so that the whites were clear in the gloom. She uttered one piercing scream and straightened out as her heels drummed the floor. Then her body went rigid and stiff. Tempest shook her, but she did not move.

From her reading, Tempest knew that this must be some version of the falling sickness, but she was unacquainted with anything to help Savora except to make sure that she did not swallow her tongue; her jaw might have been nailed shut, so clenched was it. Strong spirits would help if she only had some. Brandy or rum ought to be available here on the ship in plenty if all the tales about sailors were true.

She paused only to snatch up the shawl from the floor and wrap it around her head and shoulders before dashing out into the tiny corridor that led upward to another level. Such was her anxiety and rush that she did not at first notice that the ship was pitching less and she could make her way more easily. Her one overwhelming concern was for Savora.

As Tempest went, she regretted a fact that she had previously taken delight in. Their cabin was virtually isolated from those higher up and this had helped preserve their privacy. Now she scrambled up the ramp, bent almost double against the motion she expected any minute to dump her forward, and hammered as hard as she could on the first door in front of her. There was no answer, so she whirled and crossed to the next. This time she not only hammered with her fists, but kicked and cried, "Open! Open! This is an emergency!"

The door was jerked forward so swiftly that she fell with it and would have continued on to the floor had not a hard pair of arms caught her. She looked up and saw the arrogant, annoyed profile of Justin St. Trevian. His hair was rumpled and his eyes were lazy. A ruffled white shirt was tucked into the green trousers. One hand held a quill pen, and beyond him, on a table bolted to the floor, were sheets of paper filled with writing.

Tempest righted herself before his touch could shake her. "Forgive me, but do you have any brandy or strong drink? I must have some. It is urgent."

"So I gathered. Have you suddenly found yourself with a lack? I should have thought your faith would comfort you, Mrs. Hutt." He mocked her easily, one hand sweeping back the tawny hair as his mouth curled downward.

"My companion is stricken. Please." Tempest saw a flask on his bed, nestled in a cradle of pillows. Did he sleep with it? She pointed. "She will not require much."

He reached out his hand and jerked the shawl from her head so quickly that there was no time to retaliate. She felt him take in every inch of her body under the loose white blouse and ill-fitting skirt of Savora's that she wore. She knew her eyes were shadowed from weariness and her hair was fastened in one long plait down her back. In another circumstance she might have recoiled from the scrutiny but now she pushed past him, walked over, and picked up the flask, noting with satisfaction that it was nearly full.

"There will be ample enough for your wishes." He stood with her shawl in his fingers, watching her, his brow furrowed. She started out but his voice, a totally different note in it, caught her.

"Have we met before, Mrs. Hutt? You seem familiar to me now that you are unmuffled and that determination is gone from your voice. You are feminine this way. But how could it be?"

He did not remember her at all. Why should she be furious when this meant that she was safe with him? No matter that his face dogged her dreams. "We are strangers, sir. I am a married woman and would not have approached you except that this was the first door and a dire emergency."

"Is it so? Then I will come with you and assist. I have some small knowledge of the medical arts." A bitter note edged his words, but the mocking smile never changed.

"As you wish." She dodged him and went toward her cabin, his footsteps hammering like nemesis behind her.

Savora lay as Tempest had left her, but in the strong light of the lantern that Justin held high, her skin was no longer ebony but dusky. Tempest knelt down and tilted the flask to the unresponsive lips, which were flaccid to her fingers. Savora's breath was shallow, barely causing her chest to lift.

"Let me." The calm, authoritative voice bore no trace of mockery now as Justin sat down and lifted Savora's head to his lap. "Bring whatever coverings you have in this place. She needs warmth." When Tempest thrust cloaks and the blankets at him, he piled them over the girl, pressed on the angle of jaws and neck until her mouth moved as a small bird's might. Then he gave her small doses of the spirits as he murmured, "The storm is going. We are all safe. Safe. Safe. It is all right. Your mistress is here."

At the snap of his fingers, Tempest leaned over Savora. She murmured the same words he had spoken, while he gave her more liquid. It was with great relief that she saw the great eyes open and focus.

Savora whispered, "All right. Safe." Her head went to the side and her whole body relaxed. Tempest's gaze flew to Justin, who smiled, a softening and illuminating of his features that touched her with warmth.

"She will sleep and waken normally. She has had a shock; this is not the falling sickness in and of itself. What happened?" After Tempest's quick account, he nodded. "The other voyage was likely painful and this brought it back. And she feared for you, of course. She is fortunate in her mistress."

"I am fortunate in her." Tempest spoke soberly. She did not

mean to tell Justin of Savora's cries to the savage gods. That was their secret.

He rose and now his eyes mocked her. "You have taken my fine imported brandy, disturbed me at my letters, and made me practice a forgotten art. I demand payment, Mrs. Hutt."

Tempest drew herself up proudly. "We are poor as you can see, Mr. St. Trevian. Savora is a free woman. When we arrive in Jamaica . . ."

"I know. You, your husband, and all your faithful band will pray for me. Well, I take the here and now always. These tropical storms rise and fade with such intensity that I think I can predict only a little turbulence. Come and walk with me on the deck. Let go your prim way for the moment. I promise that you are safe, and I am minded for a bit of conversation." He smiled again, and this time there was a challenge in his eyes.

She could not resist the thrust. "The ladies you escorted earlier will not miss your company? I should not like to feel that I intrude."

His grin flashed. "You do not. You are unworldly, Mrs. Hutt. Remain that way." He held the door open and motioned for her to precede him.

Tempest started for her bonnet but changed her mind. It looked so ugly and she knew few would pay any attention to her at this hour of the night. His nearness was rousing her blood to fever; she dared much to go with him and still she knew that she must have this moment in spite of what all reason told her.

Justin was watching her intently. "Would you permit me to address you by your first name just for tonight? You know, I am sure that we have met—if I could ever recall. Something about your face is so clear." He shook his head in annoyance.

She had to divert him. "Let us go quickly. I must get back. And my name is Martha." It was the best she could do on such short notice. Anyone might have mentioned the player girl Miranda.

He rocked with silent laughter as he drew her into the hall. "Martha the faithful, the devoted. Are you so?"

With his fingers on her arm and his warm body close to hers, Tempest felt her pride to be her only shield on this night of storms. Would it be enough?

5

In the Balance

Tempest and Justin stood together under the wooden awning that projected out over the highest deck for a short way. There was a stout railing there as well, and they held on to it. Clouds scudded before the wind that whipped the ship over the high creaming waves, but the force of this storm was gone as he had predicted. Sailors moved about below them but paid no attention to the dark figures. The sails blew full from the masts, and far beyond, there was the faint glimmer of a star.

Tempest drew deep breaths of the fresh, tantalizing air that seemed to carry the promise of far, exotic places. In the aftermath of fear and worry it was wonderful to relax a little and let the time carry itself. She would never see this man again after the voyage. What fun she and Morna would have with speculations about him!

His voice was soft and easy, nearly reflective, as he continued to speak as he had since their arrival up here a few short minutes ago. "The islands are fantastically lovely down in this part of the world and some of them are so unspoiled. Islands have a fascination for me: Crete, Delos, Majorca, Sardinia, Ireland, those sea islands of Georgia. I remember once on Delos . . ."

He talked on and on, but Tempest noticed that the flow of words contained little that was personal. He was an excellent raconteur, skilled in the use of words and manipulation of individuals. There was something fascinating about him quite apart from his appearance. Perhaps he was a gambler, a wealthy landowner seeking excitement, the black sheep sent away for his sins.

When he paused for breath, she asked, "You are truly well traveled, Mr. St. Trevian, and may one ask what your ultimate destination might be?" He had accused her of primness and so she acted. "You know mine and the why of it."

Justin looked down at her and smiled that strange twisting of the lips that held no mirth. "Why, Jamaica, of course. Haiti, possibly, and the other islands. Eventually New Orleans, Mexico, who knows. Wherever Jacky will take me." He put one hand on her waist and tilted her chin up. "You could be fair if you wished it. Do missionaries have to be drab and weary all the time? Would your husband not wish to dress you and admire you?"

"I am no doll." Tempest knew she should turn away, but she could not.

"I can see that. You are a woman as other women." His gaze went over the loose blouse that did not fully conceal her upper body. "And yet there is more about you." Now Justin was almost musing. "A quality of mystery that intrigues me. Were I not otherwise committed, it might be different."

"I must go." His idle words stung and hurt. "I must see to Savora."

"See to me instead." With one smooth, practiced gesture he swung her toward him, hard against his chest, and that firm mouth closed over hers before she could even begin to struggle.

Warmth suffused Tempest and ran over her flesh, which seemed to melt into his. Their tongues met, twined, and probed. She smelled him, was enveloped by him, and wanted him with a fierceness that was a dagger in her body. Tempest was only dimly conscious of the cool wind against her hot skin and the fact that they stood on a public deck, where the captain might emerge at any moment. Justin's hands were iron bands to sink into her skin and hold her as a willing, eager captive. She locked her own behind his neck and drew him closer until she could feel his growing manhood. His powerful body bent into her slim one as the phrase "one flesh" rang in the part of her mind that could still think. She wanted this man as men were said to want women and were free to take them. She was not sure she even liked him and certainly she did not love him, but that had no bearing. The roaring longing must be satisfied.

She moaned as his hand went down into her bodice, drew the cloth aside, and closed on her breast. Her back arched as his kiss grew even more demanding. Her mouth was filled with his tongue as his fingers first rotated her nipple and then squeezed it with a sensation that was first pain, then kindled an already blazing fire. There was nothing in the entire world but this feeling that was surely a foretaste of glory to come.

Then he set her back from him so suddenly that she cried out. Her very nerves were pulsating at the interruption and her skin grew clammy as she stared into his hard face. His nostrils were spread wide. A pulse hammered in his temple as he tried to control himself, but when he spoke, the words were little more than a whisper.

"I remember! The night of the sailing! You were up here and we began this thing. I invited you to come to my cabin and you refused right royally. I was very drunk, but now I recall. Why were you so hesitant? Why do you wear the missionary guise? Is the trade better that way? Martha indeed!"

The implications of his words stunned Tempest for an instant and she said, "I do not understand your anger."

"Then I shall enlighten you." He spoke more precisely as his fury deepened. "You are no quiet missionary, for all that you look the part. No, those other women at least have the decency to be what they are. You are outwardly meek, but your eyes sought and lured me. Your flesh demands my touch and fires at it. Did you think to become my mistress and that I would set you up? You are inventive, I will give you that!" He turned to one side as if to wave her by.

Rage overtook Tempest and swamped her. "You think to call me tart because you stirred my senses! A man can take his pleasure and be thought the better for it, but a woman is a tart, is she? What do you know about the feelings of a woman? Can a missionary not be a woman and yet serve? Do you think every woman is enthralled by you? What makes you such a prize? Your mistress? I pity the poor women in all their numbers!"

"The word *tart* is yours, madam. Would you prefer Magdalene, in honor of your assumed calling?"

Tempest slammed her hand, nails curved, onto his smooth, unblemished cheek with such force that he reeled back. She felt the shock of the blow all the way up to her shoulder.

They looked at each other for a second. His fist clenched and she knew it took a great effort of will for him not to strike her in return. The other hand rested at his hip, where a sword would normally hang.

"I will bid you good night now. I trust you will excuse me if I do not see you to your cabin." Justin gave her a correct bow, his face icy and unreadable in the gloom that surrounded them now.

Tempest walked past him, her back straight and her head high.

Once back in the cabin, Tempest would not let herself weep. Humiliation and anger fought the fascination that Justin St. Trevian caused in her mind and the passion of her hot blood's first true rousing. She came by it naturally, she told herself. Had not her own father, sent to England to find and wed an heiress that the family fortunes might be recouped, chosen an American girl orphaned by war and refused to be separated from her in spite of paternal rage? And her grandmother, married once in duty and widowed by a lone Indian, took a man younger than she by some fifteen years as her second husband and went with him to France, where both died of the fever. A passionate breed, Tempest thought, and she was the last. The stories that horrified Great-aunt Hannah now returned to give her strength.

In the course of what remained of that long night, Tempest passed through the crucible of her own testing. "I will make the name Mallory ring in the true theaters! Every emotion, each experience, all thoughts and knowledge, the things I have known in the past, those I encounter in the future, everything shall be used to enrich any portrayal I do. Whatever it takes to become an actress is what I mean to do. I do swear it. That is my goal!" She had always wanted to be an actress, not simply a repertory player, and she ever loved rendering a good performance with anyone. The deep determination had been born early and did not falter, but now she regretted that she had not run away earlier. The episode with Justin made her aware of the passions within her. She would rule them and use them; they would not rule her.

With that firmly in her mind and heart, Tempest turned onto her side and slept with no dreams.

Rage stormed through Justin as he strode through the corridor. Women did not reject him, not did they ignore his interest once he showed it. Who did that red-haired wench think she was? He'd show her a thing or two. From now on, he'd devote all his attentions to Bess and Lila. They understood how things should be. There would be no demands from them once the *Corinthian* was in port. Their husbands or lovers would meet them and no questions were to be posed on either side. You took pleasure as it came; men knew this and women ought to, but only a few could be honest. He slammed one hand against the other and concentrated on Lila's heavy white breasts, those long smooth thighs Bess had, the delights he'd sampled only yesterday.

That girl was no innocent for all she tried to act as if she were. Look how she'd responded to him! Ignore her for a while, let her see him with the others, and then see how she reacted. He grinned to himself; that technique had worked many times. He tried to forget those brilliant gray eyes gazing into his and the lash of her scornful voice even as his lips burned from their mutually ignited passion. She thought she was different, did she? Once he'd thought that of himself, believed in the love of one woman, and that was too long ago. The boy he had been learned better. Libertine? Rake? Better names than fool and idealist.

Their door was discreetly ajar, but he gave a perfunctory tap before entering. Immediately Bess and Lila rushed toward him, brunette and chestnut curls tossing, ripe bodies gleaming under loose robes, mouths red and avid. He'd wanted them, enjoyed their knowledge and experience, given and taken eagerly. Why now did he want to draw back in spite of the ache in his loins?

"We knew you'd come, but you were cruel to keep us waiting so long." Bess flicked the buttons on his shirt and let her long fingers move inside it.

Lila was the slimmer of the two, but her rosy nipples and rounded full bosom gave her the look of an earth mother, a mighty goddess of fertility. She bared herself to him now and Justin remembered how her softness had excited him nearly beyond endurance. Now he wondered how another graceful body would feel and whether she would ever give him such a hungry look as these women turned on at his mere entrance. Justin shook his head angrily. What was wrong with him? Hadn't he learned that too much thought was dangerous? Pleasure and the moment; that was everything.

He was not aware of speaking aloud until Lila cried, "Of course it is! Justin, are you just going to stand there?"

He put his arms around them both and smiled suggestively into their eyes. "That wasn't really what I had in mind, but if you ladies prefer it . . ." They began to giggle and he moved them toward the wide bed. "I think a bit of relaxation might be in order, don't you?"

Moments later they were tangled together in a heap of white limbs, tossing hair, and knowing hands. Justin's lean, tanned body wove between them in a rhythm of excitement. Now his head was at Lila's tufted mound, while Bess touched his shaft with eager pumping motions to set him aflame. He came to the brink and held back deliberately, fending them off.

"Let me see you. Together. You know." This was part of the games they played with each other, this coy innocence. Ordinarily it amused him, but now he could see the red-haired girl in their places and savage desire mixed with rage inflamed him all the more.

Lila and Bess were kissing now, but their movements were slow as they watched him. He interrupted at different times, never the same. This could, and usually did, go on for hours, but now he needed culmination. His voice was hoarse and reasoned thought left him.

"Now! Now! Come on!"

Bess kissed him feverishly while Lila's mouth tormented his stomach and slipped lower, tantalizingly lower. His hands went out to them and then they moved together in a timeless whirling satiation where individuality was lost and release was boundless. Justin's body seemed to tear free and float outward. His women were shuddering in their own aftermath as they clung together.

What untried, skittish girl could match this? He would make the opportunity to show her just what she was missing, and in the end she would be just as eager as Lila and Bess. Justin shifted to a more comfortable position and ran an exploratory finger down a smooth, soft back. Enjoy this for the moment and bide his time. He'd do that, but in the end he meant to have her, no matter what the cost.

He drifted, and her eyes went with him into oblivion.

In the next days the *Corinthian* drifted smoothly over blue-green water of such clarity that the distant bottom of the sea seemed to appear. The air was hot, brushed with fragrances and shimmering before them. Clouds mingled with the sails in the brilliance of night and day. Great fish jumped ahead of them and smaller ones followed behind. Now and then islands came like shadows on the horizon, fading out of sight with their passage.

The ship made a landing three times, always at night. Once Tempest and Savora tried to go on deck during the pause but were turned back by one of the sailors, who was adamant in his refusal to allow them. When Tempest asked where they were, he glanced furtively about and said, "Round Cuba somewheres, I reckon." But the next morning the wide sea was the only horizon.

They stayed on deck as much as possible, for the cabin grew unbearable in the heat of the day. In the twilight or in the very early morning, they would often see Justin watching the distances with his spyglass. He would incline his head coldly, but generally he ignored them. Sometimes he was with the captain, at others with the two women, who never failed to stare at Tempest and sniff disdainfully. The older twittered on about pirates and was doing so one afternoon when Tempest, gazing out to sea, thought she saw sails on the horizon and realized then that what she had considered to be low clouds on other days were in fact ships.

"Pirates?" She whispered the word to Savora, not really expecting the other girl to answer. Savora had been withdrawn since her attack, which she said she did not remember. She disappeared often now and returned to sit staring into space, a vague smile on her lips. When questioned, she was always noncommittal.

"I think the pirates and our worthy captain understand each other, ladies." Justin's drawl, light and mused, floated across to Tempest and Savora. His eyes brushed over them and one hand went to his mouth to hide a yawn.

"They won't attack us." Savora sounded very sure of herself.

"How do you know?" Tempest could not help the note of annoyance in her voice.

"I just hope they won't. I just think things will be all right." Savora would not meet her eyes, and she clenched her fingers together convulsively.

Tempest missed the sharing of a few days ago and thought unhappily that she was not the only one who had secrets. How good it was going to be just to talk to Morna! Still, it was through Savora that she knew even a little about Justin St. Trevian. When she mentioned to Savora that he had tended her during her spell, the girl had volunteered the snippets of gossip about him that she had heard in the kitchens while she obtained their food.

It seemed that he often traveled on the *Corinthian*. None knew his business, but all could attest to the fact that he and the captain argued violently in other languages. He did have some land in Jamaica, more in Louisiana and the Carolinas. He gambled, wenched, and drank more than most of the sailors, but was thought to be aloof and cold. It was not known whether he was American or English; part of his ancestry was French and there were rumors of a scandal in New Orleans, that most permissive of cities, which had forced him to flee.

"Gossip will say anything." Tempest had been fascinated, eager for more.

"Yes." Savora said nothing else.

Ever since Justin mocked her missionary guise, Tempest had tried to be very discreet. She and Savora still quoted verses and sang in low voices, but she wore the concealing bonnet and gown all the time, feeling safer as she did so. Soon the voyage must end. Soon they must be free from this prickly atmosphere and the necessary confinement. And still it had been benison and luck that they were on board the *Corinthian* at all.

Tempest walked, watched the ever changing sea, studied the sky, recited to herself every scrap of poetry, all the lines of the heroines she had ever wanted to portray that she could

remember from all her reading, and fought back the shattering
feelings experienced each time she saw Justin—which, thankfully, was not that often. In the long moments that remained,
Tempest worried about Savora, who was losing weight and
whose smooth shiny skin was almost sallow. How could this be
in the relatively few days of the voyage? "Let Jamaica come
soon." Each night she whispered the words into the clammy
darkness of their cabin, believing that her friend was slipping
away from her into some vortex where she could not follow by
Savora's own choice. At such times she thought of Justin's
warm, companionable voice against her ear as it had been that
night when he talked of his travels, and was almost able to
persuade herself that most of all she regretted the loss of what
might have been a true friendship.

The call came very early and was no more than a banging on
their door followed by, "Get up! Cap'n wants everybody ready
to get off soon's we land!"

Tempest sat up, rubbed the sleep from her eyes and,
knowing the answer already, still had to ask. "Land where?"

"Montego Bay, Jamaica! Couple of hours, no more!" The
man clomped away and a few minutes later she heard him
calling above them in a more civil manner to those who had
apparently paid more and thus were entitled to it.

Savora had risen and was looking at Tempest with a kind of
desperation in her face. "What will happen when we get
there?"

"We'll find someone who'll take a message to Morna, of
course. They live on this side of the island. There should be no
problem." Tempest plunged her face into the small amount of
water grudgingly supplied for washing, then lifted her dripping
face to Savora. "What is the matter? Can't you tell me? Has
someone insulted you, bothered you?"

"It's nothing. Seasick." Savora turned her back and began
to collect their few belongings. "I took your gown up to air it
last night. At least it'll be fresher. No use trying to sponge it off
any more."

"I don't care about the silly gown. We're talking about you,
Savora." A fearful certainty rose in Tempest's mind. "Has one
of the sailors tried to bed you? Rape you?" What if Justin had
dared to touch her?

"That happened long ago. It would not matter." Savora's

tone was quite detached. She might have been speaking of another person. "Let's go up on deck. Please, Tempest. Please, Mrs. Hutt." Her smile was nearly that of the bold girl who had demanded freedom only days ago.

Tempest ceased to press her. All that mattered now was landing and making contact with Morna. Would the very few coins she had left be enough? And they in American money. Jamaica was British. She would deal with that when they arrived. Now the moment must be savored. Suddenly she was frantic to get on deck. In that part of herself that was always ruthlessly honest, Tempest knew that she wanted to see Justin St. Trevian one more time.

She pulled on the gown for what she sincerely hoped was the last time, plaited her hair back, and pulled the shapeless bonnet into place. "I'm giving the missionaries a bad name with this garb."

Once Savora would have responded with a saucy quip; now the corners of her mouth barely twitched. "I am ready." She waited to walk behind Tempest as a servant was expected to do.

Tempest saw more of the other passengers in the next hours than she had for the entire voyage. There were relatively few of them, mostly older and with a generally prosperous appearance. She was given assessing stares, a brief nod or so, and then ignored. Justin and the two women were not in sight. Several bearded men, whips coiled at their waists, walked together and talked in low whispers. They dealt with slaves and that mark was on them. Tempest guessed they handled the slaves in the hold and wondered what would happen if they knew Savora was a runaway.

Tempest scanned the horizon while tasting the salt air on her lips and drinking in the incomparable beauty of the azure sea and sky. This was the true adventure, the beginning of her life as she chose it, and all her being rose to the challenge. She smiled as she thought of how the description of their arrival could be described to Morna and the pleasure they would both take in it. What would her husband be like? Strange that she had never really written much of him.

"Land! Land!" The cry rang over the *Corinthian*.

Tempest looked again into the distance and saw a line of green with a mountain mass beyond. It faded as the ship veered, and there was only a shimmer of blue-green so intense that her eyes ached. "The beautiful land." She whispered the name she had heard it called, wondering if this were an omen for their reception there.

And thus they came to Jamaica on an early spring morning.

6

Hammer of Fate

Jamaica, West Indies
April 1831

A rush of impressions reached Tempest as the *Corinthian* docked at the port city of Montego Bay. Ships of all types dotted the area and the wharves beyond swarmed with activity. Tall trees of a kind unknown to her shone brilliantly green in the streets of stone and others fringed the shores. Great hills rolled upward into others crowned with forests as the shades of green varied into the blue of the ocean at the side. She heard a snatch of song in French, the clipped English sounds of orders being given, and protests rendered in a language she did not know. The air smelled of spice, salt, and flowers.

Tempest saw that few of the passengers were to debark but all had come up to watch. An older couple, two men who must be gamblers, and a lone elderly man went before Tempest and Savora down the gangplank. Behind them were the cries and orders of the handlers as the hold was readied to discharge the slaves. Tempest felt her stomach writhe; that was one thing she did not wish to see.

A familiar voice laced with laughter reached her ears, and she could not help turning toward it. Justin St. Trevian, elegant in a yellow that just matched the paler tones of his hair, was saying something to a sailor who was struggling with a huge box. "Think how happy the contents of that will make the ladies, my man. Just a little more gently there! Ah, I see my carriage just arriving!" The women who had been with him on the voyage were now far behind and one was waving to a fat man in the edge of a group of onlookers. They paid no attention to Justin. Evidently, that little game was done.

Justin caught Tempest's stare, and the mocking grin touched his mouth. She felt the coursing warmth of her blood, but his gaze swept on over her as he waved at his servant, a young black man now tethering the horses that drew the carriage. "Hannibal, hurry up!"

Tempest wished she had not looked for him. Now he would think she yearned after him to the exclusion of all else. Hurriedly she went down on the wharf and past a bored official, who glanced at her, ignored Savora, and jerked his head to the left when she asked the direction of the main street. Now to find someone to take a message.

The ground seemed to sway under her just then and, alarmed, she tried to steady herself. This country was prone to earthquakes; was one about to occur? Her legs trembled again and she recalled the motion of the ship. She would hate to wobble around the city as if she had been tippling.

"Help you, mum?" The boy at her elbow might have been eight or nine. His face was dark and serious, but his black eyes danced. Several others stood a few paces away. Apparently, a rush had been made to assist the newcomers and thereby gain a few pence. The others who had come from the *Corinthian* were brushing more youngsters back.

"Do you know a plantation called Cloud Ridge?" At his nod, she went on. "I need you to take a message to its mistress, Mrs. Robert Dornier, and give it only to her."

"That's a good way, lady." He looked as if he intended to refuse her.

Tempest was to learn that this was standard behavior and now she suspected as much, but she had nothing with which to haggle. She showed him the coin in her fist. "There will be more for you, I promise."

He grinned wisely and held out his hand.

"Say to her that Prospero's daughter has been swept here and waits on the beach, that it is urgent for sanctuary. Can you remember that and repeat it just as I have said?" She and

Morna had once made codes out of most of Shakespeare's *The Tempest*; that particular statement meant one or the other was threatened by teacher or authority, and to come at once. She could not say why she exercised a girlish game now, only that it seemed necessary.

"Yessum!" He repeated it several times, running the words together in a singsong. "And you goin' be yonder?" One arm whirled, windmill fashion, toward what Tempest assumed must be the road to the beach. She nodded, and then he flashed away in the direction of the inner city.

"Now we wait." Savora sighed out the words and followed Tempest along the narrow street in the direction the boy had pointed.

There was a clatter of hooves behind them and Justin, face stern under a wide-brimmed white hat, tall in the saddle of a great roan, leaned toward Tempest. "Mrs. Hutt, if your husband is delayed, I would advise you to go and wait near the ship. Roaming around is not a good idea. He is coming soon, I assume?" The mockery was in his voice again.

"You need not concern yourself, Mr. St. Trevian!" Tempest looked into his face boldly and let her fury show. "Surely you have affairs to which you must attend. I advise you to seek them."

Red flared in his cheeks and the tawny eyes went flat. "A good idea." He wheeled his horse and left as rapidly as he had come.

Tempest watched his departing back and tried to think that she had hurt him. But the pain was in herself.

They walked confidently, but now Tempest was aware of eyes following them. A heavy man on a white horse rode past, staring; another crossed to the opposite street, contempt flaring in his eyes. Blacks obviously on errands looked up and several giggled, commenting in the language she did not understand. A white woman, several children at her heels, smiled faintly and gestured toward a church spire far ahead. A roar of drunken song came from a tavern off to the side. The girls quickened their pace.

It was the scent of the sea that led them to it a few minutes later, and they sank down under a palm tree, one of many growing in a circle on this part of the small beach that looked as if people came frequently to swim and relax. Fortunately, it was deserted now. Tempest unfastened the neck of her dress, removed the bonnet, and let her hair float free on the warm wind. Her shoes and stockings followed as she went to wade in the water. Savora played with some tiny purple flowers in the sand, looking out to sea with the enigmatic expression she now assumed so often.

"All we can do is wait. I wish we could have taken a horse or hired a carriage, but with no money and this unknown territory . . . surely she will send one soon." Tempest paced up and down, willing herself not to worry yet.

"I hope before night. That Mr. St. Trevian might have helped us." Savora swung around to search Tempest's face.

"He is a scoundrel!" Tempest was not about to admit the need of assistance from Justin, although that could have been the wiser course.

The day wore on, growing fiercely hot at noon. Some children came down to swim, looked at them shyly, and withdrew to speculate. The sounds of the town abated so that the only sounds were those of the waves. They did not talk; the chance had been cast and waiting left no other choice. Tempest thought of fresh cool water and food of any sort. That on the *Corinthian* had been bad enough, but at least it stilled the pangs.

The sun was dropping in the west before they heard the sound of wheels and a horse's neigh. Tempest jumped up quickly and shaded her eyes with her hand. The carriage that approached was ornately equipped and driven by a slave dressed in white. The symbol on its door was that of a cloud spanning a hilltop, very like the drawing Morna had sent Tempest in one of her letters. The wheels were set high and wide, the better for going over rough roads. The horses were both sturdy and beautiful.

"It is she! Morna is here! Savora, come!" Forsaking all caution, Tempest caught up her skirts with both hands and ran out to the road in her bare feet, hair whipping over her face. "Morna, thank God you have come! Morna, it is Tempest!"

The door swung wide as Tempest approached and an incredulous voice demanded, "Are you the sender of that ridiculous message? Pray explain yourself at once." She stared into the face of the carriage's only occupant, a man in early middle age.

"I sent it to Morna Dornier, yes." Shock made Tempest speak coolly as her head went back to look him straight in the eyes. "May I ask your name, sir?" She thought she already knew, but confirmation was necessary.

"I am Robert Dornier, and those matters which concern my wife are naturally mine as well." He had very pale blue eyes, short, straight pale brows and hair that must have been golden in his youth but was now somewhat faded. Barely taller than Tempest, he held himself in a commanding manner. His skin was weatherbeaten and lines radiated out from his eyes. He wore white against the blistering heat. "Who are you, and what does the message mean?" His voice sharpened; clearly, this was not a man who encouraged levity.

"Tempest Mallory. Morna and I have been friends for years. Has she not spoken of me?" The hurt bit deep. He was studying her face intently, and try as she might, Tempest could not conceal her feelings.

Now he shrugged. "Casually, perhaps. I do not remember. But why have you come here? And in this garb?" His brows rose as he glanced past her to where Savora stood. "Your slave?"

Tempest felt as if she were struggling in the dark. Instinctively, she felt that she must go carefully before this man who, as Morna's husband, should be her friend. "Morna spoke of inviting me here. I am afraid that I simply longed to see her. I just closed our house, my relatives were visiting other relatives, packed a few things which were unfortunately lost overboard in a storm, and took the first ship."

"From?" The word rapped out at her.

He must know she was lying, but why did she feel the urgent need to do so? "Norfolk. It had come from up the coast, you know." She had to turn his train of thought. "Savora is a freedwoman who came with me of her own choice. She is my friend." And probably the only one, she thought almost bitterly.

Robert Dornier's eyes raked them while Tempest wondered how long he meant to keep them standing this way. She was hot, tired, dirty, and hungry. Even though they had not been invited, what sort of gentleman would treat a visitor in this manner? Nervously, she hurried into speech.

"The message was just a game we used to play. I thought it would amuse her."

"It did not amuse me." He stood aside from the carriage door. "Get in. I have not met any of my wife's friends before."

Tempest was in the carriage and sitting down with Savora opposite her before she realized what the intonation on "friends" and this suspicious attitude must mean. Dear God, he thought Morna had a lover! She caught the roll of Savora's eyes and knew that the girl understood the same thing. She put one finger to her lips and Savora nodded in agreement; they must be silent and await developments. Then the carriage started as Dornier swung up with the driver.

At any other time Tempest would have been delighted with the journey through this new and colorful land glimpsed through the windows, but now her mind was alive with concern for herself and Savora. She knew that she could earn a living somehow if only she had a little to start with, but what if they were considered fugitives in a strange land? Suppose this man would not let Morna assist them? It was even possible that he kept his wife under lock and key! Then she smiled at her fancies; she had been reading too many romantic and mysterious tales.

Tempest forgot many of her worries as they traveled on. The gleam of the distant sea, several tumbling gorges, the proliferation of vegetation and flowers, the distant roar of a stream, and the very untamed beauty of this country drew at her. She wanted to explore, roam as she willed, savor this intoxicating place. The road curved and she saw various crops, all under cultivation, and tried to recall the principal product of Cloud Ridge. Sugar cane, was it not? Her mind blurred with exhaustion then, and she longed for their destination.

The carriage jolted to a stop and Robert Dornier leaned in. "Refresh yourself. Clothes will be provided and someone will come for you in thirty minutes." He extended a hand to Tempest, who was surprised that she had fallen asleep. A slave holding a tray stood just beyond him and, at his gesture, offered her a goblet. "Your girl will be tended." His emphasis was sardonic.

Tempest drank the watered wine thirstily and gazed up at the shadowed white house that rose several floors and melted into the surrounding trees with a graceful air. Beyond and around it, the lawns stretched out, sloping downward from the elevation where the newcomers stood. Elegance seemed to surround Cloud Ridge in the twilight and was echoed in the blooming white flowers on all sides.

Now a black woman, thin and tall, touched her elbow and Tempest followed numbly. She felt as if she were playing a role, watching herself from afar. In that manner she noticed the bare white room off the back of the house where she was bathed in cool water, allowed to do nothing for herself and for once content to have it so, given sweet cakes with more wine, and had her hair shaken out, then combed thoroughly. She was given a simple cotton gown, which hung loosely over her slenderness, and soft slippers. One of the delicate white flowers was tucked in her hair. The slave held up a half mirror and Tempest saw her newly thin face with the soft hollows under the cheekbones and her loose hair a leaping fire against the stark white gown.

"Good. Very good." The slave spoke her first words in precise English as she opened the door to admit another woman, who beckoned Tempest to follow.

Tempest felt her spirits lifting again in relief at having a bath and food, not to mention being rid of that old gown. She barely noticed the halls and beautifully appointed rooms through which she was taken; there would be no way to find the end of this maze without help.

Her escort paused before a mahogany door, knocked, and turned its handle for Tempest to go in before she glided away. She stepped over the threshold into green and white spring touched with gold. Glassed windows stood open to the air and were hung with yellow. Flowering branches brought the world inside. But the center of the room was the tall bed piled with pillows, canopied with pale green, and the cradle beside it. A woman sat watching Tempest approach, and in the far shadows, Robert Dornier stirred.

"Prospero's daughter has come." Tempest said the old words as a lump came into her throat. Silence hung for a long moment. "Morna, do you not know me?"

Morna Dornier let both hands rise to her face. Tempest saw the gauntness of them, the thin neck, and the wealth of blond hair that seemed to lack any vitality. Only the snub nose and generous mouth remained the same. She spoke, and the incredulity mingled with gladness. "Tempest! You came so quickly! I was sure I had not yet posted that letter. You have to see our son. Come and look!"

Tempest lifted her eyes to Robert, whose face remained impassive. Emotion overtook her as Morna stretched out her arms. She came to the bed in a quick rush and folded her friend in her embrace. They held each other while Tempest tried not to be aware of Morna's fragility or the heat that radiated from her body.

Then she admired the baby, Robert Dornier II, extravagantly, although he seemed to be a wisp for the four months of age. "And of course we are going to have a nursery full. Really, Tempest, now that you are here we must find a husband for you! It is the best and only way for a woman to live." Morna ran on until she began to cough and her pale face bloomed out in splotches of red.

Robert started toward her, but Morna waved him back and reached for Tempest's hands.

He said, "I'll get your maid."

Morna's struggle for breath slowed a little as Tempest leaned over her, having no idea what to do. "Closer, closer. He'll be back in a minute. Help me, Tempest. He's trying to get rid of me. I'm weak, you see. Too weak for him." She began to cough again, shaking against Tempest.

"Morna, this has been too much for you." Robert Dornier came back and stood looking down at his wife with anguished eyes.

Tempest gazed at them both while the warm wind blew in the fragrance of the countryside and the tall candles flamed upward. What waited for her in Jamaica? What was happening to Morna? Mingling with the pity for her friend was the determination that she, Tempest, would stand alone and rule her destiny.

7

Dragons in their Pleasant Palaces

"Madam has a lovely figure as is, but will she not just try the gown with this corset? It will make all the difference." The little dressmaker sounded as if she were about to weep.

"Between breathing and not breathing. I know." Tempest fought against the impulse to laugh. "You are preparing so many things for me that I am worn out with all the fitting. I know you must be with so much work. What about another day?" She had to escape this pulling and plucking at her or soon she would screaming down the hill.

"But the ball gown? The meshing of the green and gray has to be just so. Madame Dornier said it must be perfection, and your waist ought to be even tinier . . ." Miss Adelisa ran both hands through her dark hair and grew even more distraught.

"I trust your genius with the needle, but I will not be dressed up and miserable. Make it so that I am comfortable." Tempest cocked her head. "I think I hear Morna calling. You do the best you can. The ball isn't for another few weeks. You will excuse me?" She was already opening the door out of the sewing area. "Tomorrow or the next day, I promise!" Then her escape was made and she was running lightly over the polished floors and up to the balcony, where Morna always sat in the afternoons.

The day and evening of their arrival in Jamaica now seemed part of a bad melodrama. The past ten days had been delightful and serene. True, Morna kept to her bed much of the time or rested on couches, but she was always about in the early evenings, smiling and gracious, concerned over small matters, interested in Tempest's day as well as that of her husband. She had listened to Tempest's story of their adventures without asking any questions. "You are here and that is all that matters. If there are any problems, Robert will attend to them." It took Tempest only a short time to realize that little outside her immediate circle interested Morna, that the gay friend of her youth no longer existed. She cried out with horror over Tempest's slightly sun-warmed skin and the lack of smoothness on her hands. Her hair was treated, combed, and scented by two slaves. Creams were produced, and she was given double helpings of rich food to take away the willowy look. Morna herself ate almost nothing. Gowns were commissioned and Miss Adelisa brought from Montego Bay to fit Tempest. There were to be parties later on, and a ball—nothing elaborate, Morna explained—would introduce her to the planters, who would then be vying for her interest.

"I am grateful, but I can never repay all this. What will Robert think? Anyway, you should regain your strength." Tempest knew she could not explain the discomfort she felt at all this lavishness that was rained on her. Savora, too, had profited, for she was studying dressmaking and Miss Adelisa said she had great promise. A shop of her own was a possibility for the future.

Morna brushed away Tempest's protests, and when she alluded to the plea for help of that first night, said uncomprehendingly, "I do not understand. I have everything I have ever wanted. My health is getting better. Having Robert's son took a great deal from me."

Tempest had never really shared much with any except the young Morna and Savora. Even then there were reservations. Now she was in Morna's world of beauty, riches, and pleasure with a slave for her every bidding but she no longer knew her friend. Savora was remote, agreeable, but somehow set apart. She would discuss nothing with Tempest.

Strange as it might have seemed to her on the first night, Tempest felt closer to Robert Dornier than any at Cloud Ridge. He was aloof, polite to her as a guest in his house, and never spoke of the tale she had told him or of the rate his money was being spent on a stranger. But he talked of shipping, the sugar cane crop, difficulties with the slaves, his son and what he would be heir to, the place of Jamaica in the world, and his reserved face lit up with the pride of the great landowner bestride his world. Morna listened but made few comments. Tempest tried to speak knowledgeably, but she knew too little of Jamaica. He attempted to enlighten her at times, but Morna interjected remarks about fashion or health and their attention came to her and remained there.

Now Tempest paused at the edge of the balcony over which a huge flowering tree drooped. Morna slept in a lounge chair while two slaves fanned her. Tempest had established the custom of reading aloud in the afternoons from the light romances Morna loved, but their cloying sentiment soon reduced her to complete boredom. How people could change! What had happened to Morna's mind? Domesticity had trampled it out so that no thoughts were left.

She spoke to the ever present slave girl at her heels. "I go to walk in the gardens and later I will rest in my room. Please see that I am not disturbed." It was not the cool white sanctuary of that retreat she meant to seek.

Fifteen minutes later, skirts bundled high, Tempest left the orderly rose garden with its interspaced beds of lilies and marigolds, slipped between arbors of twining vines, moved along the expanse of lawn, and took the path to the woods. She was glad that she had put on the simplest gown she had, one Morna had given her to wear while the new ones were being prepared. It was dark, with full, loose sleeves and a swinging skirt, which, being too short, left her ankles bare. Morna deplored her appearance, but Tempest found it comfortable and in this climate that mattered most to her.

This was the first time Tempest had had an opportunity to explore any of the country around Cloud Ridge and she meant to make the most of it. She walked now among trees so tall and tangled that the shade they offered was shiveringly cool. Flowers spangled over them and birds sang in the depths. There were occasional meadows where grass grew high, rocks lined the edges, and the very sky seemed to bend closer. Then the sea scent came to her as she breathed the mingled woods odor. Far in the distance rose the great hills leading to the mountains.

Tempest lost all idea of time as she wandered, but the sound of water lured her into a deep copse and she realized how thirsty she was. A tiny trampled path led downward and she was following it when she heard voices in a dialect she could not understand. In one instinctive motion she moved behind a large prickly bush and flattened herself to the ground. She was not conscious of any fear or surprise; the tone of the voices held a subtle menace to which she reacted.

When Tempest looked up she saw three men and two women, all black and armed with guns, walking single file just beyond where she lay. One of the men had a branded *F* on his face which covered the remnants of his nose and reached above his eyes. One arm was shorter than the other, but his powerful bulk and bitter gaze seemed to compensate. He towered over the others, a natural leader who caught the gaze and held it. One of the women, very slender and wearing gold hoops in her ears, spoke in words that Tempest could catch for they were a mixture of bastard English and pidgin French.

"Why wait? Burn and kill! Time for revenge, I say!"

The others paused to wait for the leader's answer and Tempest thought she had never seen such barely repressed fury. His big hand went out as he waved back in the direction they had come, then drew it across his throat in a cutting gesture. She wanted to duck her head and could not.

"That and more. But when I, Felipe, say." The words were flat and low, but the others moved back. The woman who had questioned stared at him for an instant before bowing her head. He directed a stream of words at her that came too fast for Tempest to catch as they walked away. She saw the woman's back above the garment that just circled her waist. Long ropy scars covered it and stood high above the rest of her skin. She had been beaten many times in the exact same places.

Tempest lay still for several minutes after they went their way. She had heard comments about slave rebellions all her life—it was the thing slave owners feared most. Great Aunt Hannah's slaves were too old and too few to consider seeking freedom, but Savora had once spoken of it to Tempest. Flight had proved the better part. She knew that most slaves were not mistreated for the simple reason that you did not destroy valuable property. Were these outlaws planning fire and destruction or speaking idly on some time taken off from duties? Yet she had not misunderstood the words or the intent. Murder shone in the eyes of those who had spoken. She rose cautiously, knowing that this was a matter to lay before Robert Dornier.

Tempest set out in the general direction of the plantation, but now the woods in which she had taken such pleasure seemed a trap to delay her and she was still very thirsty. She expected someone to challenge her every step and had to fight against shrieking when a bird flew up in her face when she rushed into a dense thicket.

She crossed two small meadows and went down toward a glen where a brilliant growth of flowers and trees seemed to indicate water. She was not mistaken, for here a stream meandered between sheets of moss-covered rock to a wider pool nearly hidden under a flood of blue blossoms. Ignoring the beauty, she knelt down and drank of the icy water. It was so vitalizing that she pulled open her collar and splashed her neck and bosom, drank again, then showered herself as she slapped both hands in the stream. Her skirts were hot around her legs, so she drew them up, sighing in relief as the breeze struck her skin.

"Why don't you take a swim? The water's fine. In fact, I vouch for it." The slow, drawling voice came from behind her.

Tempest sprang to her feet, barely holding back a scream. Justin St. Trevian stood in the mingled light and shadow, wearing only a brief loincloth. His hair was partially wet and curled over his head in golden auburn waves. His tawny eyes were filled with laughter, which turned to incredulity as he recognized her.

"What are you doing here?" She could not help but stare at his tall, muscular body, which was darkly tanned all the way down. Several white scars criss-crossed his chest and curved around his narrow waist. He might have been an old pagan god surveying his domain, so at home did he seem in it. Apollo, thought Tempest, vowing that she would not look away.

"My dear Mrs. Hutt! Are you in these woods looking for souls to save? Where is the zealous Mr. Hutt?" His tone was one of good-natured raillery; they might never have faced each other in anger on the deck of the *Corinthian*.

Tempest thought of explaining her true circumstances, but caution held her back. Robert Dornier might not press inquiries for his wife's sake, but Justin, perhaps curious or simply annoyed, might have no such compunctions. She must be civil and agreeable, then leave as soon as possible.

"A pleasure to see you, sir. I came for a walk and thought to gather herbs."

His brow crinkled. "With no basket? And in this part of the country, where runaway slaves often to come seeking to recruit others from the plantations? Successfully, I might add."

Tempest could not doubt that she had encountered such a party. She had to say something to distract his attention from the neck of her gown and her bosom, which felt exposed. Yet if she fastened it, that would only emphasize the discomfort. "I must be getting back. It grows late. The beauty of the country fascinated me and I wandered too far." She felt the blood hammering in her ears and wondered at the breathlessness of her voice.

Justin stepped closer. "I know of no missionaries around this area. Chapels, yes, but regularly watched. The plantation owners do not like their property . . . disturbed." There was an odd intonation in his voice as he watched her. "They do not care for the activities of the missionaries, either. Have you and your husband not found it so?"

"I have to go." Tempest started around him, but he clamped hard fingers on her arm.

"Little fool, do you know what could happen to a lone white woman out here? When I think of the stories I could tell you." The amber eyes suddenly glittered down into hers. "Ah, but you are not alone, are you? You met your lover here or you are about to go to him, is that it?"

Tempest was so angry that she could not speak. She felt heat suffuse her face as it always did when she was furious. When she jerked in an attempt to be free, Justin laughed and put the other hand behind her head to pull her closer.

"Hit the mark, didn't I?"

Then his mouth closed over hers and he held her imprisoned while they kissed. Tempest twisted her head, but even as she did so she knew that she did not really want to escape. His tongue probed hers with light movements while his lips moved silkily. The faintest burning began in her loins. Her breasts ached for his touch. She could not breathe. Her very air was being drawn up into him and yet she let her tongue curl tentatively around his so that their mouths locked together all the more tightly.

Justin moved his hand into her open dress, found her nipple, and began to rub it. This added to the building fire which grew when she felt the bulge of his manhood against her legs. She heard herself moaning a little and the harsh sound of his excitement clutched at them both. It felt to Tempest that she would die if they stopped now, and still they had to do so. She was a virgin; how could she consent to despoilation?

Both hands were touching her breasts now, gently and then harder as their ardor grew more powerful. Tempest held him hungrily in her arms, delighting in the feel of his body and marveling at the smoothness of his skin. Her fingers caressed him while all her senses came alive in a way she had never before imagined.

They paused to catch their breaths but continued to hold each other.

Justin spoke hoarsely. "It's private in yonder. Will you come?" He ran his fingers softly across her bare erect nipples and watched her shudder with pleasure.

Tempest was conscious as never before of her surroundings: the fragrant flowers, the rush of the stream over tiny white pebbles, a swaying bird on a branch just beyond them, the sensual feel of warm air on her skin, and most intense of all, the passionate man who held her as he asked for what she longed to give. And that, after all, was the deciding factor. He could take her and she knew that she would yield, that she could weep in maidenly distress thereafter. But she, Tempest Mallory, made her own decisions and stood by them. She wanted this man and had ever since she first saw him. Men made such choices all the time and were not the less. Why not women? Why should her first lover not be such a one as Justin St. Trevian?

"Show me." She spoke the words with all their layers of meaning very softly as she looked straight into his eyes. He should not mistake her purpose, nor would she turn away from it. Tempest knew all that happened between men and women.

Savora had been quite explicit on the subject, speaking of the pain that became pleasure and of the bitterness that could come from the cold taking of an unwilling, unknowing body. The girls in the school and convent had been equally frank. Women were not as sheltered as men often liked to think. Now she, Tempest, was to take her first lover.

Justin released her, smiling. "Gladly. But one thing. I know Martha is not your name. What is it?" He laughed with her in amusement and the anticipation of what was to come.

"Miranda." It was true. Tempest Miranda Mallory, from her parents' love of Shakespeare, whom they had quoted incessantly.

"Miranda." It was warm on his tongue as he took her hand and led her under the overgrowth of vines and branches, around a grouping of large trees at the edge of a rock formation that was covered with the same blue blossoms abounding in this area. Just beyond, there was a pool into which the sun reflected. Several vines trailed along one side and covered the stones with lush green ropes. The other side was in the shade, mossy and soft, a delicate couch. It was a bower such as lovers might seek. Looking at it, Tempest was grateful for the beauty.

Justin swung her up in his arms, kissed her deeply, and sank down on the moss. Then he very slowly began to unfasten the remaining buttons keeping him from her body. When she was naked to the waist, he bent and took her left breast in his mouth for the full length of the nipple. His tongue sought it as earlier it had sought Tempest's tongue. He smoothed the flesh of her side with one hand while she caressed his hair and neck. Her back curved toward him as her head went back in the rising ecstasy. Far up in the sky a dark bird rode the wind currents, plummeting downward with a call that matched her own unsounded one.

8

Covenant of the Flesh

Justin's mouth moved over Tempest's skin, kindling tiny fires that threatened to grow into one mighty conflagration. They lay together on the moss with their bodies pressed close. With her eager help, he had removed the last stitch of the few clothes she wore, admired the slender rounded curves, pulled off the loincloth to show his bronzed leaness and powerful shaft erect and throbbing, and come to her with all the hunger of a man who could not wait.

Tempest was a little fearful at the thought of what must happen next, but the throbbing of her flesh had taken over. He placed her hands on him, smiling a little at her hesitancy, and put his own fingers deep into her hot womanhood, which had been long wet with anticipation. She leaned over and kissed him, wondering what it would be like to touch that pulsating core of him with her lips or taste the flow of his power. She looked up at him and saw in the darkened amber eyes that desire could wait no longer.

"Miranda! Come here!" He pushed her back and rose above her, sweat beading his brow. Man the impaler and woman the receiver; Justin, the man she wanted as she had never in her life hungered for anything before.

Suddenly it was too soon. Tempest tried to roll away, but her choice had already been made. She smiled at Justin then and lifted her arms to him. He fitted his mouth to hers in one long, explosive kiss which made her shake with pleasure. Then he was spreading her legs wide as she arched to meet him.

He penetrated her so deeply that Tempest felt the shock even over the lapping waves of desire. She thought briefly that she would have preferred his fingers. This was pain just as it had been described. His mouth had locked hers; now he held her more firmly and when she twisted about, his eyes glowed as if this enhanced his delight. He withdrew a little and began to move up and down on her, riding her thighs as expertly as he might a horse. It hurt and she put one arm up on his shoulder as if to stop him. He grinned and moved the harder. The frenzy of passion was upon him and he could only go with it.

Then Tempest felt the drawing sensation. It was as if something were just opening inside her. Each thrust brought her closer to an edge, toward a pinnacle of a thing not yet experienced. Pain vanished; she grew heated and clung to Justin as they rose and fell together. He filled her. She opened the wider to receive and hold him. She would not let him escape. The were linked in this sweet immolation.

Justin went rigid, gasped, and fell back from her all in one swift motion that left her shaking. He frowned and put one hand over his eyes. His seed was spilled, and Tempest, still in the first hunger, turned on her side away from his gaze. The silence was so complete that she could hear the faint rasp of a lizard on the stone just beyond them.

Justin touched her bare back and his voice was softer than she could have imagined. "Miranda, you should have told me. I never thought to find you virgin. A married woman, or at least one of experience . . ." He let his words trail away on a rueful sigh. "Will you forgive me? We all have our reasons for what we do, don't we?"

Tempest faced him then. He sat cross-legged and serious, his eyes gentle, the long hands that had promised such delight now cupping his chin. The scar on his cheek was white, reflecting emotion. "Justin, please believe there is nothing to forgive."

"Oh, but there is. I want to take you back to my house. It is a long way, but my horse is tethered not far away from here. I want to know about you, to teach you, and have you for my own."

"Your mistress, you mean?" Tempest tried not to think of the pleasure that being with him day and night would bring. "Once you hated that idea." Did he mean he would dispossess his other women for her? A flower plucked and discarded after a short period of fondling?

Justin's mouth quirked upward. "But now I do not. Why should that surprise you? You are beautiful as you are, but I could dress you, show you all the ways of love. This is a lovely land, Miranda, and we could have it together."

A virgin was a rarity for him. The words almost came to Tempest's lips, but she bit them back. She must not destroy the moment of their coming together. What if she confided in him? Sought his friendship? What was there to lose? Certainly much could be gained. She opened her mouth to begin, but he was speaking.

"And afterward, I would make sure that you were amply taken care of. A new start any place you chose and enough money to ensure that you find a good husband." He was leaning toward her eagerly, the touch of his hand burning on her arm.

"Afterward? Husband?" Was she reduced to just repeating his words? The banked desire rose in her again as she moistened her lips.

"Yes, of course. I must go to New Orleans to wed, but that need present no difficulties for us. Naturally, a woman must be married. But then you know that."

"Naturally." Her mouth was stiff and she felt the beginning of tears. Use and discard her, would he? But, to do him justice, Justin seemed concerned and caring. He probably thought he was offering her a marvelous opportunity. But she was a woman with a will of her own and she would make her destiny as a great actress. That resolve was now stronger than ever. "Of a certainty."

He was drawing her closer, the amber eyes gleaming into hers and threatening to drown her. "I almost thought you were a missionary. I'm glad you aren't. Hard times are ahead for them here. But we have other things to do, you and I. I want to know everything about you, Miranda. Will you tell me?" One hand brushed back the red hair from her forehead, and the tenderness of that gesture shook Tempest to the core.

A breeze rustled the leaves close to them as a bird call came piercingly sweet in the still afternoon heat. Justin ran his finger over the curve of her mouth, around her chin, and down her neck. His white teeth shone in the half smile that was so much a part of him. Tempest bent her head to kiss the caressing hand that turned and lifted her face to his.

"Miranda, you haunt me. I feel that I know you and still you are an enigma."

"Yet we know so little of each other." She whispered the words.

"Let me hold you, sweet. Let me show you love." He set his mouth on hers with no urgency but with all the cherishing of a dear lover.

Then began the time that transported Tempest to a delight of mind, heart, and body in a fusion so complete that she wanted to weep. Justin's hands and mouth were everywhere on her skin, breasts, soft mound, toes, and back. Always, his eyes adored and promised her. He kissed her nipples, took them between his teeth gently, and moved the tip of his tongue over them until Tempest clutched his shoulders with both hands and called out his name in her demand. They locked together in a passionate kiss that went on and on. Tempest put her hand on his shaft to find him erect, ready for her. Now she was doubly ready for him. Her whole body throbbed with eagerness for consummation.

But it was not time. Justin took up, held her at a plateau while he touched and fondled. His tongue went at her mound softly at first and then like a tiny blade that promised his mightier thrust later. Tempest held him, returning his kisses, lavishing her own on his powerful body. Once, greatly daring, she put her mouth to his shaft, circling it with her lips and moving quickly back as it pulled upward.

"Later, my darling. This is for you." Justin kissed the top of her head as he drew her about so that she sat facing him with her legs around the curve of his buttocks. "I won't hurt you."

"I know." Tempest did not care. She was one pounding, aching hunger that must be assuaged. Her flesh was alight with a fire that was approaching incandescence. She saw that Justin held back with an effort. His brow was furrowed and his eyes were almost dark. He was swollen large with leashed power in restraint.

Now he boosted her a little as she placed her arms on his. Very slowly she lifted and came down so that the entire length of him was in her, filling her in a way that was the beginning of pleasure and the bare edge of pain. They moved together in a rhythm that stirred and drove, revitalizing itself with every motion. Tempest rode him easily, up and down, enjoying the withdrawing and filling that took her higher each time. Then she was at the height. Something inside was about to burst free; if it did not, she would die.

"Now!" Justin raised himself with her and this joining was hard where all the others had been gentle and tantalizing. He pulled her back with him so that she lay on top of him, his arms around her while his body still moved with hers. "Now and now!"

Tempest barely heard his words for she had plunged straight into the sea of fire that waited. She soared, tightened, and rose again. Her flesh convulsed and the world blurred. She and Justin were the core of each other; nothing else existed. They clung together and breasted the wild storm of their passion.

In the aftermath, Tempest heard herself murmuring Justin's name and his response.

"Rest, love. It is all right."

The soft words of reassurance bore her on their tide and she fell asleep in his arms with his lips on her brow.

A cramp in her fingers woke Tempest with a start. Justin slept soundly beside her, one arm on his chest, the other on his stomach while he clasped her hand. His face was smooth and very young in the dappled light from the late sun as it filtered through the flowers above them. A low rumble of thunder came from the distance, but it did not rouse Justin. Tempest let her eyes roam over his long, tanned body, which had given her such pleasure. The carved lips were gentle in repose just as they had been when he had spoken tenderly and given her understanding in the ways of passion.

She pulled her fingers free very slowly so as not to wake him. He sighed and his mouth formed a name before he turned on his side and fell more deeply asleep. She did not think that name was Miranda. In her mind Tempest spoke to him while she scrambled into her clothes. I have to go. You want a mistress for a few days or months. You have many women and will have more. For my own sake and that of my ambition, I must be for myself alone. Justin, Justin, Justin!

It would be so easy to wake him and go with him. What ties were there, after all, to Morna? They were strangers. But then so were she and Justin. She had chosen to savor the delights of love with him and she would never regret it. If she went with him now, Tempest knew in some way that she would the lesser. I go alone. Grandiose perhaps, but was she not to be selector of her roles?

Tempest looked once more at Justin, drinking in the memory of him for all the long nights and days of the future, then she turned and ran from the place of their happiness.

She did not know when the tears started. Suddenly, they were raining down her cheeks and sobs were rising from her chest into her throat. She did not look where she was going, nor did she really care. The thought crossed her mind that Jamaica might be filled with snakes and wild beasts, all massed in this particular spot, and still she would face them weeping. Weeping. Surely that was a delicate word for what was happening to her! Howling was more like it. Something in her decided that was very funny indeed, so she sat down under a swirl of vines to laugh. Only tears came, but she shook with them.

Tempest could not have said exactly why everything seemed to merge into this unbearable *tristesse*; the French word exactly fitted the way she felt now. She had never been one for tears and had not wept since the death of her parents, but at this time it was for them, for Great-aunt Hannah, Morna, all that the future might offer up, and her own self-imposed loss that she agonized. Clarity burned in her as she saw the struggle of that future: the repertory plays if she were uncommonly fortunate; the necessity of beginning as a singer or dancer, with the free use of her body expected; the need for lessons, connections, opportunity. Talent and will could never be enough if one was a woman. An actress was always considered in terms of some husband or protector unless she was truly phenomenal. Sarah Siddons and Fanny Kemble came to mind immediately as exceptions, but they were products of notable families.

Thunder rattled close by and her head jerked up. On the right, it had come. That was a good omen if one trusted the

Greeks. A breeze sprang up to dry the tears on her cheeks and hands. She realized that she was very tired; there were no emotions left to feel. She was simply passive; the bout of self-pity departed as quickly as it had come. Obstacles were there, but they must be accepted or overcome, even ignored.

Tempest rose walked on, uncertain of the actual path, but reasonably sure that Cloud Ridge was in this direction. She had no idea what she would say to Morna; that would have to be faced when she arrived. The sun dropped as she moved along, and by the time she came out into one of the little meadows that was familiar, high clouds edged with purple were building in the north. The air was still and heavy, but the freshness of rain was in it. A flock of small birds flew upward, the sun glinting on their dark feathers. There was another rumble of thunder and they scattered in all directions. Justin would probably be awake by now. What was he thinking? She must not let herself speculate on that. She went faster, concentrating on nothing else.

The red glow was still visible behind the trees when Tempest emerged from the undergrowth to see the vista of Cloud Ridge before her. The placid gardens were just to her left, and she could see a tall black figure bent over one of the rose bushes, apparently tending them before the rain. She hoped that she would go unnoticed until she reached the house. The Dornier slaves were far too well trained to ask questions of a guest and Morna might not have missed her, but she did not want the sharp eyes of her host to rake her again.

"Evenin', mum." The man stood up to his full height and bent his head respectfully. He was so dark that his skin was glowing ebony. He had an arrogant nose and a jutting, forceful jaw. Thin white trousers and shirt could not conceal the muscles of his powerful body. The eyes that lifted to meet Tempest's were hooded. He was one of the men she had seen with the branded man who called himself Felipe earlier in the day.

Questions raced through her mind. Renegade? Dornier slave? Was there any chance he could have seen her? One thing happened after another, and all she wanted was to sink into a hot bath and bed. Sleep and blessed oblivion—the most desirable thing in the world.

"Jason! Jason love! It's all right. You can come now." The

low voice carried clearly in the quiet and came from behind a stand of ornamental palms. A second later, Savora came running around it.

The dark man rapped out what seemed a command and she stopped, her startled eyes going to Tempest. She wore a loose tunic dress of pale green which showed the richness of her body, but it was her face that held Tempest silent. The great eyes glowed with brilliance and the curve of her cheeks and mouth were tender. The lost, pensive look of the past weeks was gone. The time with Justin told Tempest what she knew now. This was Savora's lover, and she had come to him for their consummation.

Savora's head went up as she said, "Miss Tempest, I wondered where you were. Mrs. Dornier wanted you, but I said you were off by yourself reading. She said you always were funny that way. Jason, this is my . . ."

"Friend. Not mistress, but dear friend." Tempest broke in to say the words as compellingly as she could. No one could miss the tensing of the huge shoulders and the glitter in Jason's gaze as he observed her disheveled appearance and tumbled hair. She certainly did not resemble a lady of any sort. All her heightened senses told Tempest that she was in danger from this man.

Several of the darkened windows of the great house flamed into life above them, and a figure could be seen walking back and forth across one of them. One voice called out to be answered by another as a snatch of song drifted down to the garden. It would have been peaceful enough except for the three who stood in dangerous silence.

Jason said, "Friend? Who can be friend to us, Savora? Pick your words more carefully."

"Go, it is not safe. Especially now." Savora turned to Tempest and spread both hands. "You have not seen him. I came to fetch you and we return together, is that not so?"

"It is so." Tempest saw the murder flame die down in his eyes as he reached out a hand toward Savora and stopped but not before she saw the tenderness of the gesture.

"We will meet again." Jason whirled and vanished into the shadows of the wood before either woman could speak.

Tempest stared at Savora questioningly.

"He is my husband, Tempest. And he is a rebel. Our lives rest with you."

Tempest had thought she could bear no more, but now she put her arms around Savora. There was love between them, and love is trust. "I understand. Tell me about it, and when you are done, I must tell you what has happened to me."

Thunder hammered down and the rains began.

9

The Rarer Action

Hot water sluiced down Tempest's back as the fragrance of lavender drifted up. She dipped a hand down in it and traced the drops over her breasts, which bore the faint imprint of Justin's fingers. Then she shifted in the wide wooden tub so that she faced Savora, who was reaching for yet another pitcher of water.

"That's enough, thank you. Then what happened?"

They were quite alone in the anteroom off Tempest's quarters, but Savora looked around apprehensively, sipped some of the wine Tempest had poured for them both and sighed. It had been easy to obtain privacy. The master was out, Morna was resting in her rooms after being assured that her guest was all right from her nap in the gardens and subsequent drenching, and the slaves had been sent on their well-trained ways.

Savora had already told how she met Jason on the *Corinthian* when she wandered about. His English master had died unexpectedly in Norfolk some months previously. There was no kin to claim his belongings and Jason took the opportunity to flee, but he was apprehended and sold at auction to a cruel planter, who, unable to subdue him and angered at his refusal to act as stud, sold him to the first bidder, who happened to be a representative of Captain Jacky of the *Corinthian*. It appeared that the captain was a smuggler, slave trader, and trickster par excellence. Jason had been agreeable, a trifle foolish, and due to his size, considered a prize. He was fettered but knew how to release the chains. He and Savora met when they could and fell instantly in love.

"I may have his child. I hope so. He was bought at a secret auction by one of the planters around here, a Mr. Robertson, but ran away on the first day. I met him and went to the missionaries, most of whom are very sympathetic and hate slavery. We told them part of the truth, and were married. Jason lives in the woods and comes to me when he can." Savora drew a halting breath. "I said earlier he is a rebel, but what he wants, what we both want, is just to live in peace and freedom." Her eyes challenged Tempest. "What will you do, my friend, my mistress?"

Savora often talked that way when she was most unsure of herself. The transforming love she felt for Jason burned in her face.

Tempest said, "Listen, Savora." She told her about Justin and the afternoon and all her conflicting feelings. "But I could go no further; I could not be one of many. I do not love him, of course, but he is excitement, flame in the blood." Why did she feel this sense of betrayal toward him? The vision of his face and the tenderness in the tawny eyes made her pause. "He is betrothed in New Orleans."

"On the ship, they said he had a reputation for a fancier of the ladies, that he has little money and will do anything to get it." Savora saw the look on Tempest's face and knelt beside her, instantly contrite. "It was best to get it out of your system. There are potions to see that you are not with child. You'd best not wander around alone from now on. I'll talk to Jason."

The bond between Tempest and Savora was now stronger than ever by virtue of their sharing, but Tempest found that she passionately envied Savora the love of Jason. If only she and Justin had loved each other for just a short time! Then she thought of his gentle lovemaking and the ascent to the heights, his caring and concern that all be pleasurable for her, the hunger held in abeyance. Justin was surely a man who took what he wanted. Had there not been something other than the hunger of the flesh? Then Tempest had to smile at her romantic fancies. She, no less than he, had taken what she wanted and with that must be content.

Tempest had believed that she would never sleep, exhausted though she was due to all the happenings of that one long afternoon, but once ensconced in the high white bed shrouded with mosquito netting, oblivion came down. She walked in dreams with Justin, lost him in fog, stood alone on a stage with skeletons for audience, sailed a dozen ships and came at last to a swampland where a pirate demanded gold and wore Justin's arrogant grin. He clamped a hand on her shoulder and called her name over and over.

"Are you going to sleep all day?" The question was repeated several times as Tempest twisted back and forth to avoid it. "Tempest!"

She opened one eye, shut it against the morning light, then opened both and looked into Morna's face. The blue eyes were livelier than they had been since Tempest's arrival and the blond curls, arranged in an elaborate hairdo, had more sheen. There were red flags in her cheeks, but her skin was no longer chalky.

"What time is it? Are you all right, Morna?" Tempest sat up, forgot that she was nude under the sheet and jerked it higher. She always had hated to sleep in any sort of nightwear.

"Ten o'clock and I'm fine. Haven't I told you my strength is coming back? I've come to have coffee with you." She motioned to a slave just behind her, who set a tray of that liquid and rolls beside Tempest, fluffed the pillows behind her, placed a chair for Morna, and tiptoed away.

Morna cocked her head to one side and surveyed Tempest. "Your gown for the ball will soon be ready and we've set out invitations. It will be in another two weeks. It's going to be such fun, don't you think?" The limp way she sat in her chair belied the bright words. "This will be the first party since well before young Robert was born. I vow, I've missed our social life. You'll love the Robertsons, the Marbons, the Henrys; she's a cat, of course, but so amusing. Mrs. Marbon's nephew is visiting from Philadelphia, but he's always talking politics. You might like him—you're so serious now."

When Morna paused for breath and to sip her coffee, Tempest said, "I hope you're not doing this just for me. I really don't think you are well enough and it is pleasant being here. I cannot express how grateful I am that you and Robert have made me welcome after the way I came." She hesitated, wondering if she dared express her true desires.

"I always wanted you to visit and after what you told me about your aunt—that awful marriage and all—Robert and I want you to feel that we are your family. He is such a good husband! This is the most marvelous way to live, everything I've ever wanted!" The red marks were brighter on her cheeks as she spoke. Tempest doubted Morna knew she repeated these remarks every time she was around her friend. "Jamaica has any number of eligible gentlemen. We'll find one for you, wait and see. He will have to be special to be worthy of you!"

Tempest spoke gently as she set her cup down and pushed the red hair back from her face. "Morna, I don't intend to marry. You know I've always wanted to be an actress and now I am more determined than ever. We talked about it so much in school, and you remember how we vied for the best parts. I was serious about acting then, and I've never changed."

Morna leaned forward. "But this is real now. This is the rest of your life! A good husband is what every woman should have."

Tempest had the sinking feeling that nothing she said would make any difference. Morna was barely listening now and still her face had an expression of interest in it. The real woman was somehow far away.

"Let me work for you and Robert. I am a poor figurer, but I write a good copperplate hand and I believe I express myself well. This is a large plantation, there must be irksome business details I can handle. When you have guests, I can recite and sing. If there is any sort of theater here in Jamaica, I could act there and get some experience. I need to save money, Morna, and learn about the craft. Then I can go to one of the cities where actors get ahead and are honored—New York or Philadelphia." Not New Orleans, she thought, for Justin would be there with his wife. "I could give good service."

Morna looked closely at Tempest and gave a little trilling laugh. "I am sure you will forget all that foolishness after you have been here for a time, dear. I could never let you work in the way you speak. Robert would never permit it. You are our friend, our guest. Now, you relax and think about parties.

You've never had a real chance for fun, Tempest, and now you will."

"But how can I remain here this way?" She had expected Morna to react this way but now that the moment was here, it was still hard to believe.

"Nonsense! You lived in Virginia and so did I. Guests came and stayed for years, became actual members of the family in fact. You are welcome here always. And anyway, you'll marry soon." Morna snapped her fingers, the sound loud in the silence. A slave appeared immediately and extended an arm to help her rise. "Robert wants to show you around the plantation this afternoon. He will be ready at twelve on the portico. Oh, wear a hat and gloves. We can't have your skin spoiled. We'll talk some more at dinner. Darling, it is so good to have you here!" She kissed Tempest on the cheek and departed in a swirl of skirts.

Tempest wondered why Robert and Morna both were approaching her on the day after her adventure with Justin. Could they know something of what had gone on? It seemed unlikely, and yet it was possible. Her failure just now with Morna confirmed that nothing of the old friendship remained. They were two people who had once known each other well. She could not accept what Morna and, through her, Robert offered. Very well, try him. She would be practical and reasonable; a businessman should respond to that.

On the stroke of twelve, Tempest was waiting. She did not know if Robert planned to ride or be driven, but her dark green riding habit with the tiny waist and tawny piping on sleeves, skirt hem, and jacket should be suitable for either. Her hair was braided around her head and a few curls hung at ears and neck. A hat of lighter green was perched slightly over one eye. A veil of the same shade ended at her chin and tickled her nose. Boots and gloves of a fawn color completed the ensemble.

"I assume you ride, Miss Mallory?" Robert Dornier, immaculate in beige and brown, strode toward her, gloves and hat in his hand. "I have taken the liberty of having the horses fetched. We can go by carriage if you prefer."

Tempest had been taught to ride in her earliest youth, but there had been no opportunity since her school days for her to do so. She hoped that this was something a person did not forget. Now two slaves brought a chestnut mare up and stopped before her. "She is beautiful, so sleek and elegant! What is her name?" She did not try to conceal her delight, and the horse seemed pleased also as it nudged her shoulder with a friendly nose.

"She is Hera and she belongs to you if you find her suitable. If not, there is a stable from which you may choose." Robert swung easily into the saddle of his gray stallion and smiled down at her. His eyes were ice cold.

Tempest thought he knew she would protest. She inclined her head as the slave helped her into the saddle. "Queen of the gods. It is truly her name! I adore her already and shall be happy to ride her while I visit. Thank you."

"Come, then." Robert's lips twitched as if he hid a smile. "There is much for you to see." He started down the drive at a decorous pace.

Robert and Tempest rode abreast while he kept up a running comment on Jamaica, its history, products, and culture. She was given no time for comment or question. He was a man in love and obsessed with the object of that love. Cloud Ridge was a fully producing sugar cane plantation, although vegetables and fruits were grown as well. They passed fields of green cane situated on hills of fertile soil and valleys of the same, water and windmills, oxen for use in working the ground and slaves at their toil. He pointed out the various buildings, curing and distilling houses, the overseer's quarters, slave areas, the carpenter's quarters, and those of the other skilled workers who lived on the estate.

"We use the best land for the cane, of course, and allow some to lie fallow or use that for pasture. The land is cleaned and turned up about twice a year." Robert broke off and studied Tempest. "Are you growing weary? I should not have brought you out in the heat of the day. Had you been a European I would not, but since you are from the southern states, it seemed all right and this is the only time I had free."

"Not particularly weary, but hot." Tempest stripped off her gloves and patted Hera's side. "Could we rest for a bit in the shade?" She pointed toward a spreading tree on the edge of a small rise. Behind it the landscape rose and fell in gentle undulations before becoming stark with the path to the mountains.

Moments later she was sipping the water, now tepid, which

Robert had so thoughtfully provided. She had to speak before he began to tell her at length about the harvesting of the cane. Once she would have found such data fascinating since she knew only of the cotton plantations of her South country, but now the coil in which she found herself must take precedence over everything else.

"Robert, if I may call you so, there is something I have been wishing to speak to you about." Once launched, Tempest let the words pour out. He watched her quizzically, reminding her unpleasantly of boys she had seen impaling bugs on pins. Just yesterday another man had watched her and she had found that scrutiny glorious. Justin. Justin. His name rang in her heart as she looked Morna's husband in the eye and felt the chill.

"Enough, Tempest. I should have spoken to you before. Matters ought never to have come to this. Was Morna very upset?" His voice roughened with pent-up emotion.

"I think not. But she is so different from the girl I knew."

"She would be. Her body is frail and her joints give her pain. The morning fever wastes her. The doctor tells me that she will not live long and should be humored in all things. There is no cure. My son has the same illness." Robert controlled his speech. The flat statements could have been made about another person, not the wife who so loved him. "No son of my body to take over Cloud Ridge. That is a bitter thing."

Tempest jumped to her feet as things became plain to her. She wondered that she had not seen them all along. "Poor Morna, my poor friend! Does she know?"

"Of course not. Sit down, Tempest, and compose yourself. You must act as if nothing has happened. Let her take delight in you, for she will see herself as you are." His eyes went opaque as he stared at her face and body. "Lovely and alive and strong. You bloom in this land."

Tempest felt her skin crawl. He had looked upon her with desire and Robert Dornier was total master of his domain. Turn it aside and quickly. Let him think she was a simpering fool. "Oh, Morna! I shall weep when I see her! She thinks she is getting better. How can I conceal what I feel?"

He stood up. "You will have to. I assume there will be no more talk of leaving while matters are as they are? For her sake?"

"For her sake. May we go now?"

He caught her arm, his fingers digging into her flesh. His face was set in hard lines. "She must not know. There must be no mental strain on her; it will take away from her strength. Compose yourself."

Tempest was uncertain now. Was she to be one of those women who read male fascination into every glance and idle word? There was nothing in Robert's voice or manner now to suggest an illicit interest, and he was a man to whom emotion came hard. But still, that glance had been as startling as a reared snake's head in the moment before it strikes.

"What is the name of her illness? How many doctors have seen her? Morna was always strong in her youth, and her family was not prone to protracted sicknesses."

The skin around Robert's mouth went dead white and his sentences pushed through stiff lips. "You are her friend. I must remember that it is your right to ask such a question. I hope that you will consider the fact that it gives me pain to answer them and discuss my wife in this way. It is a combined ailment of the blood and joints. A doctor in Paris first confirmed it, and two others here concur. Will that suffice for you?"

Tempest knew it was time to back down. "Of course, Robert. I did not mean to badger you."

"Do what she asks of you. We understand each other, she and I." He tried to smile at her, but failed. "Who knows, Tempest? You may yet fulfill her wish and find a husband here."

"I want no husband." Tempest clenched her fists in the skirt of her riding habit and wondered if she dared mount Hera. Anger at her own hesitation swept over her and she was on the horse's back in one fluid movement learned long ago. "I wish to be alone, Robert. I am sure you understand."

Robert Dornier surveyed her leisurely. "It is for you to understand, my dear, and you will, in time's fullness."

His words drummed in her ears while Hera took the road back to Cloud Ridge.

10

Crescent Powers

"I know it must be awfully boring for you, Tempest, but after
the ball you'll have so many invitations you won't know what
to do with them. We have concerts, assemblies, horse races,
dances, visits back and forth." Morna leaned over Tempest and
made a face at her book. "Shakespeare again? Men don't like
to talk about things like that. Small talk, that's what you need
to perfect."

Tempest shut *Othello* and rose to put her hands on Morna's
shoulders, already thinner in these past few weeks. "Sit down
and rest. You're going to be lively for the party, aren't you?"
Morna smiled up at her and in that expression Tempest read the
old stubborn one of their youth. She had tried to cosset her
friend, avoid Robert, and not think about Justin in these past
days. Her flux had come. She was not to bear Justin's child and
thanked heaven for that. The thought had not crossed her mind
during their interlude. Robert's library had proved to be a
salvation. It was very well stocked with philosophy, religion of
all types, texts on farming, poetry, fiction, and drama as well as
art and manners. She shut herself away here and read by the
hours. When the longing came to go into the woods, she fought

it back. She knew that she would look for Justin and that must not be.

Morna was laughing now. "You can't see my gown. It's to be a surprise. Yours is gorgeous. Robert is fetching that special hairdresser all the way from Kingston for us. Isn't that marvelous!" She prattled on while Tempest nodded and smiled at appropriate intervals. "Come and let's go look at Robert. He's such a good, quiet baby, don't you think?"

Did Morna not wonder at her own gauntness and weariness, the fevers that were more frequent and that repeated themselves in her child? If not, Tempest thought she herself could only be thankful. Morna professed her pleasure at Tempest's abandonment of the idea of acting and leaving. Robert was agreeable around them both, but remote with Tempest. Their exchange on the hill might never have happened. Tempest felt imprisoned; this was a stalemate that would end in the death of a friend and the loss of something never fully realized. She and Savora were closer than ever, but not even to her had Tempest confided Robert's words. That must be her own burden.

There was a knock at the door of the library just then, and a slave entered. "Master Clement has arrived, madam. He says he is exhausted and must rest immediately." Her voice quivered with what might have been laughter and vanished at Morna's stern look.

"The hairdresser! He is very temperamental. We must be very patient." Morna winked at Tempest, who smiled back, glad for the camaraderie of the moment. "Show him to his room and give him refreshment." When the slave vanished, she put her hand to her head and sank into a chair.

"What is it?" Tempest knew very well that the afternoon dizziness was upon her. They had their pretense to play out. She crossed to a table and poured out a little wine, which she handed to Morna. "To the ball! May it be an occasion to remember!" She thought then that she made a prophecy.

Four afternoons later, Tempest sat having her hair done by Master Clement, who was already enraged by her request for something simple. "An elegant froth of curls, swirls at your neck and ears, the whole dressed with jewels and feathers. Only think!" At her barely repressed shudder and firm no, he grew sulkier still. He was barely five feet tall, with fiercely curled black hair and sharp eyes, but his mutters and snorts made her jump even as he finally obeyed. "The very idea! You will look a veritable sober matron at the ball tonight!"

Morna had been resting for the past few days, and Robert remained in unusually close attendance. Knowing how much she wanted this to be the event of the year, Tempest had expressed eagerness and enthusiasm before them both and now she was nearly as excited as she should have been for her first social occasion in this new land. But still, she feared greatly for Morna.

It was nearly twilight when Savora came to help her dress. There was a satiated look about her that made Tempest ache for Justin. How long did it take for such hunger to fade? She pushed back the thought and slipped into the thin petticoats, gossamer stockings, and low slippers that lay ready. She did not intend to wear anything to pinch her body into another shape, regardless of the fashion. Savora now lifted the gown over her head and settled it into place, fluffing the skirts out. She lifted her face to Tempest, who saw the stunned look there. Slowly, she revolved to the mirror and stared in her turn.

A tall elegant woman stood there, bare arms gleaming in the light, her slim throat ivory pale. "I am so different!" Tempest took a dance step, one of those taught to her long ago and now probably out of date, and watched the gown drift like smoke over her body. Madame Adelisa, prompted and cajoled by Tempest, had done herself proud. The soft material, shading from palest gray at her bosom to sea-green and white at the hem, gave the firm rounded curves of her body full vantage while artfully showing the innocence of a young girl. A leaf-green sash circled her small waist and emphasized her bosom delicately.

Her flaming hair was pulled severely back from her forehead and dressed in a coronet of braids. A few curls rested at the nape of her neck and several were so arranged behind her ears as to curve forward toward her shoulders. The severity of the style was thus offset. Her lips shone naturally pink and her skin still had some touch of the sun, so it gleamed honey warm. Tempest saw that her eyes were a deep gray in contrast to the gown and her cheekbones had little hollows under them, which lent allure to her face. Savora had touched the birthmark, the cleft in her cheek, with a bit of rose shading so that it became a beauty mark such as ladies often wore. In one hand Tempest carried a long-stemmed white rose. Morna had sent several necklaces of diamonds, emeralds, and pearls as well as bracelets, rings, and pins. Even though she admired this largess, Tempest knew she did beautifully as she was. Come what might, she was determined to enjoy this evening.

The hush when she descended the staircase, the admiration in Morna's eyes, and the stupefaction in Robert's gave her even more confidence as she was presented to the assembling guests in the parlor. Names ran through her brain in a blur while she smiled, nodded, and made decorous remarks to older gentlemen and their ladies, who viewed her sharply. Several young men circled about her immediately, seeking the opportunity to bring fans, tea, or wine. Some of the young women remarked on her gown while fingering their elaborate ones.

The floors where the company would dance later were polished to a high gleam and the flames of the candles reflected in them. Golden curtains moved in the breeze from outside while individual fans operated by slaves in white gave cool air to the rooms. When they went in to dine, the huge table was laden with all manner of rich foods and sauces, fine wines were offered, and musicians played softly in an alcove. A great wooden fan hung above them, pulled to and fro by two slaves. No expense or effort had been spared for this party.

A deaf old lady sat on Tempest's left and bombarded her with remarks about Italy, which she appeared to think was her home. These ceased abruptly when the beef in wine sauce and roasted piglet were passed her way. It was then that Tempest's other partner, an English lord living here these twenty years for his health, Sir Herbert Shurden, engaged her in conversation. He was both urbane and witty, carrying his seventy years with distinction. His wife eyed them across the table and returned to her animated conversation with the Henrys' nephew, who was visiting from Philadelphia. He was a thin young man in his twenties with anxious brown eyes that remained fixed on Tempest. From her end of the table, Morna, brilliant and apparently healthy in blue satin with sapphires, gave little peals of laughter and saluted Tempest with her glass.

"Will you be staying long, Miss Mallory?" Sir Herbert said. "If I may so boldly remark, you grace our island. Our community in this section of it is rather inbred and we are always delighted to have newcomers, especially young ladies." His chuckle invited her to laugh with him.

"The length of my visit is rather indefinite." How fearful to think it was measured in terms of Morna's life! He knew, as did all the guests, that she and Morna were old friends and had attended school together for a time. What if he began to ask personal questions as old gentlemen sometimes did, knowing they could get away with it? "But Jamaica fascinates me. Let us talk of this lovely land. What of the arts here? I am so interested." That should distract him and please his wife, who was now listening avidly. Tempest smiled demurely at her, received a cold nod, and fixed her limpid gaze on Sir Herbert.

By the time the desserts of cakes, tarts, and varied puddings arrived with appropriate wines, Tempest was innundated with more information about intellectual affairs in Jamaica than even she, who cared passionately about such matters, wanted to know in one evening. Morna had told her in passing that no theatrical company nor its like had been here and that it was not missed. "I would not speak of the profession here; the idea is rather shocking to the genteel." She had gone on to speak of other things, and Tempest had not pursued the discussion. But now the impulse seized her. This was a man of influence and personality. Why not try?"

"No theater here? How surprising. The drama is one of my great interests. You will think me overbold, Sir Herbert, but I have often longed for the opportunity to both see and perform the greats of past days." She tried to keep her tone light and a bit pedantic, but she could not be casual about her ambition and the sharp old eyes of her listener narrowed, then took on fire.

When she stopped to catch her breath, Tempest saw that all the people at their end of the table had paused to listen in mingled interest, surprise, and shock. Several of the men glanced at her more boldly, and one lady tittered. Her cheeks reddened. Sir Herbert finished his wine, allowed the slave to refill the crystal goblet, and spoke rather loudly.

"Well, my dear, we do have similar interests. I've seen the best in Covent Garden and a lot of the worst elsewhere. Would you do a recitation, a bit of music, for an old man? Humor me, as it were?" He let his gaze sweep the table to pause on his host and hostess. Robert nodded, waving one hand at Tempest. The guests buzzed, fascinated by the exchange.

"It will be my great pleasure, Sir Herbert." If he expected a bit of sentimental verse and a nasal song or two, he was in for a shock! This action might be unwise, but what actor ever missed a chance for the limelight?

The gentlemen retired for brandy and cigars while the ladies went apart. Morna was enthroned in a tall chair in the drawing room and she kept Tempest beside her, managing to whisper at one point, "Don't be too bold, dear. Just relax and let the men talk."

Nothing could have annoyed Tempest more; she knew her conversation was far more interesting than that of most of the men who had bantered with her. Now she nodded apparent agreement to Morna who, after all, was showing her the way of polite and dull conversation. The talk of gowns, shopping, lazy slaves, and babies had to end sometime. Snippets drifted to her ears and then words of real fascination struck her so that she looked for the speaker.

"It is not to be tolerated, they say, and they are right! The slaves have souls, too. The missionaries say we treat them as inferior animals, not even protecting their bodies properly. We know slavery is wrong." The woman was in her forties, very thin and intense, her hands twisting in the skirts of her brown silk gown as she talked. "We are going to free ours. There's no real choice!" Her head went back as she looked at the horrified gathering.

There was a collective gasp of rage and several voices rose at once.

"Give up our property! You're mad, Mina Entwright!"

"I've never heard such rot! We've worked for what we have."

"Next you'll be advocating we make them equal with us!"

Morna's light, sweet request rose over them all. "Now, now, this is a party and there'll be no serious talk. I forbid it. Shall we join the others for recitation and music?"

Tempest thought she would like to talk to the daring Mrs. Entwright, who was being steered apart by a tall, angry woman whispering as they walked. It was a vexed question, that of slavery, and her relationship with Savora made the matter very personal for her.

Robert escorted his wife and Tempest into the Golden Room, as the dancing parlor was called, just as the musicians began to play a lilting country air. His face was red and one corner of his mouth twitched convulsively. He turned to answer a greeting from a man close by, and Morna spoke to Tempest quickly.

"He's been arguing about slavery, too. What a wretched business all this interference is!" The red splotches were mounting on her cheeks now under all the powder, and little beads of perspiration stood on her forehead.

Hurriedly, Robert seated her, took Tempest to the pianoforte, gave her one of those challenging looks that both irritated and unnerved her, and held up his hands for silence. "Miss Mallory will now entertain us."

Sir Herbert was watching Tempest eagerly and she suspected that due to his interest, the guests were quieter than they might otherwise have been. Several of the men looked angry still; their discussions must have been heated. Were there many who felt as Mrs. Entwright did?

She spread her skirts out, sat down, and played the first notes of "Lord Randall." Her voice was not strong, but it was pure and clear. The compelling ballad was one of her favorites and she moved with it to the tragic end. Then, not looking up or giving her audience time to applaud, she launched into Desdemona's green willow song from *Othello*. The haunting refrain made her remember how she had once wept for the sad heroine. Now she half regarded her as foolish, mad for love's sake. The silence came and drew out, her supreme compliment. She smiled as she acknowledged the applause, which began with Robert and continued. The look of naked hunger he gave her was at once masked. She hoped that Morna had not seen.

"The recitation!"

It was Sir Herbert, and those around him repeated his demand. It was flattery and Tempest knew it, but she was intoxicated with the delight of performance. She held up her hand for quiet. Instantly, she was obeyed. She came around to face them, her smoky skirts reflected in the polished floor and her head high. The only sound was that of a door opening and shutting somewhere and a muffled tread that ceased as a rug was encountered. Tempest bent her head as if in thought, savoring the moment when she held these people in the web of growing illusion.

Then reality faded for her as she stood tall and straight, a goddess invoked, her voice a trumpet of entreaty and demand as she cried, " 'Let me entreat you soften your indignant grief . . .' " and continued Pallas Athena's speech before the Furies in the play of the same name. The words came of their own volition, just as she had learned and used them long ago in school and for her own comfort against Great-aunt Hannah's strictures. " 'Calm this black and swelling wrath!' " She was herself and yet not herself in this transportation and power that was both talent and necessity for Tempest Mallory. One day she would do this on stage. The goddess took over and swept her forward with " 'destructive boldness, kin defying kin . . .' "

There was a movement at the entrance to the parlor, but only Tempest saw it. The others leaned toward her with rapt faces that were one blur in the flickering light of candles and golden curtains. The scents of wax, perfume, and roses mingled with the earth fragrance brought by the breeze. " '. . . Bring victory . . . enrich my people . . .' " On and on her voice pounded toward crescendo as she watched the man standing very still, his hands on both hips.

His tight trousers and matching coat were of tawny-gold, which picked up the same shade in his hair. Ascot and waistcoat were a darker shade of auburn, and a green stone flashed on one finger. The slashing brows were raised and the cruelly sensual mouth quirked downward. He managed to look bored, arrogant, and aloof at the same time. Every other man in the room was dwarfed by his height and air of insolent command. Justin St. Trevian had arrived.

His expression did not change nor did his stance alter, but Tempest felt the suppressed rage stretch out toward her. It was as though she had been ordered to yield. Her pulses hammered and she felt all her senses quicken. A warm wetness came to her palms and her breasts when a memory of their passion in the secret place rose up in her mind. Outwardly she stood relaxed in her role that was part truth.

It was time to end. She sensed the first touch of restlessness among the guests. A few matched phrases brought Athena's triumph even as Tempest was more acutely aware of the coiled fire Justin exuded. " '. . . Let the flaring lights move on

. . . gather with gladness,' " while goddess and chorus proclaimed the " 'reconciliation of gods and fate . . . to crown the song of joy.' " Her voice rose as the Greek chorus might have, and fell away. She did not bow, for her role was yet upon her. Head up and chin level, she gazed into Justin's eyes.

"Bravo!"

"Bravo, indeed."

"Splendid!"

"Who was she supposed to be?"

"Who wrote that?"

"Excellent."

The comments swirled about her, but she heard the drawling voice pitched so that all the room could hear.

"Dreadfully sorry I'm late, Robert. Who's the player wench? Maybe you'll introduce me later?"

Someone tittered, and Justin grinned wolfishly. Morna looked ready to faint. Tempest let a slow smile flit across her face while her fingers moved casually over the petals of the white rose she still held.

"Tempest Miranda Mallory, guest of this house and Jamaica, formerly of Virginia and Georgia." She gave him another long glance and had the inestimable pleasure of seeing a wash of color on the high cheekbones before she turned to Sir Herbert, who had just come up. "May I trouble you to fetch some wine, my lord?"

Justin spoke for her alone. "Checkmate!"

11

Precipice

"I vow it has been long since you visited us, Mr. St. Trevian. I
am annoyed. Really, I am!" The high sweet voice cut across
the rising whispers of the guests and caused their fascinated
eyes to swing toward Morna as she advanced toward Justin.
Her steps were slow and the high color burned in her cheeks as
well as on her neck, yet she was in perfect command of herself.
"Now you just come right along and sit with me and tell me all
about your travels. Every word, mind you! And you shall have
only sherry to keep me company, for that is all I'm allowed to
have. Is that a penance, sir?"

Justin smiled as he went to meet her and made a perfectly
executed bow. His voice held just the right shade of chagrin
mixed with pleasure. "On the contrary, madam, you do me
more honor than I deserve. I must ask your forgiveness for my
tardy arrival and remarks. It has been far too long since so
gracious a household and lady welcomed me." He presented
his arm to her. "Will you permit me to escort you to a chair?"

Tempest was thankful that Sir Herbert returned at that
moment with the wine she had requested. His stocky figure
shielded her as he began to remark on other versions of *The
Furies* he had seen, including one in Athens.

Robert must have spoken to the musicians, for the strains of a lively country air filled the room almost immediately. Out of the corner of her eye Tempest saw him maneuver Lady Shurden onto the floor as he called to his guests, "Come and join us!" He swung the worthy lady in a fashion that made her gasp and laugh even though her face was faintly shocked. Some obeyed as their eyes no longer stabbed toward Tempest, who supposed that Morna must have taken Justin to a suitably public place.

". . . bad breeding there, for all his airs. Gentlemen are getting fewer all the time." Sir Herbert's jowls were redder now and his faded eyes snapped with anger. "I wonder that the upstart was even invited."

"Why was he, I wonder?" Tempest noticed that her voice was mildly curious and quite composed. She concealed the shaking rage she felt, knowing that she did it well. Just view all this as good practice for the stage, she thought. Her fingers itched to claw Justin's arrogant face even as her breasts tingled when she remembered his mouth on them.

"Something to do with business, I'm sure." Sir Herbert's voice was disdainful. "I can recall the days when that was a thing apart from one's social life and the ladies of the family were not subjected to rude company. It is not that I criticize my host; you must not think that, my dear Miss Mallory. Quite the contrary. Mr. St. Trevian has methods of business . . ." A cough at his elbow made them both turn to face a pink-faced young man who was nearly a head shorter than Tempest and whose brow was moist. "Well, what is it? Well?"

The young man gulped. "I just thought . . . I mean I don't want to impose or interrupt, but I, well, wanted to ask the lady to do me the honor." His words ran together as he gazed at Tempest. His flush deepened when Sir Herbert scowled. "Excuse me, please. I forgot myself."

Tempest sternly repressed a giggle as she dug her fingernails into her palms. Sir Herbert was about to let some information about Justin fall. Why did this boy have to come up and distract him? She looked at the older man in appeal, but he took it another way.

"Think nothing of it, lad. Musn't monopolize her after all, you know." He stepped back and bowed to Tempest. "We'll talk again about the state of drama. You have a power that ought to be put to use."

The words were utterly sincere and Tempest knew it. Pride and delight made her cheeks flame. Admiration burned in the eyes of the boy, who began to murmur polite phrases. She spoke abstractedly while she put her hand in his. "I hold you to the promise of our future words, my lord, and I thank you for the compliment."

"It is only truth, Miss Mallory." He lifted a hand to signal the slave who was carrying several decanters of wine.

"You do me too much honor, Miss Mallory." The boy's voice failed him again as he tried to move away with her, and she did not catch his name. He handed her in and out of the motions of the sprightly dance with a skill that seemed to take all his concentration, for he said little else. They nodded and smiled at each other during the various passages and soon Tempest allowed herself to forget everything else except the music as she gave herself up to it.

When that dance was over, another young man presented himself and there were others behind him. It seemed that in this fairly close society a certain informality prevailed and introductions were not always performed. Married women danced with their husbands and others in turn. Unwed girls, of whom there were only a very few, were in great demand. Tempest lost count of the names and faces. For this time it was enough that she was young, fair, and vied for; she held herself partially remote and this appeared to excite more interest. Robert claimed her once and she had to force calmness at the veiled hunger in his eyes as well as the greed in his hot fingers. She went eagerly to the next hand held out to her and recoiled at the last second so that the figure of the dance was altered.

"Why, Miss Mallory, have I caused you to stumble? If so, I must ask your pardon. Would you care to sit out this dance? Perhaps it is unfamiliar to you?" Justin was standing in front of her, his face the very picture of concern, the tawny eyes slightly narrowed and glittering. "I owe you my respects and several apologies. Will you permit me to give them?" He put one hand on her shoulder to draw her out from the couples who were watching just as avidly as those on the sidelines. His mouth quirked downward so that he might have been either amused or enraged, but the power of him reached out to surround Tempest.

She tilted her head back and let him wait for a minute that seemed to stretch out into infinity. Then she gave him a smile that was identical to his, even to the quirk. Her fingers brushed her skirts as she shrugged away from him. "Our host and hostess may present you later, sir. I fear that I am quite tired and plan to spend the rest of the evening in their company. Now, do excuse me."

Turning around abruptly, Tempest walked away without a backward glance. The sound of his laughter followed her as she went. Where in God's name was Morna? She would join her and stay there. How could one man's touch draw all her flesh into one naked yearning? How was she to fight against it? She did not want Justin to have such power over her.

Tempest was conscious of the glances that followed her and was well aware that some of them were speculative, but the high tide of excitement that had bouyed her up all evening still held. She did not think for a moment that Justin wanted to offer any apologies; if anything, he wanted to mock as he had done earlier when he called her a wench. Would he approach her again? She hoped that he would and that he would not.

The music altered suddenly and the soft strains of Mozart drifted across the great room. People moved together, separated, stood apart to listen, and the sounds of conversation were muted. Tempest saw Morna seated in a curtained recess while she sipped from a tall cup. A slave stood beside her waving a fan. When she approached, Tempest saw that Morna's face was drawn and so white that the red of her cheeks seemed the grossest paint instead of fever.

"Morna, you ought to be in bed! Let me help you there." She kept her voice low and urgent.

"I can't. I have to stay up until the guests leave. Robert said I had to." The brilliant eyes, too far dilated, burned into Tempest's and the thin fingers trembled convulsively on her lap. "That won't be for hours yet. There will be a great deal more dancing, and you must dance with all who ask you. Soon someone will be offering for your hand. Robert says so and he is always right."

"The devil with Robert!" Tempest fairly hissed the words. "You've got to rest!"

"Ah yes. Forever!" Morna laughed low in her throat and the sound was ugly. Her tone changed. "There's no air in here. Have you noticed? There's no air at all. Is he coming this way? Where is Robert? He must not see me unwell. Poor man, it distresses him so."

Tempest looked at the slave, who stood impassively swinging the fan. What did she think of all this? "Go to the tall man in tawny yonder. Mr. St. Trevian." She spoke quietly but firmly, hoping that Morna would not protest. Oddly enough, she did not doubt that Justin would confront Robert if the need should arise. "Say that the mistress wishes to speak with him immediately. Go!"

The slave skittered away, and Tempest bent to touch Morna's hand. It was hot and moist, thinner with each day. Her neck was almost scrawny now that the thin scarf of material from her gown was pulled aside. "We'll get some air. You'll feel better; just wait and see."

Morna pulled herself up as if to speak but abandoned the effort. Her breath came raspingly.

The guests were dancing again to music that Tempest did not recognize. She was grateful for the covering liveliness of it when Justin came toward them, a wineglass in one hand, and followed by the slave, who carried a half-filled decanter. One questing eyebrow rose when he looked at Tempest, but when his gaze fell on Morna, all latent amusement left his face.

"She is ill and feels that she must remain here as long as Robert does. He has ordered it, I believe. Will you take us into the garden for air? Support her. Laugh and chat. Bid the slave follow. Morna can bear no excitement." Tempest rapped out her words. This was not a time for asking. Only Justin was strong-willed enough to regard a request that might compromise them all should Robert choose to object to it.

"What has she been given? Who is her physician? The man wants whipping!" Justin's low voice was ragged with anger that reached his eyes and turned them into pits of flaring amber.

Tempest was reminded once more of the lion surveying his prey, but a flash of movement in their direction made her aware that there was no time to lose. The boy who had first danced with her was coming toward her with a look of concentration on his earnest face.

"Outside, please! Justin, say something. Anything!" The

boy was near enough to hear now. She let her voice rise high and lilting. "The roses are even lovelier by torchlight and moonglow, if you can believe that. Just think what a yellow gown in that shade would be! Morna, do you think one might be made up?"

Justin followed her lead so naturally that he might have been born to the role. Tempest wondered darkly if indeed he had.

"I must see such celebrated flowers. May I now or would the imposition be too great? I vow, ladies, they could not be fairer than your own delicate cheeks. Just outside for a moment and then back? Just to gratify a guest who has been remiss?" As he nattered on, Justin gripped Morna's arm in his and nearly supported her to her feet. Tempest went to her other side, giggling and chattering inanities, and did the same. Together, the slave close behind them, they moved toward the closest door and onto the veranda.

"Miss Mallory! May I claim the pleasure later?" The boy— what was his name?—was certainly not reticent.

"Yes, of course. I look forward to it." Tempest would have said anything to get rid of him. He grinned and sniffed but moved backward, the look of eagerness never leaving his face.

Another instant and they were in the cool, flower-scented air, down the steps, and on the path that led toward the garden. Justin swung Morna up into his arms and carried her to a stone bench that was half shielded by shrubbery. Taking the wine from the goggling slave, he poured some into his glass and put it to her lips. Morna drank, choked, and began to shudder but she was breathing deeply in an attempt to get air. With an oath, Justin produced a short knife and slashed downward so that stays and gown were ripped in one motion. He bent her forward and back simultaneously until her breathing was regulated.

"Will she be all right?" Tempest wondered at the practiced quality of his actions and remembered how he had tended Savora during the episode on the *Corinthian*. "She has strained herself too far." Dread hammered at her as she looked at Morna's skeletal face in the moonlight. She could not doubt that Robert had told her the truth.

"She ought to be in bed, given restoratives, tended, and kept calm. The stimulant is wearing off, and these are the results." Justin gritted his teeth. "She cannot endure such shocks to her system. Robert must be informed! You, girl!" The slave rolled her eyes at him and backed away. "Get some help and escort your mistress upstairs."

"No! I won't go. I'll just rest here and I'll be all right. You cannot make me." Morna's voice shook, but her gaze burned at them. "The slave shall bring me a shawl and we will talk here for a time. Then I can retire. I'll not be driven from the party. Robert would be furious, you see."

Tempest started to protest, but Justin's hand clamped her wrist with such force that she was silenced. He said, "I advise against it, but you must do as you think best." He was soothing and gentle as he watched her distraught face.

The footsteps were so soft that they did not hear them until the deceptively calm words rooted them in their places. "What have I interrupted? Morna, the guests are asking after you. Tempest, did you not promise a dance to young Louis Watt? And Justin, I suppose you know that I could call you out for this?" Robert waved one hand at Morna, whose state of undress was all too apparent in the night brilliance. Robert was smiling as if something in the scene pleased him very well. He was no longer the polite host; now he was lord of the manor, the absolute ruler. "Explain yourselves immediately!"

Tempest felt the pleasure coil around her and knew that danger encompassed them all; it had been planned that way, for one of the confrontations was about to take place. Justin's brow was furrowing while one hand went toward his waist, where a sword would customarily hang. Morna gave a little cry and collapsed in the arms of the slave. Robert looked at Tempest with the beginnings of triumph in his face. In the white house beyond them the guests and witnesses danced to a merry tune. Was it purposely just that loud?

No man manipulated Tempest Mallory! She felt the reviving flick of rage as she stepped quickly between the two men and put her arm in Justin's. Chin high, smile firmly in place, she faced Robert and let another Tempest take hold.

"I vow, I don't know what all this is about, Robert. You've no call to fuss at Morna or Justin. I wanted to see the flowers and I asked her to come with me, so he came as escort. I had one of those little plums that were so good—remember—and I offered it to her. She choked and he just saved her life. That's all. So blame me if you have to. I'm so sorry but she's forgiven me and maybe you will." She held the hard smile, but kept anything he might say at bay. "She needs to rest, naturally. Do you think we might go and dance? Surely it will be all right now!" Let them think her heartless or foolish at the very least. Even hysterical. The crouching beast must be disarmed. Her voice went high and a bit shrill. "Come, Justin, you have boasted of your dancing skill and now I claim that test of it. Morna darling, you'll be fine, we know it."

"Go on, Tempest. Please do." Morna was already stronger even as Robert's frustration was evidenced by the tensing of his body when he swung toward her.

"Where's Robert? He has this dance with my wife!"

"Robert? Are you out there?"

"Hurry up, you lazy things! Madam, she this way!"

The cacophony of voices swelled up against the now soft music that floated out to them. Feet scrunched on the path, and Robert was called again.

Tempest cried, "Come, sir! I demand my dances!" Shameless was what they would brand her, but intuition told her she did well. She held Justin with as strong a grip as he had grasped her, and he would have been hard put to wrench away.

Robert snatched off his coat and placed it over Morna's shoulders just as several gentlemen and slaves rounded the nearest bush, pausing to stare at the tableau before them.

12

The Spun Web

The last notes of "Endearing Young Charms" dropped into a well of silence as Justin dropped Tempest's hand to bow correctly, formally, before her. It was very late and the dance floor was nearly deserted. A few yawning men and their watchful wives sat at one end of the room. Robert talked with Louis Watt, now quite drunk, but still able to yearn after Tempest, in an alcove. The musicians seemed exhausted, but they were slaves and had little choice as to continuing.

"Surely this is enough, madam?" Justin straightened and stared at her, his face emotionless, something very like distaste glittering out of his eyes.

Tempest left the smile pasted on her lips while she fought the irresistible urge to slap him. When they first began dancing over two hours ago, she had whispered to him, "Play this out with me, whatever you think, for now. I will explain later. For Morna's sake." His words had flayed her, although she had not really expected him to play the gentleman. The quizzical gaze had drifted over her as the aquiline nose tilted. "There is nothing to explain. The situation is perfectly clear. Robert is extremely wealthy, and his wife ails. You really ought to be less blatant, my dear. Shall I vouch for you as a . . . partner, or does he think you virgin?" At her gasp of rage, his face went steely and he swung her into the first motions of the dance. "No point in discussing all this. I am easily bored, and you are a very crafty woman. Remember this, however. This community does not condone murder." He would say nothing else to her, and after her flurry of shock and denial, she had not tried. They exchanged inane remarks where others might overhear them and danced on; Justin would let no others claim her and people had whispered. Once Robert approached, but Justin only laughed as he took her in a series of spins. That time she was grateful.

Now she answered, "Enough and beyond, sir. Doubtless my reputation will be in shreds for what we have been doing." At least Robert had not pursued a quarrel with Justin and allowed Morna to leave. The guests thought nothing of their venture in the garden; they would not gossip there, at any rate.

"Doubtless. I suggest that you remember my words. Hanging is a most uncomfortable experience." He smiled politely as he spoke.

"I bid you good evening, sir." Heedless of what anyone might think, Tempest picked up her skirts and ran from the room. Justin St. Trevian should be made to pay for his insults! Her skin quivered and she longed for his touch, the hardness of his body on hers, and the savagery of his kisses. She knew he suspected her of much that was nefarious, but his cold manner had not hidden the eagerness of his flesh.

Tempest made Savora sleep in the room with her and stationed another slave just outside the door. She expected to toss for hours as she relived the fascinating and terrible evening with its unresolved dangers, but sleep caught her as soon as she lay down. In her dreams she gamboled with Justin in forests where the lions came to join them and were as pets. Love and passion were mingled for Tempest and Justin then, and in the depths of what she knew to be fantasy, there was no other man for her.

It was still early when she woke from a particularly passionate episode and knew that there would be no more sleep. Savora was gone, but then she often was these days. Their old closeness was gone, yet Tempest could not regret the love which had been so hard won for her friend. Now she jumped up, splashed water from a nearby pitcher over her face, combed her flaming hair back from her face, and pulled on a thin white dress with a full skirt. She wanted to be outside, away from anyone. Her next course of action had to be decided.

The great house was silent as she slipped through the corridors. She saw no one but knew that the slaves had been hard at work, for everything was tidy and polished. Bowls of flowers scented the air and the floors gleamed. Once outside, Tempest kicked off the thin white slippers she had put on, thrusting them out of sight under a bush. Then she pulled her skirt up, hitching it through a cord she had brought for the purpose, and ran as hard as she could away from the cultivated beauty of Cloud Ridge.

The morning sun slanted down warmly across her back. The air was fresh with flowers and the odor of earth. The tang of the distant sea was in the breeze. It was as if the world were constantly renewing itself; ugliness was not possible in this beauty. Tempest thought now, as she often did, that she could very easily be a nature worshiper.

For all her swiftness, she was still within the tended meadows and gardens of the estate when her bare foot caught in a root and sent her sprawling. One of the oaths she had learned from Savora took the rest of her breath and she sat up to examine the tiny purple flowers upon which she sat, their petals already staining the fabric of her dress.

The thoughts that she could no longer hold back now overwhelmed her. Morna was being given some sort of drug to both stimulate and strain the illness she had. Had Robert brought on that sickness by some artificial means? How did Justin dare speak of murder as he had to her? It was painfully clear to Tempest that he believed she and Robert were having an affair, that they had known each other previously and were planning to set her in Morna's place in a future time. By telling her of his suspicions, he hoped to forestall Morna's death. Robert had been ready to fight with Justin in front of Morna and perhaps shock her into an attack, which could easily be fatal. But she, Tempest, had prevented that. Morna was afraid of Robert and still she cared for him. That much was obvious. If she could just talk plainly with Morna! But no woman, even a healthy one, could endure calm talk of deadly illness, possible murder plans, and the defection of a beloved husband without firm proof and a steady mind. None of that was present.

Tempest sighed, massaged her toes, and started to rise. She would tell Savora all she knew and together they would mount a watch over Morna. Meanwhile, she must avoid Robert while cementing a closer relationship with Morna. She hoped that Sir Herbert would visit often. In addition to all his talk of the state of the theater in various cities and his apparent interest in her skills, had there not been some mention of his connections with the courts? A magistrate, perhaps?

She bent over again to select one of the larger of the flowers to carry with her as she roamed in blessed solitude. Why had Justin not let her explain? The familiar swamping fury rose up along with the hunger she felt for him. Certainly he had no right to make such assumptions about her, and he had made no effort to help Morna!

Suddenly something cannonaded into her from behind with a powerful force that threw her flat. Feet trampled her back and hot breath bathed her neck. A low growling began as the monster pawed at her hair. Tempest was overcome with a rage that abandoned all fear. She could not scream and fight at those who sought to use and destroy her and Morna, but this wild animal was a another matter! She rolled over in one lithe movement that briefly unsettled the thing so that she saw white fur, hungry black eyes, and long gleaming teeth that seemed ready to close on her flesh.

The beast was huge. It had tiny ears, a wide muzzle, great paws, heavy shoulders, and a veritable explosion of snow-white coat, which shone in the sun. She had never seen anything like it. At her slight attempt to sit up, it made a low sound in its throat and sank low as if to pounce. Thankful that it did not and looking about for a rock, a stick, or anything to divert that deadly attention, Tempest said, "What sort of monster are you?" Did animals delay eating you if you spoke to them? Fairy tales rang in her mind and she thought that she was probably close to hysteria.

The thing came closer and sank down at her side. Now it was whining and the long rope of a tail began to beat the ground. One massive paw patted the edge of her skirt. Tempest put out a tentative hand and was swamped as the beast rolled over on her. She began to laugh and this threw it into transports of barking that nearly deafened her. She put her hands in the strangely silky fur and laughed until her sides ached. "Monster! Monster!" The long tongue ran over her hair before the barking started again.

"Aristotle! Aristotle! Come here this minute! Bad dog!" The familiar voice, now shocked but with threads of laughter running through it, rang from the distant copse. "Lie still! He won't hurt you!"

Tempest looked up to see Justin running toward them, his hair tossing over his high forehead, the full sleeves of his white shirt rolled back and the loose trousers emphasizing his maleness just as the tight ones had done the night before. Her blood sang with excitement. She could not stop laughing, and the dog was growing more excited at the sight of his master. "Aristotle!" Justin called his name again and that sent Tempest into another paroxysm. The idea of naming so peculiar an animal after the great Athenian seemed to cap the entire episode.

"Are you all right? I am so sorry . . ." Justin paused a few feet away and stared at them in undisguised horror. "Madam, what are you doing out here? Suddenly you are everywhere I look. I fail to see how you can pursue your schemes out here." His voice was so sharp that Aristotle backed up and howled. The sound was so mournful that Tempest laughed again, and this time Justin had to join in.

She took advantage of the lull to rise to her feet and fling her hair back. Dignity was hopeless to achieve; she could not pull her skirts down, since they were so firmly girded up to free her calves and ankles. She caught Justin's eye and struggled not to giggle. He fondled the dog and bent over him, but his shoulders shook.

"Justin." Tempest wanted to try to talk to him, but her tongue went solid in her mouth. Time seemed frozen around them as all sounds faded in the brilliant morning. Nothing existed except the man who was walking toward her, his face still lit with laughter, his eyes burning into hers. She went to meet him, her arms raised to hold and caress.

The strange power that each held over the other ignited at their touch and fused into one column of desire. Tempest felt the bulge of his shaft and heard the hammering of his heart as they stood locked together. She answered his mouth with her own and demanded of him at the same. Her hands pulled him even more closely to her while the honeyed desire flowed. Tempest arched her back so that she fitted tightly into him. Her breasts tingled with a life of their own, throbbing for his touch. Her legs weakened as she shook with the force of her passion. She wanted nothing but to lie with him this minute and know the consummation of their mutual longing.

It took all of Tempest's will and strength to finally pull back. She knew in the deepest part of her mind that she must not give way before this onslaught to her emotions. When she came to Justin again, if ever, it would be with reason as well as passion. A free choice, not a savage hunger that overwhelmed all else. She could do no less and be Tempest Mallory.

Justin tried to bring her fully to him again, but she forced herself to struggle. "It's all right. No one will see us. We can go back up in the cool woods." His sun-darkened face, brows quirked, bent to hers earnestly.

"I can't." How could she explain what she did not fully understand?

"Why not? You had no difficulties before." He was trying to control himself, but his eyes were beginning to flash with anger and his grip tightened on her arms. "Why be coy now?"

He was not used to being crossed. Doubtless, women fell before him in their eagerness. She was not one of them, and he should be apprised of that fact. "I am not what you think." The feeble words were all that would come. She felt the weight of Aristotle against her legs and was vaguely comforted.

"What I think does not matter right now. We are here alone and you want me as I do you. You were made for pleasure, don't you know that?" He grinned lazily. "Really, my dear, you should have accepted my offer to be my mistress for a time. I'm afraid it no longer holds now that you're so involved with Robert; he can be deadly if thwarted. I've no wish to be ambushed on a lonely road or have to watch my back all the time. But a little dalliance, discreetly, can add a fillip to life, agreed?"

Tempest jerked free and moved back. "I have heard of people being attracted to each other even though they have a mutual dislike. While I cannot deny a certain power, I must own to a strong and avid distaste for you, your speech, and your mind! Find another with whom to dally! And I want you to know that I strongly resent those ridiculous and false charges you made last night about murder and hanging! Morna is my old school friend who invited me here. I first met Robert then. I would never have anything to do with him! She is gravely ill; that I do know." Despite her efforts at control, her voice shook slightly.

"He wants you, and she is being dosed." Justin spoke flatly, his eyes never leaving her face. "Robert and I have done business together and will continue to do, but he is a swine. She welcomed me into her home on several occasions and gave me all honor. For various reasons, that is not a thing too many hostesses feel free to do and maintain their places in the correct society. I will help her if I can." He was serious now, the thwarted passion fading. "Indeed, I fear that I am to be a houseguest for the next few days on her invitation. Does that frighten you, my schemer?"

"I welcome anything that will help Morna."

"Then if you care for her, leave that house. I can well imagine that you will receive an offer or two of marriage and many a proposition because of last night. The short Mr. Watt, for example, is both wealthy and malleable. We could still enjoy our games together. He is somewhat stupid. A rich and foolish husband would work out nicely." Justin surveyed her and snapped his fingers at Aristotle, who gave a short yip, leaning more heavily against Tempest. "That is, of course, if what you tell me about caring for Morna is true." Sarcasm lined the words and his mouth drew into a hard line so that he seemed older than the man who had kissed her only minutes ago.

Tempest spared time to reflect that Justin seemed capable of arousing only two emotions in her, passion and fury. They were bred of each other and fed on that. He could be a powerful ally, but he must be won to her side. She could not afford to give way before his scorn or yield to him again. Yield, in truth! Her mind told her that theirs had been an equal coupling, man and woman in mutual delight. When the time came, she would have that pleasure again, but it would be of her own choosing. Now she controlled herself as she must.

"I want to marry no man. I will be an appendage to none but a person in my own right. I mean to be an actress; that has always been my ambition, and I intend to realize it. I have reason to think that I can do well."

He interrupted her. "An actress! You play your several roles with me, Robert, Morna, and that gaggle of foolish men very well. Do you really not know that actress is often just another word for prostitute?"

Again she must hold her temper back. "Of course I know it. But you thought me to be a missionary on the ship, did you not? And you saw me be the foolish girl at the party as well as Pallas Athene, and saw how I came between you and Robert when I knew he meant to try to kill you? Or did you not know that, my wise man of the world?" Her tone was a parody of his.

"I suspected as much now and then." His look was distant and icy. "Robert and I, along with the worthy Captain Jacky and others, do engage in the illegal slave trade, a most profitable business." He waved in the direction of the hill over which he had come. "I have bread and cheese yonder. We can drink from the little stream. I will hear your tale, and believe me, I will know if you lie." The muscles rippled in his neck, but otherwise he held himself apart. His very stance was a threat.

"And I will hear yours. A truth for a truth." She could be as firm as he, although she knew that violence was very close to his surface.

"I do not bargain."

"Nor I." She stared him down, waiting for his next move.

13

Fortune the Oppressor

It was Aristotle who broke the deadlock between them as, eager for attention, he loosed several loud, mournful howls of a particularly penetrating variety. The superstitious might have suspected the presence of any number of night demons lingering in the early light to catch unwary souls. Both Tempest and Justin put their hands down to silence him and he reveled in the attention. Minutes later, they were all sitting under the spreading branches of a tree that sheltered them from anyone who might be passing by, and the dog was spread out accepting homage as his due.

Justin's lean face showed amusement as he stroked the kinky white fur.

Tempest said, "You are a contradictory man. I would have expected you to have an aristocratic wolfhound or some savage brute devoted only to your whims."

One corner of his mouth went up. "I found him in Boston. They wanted to drown him because of the mixture he is. He looked so wise and accepting before the would-be drowners that I could not resist the name. I gave gold and have never regretted my rescue."

He said nothing for a short period, and during that time

Tempest stared off into the green thickets heavy with the scents of summer in this month of spring. She knew Savora would keep her secret if she found her gone, and after so late a party, everyone must surely sleep late. There was no reason for her skin to crawl suddenly as though clammy hands had been laid upon it.

"Tempest Miranda Mallory." He whispered her name so softly that it could have been blown on the wind. The tawny eyes were gentle and it seemed to her that they probed toward the very center of her being. It would be so easy to lean toward him and take the warmth growing between them in the wake of their last exchange, but she thought he attempted to manipulate her.

"My parents loved the drama and that play. I am told that some of the lines from it made up my first words. That was probably a tale." Tempest kept her voice light as she launched into the story that was not so difficult to tell after all. She did not give her aunt's name or Savora's true state, but she gave the rest fairly accurately, stressing the attempt to have her married, the penalty that would have been exacted had she remained, and reiterated her own determination to be an actress. It was only when she came to speak of Morna as she had expected her to be, the loss of the friendship, and the fate now so close that Tempest's nerve faltered. She bent her head to hide the sheen of tears and feigned great interest in Aristotle's ears. "I will do what I can for you until it is ended. Then I will get work of any sort here in Jamaica until I can save enough to go to one of the American cities where there is active theater."

"Better think about the rich husband." Justin leaned back on both hands and regarded her cynically. "It seems that money rules us all. You have probably been partially honest with me." He held up one hand to still any protest she might be preparing to make. "If you are in league with Robert, you conceal it well. It really does not matter so long as Morna lives out her days in reasonable peace; you and I are united on that. Her illness is mortal and must be left to run its course with no more stimulants, which can only hurt."

"How can you be so sure of all this?" Tempest would not try to argue with him. She was drained by her recitation and for the moment it was enough to sit here in the green peace, feel the breeze stir her hair, and watch this man, whose strange mixture of arrogance and gentleness would never cease to stir her.

His face went hard as he stared past her into another time. "I once studied medicine. In Edinburgh. I learned much while there." His laugh was harsh and the slim, well-shaped fingers clenched together in a fist. "Not one of the lesser things I discovered was how important it is to be wealthy or at least to have the appearance of it. Cassandra . . ." He halted, his face nearly white under the tan. The moment stretched out while Tempest looked anywhere except at his eyes.

In an effort to distract him from whatever memory gnawed, she said, "Then we are allies of a sort? That is what you mean to suggest?" She could not help but wonder who the woman called Cassandra was and what she had been to him. He had certainly shown his interest in many ladies and made no secret of his worldly inclinations. Why did she feel this sense of loss, of danger nearing them both.

When Justin spoke again, his tone was casual and his brow was smooth. "In a way. I go soon to New Orleans to marry the heiress to whom I have long been betrothed. I have invested money there and have part interest in a plantation operated by my cousin, Dominic. Sugar cane, just as here. We've been involved in a few dealings in our time, but not enough to really lead the lives of gentlemen in that society. The small plantation I have here doesn't pay for itself. So what's a man to do?" He gave her a wolfish grin. "A woman can always use her body, can't she?"

"I doubt not that you will use yours. The heiress means to supply your needs in these respects?" Tempest relished the jab.

"I'm just being honest with a fellow schemer. A rare luxury, that. She will have a, shall I say, presentable husband and an understanding one. We share name and wealth. So long as she is discreet, she may do as she wishes, and I, of course, do not plan to alter any activity I find pleasurable. If you marry and remain here as I advise, we can see each other on my necessary journeys here. What do you think?"

"I think you evade honesty and seek to shock me. You do not succeed."

"Do I not? You want honesty, you think? No woman wants that. She wants honeyed lies, tales touched with little truth, facades. You are no different for all that you think you are. You were virgin when you came to me, but you have used that virginity and can simulate it again when you come to the pass. Actress!" His laugh was bitter. "A net for your quarry, that is all you mean by that ambition!"

Tempest stood up very deliberately, unfastened her skirts, and let them fall to her feet. She smoothed her hair back as she surveyed him lounging there. "I will leave you to your musings, Mr. St. Trevian. They do not interest me. I say this, however. Money does appear to interest you greatly. May I ask why you do not practice medicine or work your various plantations? Is work so foul a word?" She wanted to strike at him for his denigration of her ambition. "Or is selling yourself easier?"

Justin rose, his face a mask as he stared down at her. His eyes went flat and were almost yellow. The breeze tumbled his hair and blew the collar of his shirt against the brown neck. His lips went thin so that the points of his white teeth shone. He made no move, but she sensed the swelling contained rage that was all the more fearful for being so. When he spoke his voice was very soft, but underneath was the venom of the years.

"Because a woman lay dead at my hands because she trusted a skill I thought I had, because a lying bitch thought to use me and left a husk, because sugar cane and cotton are less important than human life. Mostly because there is very little that truly matters in this world and less of that every day." His brows drew together and the pulse began to hammer in his throat. "I would bid you good morning except that I think you will understand this better."

Tempest did not draw away when he reached for her. She could not move before the wave of bitterness that swamped her. His hands were hard and demanding, his mouth savage on hers as it ground into her teeth and lips. He meant to hurt her and she sought no defense against it. Her arms went around him as she held him to her in an intensity of caring that shook her through and through.

Justin set her back from him. "Damn you! Damn you!" He lifted one fist as if to strike her. "Bitch!" Snapping his fingers at Aristotle, he turned his back on her and strode swiftly away.

Tempest had to have action after such a struggle. She did not really care who saw her or what they reported to whom. She was an actress, was she not? Very well, she would have a tale ready when the time came. She began to walk as fast as she could in the opposite direction from the one Justin had taken.

In spite of all that he had said to her, Tempest found that she could not believe Justin either the total materialist or cynic he appeared. There was an unhappy love affair, perhaps his first, and he recalled it painfully; in later years she might think so of the short relationship with him. A dead patient was another matter for an idealistic physician, but surely that was long ago? No, there was far more to this man than appeared on the surface. He had been tender with her in the first shared passion, but he had rejected her wordless comfort just now. Arrogance was his armor; could she do less when next they met? She, too, knew the safety of subterfuge.

Tempest had no idea how long she walked or where she went. Her thinking mind retreated as she submerged herself in the still beauty around her. The day was growing hot, but birdsong spiraled up toward the cloud-freckled sky and a few branches of pink flowers were rifled by an errant breeze when she paused beside them. The grass had been trampled down, cut in places, and some of the shrubs had been pruned, leaving the odor of freshness and drying to carry on the air. The limits of the plantation were being extended, she thought, and perhaps this would soon be parkland. This country was so lovely. She longed to see and bathe in the sea, to explore and enjoy the land, and be free in a setting she had never known. As it was she was battered by conflicting emotions and struggles. She must try again on her own destiny if she was not to be submerged. Idea after idea came and was discarded as she walked all that long morning and into the afternoon, but when hunger and thirst finally drove her back to Cloud Ridge, her plan was laid.

If the house slaves thought anything about one of the guests entering, dusty and hot, from the back doors, inquiring sharply about the health of the mistress, and hearing that she took tea on her balcony with reasonable health, then going there as she was, they were far too well trained to show surprise. Tempest looked at the smooth, hidden faces and wondered what they were really like. She wanted to confide in Savora but knew she dared not; her friend's every concern now was Jason, whom she loved and who loved her in return. Tempest knew that she would not change her freedom for love's captivity, but she did feel an uprush of envy at this moment.

"Where in heaven's name have you been? I thought you would have been sleeping late after last night. Tempest! You look wild, distraught. Has something happened?" Morna half started up from her couch and the delicate cup wobbled in her thin hand. Her hair was arranged in curls around her face with a blue ribbon binding the back. Her blue morning robe foamed about her body in crisp ruffles. The skin of her face was blanched. Dark circles lay under her eyes. She might easily have been fifteen years older than she was.

Not for myself alone. Tempest accused herself briefly of selfishness at the course she meant to take, but in it lay some peace for Morna and protection for one alone as she was. She looked straight at her friend and said, "Morna, first of all I want to thank you and Robert for the unquestioning hospitality you have given me and the true welcome I feel. The party was delightful, but I fear that I may have behaved inappropriately at certain times. I have been thinking of the advice you both gave and which I thought to ignore. I have been walking since first light, thinking. You remember that was my habit?" Tempest knew she would not. Likely, she could recall little now.

"Of course." Morna nodded, trying to smile as she shifted position and twisted uncomfortably. "You are my friend, Tempest. Why should you thank us for having you here? If anyone was shocked at you—which I doubt—it would simply be because there have been no faces such as yours in our relatively small society recently." She gestured toward her long mirror. "But only look at yourself! What deep thoughts required such effort?"

Tempest did as she was bidden and could not restrain the laughter that was a welcome release from the tension of the morning. Her face was smudged and dusty; her hair flamed in loose tendrils, and the white dress was stained with grass. When she looked closer, Tempest could see the strain her eyes held and the pinched look of her nostrils. Justin had left his mark.

"Perhaps you are right when you say that I should consider the possibility of marriage. I met several pleasant gentlemen last night. It is such a struggle to be alone. Of course I still want to be an actress, but I would like to experience such a life

as is possible here. Naturally I couldn't rush into anything."
Tempest paused to gauge the effect her words had on Morna
and was relieved when the bright smile came. "I'll need your
help, though. I really am not sure how to entice gentlemen
without being thought bold. What do you think?"

"How exciting! How very wise of you, Tempest! Marriage
is the only goal for a woman—you'll see. I've been so
fortunate. We must plan. I'll tell you who is really eligible;
we'll have other parties, and callers will come." She clapped
her hands in glee and was suddenly young once more. "But
you shouldn't encourage Mr. St. Trevian. He has a bad
reputation with the ladies, although he's always the very soul
of politeness to me. Anyway, he's masterful and you don't want
that. Now young Watt . . ." She broke off with a laugh as
Tempest held up one hand.

"You're going too fast. I'm only thinking right now, not
launching a campaign." It would work; she knew it would.
Here was a reason to stay close to Morna and observe what was
going on at first hand. There must be opportunities to view
what Morna was given that brought on excitement and
alternate weakness. Thanks to Aunt Hannah, she had some
idea of potions—pray that she knew enough to help. Robert
could offer no objections. Had he not suggested she find a
husband here in Jamaica? But he meant her for himself as
mistress, possibly as wife. All her knowledge told her that. She
would buy time for herself and Morna, playing each day as it
came.

"You were much with him." Morna was shrewd in spite of
the physical discomforts that sapped her attention, and her eyes
were sharp on Tempest.

"He is a rude, overpowering man. I dislike the type and I
wanted to see if there was anything to him. You must admit he
is very handsome, but that is all." For the moment she meant
every word. "He does business with Robert and took care to
make sure I understood that."

"I think he knows his place." Morna nodded, satisfied.

A burst of laughter and some farewell greetings rang out just
then, and Tempest crossed to the open window in an effort to
control herself. What was Justin's place in the ordered society
Morna took so for granted? Her tone had been casually
dismissing. Business was one thing, proper folk another. The

arrogant Justin would have found that amusing, but Tempest was furious for him and with herself for being so.

"Goodbye! Such a wonderful time. You and your family must come to call." The farewells of a portly man and his wife whom Tempest could not remember rang out as their carriage drew up, and Robert's deep voice responded in kind.

"When my wife is better, we will come. But you must understand . . ." The words trailed off into lower tones which seemed to subdue his listeners. Tempest could see him only in profile, but the set of his features was hard.

She turned back to Morna with her role firmly in hand. There was no doubt that the curtain for the final act must soon rise.

14

Let My People Go!

"Naturally, Mr. Shakespeare's history cannot be regarded as accurate, but his plays of that sort are so masterly that one fails to care. When *Henry V* is considered . . ."

You consider him. In another minute I'll be asleep. Tempest wished she could speak the words aloud just to see the respectful look on Lucius Hurst's face fade into shock. The Henrys' nephew from Philadelphia was in Jamaica for a long visit, and while his passion was old naval battles and botany, he was given to long dissertations on Shakespeare and the Greek dramatists when visiting the Dornier household and Tempest. He discoursed and she was expected to listen raptly. Now he paused to catch his breath, fixing her with an expectant look.

"Of course. You make matters so clear, Mr. Hurst." It did not matter what he had been saying; she had lost count of the times she'd spoken so to him, Mr. Watt, Mr. Ratcliffe, Mr. Jordan, and several others who had come calling in the past two months. Insipid, all of them, boring, boring! And they thought so much of themselves that they expected her to be overcome with the slightest attention! Mr. Jordan and Mr. Hurst barely shared a chin between them.

"Thank you. *Richard III* leaves one in doubt regarding

certain salient facts. I will venture to point out that dramatic veracity is not often a feature there." On and on he droned.

Tempest clenched one fist into a ball under the spreading skirts of her green gown that almost matched the leaves of the arbor where they sat. The late afternoon air was hot, but two palmetto fans operated by the chaperoning slaves, Marty Dee, and her young daughter helped to cool them. She fought back another yawn, saw Marty hide one in her turn, and tried not to giggle as their eyes met. Surely he must leave soon. Due to Morna's delicacy, guests paid short calls, departing soon after afternoon refreshments.

There was a far off booming sound, which repeated itself several times before cessation. Tempest saw Marty come to alertness, which was instantly hidden. She had heard the sound in the nights of late but only once in the afternoon. When asked, Savora simply said, "The drums call to those who can answer. I can say no more." The other slaves appeared to take no notice. Now Tempest wondered, for she knew the planters feared rebellion above all other things and talked of it wherever they gathered. There were sections of Jamaica where the runaway slaves went—encouraged, it was said, by the missionaries, who taught them to think they were as good as their owners—and no white man might go except in peril of his life.

"Excuse me, but I have an invitation for you." Robert was hidden by the sun's glare and startled Lucius so much that he stumbled over his lecture and came hurriedly to his feet. Robert ignored him just as he did the slaves and fixed his gaze on Tempest. Only she could see the thwarted anger in him. "Flattering, but I doubt you should accept it." He extended the envelope toward her with one hand and waved the other in the general direction of the hills. "We may have to lead another expedition to try and exterminate those rebels. A good hunting, you might say."

Since the party, Robert had three times found Tempest alone and spoken to her in the same vein about Morna's illness, his need for strong sons, and her own fascinations. Once he overpowered and kissed her, his desire so strong that only the chance of a slave approaching enabled her to break free. After that, she kept a slave or Savora with her, stayed with callers or around Morna. His eyes would rake her even as his hands sought her shoulders, patted hers, or gave the casual greeting. Such a nature, cold and determined, could be ruthless.

"Since you have read it, please tell me the contents." Tempest let the acid flow through her voice. No one would think it odd that he read letters addressed to her. He and Morna were the guardians of a young, unmarried girl. What more natural?

"Sir Herbert Shurden and Lady Emily give you greetings and ask if you will spend several weeks with them very soon. He suggests that you might find it interesting to participate in some dramatic recitations from the classics and sing at some socials they will give and to which they will go. This will greatly aid in the advance toward an able company of thespians in Jamaica, a cultural endeavor long lacking and which you will grace." Robert gave her time to read the lines before he added, "I sent your regrets by the same messenger. They live out from Montego Bay in another direction. These are dangerous times for travel. The deep heat of summer stirs the savage blood of the slaves. In the cooler weather, perhaps."

He gave her a little smile, then favored Lucius with a look that made him babble agreement and mention leaving. Tempest nodded absently at her suitor, who tried to reassure her about Jamaica. She was reminded of the horseflies and how annoying they could be. Robert was enjoying the effect he had created, but she was determined not to give him any more satisfaction.

"I will bid Mr. Hurst good day and go to Morna. She does seem stronger, does she not? Mr. St. Trevian promised to call today or tomorrow and I will sit with them; she does so enjoy his tales of travel. It will be interesting to hear his opinions on the slave situation."

"St. Trevian comes here often? His reputation is shocking!" Lucius stepped back a few paces and gaped at them.

"He has beautiful manners." Tempest made the statement as guileless as she could and smiled at them both. Justin came to call at least twice a week, varying the times so that they never knew when to expect him. Two slaves remained in the room while he talked to Morna, and very often Tempest was called to come in by her friend. His attention was always given to Morna, with only the most chill and correct courtesies to Tempest. There had been no personal word to her in all the two months since their last confrontation.

"The man is a common adventurer, but I can deny my dear wife nothing." Robert extended his arm to Tempest. "I will escort you back, my dear, and then I must question some of the slaves who have been sullen lately. They will know something about those drums and I mean to know it. A good taste of the whip is what they want."

Tempest looked over at Marty and her daughter, but their faces were impassive. What did they feel when they heard themselves mentioned as if they were not there? They were possessions only, just as she had been in the eyes of Aunt Hannah when marriage was considered.

None of her feelings must show. She took Robert's arm lightly and extended the other to Lucius so that she moved between them. "I am eager to visit Sir Herbert and his lady; it is so kind of him to think of my interest in the drama. I wonder if any gentlemen could come so far to call? Ah, but I'm being bold!"

"You could never be so. May I come?" Lucius said yearningly.

Tempest batted words about with him, but she felt Robert's stiffness and his leashed anger. Strange that he had never actually voiced his intentions to her and yet she knew them as surely as though they had had hours of conversation. If only she and Justin could have had such perception of each other. She could not doubt Justin's true concern for Morna or the fact that she was better since his visits. Morna drank much less tea, adhered to a regular schedule, rested far more, and ate apart from the others, often with Tempest, who sought her company for most of every day. Some of the ladies in their immediate neighborhood who came to call commented on the color in her face and the weight gain, not seeing the remission before catastrophe. They remarked, too, on Tempest's need for a husband and the generosity of the Dorniers to her as well as the various merits of those who came to call and how a woman must be exceedingly cautious with gentlemen lest she give them the wrong idea. Tempest was usually bored, but she never made the mistake of allowing them to know this. The time might come when she could use allies against Robert.

The drumbeats started again as they walked. The sound was steady and ominous in the golden afternoon. Robert snapped out an oath, then left them without apology, calling for his horse and body slave. Lucius took his leave reluctantly, but Tempest knew it was because he was afraid and not due to her charms. Three of his uncle's husky men had come with him, but who knew whom to trust when it came to one's life?

Tempest stood alone on the path and listened to the drums. She had reason to be thankful for them. Both men were gone and she might have some time for herself. It was highly unlikely that Justin would come this late in any event. He had been careful to be the very soul of circumspection. If there were trouble with the slaves, would he be safe? Or any of them? She had heard tales of rebellions all her life and never known of a true one. Why did this deadly certainty fill her now?

"Marty! Marty! Will you go and find Savora for me? Tell her I am out here; I'll wait." If Savora would tell her anything. They had come far from the camaraderie brought about by adversity. In recent weeks Tempest knew Savora watched her with suspicious eyes, although the reason escaped her.

Marty nodded, walked a short way, paused, and returned to stop before Tempest. The usually impassive black eyes were alive and watchful now. "Her not here, Missy. Ain't see her not all day long. No good to look, either."

Tempest felt some of the fury that owners must feel with recalcitrant slaves. "Go do what I said. Now!" Suddenly she had a desperate need to see her friend, yet she did not want to enter the house and seek her.

"Yessum." Marty and her child went slowly to obey, but there was resistance in every motion.

The drums slowed to a dragging beat and stopped. The only sounds now were those of two small birds in the tree over her head and the distant lowing of a cow. The fragmented clouds in the distance blew before the rising breeze and the intoxicating scent of flowers came to her. Tempest would not have ever said that she had any sense of the future, but she knew what Marty said was true. One friend was gone from her. Savora had begun to part from their closeness on the *Corinthian*. It was useless to mourn for what was done.

"Miss Tempest! Come quick! Miss Tempest!" The scream shattering her resignation seemed at first to come from inside the brain. Then it came again and again, that repetition of her name as though that was all the screamer knew. The dreaded thing had come; they were face to face with the unnameable.

Tempest did not waste breath calling out. She started to run, fell over her skirts, caught them in both hands, and ran with all the strength she had. It was Sunday and many of the slaves were allowed to rest in the quarters far beyond the house. There were few enough of them about now, but those who were stood clustered about the limp body that lay just inside the dim parlor where the dance had been held.

"Morna!" Tempest knelt beside her, feeling for the pulse, which gave a faint, thready beat. "Darling, it'll be all right." She looked at two of the shaking slaves. "Send someone for the master immediately! Bring brandy, something to cover her with, and pillows for her head. Get the doctor and make him come with you; I don't care how long it takes. Hurry!"

"Ma'am, Miss Tempest. That Savora, she nowhere. Jus' gone and so's her stuff. All gone." Marty looked from Morna to Tempest in what might have been triumph.

"Her choice. She's a free woman. Now you go to the kitchen and have some nourishing soup prepared." Tempest lifted Morna's head onto her lap and began to murmur soothing words. The several slaves to whom she had not given orders huddled together, staring with fearful eyes.

Morna's lips were dusky and the circles under her eyes were now black. Perspiration stained her gown and dripped from her face, but she was shaking with a chill. Blood oozed from her nose and there was a puddle of it on the floor. Her lips moved as she tried to speak, then her whole body shook with the effort of it.

"Don't Morna. Just lie quietly. You'll soon be comfortable, I promise." Tempest tried to make her voice low and soothing, but it broke before the certain knowledge that her friend knew just what was happening.

"Killed me! Killed me! I knew. No hiding it." The words came out in a shriek that caused the blood to flow copiously. "No more! Please no more!" Morna began to sob and mutter incoherently just as the other slaves returned with the things for her comfort that Tempest had ordered. They could not help but hear and awed stares rested on Tempest. "I knew all along. You and Robert! You and . . ." The trembling voice faltered and stopped. Morna gathered her last power. "Prospero's daughter. Urgent for sanctuary." Blood came in a jetting stream as breath left her.

Tempest sat there on the polished floor, her dead friend's body before her, her own skirts soaked with Morna's blood, and felt the silent accusations of the slaves. She wanted to run crying and screaming from this place, but that indulgence was not a thing to permit herself. Morna had known all along about her situation and Robert's intentions; Tempest suspected that he had given her something to aid the eventual process along and could only pray that Morna had not been that aware. She had gasped out their childish danger signal only at the end. What agonies had been meted out to her before it came?

"Where is the master?" She heard her voice come out reasonably steady. "Is he on his way?"

"Dey lookin' fer him. He off in 'em hills." It was one of the older slaves, Lena, who volunteered this information. "Ma'am?"

Tempest stared up at the woman, observing that her dark face was nearly gray. "Send someone for the nearest neighbors. Bring them back with you. Mrs. Dornier is dead." She pulled herself free and reached out for the sheet Lena held. "I have to cover her."

"Ma'am." The next words came with a rush that sent the superstitious slaves reeling back, some crossing themselves, others muttering in a strange language. "De baby. He in bad way." Shaking her head, Lena began to weep. "He bad off. All in one time. Evil!"

"Get his nurse and everyone who know anything about children up there."

"Won't do no good. House cussed."

Tempest wondered if she was going mad. Death and impending death and now a curse? "I will come. If I hear any more talk such as that, you will pay for it." Would firmness make them help her? Surely some fondness for the Dorniers had to be there.

"Drums say 'let my people go.' He don't. Nobody do. They pay. Their Christian God said it." The words came from Marty Dee, who appeared a woman transformed by determination as she faced Tempest. "Baby die and lots more."

The others murmured agreement. Tempest took a minute to wonder if anyone had been sent as she commanded. Her head went high as she placed both hands on her hips and gave them look for look. "I am going to tend young Robert and you are all going to help me if I need it. Is that understood?"

The silence was long in that place of death. Tempest did not move or alter her expression. A tiny, gasping wail reached them and subsided.

Lena stepped toward Tempest. "We knows, Miz Mallory." She glared at Marty, who moved back a few paces.

In that partial victory Tempest began another battle.

15

The Ancient Life-Giver

"May He who gave these lives and now has taken them for reasons we poor mortals cannot comprehend look with compassion upon these mourners and give them comfort."

The rites of the Church of England rolled inexorably on, but Tempest heard little of them. She was in a tight locked cage of despair and the outside world was one of shadows. The two coffins beside the waiting graves, the tossing of her black gown in the grass-scented wind, Robert's haggard face, the passive eyes of the neighbors, Zard Finguson and his wife, who had stayed at Cloud Ridge in the day and a half since the two deaths, a few other friends who had heard the news, and Justin, austere in gray cloth, seemed players in a drama from which she hoped soon to wake. Even the low tapping of the drums could not rouse her interest. Always she stood over Morna's body; always she watched the strangling of the child as it fought a losing battle for breath, and always she saw Robert assess her over his dead. If only she had not come to Jamaica! If only Robert had not lusted after her! Blame and blame again were not enough for Tempest in this time when she could not even weep.

Robert had ordered the services done as quickly as possible, only sensible in the summer heat, and outside just, beyond the rose garden. He could not bear the presence of people, he said, and must go off alone as soon as he could. Tempest would remain with the Fingusons and he would see her on his return. She had not cared; he was far removed from her. Morna and her child were the reality. Would the scenes of their deaths play forever in her head and haunt the fitful sleep that was so hard to obtain?

"Let us pray." The final words were being said. Everyone bent obediently except Tempest, who only stared straight ahead into Morna's eyes that only she could see.

People scattered swiftly before the grave filling began. Tempest saw Justin say something to Robert, who shook his head before they galloped away in opposite directions. She returned with the Fingusons to their modest house, refused their offers of food and drink, tried to be polite when they offered to pray with her for the souls of the departed, and kept saying, "I have to walk and be alone. I'm sorry. I have to be." Then she walked up and down in their arbor, picking at her gown with fingers that seemed too stiff to move.

A slow hour passed and then another. It was no use. She must exhaust herself and get out into the woods or meadows. A hundred slave rebellions would not matter. It was getting on for afternoon. The Fingusons, both elderly, would be lying down and their slaves surely cared nothing about watching her.

Tempest took the first path away the house and was soon in the uncleared woodland, but for all the comfort it and solitude brought, she might have been surrounded by people. The humming insects, swaying trees and tumbling vines interested her no longer. She saw Morna's dying face and the beauty of the world was dross before that.

She walked rapidly up the summit of a hill and looked down into a small valley that was filled with huge trees, the branches of which looked to be smaller ones. Creeping vines twined to their heights and brilliant flowers of pink and purple flamed in the summer sun. A subtle spicy odor hung on the air. Silence was heavy around her. Not for the first time she reflected how quickly one could become used to the drums.

"You are the very devil to catch up with. No lady walks so fast, don't you know that?" The cool, amused voice came from just behind her.

Tempest felt nothing, not fright, anger, or even curiosity. She turned slowly and looked at Justin, who leaned against an outcropping of rock and regarded her steadily. His decorous suit had been exchanged for loose white trousers and shirt. He was barefoot. A long knife was thrust in his belt and one hand lay casually on it. The sun struck sparks in his tawny hair so that his dark brows made a strong contrast to the fairness.

"What do you want, Justin? I do not wish to spar or fight with you. I cannot. Leave me in peace."

"Peace, Tempest?" He scowled at her. "You are ready to explode."

"Then let me." She was running out of words. She had to get away from him. "Go seek your women. Go to the devil. Let me be." The words rapped out flatly in a rudeness that might have horrified a week ago and now were commonplace.

He said, "I have to talk to you. There are things about Morna's death that I must know, and you are the only person who can tell me. If a crime has been committed, and I think it has, the perpetrator must be punished." He took a step toward her and she recoiled. "Come, don't be silly. I won't hurt you, and this is necessary. I could hardly call on you at the Fingusons."

"It doesn't matter what happens." Morna's dead face was receding before Justin's sun-browned one.

"If you believe that, you are destroyed in truth. Where is the bold girl of the hillside and parlor, the actress-missionary, the fighter?" His words affected her. "I know you feel sorrow for them, Tempest, and that is natural, but they had the same sickness and it was only a matter of time. If Morna's death was premature, there is still an accounting to be made. Listen." The long fingers reached out and took her chin, holding it so that she was forced to look at him. "You have to talk to me and I am determined that you shall. Do you understand me?"

His insistence was shifting the deadly visions as her anger tried to surface. Once she had been bold, just as he said. How long ago and in what life was that? "No!" It was too much. The shade of the trees close by beckoned, and she started toward them. His movements behind her were like those of the ancient nemesis as he followed.

They ducked under some outspread branches and went into a green cave of filtered light which was hung with purple flowers outlined in white from the heavy vines winding to the top of this particular tree. It was so quiet that Tempest heard the faint hum of several bees hovering over one of the blossoms. The ground was very soft due to the leaf bed, but she resisted an impulse to sink down.

"Well, madam? I am waiting." The arrogant tone, his piercing gaze, the indolence of his pose as he leaned against the huge trunk suggested that he had all the time in the world to wait.

Tempest felt the stemmed tide of her emotions stir into a self-protective rage. Her hand went up and back, ready to slash at him. Justin came erect and waited for it to land. He made no effort to protect himself. The weight of her arm was too much for her and his very stillness made her pause.

In that moment Justin spoke. "She bled a great deal, I suppose. And there would have been pain. Much?"

The savagery of it cut into Tempest as though he had rammed his own blade into her shoulder. Time swung back and she was running up the path to Cloud Ridge in answer to the cries that could have only one meaning. She stood before Justin and let the words come. Her conscious mind marveled at what she said, told her to be cautious for what she might regret later, but nothing could stop the tearing pain that must be alleviated, pain and guilt that must be set free.

She went down into the dark world of despair and unending loss. The tragedy of Morna Dornier and her child became that of Tempest Mallory. Robert was larger than fiend and his probable plotting became diabolical. Twice over, the final scenes replayed themselves as the bright day faded for her.

Strong arms were holding her and her face was pressed against Justin's chest. She heard the hammering of his heart as he touched her hair in slow, soothing motions. He was whispering, "Say what you have to, but let it come. Don't lock yourself away." The tenderness in his voice was like nothing she had ever heard from him. Surprised, she raised her head and looked up at him.

His eyes shimmered as if they were jewels and his predator's appearance was softened by warmth. His mobile mouth lifted at one side, causing the scar on his cheek to gleam white. Tears blurred her sight of him for an instant, and he bent to touch her lips with his. A thin trickle of fire ran through her veins. He drew her close in a comforting gesture, holding her as he might any young bereft creature.

"Forgive me, Tempest, that I had to do that to you, but I of all men living should know the damage silence can cause. I did not mean to be cruel, little one. Will you try to believe that? Do you think you feel able to come and rest under this tree for a while before we return? There is much that you need to understand when you are able."

Tempest put her arms around his lean waist, resting her open palms on his back. The muscles contracted under her touch through the thin material of his shirt. The darkness and visions of death receded. She could feel and reach out; she lived and was beginning to realize it.

Justin moved and she held him the more tightly. He put his hand on her neck, then thrust it up through the masses of her hair so that it tumbled free over her shoulders and down her back. "You'll get a headache wearing it up that way." He was whispering near her ear and his breath tickled gently.

Tempest said, "My neck is stiff." He moved her back slightly so that he could look into her eyes. She tilted her head, turning it from side to side against his fingers. They stared at each other in growing intensity. "Yes." She breathed out the word as he gave a half smile.

They came together so carefully that delicate hands might have fitted them that way. Justin's mouth caressed hers and she responded, content to let the banked fire smolder. She felt his manhood rise against her thighs and press through the thick gown and numerous petticoats she wore. Her breasts began to throb as if in anticipation of his hands there. She ached for him, for the thrust and possession that would encompass them both. Why was he delaying? She had to have him. Her skin was prickling and burning with desire; surely he felt the same way!

He released her lips and trailed kisses down the side of her face, across her neck, and at the collar of her gown. There he paused. "You want this, too? Be sure."

Why was he so hesitant when she was inflamed? His body told her that he wanted her and he had taken her from that netherworld of horror into this honey sweetness. If the decision was to be hers alone, then she would gladly take it. Her fingers went to the buttons while she kept her gaze on him. No words were necessary. She could not have voiced them, for her tongue was dry in her mouth.

Justin spoke for them both and now the tenderness was gone. Another look was on the dark face, one of determination mixed with speculation. "Let me disrobe you. No one will come here." She stood very still in acceptance while he dealt with the buttons and fastening in swift motions. The wrappings of mourning fell from her and with them all restraint. She shuddered when her breasts were exposed, thrusting herself toward him until he held them and set his mouth to the nipples for a second before releasing the rest of her clothes so that she stood naked before him in the dappled light.

"Now you." Tempest pulled his shirt free, opened it, and kissed the smooth flesh, tonguing the tiny hairs for a moment before moving on to his trouser band. He wore nothing underneath and his long shaft was high, pearl-tipped with eagerness, nested in a swirl of tawny hair. Once again Tempest shivered at the beauty of his powerful body, the strength of the muscles, and the flat planes of back and stomach. Did he find her fair? Was the recent turmoil stamped on her face and flesh? He reached out for her and all questions vanished.

Tempest and Justin stood locked tightly against each other, their mouths fastened in a deep exploring kiss, tongues tantalizing, flicking, and probing. She felt the strong push of him between her legs as her ready moisture emerged. They swayed, shifted, and allowed their hands to rove up and down in a hunger that was so fundamental, nothing could stand in the way of its completion.

She drew back slightly to catch her breath and met his eyes. Brown, erect and hard, he might have been a primeval man before his mate. Tempest straightened, smiling proudly as she shook her hair back. This prolongation and assessment came from the dawn of time also.

"I want you, Tempest. I want to plunge deep in you and feel your pleasure in what I do. Does it shock you that I speak so?" Again there was that strange speculation in his gaze.

"I want to draw the very power from you and feel it spill over into me. I want you. And I want you this very minute." She challenged him, knowing that she had to do so and had to put it in words. Feeling was running high in her. It shut out everything except the present. There was nothing in the world except Tempest and Justin, naked in the noon sun under a tree.

He smiled, a flash of white teeth that held no humor. Then he turned to spread her gown and petticoats out on the springy leaves. She came to him and they kissed again before he bore her down in one quick motion and was in the depths of her before she could cry out that it was too soon; she wanted a mutual coming and he ought to know that.

Justin came up and down on Tempest in a fury that threatened to rend and tear. He was inflamed to such a degree that there was no suggestion of the earlier tenderness; she was a vessel for him. But she would not have it so. She twisted her hips so that he paused in mid-stroke. He was very near to his culmination and she was roused to a fine pitch as well. How could she tell him to cherish and lead her to his heights? It was rather frightening to realize that she did not know him well enough to talk to him about so important a thing.

Words were not necessary, after all. He sat forward slightly and took her nipple into his mouth as he drew on it and teased with his tongue. All the while his shaft moved inside her. Tempest let her fingers play up and down his back, on his neck, and at the edges of his face. A solid, contained flame was building up in her, filling every crevice of her skin. She writhed under his mouth and touch, knowing very well that she rendered him as excited as she.

Now he drew her to his side and began to thrust in and out while she arched to meet the impact. His eyes fastened on hers and she could not look away. Something wild lived behind his face, a thing untamed and beyond knowing. Civilization was far away from them here in this bower. Tempest felt the barriers fade away; she was close to merging with this man and he with her. The pillar of fire crumbled and spread outward to engulf her. Her legs spread wider as one went over Justin's hip and they clung together in the blessed immolation, their bodies throbbing in desire's aftermath.

A few minutes later they lay apart on the improvised pallet. Justin kept firm hold of her hand, doubtless recalling their last passionate episode. She was content to be still, allowing her skin to cool, watching the play of light and shadow on their sated bodies, and enjoying the fragrance of grass and flowers in this secluded green cave. They were against the earth in the most fundamental rhythm of all, and she, Tempest Mallory, was a part of it. The place of shades had been forsaken for the house of life. She might have won through alone; she was strong in her own right and well she knew it, but Justin had shown her the way.

She raised up on one elbow and smiled at him, then bent to kiss the carved mouth. "I suppose you know what you have done?" Gratitude and rising passion were in her tones. "I think that I now know what I intend to do." Boldly, her hand reached for his shaft.

Justin quirked an eyebrow and tried to keep his own smile back, but he could not. "Whatever do you mean? I do not understand."

She put her mouth to him in such a way that he could not conceal the delight he felt. Then she sat back on her heels and gave him an inquiring look. He gave an exclamation and reached for her. She tried to dodge and they fell backward, shaking with laughter. Their mouths met and the tenderness began.

16

The Brazen Dark

"I had to make you talk about what you had been through, Tempest. Otherwise it would have festered in you. You were hurt and battered. You retreated into a place of safety and might have sought to remain there." Justin wrapped both arms around his white-clad knees and regarded her seriously. "Since you already know much of what happened in my life, I can tell you that I endured an experience very similar in the days when I attempted to practice medicine. I purged myself in much this way and found that my chosen cure was beyond endurance. But you need have no fear of me."

Because of all that they had been to each other in the past few hours, and since she remembered the bitterness he had once shown the day they met in the field, Tempest was now bold enough to say, "I could never fear you, Justin. But there is much I do not understand. Can you explain what you mean?"

He sighed and once more she saw the shadows of the past in his face. He, who had been concerned for her hurts, had not yet mastered his own. "I think that will have to wait for another time. The afternoon goes on, and even the Fingusons will wonder. Can you meet me tomorrow afternoon?" His mouth quirked upward as he reached over to smooth back a wisp of her hair. "What we do is for you to say, but I must review what you have told me and consult certain texts. There may yet be a case to place before the Governor. If so, you will have to testify."

"I will do it gladly." Her first thought was of the passion to be shared again on the morrow and she was ashamed that Morna's passing and the circumstances of it could so easily leave her. Her gaze went to Justin, who put his hand on hers.

"We weep for ourselves, not for the dead. Remember that, Tempest."

The truth had a harsh taste, but it was more palatable than platitudes. "You teach me many things, Mr. St. Trevian." Her smile belied the formal words. "I will come to you as you ask."

He understood the full meaning of her words and once again they fused in a long embrace before the time of parting.

Although she had been gone for hours, Tempest apparently had not been missed from the arbor. It was very hot and the black gown chafed her skin. She did not want to wear that shade at all, and certainly not to meet Justin tomorrow. What did she care if this community was shocked? Eventually, whatever happened, her future lay away from Jamaica. Now she could not plan; she was still too raw from the horror of Morna's death and the glory of her passion with Justin. This was a waiting time. Meanwhile, she could not return to Cloud Ridge with Robert there, nor would it be proper. The Fingusons had offered hospitality; they would understand that she had to have some of her belongings—Morna's gifts—from the plantation. She would take the small carriage and a slave and drive there, pick up a few things, and return quickly. A few books—the Fingusons had only the Bible—and some pretty gowns would make all the difference. She wanted to be fair for Justin. Was she beginning to care for him? It seemed to her that she was, but he, the arrogant and debonair, showed his own feelings as well.

Less than an hour later she was on the road as she had planned. Mrs. Finguson had professed herself shocked. "I don't understand this rush, Miss Mallory. It is not seemly to gad about as you're doing, Mrs. Dornier so recently in her grave and all. A day of prayer and fasting can do wonders for the tormented soul and that is why we offered you refuge here." Tempest had insisted and thus horrified the woman further by the presumably selfish wish for clothes. She soothed and promised to pray alone, saying that she must have solitude, but greatly appreciated the kindness of these neighbors. "Soon I plan to go to Sir Herbert and Lady Shurden, who invited me recently. They shall know of your generosity in this time of need." The carriage and slave were produced without more arguing and there was dawning respect in Mrs. Finguson's eyes as she watched her odd guest.

Cloud Ridge was white and beautiful in the summer silence, its grounds well tended and immaculate. There was no sign of the tragedy that had happened here. Robert was far away. Mr. Finguson had said something about Kingston and a time of respite for him since he had lost so much. But where were the slaves, the outside workers, the overseers? Plantation work went on regardless of the whereabouts of the master.

"Wait here for me." The driver nodded eagerly and looked around, his eyes rolling in his head. He, too, felt the strangeness of this silent place.

She went up the steps, across the portico, and up to the door. Repeated rappings brought no response, so she pushed on it, entering as it gave way without a whisper of sound. Her flesh began to crawl just as it had that day when she had spoken with Robert and again on the hillside when she had quarreled with Justin. Eerie. The house had an air of emptiness that it had never possessed; always before, there had been the unobstrusive slaves. Now there was no sign of another human being.

"Is anyone here? It's Tempest Mallory!"

Her voice rang back at her from all sides. Perhaps the slaves had run away. She did not think Robert would have given them time to mourn for the mistress. Well, it was no problem of hers. She would rush up and collect her things and be back out in five minutes. The Fingusons' house began to look welcoming beside deserted Cloud Ridge.

Avoiding all proximity to the place where Morna had lain, Tempest dashed for the stairs, shuddered at the closed door of the dead child's room, and made for her own. There was no bag or case in which to place the gowns and other materials she would take, but she was past caring. A long black cloak hung from a peg in back of a green gown. She caught them both up and spread out the cloak so that it could be folded into a carryall. Several other gowns in white, dark green, blue, and tawny, along with slippers and petticoats, followed. *The Collected Plays of William Shakespeare, Evelina,* and *Frankenstein* were piled on her bedside table and now would go with her. She picked up her hairbrush and a fashionable round mirror backed in ivory. All this was enough. She tied the edges of the cloak together and started toward the door with her bundle. She could not wait to get out of this house and into the sunlight.

Her fingers froze and her throat went dry. Robert Dornier stood in the doorway, his face impassive, pale blue eyes glittering as he stared at her. His arms were folded across his chest, and his legs were wide apart. Tempest was reminded of the Holbein portrait of the eighth Henry at the height of his power and in the middle of his wives. Robert's white suit was precise, unwrinkled; he was not the picture of despair he had been that morning.

"I just came for a few things. It's all right, isn't it? I understood that you were leaving for Kingston. Or was it Montego Bay? You need to get away, naturally. The Fingusons are so kind to invite me. We all need to try and recover from the shock we've had." Tempest moved closer to the door as she spoke, hoping that Robert would give way. She knew she was babbling, but his very calm was unnerving. *Where is the bold girl I first knew?* Justin's words rang in her mind and gave her support. Tempest Mallory did not quail before one man. She knew now why her flesh had crawled; instinctively, she had sensed the evil of his presence and recoiled. What if he had actually seen her with Justin?

"You need not be in such a rush to leave. I believe there is something cool to drink down in the drawing room." His voice was cool and expressionless.

Tempest smiled in what she hoped was a disarming way. "Thank you, no. I am expected back, and the driver will be wondering what I am doing up here for so long. By the way, where are all the slaves? I saw no one about."

The thin lips stretched out. "They know better than to intrude. And I am not noted for my kindness when the drums beat in the hills."

"I must go, Robert." Tempest had spoken softly, but now

she paused. He showed no intention of moving away from the door.

"No, my dear. You are not going anywhere." Robert came slowly toward her, hands held out to intercept any attempt to escape him. "I have waited long to have you. I mean to test your skills in lovemaking. Perhaps you will even become pregnant as a result. A man must have sons."

"Don't be silly, Robert. The driver will come up to see about me, and the Fingusons may send someone else. You are distraught. You have a reputation to maintain." Tempest knew she must not excite him. If she could dash by and run outside, surely she would be safe. He would not risk a fuss; slaves gossiped so much.

His laughter was sharp and without amusement as he stopped a few feet from her and ran a leisurely eye up and down her figure. "It is pointless to play the innocent. I know what you and Justin St. Trevian did together. Do you think you went unseen? You'll never be sure what happened to Morna either. It won't affect what we do together. I've wanted you from the first. She knew it, and so did you. Now the reckoning has come."

"Let me by!" Tempest abandoned any attempt at subterfuge. "You are acting like a madman! Do you want me to scream? Slaves talk!" .

"I invite you to do so." He put one hand on her shoulder and let his fingers trail toward her breasts. "Matters will be all the more amusing if you resist a bit. I like spirit. Morna had none, always weeping, trying to refuse me even after I gave her . . ." He broke off and glanced quickly at her face, which she kept calm by a struggle. "I knew you would come here sooner or later. I had you watched. My slaves obey me or they die and others are bought. Some have dared to run away, and they are to be hunted down like the animals they are. No notice will be taken of the fact that you are here. Your driver, suitably bribed and threatened, will return with a story of how some other neighbors arrived and, their way of life being more interesting to you, asked you to come for part of the time of sorrow. The Fingusons will not care; they dare not, for my money and influence are powerful here and in all Jamaica."

Tempest sagged backward, letting her hands slip away from the bundle. Her whole body began to tremble and she fixed her imploring eyes on his hard ones. "Robert, I cannot believe this of you." The words came in a breathy little burst as she turned her face to one side.

"You are frightened. Good. That will show you that you have a new master. I can do things to you that Justin St. Trevian never thought of doing, rakehell and murderer that he is. Be afraid of me, Tempest Mallory. You have reason to be!"

Robert came so close to her that she could smell the strange spicy odor of his breath. He bent over as if to pull her to him, but she shrank from him with a little cry. He was sweating and his eyes had an unhealthy glow. Lust poured out of him and she could see the bulge of his tight trousers.

"No. Please don't do this, Robert!"

He laughed and jerked at her waist. She came forward to him as if limp in terror. Then her knee came up with all the force her athletic body could muster and slammed into his groin. He spat a curse and doubled over with a howl of pain. Tempest hit on the back of the neck with the side of her palm in a gesture she had learned from Savora. He cried out and fell flat.

She stood above him in the safety of the moment and drew deep breaths of victory. His flagrant desire and her own acting had saved her, but now she had to gain some leeway as far as time was concerned, for she had no illusions about his determination to pursue her.

Her one thought was to find Justin, but she realized she had no idea where he lived or how to reach him. She would simply have to hide until tomorrow afternoon. Logically, the Fingusons were her hosts and responsible for her, but if Robert came searching and found her, she would be given up as only proper. A chaperon could be found and manipulated; Tempest did not doubt his power.

She recalled the scissors that had been in the drawer of the table near her bed and went to look for them. Thanks be that they were still there! Quickly, she cut long strips from the cloak and bound Robert's hands, then his feet, and tossed the remainder of it over him. His pulse was strong and steady; it would not be long before he woke. Another piece of material furnished a gag. She stepped over his body, opened the door, and peered out. All was silence. Now to find the driver and get out of this house. She wanted nothing from Cloud Ridge—only her freedom.

She ran through the house and out to the portico, but no one was there. The driver had gone. The sun was sinking and shadows were drawing long on the grounds. When she turned her head to look upward at the great white mass of the house, Tempest saw the pink reflections cast on it and wondered again at the quiet loveliness that was somehow ominous.

There was no time to waste. It would not be long until darkness, and all her instincts told her that she must leave this place at once. She darted behind a bush, dug her nails into the hem of her black gown, and ripped a long piece free so that her feet would be free. The clinging undergarments met an equal fate. She buried them in the leaves and stood up. As she lifted up on her toes and prepared to run, the drums began to beat in the hills, a beat that was no longer resigned and slow, but somehow triumphant.

17

Cave of the Dark Lord

The moon was high and white in the sky when Tempest sat up under the tree where she had sheltered earlier. The sleep that had come upon her so suddenly had been restoring and now she was surprised that, with all the recent happenings, she felt as well as she did. She smiled as she thought of Robert's rousing and the fury he would feel at his own helplessness. She knew in her heart that he had destroyed and murdered Morna. If there was any justice in the universe, he would in time pay for that sin. In the meantime, she was free and knew how to hide. She and Justin would make love, laugh and talk and plot their next moves. For this time she could pretend she was the only person in this silver night, that she ruled if she chose.

The beat of the drums exhilarated her; it was like a slow, rising fever in the blood, not unlike the lifting power that bore her along in passion with Justin. Culmination and release were promised by the drums, and the time was nearing. Tempest knew that a sensible person would be afraid, but she had fought a battle of her own and won. Now she savored that pleasure.

She knew it was not wise to wander about, but her legs were cramped and stiff. Restlessness pulled at her nerves so that she had to have some sort of action. A short walk might help calm her, and she would be most watchful. A puff of wind brought the smells of cooking meat to her nose and reminded her that she was ravenous, a state in which she was likely to remain for many hours. She must go away from any sign of activity, for now everyone must be regarded as a foe. The treetops tossed and bent over before the rising breeze as the odor of distant rain was borne in. Once more Tempest longed to explore this country with Justin, to make love and roam as she chose, to care passionately and still be free. Would he think this night was an adventure? How very little she really knew about him, after all.

She plaited her tangled hair and secured it with another bit of her now bedraggled skirt. Then she set out, moving cautiously from tree to bush and through the undergrowths, skirting the open spaces and melting to the ground at unfamiliar sounds. In a way she was reminded of the games she used to play as a child; red Indian, stalker, princess of the wilderness, bounty hunter, and seeker of the buffalo herds. Time drifted into memory and reality.

The drums were louder now and the beat was steady. It seemed to say, Come! Come! The sounds came from no discernible direction but were all around this area. Tempest knew that she must go to ground and wait for daylight; danger had moved closer in the last hour or so. Her back was aching and she was growing very thirsty. If only she could find a spring. It would be worse than foolish to go looking for one.

She paused on the edge of a small uphill meadow that was fringed with lush growth on the far side and rather sparsely on her side. Dared she cross over and check on the possibility of water there? It was rather far around, but a quick dash would bring her into the trees. The grass leaned before the wind as she watched and the moon was partially hidden behind a scudding cloud. Taking the moment, Tempest stepped out and prepared to run. In the same instant that she was limned against the dark pattern of low bushes a huge shadow rose from the distant trees and headed toward her. Two others came behind it.

Tempest took one look and ran down the meadow as fast as she could sprint. The pounding steps of her pursuers gained on her and she zigzagged in an effort to avoid them, but it was no use. She was grabbed from behind and brutally slammed to the ground. She kicked and twisted as they turned her face up and knelt beside her, but there was no escape. The three black men who held her wore only loincloths and their faces were painted with designs of red and white. The savage expressions on them left Tempest in no doubt as to the fate they planned for her at this instant. She was afraid, but the burning anger that she could be so used was suffusing her veins.

One of her captors pulled at the buttons on her bodice and said something in a strange dialect to his fellows, who roared with laughter. The thin material ripped and exposed her bosom. Another of the men started to unfasten his brief garment. Tempest writhed in a futile attempt to regain her freedom and he slapped her sharply. It was not a hard blow, but her senses swam and came back to the clear knowledge that if she were to live, all her wits must be put to use. They certainly meant to rape her, but that need not kill her. Her body alone would be violated; Tempest Mallory's very self went far beyond the flesh. Had not Savora once mentioned something of the same thing? A fragment of memory came to her then and with it the certainty that there was nothing to lose.

She forced her recoiling flesh to be still. Her writhing ceased and she went limp in their grasp. With all the power left in her voice and in the strength of years spent in the declaiming of verses for her own pleasure and dreams, Tempest released the only bolt she possessed.

"Felipe has not yet given the word to attack all the whites! Some of us hold to the cause! I am the friend of Savora, wife to Jason, and honored to them! I am of the missionaries who have helped you and risked their lives. Do you have so many friends that you can torment them?"

She was flat on her back, breasts exposed, skirts to her thighs, and clutched in the hands of men who had to be rebel slaves, but the commanding of her voice, unshaded by fear, and the calling of at least two names they recognized held them back from the rape that had been only seconds away. The largest of her captors bent over her, his face a dark moon in the shifting light of near dawn. He drew his lips back so that his teeth seemed slabs of white, making him the veritable ogre of childhood nightmares. Tempest wanted to scream with fear, but she fought it back as she stared back at him.

"You know Felipe then, white woman? And you can tell me what he looks like? Or do we all look alike to you? Someone to take orders and be whipped if we do not obey in the next breath? Tell me what Felipe looks like. I suppose you know him well?" His laughter came harshly. "If you do not describe him properly, your throat shall be slit and we will take our relief from your body in death! Slaves have to make do, you understand!"

If I live through this, any struggle to get on the stage will be nothing. The thought appeared in Tempest's mind and vanished. There was nothing else but the role she played. The branded, bitter face of the man she had seen walking with several others who spoke his name was a flame in her memory because almost directly after that had come her first passionate encounter with Justin, two months ago. "He is very tall, much more so than others, even yourselves. His left arm is shorter than the right, and his face is marked with a large *F* covering the remains of his nose and going up to his eyes. Those eyes go through you. His word is law. He gestures with a cutting motion that is habit." Tempest did not really know if this was true, but it could be and any chance must be taken. "Jason walks with him." She described him and Savora and the arrival on the *Corinthian* as well as the things Savora had told her concerning their marriage.

Her questioner flicked a finger and the imprisoning hands fell away from her so that she could sit up. He leaned close and his voice was still taunting. "You seem to know much, but I do not think you are a missionary." The teeth flashed in that merciless grimace. "You do not look or act so. I have heard their pious words, their attempts to save our souls, as they say, and they always pray. My late master was a barrister. I learned much from him before I killed him. Who are you, woman?"

"One who has suffered even as your people. Look at my clothes, the way I travel in the night. I ran from a man who sought my life after I denied him. Ask Savora and Jason if they know Miranda Hutt, the missionary. They will vouch for me to Felipe. Does a person have to be black to suffer?" Tempest did not take her eyes from his as Robert, Morna, and Aunt Hannah passed before her inner vision. They, and Justin as well, had thought to force her into a mold. Now these rebels had no consideration for any other person. Her words had rung with conviction and they felt it.

"You go with us to the cave as a prisoner. May your God

help you if you are lying to us." He looked at the others, who nodded a grinning agreement.

Tempest scrambled to her feet, wondering just what name or repetition of names had preserved her life. She pulled the rags of her bodice up and arranged them as best as she could so that she was no longer exposed. "I trust the judgment of your leaders."

The spokesman gave her a sidelong glance and for the first time his voice was not threatening. "There is only one leader Felipe." He reached into a pouch at his side and produced a folded length of cloth. "You will be blindfolded and travel as we say." Oddly, he waited for her nod before fastening the cloth in place. "Hold on as we go."

She was hoisted up to his broad back, her legs around his waist and her arms placed on his shoulders. For all that they had been so close to taking her only a few minutes earlier, the touches now were almost totally impersonal. They began to run through the warm night, the sounds of the drums magnified in Tempest's ears because her vision was blocked.

It seemed to her that the nightmare journey went on for an eternity. She bounced about in the noise-filled blackness as she clutched her captor with both arms, not daring to shift position or even move. Life was too precious, too dear, to be jeopardized by a chance action. Tempest thought of how easily she could have been dead and of what the next hours might bring. Then she fought to push back any negative idea that might undermine the role he meant to play. All she could do was fight for life as best she might, with all the powers at her command. Self-doubt must not enter in. It was pointless to think of the darkness that Morna now inhabited or of all those younger than she gone down to untimely death. While Tempest Mallory lived, she would do so with verve and determination. It might be a credo, she thought in an effort to hold her throbbing arms still.

They went uphill and down, through vines and snapping branches, across streams and over open spaces. The drums never stopped, but they were dulled when Tempest was carried by her captors into what she could only guess was the cave. Here the air was cool and she could smell water, but there was sense of overwhelming darkness with penetration into the earth. All her faculties were sharpened; now she heard low voices and felt the presence of onlookers. Once a high laugh rang out and was instantly silenced.

The man carrying her stopped so suddenly that she almost fell backward as he said, "The prisoner must see him, but she cannot in this garb. She says she is a missionary."

Another voice answered, "Soon, soon. Take her to the inner place. Clothes befitting a missionary will be found." The intonations were light and amused, but the underlying savagery there belied an obvious education.

Two turns and a few steps to the side brought them into a quiet area where Tempest was set down and the blindfold jerked from her eyes. She was blinded by the flaring torches set about and her legs shook from the sudden rush of blood to them, but she knew she must not show weakness. She gazed about as calmly as though she stood in the drawing room at Cloud Ridge.

Walls of rock reached up into murky darkness. The small area where she was formed a natural private enclosure on three sides, and a hanging bright cloth, now pulled aside, covered the entrance. A woven mat of several thicknesses lay to one side on the floor and a pile of garments was next to it. One torch set high illumined the area.

"What is this place?" She was proud of her steady voice.

"There is no need for you to know. You will do as you are told." Her captor gave that cruel grin once more. "I am Marcus. If you have lied and are proved to have done so, it will my right to destroy you. Remember me, woman. Mine may be the last face you see in this life."

It might have come from a bad play, this constant threatening and allusion to death. In that light Tempest could say, "In the meantime I would like to have some water and food. I believed you mentioned a change of clothes? And what about water to wash?"

His eyes glittered at her. "Coming now. Hurry with it. You have only a little bit before you face him." The bombastic language was gone; in its place was a quiet purposefulness that needed no support. "Be careful what you say."

At that moment a young girl entered with a pail of water in one hand, and a loaf of bread and some cheese in the other. She looked at Marcus, who shook his head. After she had set the things down and gone, he waved at the clothes near the mat.

"You have twenty minutes. You will wear what's there." He laughed and pulled the cloth over the entrance as he left.

Tempest found herself not at all squeamish about drinking from the questionable pail and washing thereafter. She fell upon the coarse bread and sticky cheese with all the enthusiasm of the starving. Did they think she would complain about such fare? When her short meal was done, she went through the garments and found out what the joke had been. They were of such thin weave that one's body could be seen clearly. Moreover, the skirts were short, brilliantly colored, and gaudy; the tops were the sort that fastened under the breasts and drew attention to them, the type of provocative clothing a dancer might wear. The trap was easy to discern: a missionary would never wear such things; a white woman who did could be branded a slut with no difficulty. Tempest knew what to expect in that case. But if she refused to obey the clear order given, Marcus would deal with her. She had no illusions on either score.

She stood irresolute for a fleeting moment. There was the most passionate regret that she had never been a true actress, and she longed for more pleasure with Justin. Pleasure, yes, but so much more than the body. She wished she could have experienced sharing, laughter, and tenderness beyond the body. Other than that—the whole of life—she might find this fate less unbearable. For now she still lived and meant to continue in that state. Think only of survival!

Hurriedly, Tempest stripped off the rags of the once respectable black gown and few underclothes. Then she put on four of the skirts at the same time, fastening them securely around her slender waist. The colors of red, orange, yellow, and brilliant green swirled together in a riot that did much to hide her nudity. She twisted several of the tops together into a halter to hold her breasts up. Then she picked up another of the skirts, ripped it open and settled the long flow of material over her shoulders so that it was both blouse and shawl. She combed her hair with her fingers so that it was loose and streaming on her shoulders and down beyond her waist.

No sooner had she finished than the curtain was ripped back and Marcus stood staring at her. Behind him were several other men and a few women. One held a torch high. Tempest revolved to face them, wondering if she looked the very fool in the bizarre garb, although it certainly made no difference.

"I am ready to see Savora and Jason. I am ready to meet Felipe."

"They are not here, but you shall surely see Felipe. You still say that you are missionary?" Marcus's gaze went to her breasts and back up. "I did not say wear all that."

"I am a missionary, and I have not disobeyed." Tempest gave him look for look without flinching. Bravado was everything here.

He snorted and motioned for her to follow him. As she did so, Tempest was conscious of the waves of animosity pouring out from the watchers. It was frightening to be so hated, and she wondered if the proponents of slavery were really aware of the magnitude. Savora had suffered, but her fury had never erupted. Who could blame the slaves; not Tempest Mallory, who had known another sort!

Never in all her nightmares could Tempest have envisioned the scene into which she now walked. There were perhaps a hundred men and women in the open area of the cave. Torches made the brightness rival the most brilliant day. Crude paintings of battles decorated the walls, which were smoke-singed. Food and drink was set about; people ate and talked; some worked on weapons or watched the others. Four men were drumming ritually, the sound full in the confined area. Two others, naked, stood beside them and swayed back and forth. But the figure reclining on a rock formation in the center gripped her attention and riveted it.

Felipe wore a red cloak and there was a band of the same shade around his head. The *F* on his face was outlined in vermilion, which glittered in the light. His small eyes rolled back and forth as he watched the people. A huge diamond shone on one hand as he slapped it into the other in time to the drums. He was magnificently ugly as he surveyed the kingdom of his domination.

Several figures stood around him, leaning forward to speak to him now and then. Their cloaks were of bright colors, but they wore masks of boar's heads with great tusks shining white. It seemed to Tempest that Felipe was surrounded by the great animals rather than his followers. At any moment they might be sent to rend her apart.

Felipe raised his head and saw her. The low, growling voice stretched across the cave and quieted all other sounds. "So this is the missionary! Come here and let me see. You are far from your church." He began to laugh without amusement.

As Tempest walked toward him, she saw Marty Dee and several of the other slaves from Cloud Ridge in the lines of those who parted to make way for her. Now her reckoning had come.

18

Bold Deception

Tempest forced herself to stand calmly before the slave leader. Her arms hung naturally at her sides and her chin was high. It was a struggle to keep from trembling, but she dared not show fear. They would expect her to be terrified, to weep and beg for release. She would not have the slightest compunction about doing so if there were any hope of freedom, but the blood lust was too high here. Time must be bought in some way, and if she must die, she would do so fighting.

"You have said you know me. I say you have lied to postpone your death." Felipe leaned forward to stare into her face. He spoke flatly and without heat, but savagery burned in his eyes. "You have not avoided it for long!" At his last words one of the men tapped a drum in a low, hammering rhythm that seemed to underscore the menace of them. "Do you think we have cause to love the missionaries that you pretend to be one of them?"

Tempest looked at Marty Dee and saw the triumph glittering in the brilliant eyes. The woman must have wasted no time in letting Felipe know who his prisoner was. Now Marty called out, "She thinks she goin' be mistress up at Cloud Ridge! Got another think comin', that she has!" Her laughter rose over the tapping of the drum and fell into silence as Felipe raised his hand.

"We're going out tonight to kill, destroy, and burn. We take back our own country and drive out those who made us slaves. No white person shall live. The missionaries want us to worship their God, and they slap the fingers of the masters here. Freedom isn't theirs to give. We take it and keep it. We kill and we keep our island."

Felipe spoke quietly, but there was no doubting his intent. Every person in that room was with him to the death he intended. Tempest felt the sickness rise in her throat and wondered if she could control it. Why had she not stayed safely on her hill until time to meet Justin? Justin, whom she would never see again. They would rape her, torture her and mutilate her flesh, degrade her completely before finally giving the mercy of death. Even in this moment Tempest could not believe the possibility of her own ending. She had to do something.

"You think to be like Haiti when they threw out the French, killed the whites, and made a separate black nation?" Her own voice, faintly conversational, rang in her ears. "Would you be king or emperor, Felipe?"

Tempest was not the only one amazed by her words in the face of horror. Felipe and those around him were gaping at her. The wearers of the boar's heads leaned closer as the leaping fires from torches glinted in the smoky air. A few murmurs rose from those nearest before Felipe glared at her and half rose from his seat. The very atmosphere seemed to thicken.

"You'll not be around to care, little missionary!" Felipe jerked his head suddenly and the onlookers moved back a few paces. "In case you've wondered, I know you're a friend of Jason's wife, but I also know what he thinks of those who have made slaves of us. Friends and relatives don't matter. Only our cause!" The last words rose to a scream and the gathering answered him with another.

The man who had taken Tempest prisoner, Marcus, now broke in with a shout, "She has lied! Let hers be the first white blood of this night!"

"Yes! Yes!"

"Kill her before we go out!"

"Kill! Kill!"

The cries rose around them and Tempest felt the perspiration drip down on her neck. Her life was likely measured in minutes or less as they whipped themselves into a frenzy that would later explode onto the great plantations of the region. What could she do? Pure panic held her rigid, and her tongue seemed to freeze in her mouth. She could only stand and stare at the madness around her.

"You would do well to be afraid." Felipe spoke almost conversationally in the midst of the pandemonium. "Your God will be angry that you pretended to be one of those who try to convert us."

Tempest looked into the fierce eyes and knew that he baited her. He wanted more enjoyment than he was getting. She forced the slow words out. "Take me up into the open air. I don't want to die in a cave."

"Kill! Kill!" The sounds hammered against the walls and into her mind. "Kill!" This was nightmare made reality. Shadows loomed high on the far wall, resolving themselves into more of the cloaked figures topped with boar heads. Was it some kind of strange ritual? She would never know. She would be dead.

Felipe had her now. "Persuade me. Why should I grant you anything?"

Their voices had reached to the others, who paused to listen. He seemed calm enough, but Tempest knew his leashed rage could pour out in the next breath. She had no plan, no hope of escape, but if she could get outside, there might be some possibility of running away. Better to make the attempt than submit to slow degradation. *It isn't real; this is a nightmare.* Her brain kept running over the words even as she tried to think and could not.

"Why should I?" Felipe was speaking louder now and there was a strange lilting undercurrent in his tone. The hunters were toying with their prey. The vermilion on his face shone in the creases of the brand and the diamond on his finger flashed prisms of light. He loomed enormous as he stood swaying back and forth, his mouth twisting at the corners. The boar-headed ones were emulating his movements, and one, taller than the others in a shrouding black cloak, was clapping both hands together in a flat, muffled sound. He wore gloves with long claws on the fingers and it took little imagination to see them running with blood.

"Because there are other gods than the Christian one. Older and more vengeful. You warned me to be afraid, Felipe. Perhaps you are the one who has reason to fear! Have you forgotten those voices that speak on the wind?" Tempest was never to know where the inspiration came from, but the names of the gods and demons that Savora had spoken in her nightmares on the *Corinthian* came rolling out. She tossed her head, whirled about so that the gauzy cloth stood out from her body and shook in appearance of what might have been a divine frenzy. For the moment she was not Tempest Mallory snatching at the slightest chance for another minute of survival; instead, she was an ancient priestess before the unbelievers and the angry gods were at her back.

Felipe and his followers gaped at her. In this instant of time they were completely held. One shouted, "How does she know that name? The god will strike her down!" But still Tempest kept up the litany as she raised her arms and cried out endless syllables that had no meaning. She could not bear to think what would happen when breath and ingenuity ran out.

Then a drum sounded abruptly and stopped. Everyone in the cave turned toward the opening. Marcus reached out and clasped Tempest, holding her in both arms as far from him as he could. They stared at each other and she saw the apprehension in his eyes, though he tried to conceal it.

"It is time to go against the whites." Felipe's voice was thick and heavy with triumph. "We shall win. Never doubt it."

"Never!" His people gave the cry with one great sound.

He turned to Tempest. "I don't know who or what you are, white woman. You will live until we are free and then you will be the first sacrifice to those whose names you cried out. But if they say otherwise . . ." He shook a fist at her. "There will be time for you later. Marcus, bring her into battle! Let her be your shield!"

Marcus jerked Tempest along with him as the people surged up the rocky paths that led outside. She went eagerly, hardly able to believe that her attempt at distraction had bought her time. Her legs went weak, but she dared not falter. Men bearing torches dashed by them while others, carrying guns of all makes, knives, swords, and clubs, followed Felipe and the boar-headed ones. The drums thundered out a war cry of blood and were answered from the throats of these ex-slaves.

They came out into the fresh night air, which Tempest drew hungrily into her lungs. She saw the fading stars in the last heavy darkness before dawn and caught the languorous scent of unknown flowers that mingled with tar and human sweat. Marcus had his knife out as he began to run with her after the army as it headed west. The rocks cut her bare feet and her breath burned in her throat, but death was held at bay for another instant. What else could matter?

She stumbled on the downward path and Marcus swung her around, nearly twisting her arm out of its socket. "Keep up or I'll gut you here and leave you!" The dark face was menacing and he touched the knife to her throat.

"Felipe said I was to live. Remember?" She wanted to rake her nails down his cheek, but there must be no yielding.

"Who did you think you fooled with that act of yours?" The tone was scoffing, but his eyes rolled back and the hand holding the knife shook slightly.

Tempest dared not answer him. The line of his balance was too thinly drawn. They stared at each other for a long moment and then his face exploded in blood. He fell backward, releasing her so that she could jump aside, twist, and roll behind a rock.

The night was suddenly silent. Marcus must have died immediately and all the others had gone on ahead. Tempest raised her head cautiously, not daring to think that freedom had come so easily.

It had not. One of the tall boar-headed figures, his black cloak swirling behind him, stood beside Marcus's body. The clawed gloves were absent, but gleaming steel flickered in one hand and the tusks shone white as the hideous head turned toward Tempest. He took a step just as she bent to snatch up a rock.

"Get away from me! I'll brain you!" That was surely a ridiculous statement, Tempest thought to herself. What good was a rock against a knife or sword? It would be better to run, but she could not go back in the direction of the cave and he blocked the path between the rocky walls. "Get away!" She heard her voice go high and shrill, but she could not will it to forcefulness. Endurance would go no further.

"Tempest! Tempest! Wait, we don't have any time to lose!"

The voice was muffled but familiar. She thought her mind was giving way under all the pressures of the past few days. The figure was pulling at the boar's head and lifting it off as she stared. She clutched the rock in fingers that were nerveless.

"Justin! Dear God! I really am dreaming!"

He stood before her, a fantastic figure in loose dark clothes, face and hands darkened, and wearing a black cap over his tawny hair. "If we don't get away from here, we'll both be dead. I'll answer all your questions later, but for now we still have a role to play. Are you up to it?" His teeth flashed white in the darkness. "You're all right, aren't you?"

"Yes!" Joy and relief overwhelmed her, so she could say nothing else.

Justin pulled her into his arms and held her so tightly that she could feel his heart hammering. Then he drew away, pulled off his shirt, and handed it to her. "That'll cover you, at least. Come on." The words were matter-of-fact, but there was a tremor in his voice. It comforted Tempest to know that he was shaken at their mutual touch. The feel of his warm flesh had stirred her even at this moment of desperation.

Then he was adjusting the boar's head and cloak as he motioned her to stay behind him. One hand stayed on his sword. Two pistols were in his belt. Tempest pulled one of the pieces of gauze loose and wrapped it around her cascading hair while they walked.

"Give me one of those pistols. I know how to use it, I promise you."

His laugh was muted through his disguise. "I don't doubt that." He handed over the smaller one and watched her check it. "Hurry!"

Night drifted into early mornng and morning into a dull gray day that hinted of rain as Tempest and Justin went through forests, along rock formations that tore at her nearly numb feet, and in icy streams, under a waterfall, skirting open meadows, and skulking behind great tree boles. Justin discarded his disguise at first light and now wore only breeches. His brown skin shone as the muscles rippled over the wide shoulders. He looked as arrogant as ever, fully in command of this strange situation.

They paused at the top of a rise and looked at each other.

There had been no time for speech previously; all their efforts
had been directed toward escape. For Tempest it had seemed
sufficient that she was away from the engulfing horror of
Felipe's cave and no longer in danger of death or rape. To be
with Justin in a shared experience was part of a dream that
exhaustion was rapidly bringing on.

"Where are we, Justin? What is happening? Tempest felt
that she was repeating herself, the words ringing in her head.
Strangely, there had been no drums since the cave. Were they
starting up again or was this part of a fire-shot dream?

Justin put his hand on her arm and looked down at her. His
amber eyes gleamed with a gentleness she had never seen there
before. His fingers burned her skin. Awareness flickered
between them like the heat lightning in the mountains.

"Tempest, believe me when I say that there is nothing we
can do about what is happening in Jamaica now. I warned those
I could, and I think the rebellion will be put down. It is time to
retreat, time to let the storm sweep over us. Do you
understand?"

Tempest's head was momentarily clear, so she could see the
pain in the depths of his eyes. A muscle in his temple jerked
convulsively and he ran one hand through the crest of his hair.
She felt everything recede before a sudden surge of desire for
him.

"Of course I do." She put her hand over his and felt him
start as a question began in his face.

"Come." He led her a little deeper in the wood at the edge
of the rise, then parted some bushes so she could see. "Look
yonder."

She saw a white rambling house with trees clustered around
it, a spread of fields, and some horses in a green field.
Flowering bushes made a pink and purple pathway toward a
rather battered iron gate. A sense of peace rose from the place
and stirred Tempest with longing.

At her look of inquiry Justin said, "Meadowlands. My home
when I am here in Jamaica. We are safe here. I keep no slaves.
My people are free, although I pretend otherwise for safety's
sake. Tempest . . ." His voice trailed off, but his eyes were
urgent on her.

She knew that she could go with him into Meadowlands and
remain untouched, that he would honor any wish she had and

not question it. He was not the demanding, arrogant man of their first acquaintance now. This gentleness was another side of his complex character. Any decision was hers to make. The future was uncertain. War could erupt here as it had in Haiti. They could be killed by black and whites alike. Ambition paled beside survival, and she had endured much.

Tempest felt a little laugh begin inside her and let it rise to her mouth. Why did she make excuses? She wanted Justin Trevian as she had never thought to want a man in her life. Let that be enough. Was she not, after all, a free woman? She would say it.

"I want to stay with you, Justin. I want . . . you." It was harder than she thought.

Justin drew her to him, delight and surprise mingling on his hawk face. "I have always wanted you, my love. Always." Then their mouths were fused in a deep kiss that welded them into one.

19

Garland of the Days

Tempest yawned and stretched luxuriously as she inhaled the scent of roses and coffee. Still more than half asleep, eyes closed against the light that pressed down on them, she enjoyed the feeling of delicious relaxation that pervaded her body.

"Wake up and drink this." The husky male voice was laced with amusement. "It's getting cold."

Her eyelids jerked open and she sat up with a start, clutching the thin white robe that was her only covering. Justin was standing beside the bed. He held a bunch of yellow roses in one hand and a cup in the other. As she stared at him, memory returning in a rush; he stuffed a pillow behind her back and lowered the cup into her lap. He grinned rakishly at the mounting color in her face.

"I will confess I've had many reactions to my advances, but never any such as yours." The amber eyes were the same shade as his hair and set off the tanned skin. He wore white breeches that molded the long flat thighs and elegant legs. His upper body might have been cut from dark marble; there was not an ounce of extra flesh on it. Tiny curls clustered at his temples as though he came fresh from his bath. He lifted one of the roses to his nose and sniffed while he watched Tempest lazily.

She sipped the strong reviving brew and tried not to gasp at the heat of it. Obviously, it had just been removed from the stove. "I couldn't help it." Her voice was defensive. "It wasn't you."

He thrust the flowers into the glass of water on the table and sank down on the end of her bed. One corner of his mouth went up in a wry grin that made her heart shake. Tempest's eyes met his and they both exploded into laughter.

They had entered Meadowlands hours or days ago. She had no idea which. In her exhaustion, Tempest had been aware of cool white rooms and wide spaces, a hot bath set out by swift-moving servants, who later settled her on a couch and fetched Justin. He had tended her sore feet, they had kissed with mounting passion, and he had started to massage her neck. She remembered the warm, caressing hands and eager lips and her own rising longing. Then there was nothing, not even dreams.

"I went to sleep on you." She thought of the bold invitation she had given on the hillside and could not stop laughing.

Justin said, "There you were, peacefully dreaming in my arms. I didn't have the heart to try to wake you, but twenty-four hours is long enough."

Tempest sobered sufficiently to drink more of the dark brew. Her hair was streaming over her shoulders and she tossed it back as she tried to hide the growing awareness of Justin as he sprawled closer. Sun poured through the open floor-to-ceiling windows and glistened on the polished planks of the floor. More yellow roses nodded from a trellis outside, furnishing the only color in this white room, with its simple hand-carved chairs and chests.

"Tempest." Justin spoke her name so softly that she could barely hear it. "Tempest."

She turned back to him, knowing well that the first move must be hers. So much was unfinished between them; so much was yet to begin. He would not touch her unless she wanted it and she had never wanted anything more. She had thought that on the hill; it had not faded. Justin could be both gentle and demanding, but what was he really like? A deliciously exciting chill went over her body.

Tempest extended the cup toward him. "Set it down for

me." He did as she asked, his gaze never leaving her face. Deliberately, she shrugged the robe from her shoulders and leaned forward so that her breasts moved enticingly. "Love me, Justin. Now." She could say no more, could put nothing else into words. Her throat was constricting and she could feel the blood hammering in her head. Mounting desire held her still.

An instant later Justin was tracing hot kisses over her nipples while her fingers roved up and down the smooth skin of his back. Her body arched toward his as his manhood grew powerful against her. She gave a soft moan when he took one rosy nipple in his mouth and began to draw on it, letting his tongue touch the end tantalizingly. Tempest began to ache all over. She had to have more and more of him. Impatience was a fever, a storm, within her.

He released her breast and took her mouth, gathering it into his and lingering over her lips as they shaped and melted to softness. It was not enough. Tempest thrust her tongue toward his and they locked together in a mute symbol of that greater melding that was to come. Now she was under him, captor and captured, woman awaiting the taking of the man. But the man was content to linger and savor. Tempest's hunger was a roaring that must be satiated. She had no time to wonder at the elemental passion she felt for this man who had first taught her what it meant. The reality was there and she must have him.

She slipped out from him, turned and knelt beside him as, half hidden by the curtain of hair, she began to trace a line with her tongue from his nipples down over the ribcage to the flat stomach and on toward the tawny thatch where his shaft rose. She touched it with the tip of her fingers and then put her mouth there. Justin shuddered with pleasure. He reached out with one hand and pushed her hair back so that they could see each other clearly. It was past the time for tantalizing. Both of them teetered on the edge of the abyss.

He pulled her toward him and she settled down, taking the fullness of his power until she thought she would split with it. Then she balanced and he held her as they rocked in the growing whirlwind, riding in the passion that seemed to have no culmination. Higher and higher they went until Tempest thought she could not bear it any longer. She would explode from within or burn alive.

Then the fire spread, peaked, and overflowed. The abyss flamed out and they fell together in release that was both life and death, a purity of feeling that transcended all else. They clung to each other, turned on their sides, and let the peace come.

Justin was lying on his stomach, both hands above his head and his face half buried in the pillows when Tempest awoke. She savored the curve of his mouth, unguarded in sleep, and the way his long lashes rested on cheek. Curls brushed the nape of his neck, making her want to run her fingers through them. She let her eyes roam over the muscular hardness of his back and shoulders, the tight, firm hips, and down the long, well-formed legs. Sunlight drifted over the little golden hairs on his body and meshed with them. Tempest shivered with the beginnings of excitement. All she wanted to do was stay in this bed with Justin, each of them taking pleasure of the other, and let time fade into sensuality.

"Why are you awake? It seems like the middle of the night."

Tempest looked at his face as he shifted toward her. There was a look of mischief in his eyes and he was trying to keep from grinning. Had he been faking sleep all the time she was admiring him? Well, two could play at that!

"I'm starving, that's why. Don't you feed your guests?" She rolled away from him and began looking for her robe. The red hair spilled over her shoulders, framing her breasts and highlighting her nudity. Justin gave an exclamation, then reached for her.

"Of course, Miss Mallory, my very dear Miss Mallory. What sort of nourishment would tempt your frail appetite? What dish shall I offer you?" Laughter sparkled in him as he caught her arm and held it. "Come here!"

Tempest swayed nearer, her lips half parted, her free hand reaching out as if to touch his face. He grinned and waited. She dodged back suddenly, snatched up the closest pillow, and threw it at him, pulling free at the same time. He gave a cry of outrage and started to get up but became tangled in the sheets. She jumped out of bed and pulled on the robe. An instant later she was opening the long doors that led to the veranda.

The summer afternoon flooded in, redolent of roses and fresh fields. A faint breeze lifted the hair on her temples and a bird sang piercingly close by. Vines covered much of this section, their deep purple blooms shimmering in the dancing light. Several battered cane chairs stood about and a low couch was placed next to the railing. She knew Justin must spend much of his time in this secluded section of his home and wondered in the same breath how she knew. So much of him was still a mystery to her.

She felt a warm hand on her shoulder and turned to meet his gaze. "Tempest, my love?" It was a question that answered itself. Her arms went around his neck and she gave herself up to the hungry probing of his tongue, the eager pressure of his hands, and the rising thrust that echoed in her own need. They melted into each other as he picked her up and carried her to the couch.

"I want you so." She heard her voice whispering the words of the hillside when he poised above her and she ran her fingers down his taut sides, caressing his manhood for a long moment before arching herself upward in the consuming need that must be satisfied. They merged, swung together, and tumbled into sweet oblivion, a sharing beyond the mind, an intense glory.

"My love?" Justin seemed half asleep, but the words could have been endearment or question.

Out of her tenderness and satisfaction, Tempest whispered, "Always, Justin. Always."

His arms came around her and they lay merged in the gentle aftermath.

This was not a time for words. Tempest knew that seriousness must come later; there was much between them to be settled, but now they could laugh, tease, say outrageous things, fondle, and touch each other in this bower away from the world. Justin brought up cold meats, fruit, cheese, and wine, which they devoured as the shadows of evening drew down. She had never been so alive or so hungry. Awareness prickled them both and desire rose many times during the night and day that followed. It was an idyll all the more precious because of the realities that waited. Tempest thought their bodies were perfectly meshed; she could wish their hearts might mingle as well, but already she knew that Justin had many barriers; there was an inviolable core to him such as she possessed. She could not reveal herself totally even in the depths of her passion, and he would not. The undercurrent of sadness this brought made their delight all the sharper.

In the early morning of their fourth day together they walked in the garden of Meadowlands with their arms entwined. The paths were overgrown with pink and white flowers, and great trees native to Jamaica created cool shade depths. A natural spring bubbled up near a rock stand. They could see the meadow wreathed in mist just beyond. Justin stood staring out at it for a long time and did not appear to notice that his hand was tightening convulsively on her slender waist.

In the affinity that had come to her in these past few days, Tempest knew that he was about to end their enchanted time. She thought that she could not bear it. Where was the bold girl who dared face what had to be and did not turn away? She was beginning to realize that she loved Justin Trevian beyond the hunger of her flesh, and her mind fought against knowing it. Face the lesser fact, then.

"We have to go, don't we? I understand, Justin." She tried to be matter-of-fact, but her voice slipped and he turned to look down at her with an expression she had never seen on his face. It was one of unguarded pain. Her resolve faded as she lifted both hands to his cheeks. Her very depth of feeling was plain, and for the moment, she did not really care.

His long fingers closed over hers, the familiar touch sending liquid fire through her veins. The dark brows drew together and his mouth was firmly set. Under the loose white shirt, his shoulders were set stiffly. "Yes, but not yet. I wanted to have this time apart with you, Tempest. Mostly for my own selfish reasons, but I don't think you've been unhappy." His teeth flashed in a grin that tried for amusement and failed. "I want you to listen to what I have to say and not interrupt until I'm done. Some of these things I cannot bear to repeat." He put her hands down gently and turned to one side.

Tempest watched bitterness cloud his eyes and understood that he was far away from this garden. She murmured, "I will do as you ask." Whatever it was, it must be borne. Her nails cut into her palms, but she gave no other sign of disturbance.

"You were virgin when you first came to me, Tempest. You are lovely and brave and intelligent. Your life ought to be filled with marriage, children, a good husband, a spacious planta- tion. Men such as I don't belong in your future. If I weren't a selfish man, I wouldn't have become involved with you to this extent.'' Justin began to pace up and down, talking in a rush of words that seemed disconnected.

Tempest slipped her cold hands into the wide sleeves of her green and white gown. It seemed years ago that she had struggled to put it on while Justin kissed her bare skin and she teased him about the assortment of women's clothes at Meadowlands. She must not give way to the feeling of savage pain replacing the happiness of only minutes ago.

Justin was going on. ''I am nearly the last of my family. We were Huguenots in Catholic France long ago and paid the penalty for that long years in the past. My grandfather and I came to Charleston, where I was raised. I studied medicine in Edinburgh, and he lived to see me take my degree. I practiced for a very short time after he died, but there was a distraction.'' His harsh laugh rang on the warm air. ''How Cassandra would hate to be considered that! Her husband was high in the English court, and she was years younger. I loved her. I wanted to marry her and I tried everything in order to have her. She wanted wealth and prestige; I determined to get them any way I could. It was a whirlwind. I was drugged with passion, drowned by that one woman. Nothing else mattered. I was that way when I botched an operation and the woman died. Her father challenged me to a duel, missed me, and turned the gun on himself. My reputation was ruined. Cassandra told me she could no longer continue our love affair, that she had never had any intention of leaving her rich husband or the other lovers she now admitted she had. I attacked her, and I think she bears the bruises to this day. My lawyer obtained my release from prison and I sailed back to America. That was years ago and I have been slaver, smuggler, gambler, have captained my own ship, now own plantations here and New Orleans, and engage in a few other dealings you don't need to know about. I will marry, as I told you, for a man must have sons, but no woman will ever have my love. I am a man whose ability for that died long ago.''

Tempest could not take her eyes from him. This was the way his face would look in age. Arrogant, sharply lined, and dark-shadowed. A man in torment and holding it before him like a treasured shield.

''You won't want to stay in Jamaica; Robert will have seen

to your loss of reputation. I'll find a companion for you and you can go to Baltimore, Washington, Memphis, or wherever you like. A pretty, respectable woman with some degree of wealth settled on her can always get married. That way you'll be safe. And perhaps we'll meet sometimes. If you wish it, that is." He stopped talking and watched her narrowly. Now that the remembering was done, he seemed almost purged and remote.

Tempest was never more thankful for anything in life than her practice with acting and the hot temper that was blotting out hurt and turning every emotion away except the swamping rage.

"I've never know anyone so arrogant, Justin Trevian! What makes you think that I have fallen in love with you that you must explain why you cannot love? What gives you the right to think you can order my life? This has been an interlude for you! Why not for me? How dare you be so presumptuous? I will go my own way, and you just try to stop me!" Hands on hips, she glared at him, ignoring the kindling anger in his eyes.

20

Bitter Confrontation

"I thought you were a sensible woman. I see that I have made a mistake. Apparently you are capable only of understanding force." Justin gripped Tempest's arm in a hard grip. "You will do as I say. It's for your own good. We leave for Kingston just as soon as my foreman gets back with the news of what is going on. The sooner you're on a ship, the better I'll feel."

"I'm not going anywhere and you're mad to try to make me. I intend to go to Lord Shurden and his wife. He was most kind at the ball and I think they will help me earn my way, for Morna's sake if not out of kindness." Tempest felt relief swell in her as she spoke. It was at least a plan for the future.

Justin gave that mirthless laugh again. "I believe you'll find his lady wife has other ideas. The gentleman is notorious for his interest in the ladies. He found your interest was in the arts and very skillfully led you in that direction. Oh no, you will discover that I really am your only chance."

"No!"

"Yes." He pulled her to him and held her body still in iron hands while his lips and tongue ravaged her mouth. In spite of all her pain and fury, Tempest felt the swelling passion rise and she yielded slightly. An ache began in her breasts and thighs as she pressed even closer. He made a low sound in his throat when her tongue met his.

"Mister Trevian! Mister Trevian, sir! There's news! Sir!" The agitated voice drove them apart as the gray-haired black man stumbled up and tried to catch his breath.

"Take it easy, Dawson." Justin pushed him down on a rock close at hand. "Rest a minute."

Tempest pulled her disordered gown into place and tried to avoid Dawson's gaze. There was an avidity in it that made her uncomfortable. Justin ignored her, bending forward to murmur to his man.

"Most the plantations all right. Few burned up. Cloud Ridge done gone to the ground, and them slaves make Mr. Dornier sign 'em free." Dawson was speaking more clearly now, and his eyes were fixed on Justin in entreaty. "That Mr. Dornier got whipped, too, before the soldiers come save him. He blamin' folks, you most, Mr. Justin, and talkin' wild about his wife and that friend of hers. They comin' here and gonna settle some things . . ." His voice trailed off in exhaustion.

Tempest said, "I'll run get brandy and a cool cloth. Put him in the shade." Justin shot her a quick look and nodded. He was calm, but she saw the pallor under the tan. Robert meant to eliminate those who could accuse him of Morna's death, and the atmosphere of a rebellion was the perfect time for it. She pulled up her skirts and ran in her bare feet toward the house, conscious of the double threat to life and passion.

During their time at Meadowlands, Tempest had seen only two or three servants and they were very unobtrusive. Food and drink appeared in the alcove of their veranda almost magically; in the distance some men had been working and some snatches of song drifted up at night, but otherwise one would never have known the master was in residence. Now she snatched up a bottle from the library table, entered the silent kitchen for water and the first cloth she saw, wondered if she should call for a servant, and then thought the house must be empty of everyone. She almost slipped on the polished floors as she rushed out, apprehension growing with every movement.

When she reached the garden again, Dawson was gone and Justin was coming up the path. There was no trace of the embittered, cynical man or the bold lover in him now. The amber eyes were resolute and his mouth was firm. He was a man in control. Looking at him, Tempest felt her own courage rise to the foremost. Whatever their personal struggles, she knew that he was a man to trust. And had he not called her brave? That was no idle compliment.

"Dawson's gone into the hills. He was feeling better. Tempest, I think you'd best go with him to the other people of my household, who'll protect you if it comes to that. Freemen aren't looked on with any favor, you know. It seems that Robert has collected a following of the most rabid planters and their cohorts and intends to settle a few scores. You and I know what kind."

"I'm not leaving without you, and you'd better accept that. Maybe we should both go." Tempest matched his firm tone and her gaze was unyielding.

"Meadowlands is mine. No one touches what is mine." His eyes rested on her face as he repeated the last word. "Dawson says some of the missionaries who've been preaching abolition have been roughed up pretty severely and a few of the planters who tried to stop this plan of Robert's were threatened. And to think that this is only one small corner of Jamaica! I fear for this country and what can so easily happen. Most people know I have a foot in several camps and have spoken for moderation: they've resented it. You'll be in danger, can't you see that?"

In all the time they had spent together, Justin and Tempest had not discussed the explosive situation that had brought about their latest meeting. It was as if both wanted to shut out reality, to immerse themselves in their mutual passion to the exclusion of all else. They had laughed, teased, played love games, and mentioned trivialities, but had always ended up in each other's arms. Tempest spared a brief instant in longing for that unspoiled delight, and then resorted to craftiness. She knew Justin well enough to know he would have her taken away bodily if she held to her present course.

"You might be right, but I've had enough of the hills. That last episode with the slaves nearly was my death. I'll hide in the house. Will that be sufficient?" She let her eyes go wide and earnest as she tried to hide her determination not to retreat.

"You'll do as I ordered . . ." Sweat prickled along his high forehead, and the long swordsman's fingers flexed as he brushed his hair back. Tension was sharp between them.

Tempest braced herself for conflict. She saw the pulse beat heavily in his neck and understood the leashed violence that was always a part of him was about to break free. "There's no time for this sort of thing." He moved purposefully toward her.

Suddenly a shot blasted the air and was quickly followed by a loud cry. Another resounded almost immediately. A flock of birds rose from a nearby tree and flew southward. The stillness was almost shocking. Even the moist, heated air was unmoving.

"They're here. Go, darling. Please." The softness in Justin's voice was almost a caress, belying the hardness of his carved face.

"Yes." Tempest gave him a hurried smile and touched his wrist. He pulled away rather than risk clasping her. He might disavow his emotion, but he could not hide the power of what they had shared together. "God keep you."

He gave that bitter grin. "To my sorrow, He may just do that."

Tempest hesitated, then turned and sped away. She would not allow herself even one look back. Let him think her afraid. Let him think she yielded. Fear roiled hot and sick within her body, but she refused to think about it. Concentrate only on what was at hand. Find some clothes she could move about in and get every weapon the house held. Nothing must distract her from that aim. Another shot came and the same high-pitched yell punctuated it. She kept going.

The next few minutes were separate short nightmares in which she skidded on soft rugs, tore open cabinets, ransacked the cool, silent library, pulled at a wall display of weapons, emptied Justin's desk, tossed the contents of several chests out, and finally, gathering up all that might be of use, ran to one of the windows that looked out on the garden, so recently a quiet and peaceful summer scene.

There was a quarter circle of men around Justin and more massed on the sloping hill beyond. Tempest thought there must be twenty in all. They stood shouting and brandishing weapons while Justin stood, sun glinting off his tawny hair and snowy shirt, with arms folded. She saw the tall figure of Robert Dornier lean toward him menacingly and heard a babble of voices in an undercurrent of savagery.

Now there was no more time. She hacked ruthlessly at the

full skirt until it hung around her knees. Two pistols, primed and ready, went into her waistband. Another set was in both hands. Long ago, Tempest had been taught to shoot and fence by an ancient relative of Aunt Hannah's who found her interest amusing. He had assured that skill in such arts did not diminish. She was about to find out.

She slipped through the grounds like a wraith, watching for invaders with every stealthy step she took. The harsh, baiting voices came to her when she advanced, and she sank into the depths of a bush that was lush enough to make it possible to see without being seen. She need not have worried. The angry planters and their minions had found a scapegoat. Some of them slurred their words in a drunken manner. Murder was not far away. It appeared there was little difference between the slaves who had taken her captive and their owners who raged at Justin.

"Nobody touched your house, Trevian! Wouldn't be surprised if those looters didn't bring some of it here. We'll just have a look in a minute or two!"

"You always did play both sides, didn't you? I remember when you had slaves for sale. High and mighty setting 'em loose later on, undermining everything, strutting around like a cock!" The speaker, a huge burly man with a brown beard, thrust his face toward Justin's.

Another joined in. "This land's not been too profitable for you by the looks of it. You always did have the reputation of a blackguard. I say you had something to do with this rebellion, even more than those misguided missionaries. What do you say to that, Trevian?"

"I say your brains are fevered, all of you. You ought to be tending your families, mending some of the practices you use on your slaves, making conditions better in general. Slavery's a thing of the past and you'll just have to realize it." Justin's voice was low and drawling, as calm as those of his tormentors were furious. He looked lean, sardonic, and unruffled in the golden light.

"Where is the girl, Tempest Mallory?" Robert's ringed hand flashed upward, and all muttering ceased. He wore a black coat and breeches. A gun rested on one hip, and there were dark smudges under his pale eyes. "I suppose you know, Trevian, that she is wanted for questioning in the death of my dear wife,

Morna. And you are now informed of the fact that you are suspect as well. Her death may have been hastened by poison. Some of us are well aware of your, shall we say, questionable background in medicine." His voice was low, as befitted a recently bereaved man who had lost everything, but Tempest wondered if she alone could read the rising note of triumph there.

"What motive have you thought of?" Justin tossed his hair back and eyed Robert with curiosity.

"Morna had money of her own. She left it to the girl, who would in turn have it in her own right. You are known to be out of funds much of the time and certainly made your desire known to my wife and the Mallory wench. Furthermore, the girl made common advances to me soon after she arrived and all during Morna's illness. I think she fancied herself mistress of Cloud Ridge, and both of you tried to take advantage of me, of my kindness and hospitality. A mistake, my dear Trevian." Robert's words died away on the still air. Those around him began to murmur in consternation.

Tempest felt her fingers twitch on the pistols. She would like nothing better than to blow the fake sadness from Robert Dornier's face and to give the death he had certainly administered to Morna. He had neatly turned the tables around on any accusations they might live to make. She had no doubt others would believe his tale.

The coolness Justin showed was nearly his undoing. Some of the men edged closer, and one snapped, "Give him what he wanted us to get! Burn all this and let's make sure he talks straight about the rebellion and your trouble, Robert! We'll get the truth." He pushed Justin and grinned. An instant later he was on the ground, clutching his hanging jaw, and Justin was gripped by four of the others.

"Go ahead. It'll be no more than he deserves." Robert restrained the elation in his voice, but his eyes blazed with it.

"One move, Robert Dornier, and I will take the greatest pleasure in shooting you." Tempest rose from the bush and levelled the pistol at Robert's surprised face. "Let him go. Now."

"Put that thing down, you fool. You'll hurt yourself." Robert smiled at her indulgently. "Don't make things worse for yourself. He attracted you, manipulated you. That can happen;

the law will make allowances.'' He took a step toward her and held out one hand.

The sound of the cocking pistol was loud in the hush. Robert froze as he stared into the unwavering barrel. She brought the other pistol to bear on those holding Justin. He was very still, but it was the attitude of the waiting lion temporarily at bay.

"I mean it. I will kill you.'' Tempest concentrated on the words, knowing that she meant them with all her heart.

"You are a slut and a liar and a murderess with that thief.'' Robert matched her tone while one hand slipped toward his own pistol.

Tempest's move was instinctive. She fired, and he whirled around to tumble into the arms of the watchers. Justin jerked free with one lithe motion. A quick stride brought him to her, and he pulled another pistol from her waistband. Together they faced the startled planters. None of them wanted to be the first to take on these two they regarded as rebels and lawbreakers. Robert had dodged at the crucial second and was unharmed. He rose now, his mouth twisted with hatred, hair falling in his eyes.

"You'll be hunted down! All of you are my witnesses! Traitor to England's power, lawbreaker, and ravisher with your slut . . .'' Robert's control had deserted him and he was falling over the epithets he wanted to lavish on Tempest and Justin.

Tempest's own common sense left her. She dashed forward and slammed the barrel of her pistol across his mouth so hard the blood poured out. "Liar! Get your weapon. I'll fight you separately. A duel!''

"You're a madwoman!'' Robert regained his balance and shouted to the others, "Take them! They can't do anything against all of you!''

They stared, but did not move. Justin's pistol was steady on the burly man, and Tempest had a fresh one at the ready. Blood lust was filling her mind. There was no other thought but that Robert must pay for what he had done to Morna and to Tempest herself.

"Did you hear me, coward? I challenge you!''

Robert burst into laughter that held a hollow note. "I don't fight with women.''

"No, you take their lives in other ways, don't you? Shall I shoot you as you stand?"

All Tempest's life came down to this instant in the hot summer sun as she stood surrounded by angry hostile men, her lover, and the man she hated more than anyone else in the world, while life and death hung in the balance.

21

Fata Morgana

"Tell them to keep away and take my challenge, Robert Dornier." Justin spoke from Tempest's side. "I have the right to defend her. She is mine."

Tempest caught the impact of his words and was shaken that he could declare himself in front of these men. His voice was filled with male possessiveness, a thing they could all understand. Robert's laughter was derisive, and his hands hung loosely at his side.

"This isn't some dueling ground, Trevian. We're going to take you and your doxy into custody." He looked at the men commandingly, but they shifted uneasily and remained where they stood. "Only two of them, and you hesitate! No wonder our plantations were sacked!" Bitterness flowed out of Robert as he half turned toward his followers, seeming to ignore the guns trained on him.

Justin glanced at Tempest and their eyes fused into one molten power transcending adversity. In that second of shifting attention, Robert whirled and fired a small gun with his left hand while the second, more powerful, one at his belt appeared to jump into his right hand. Tempest smelled burning hair and scorched cloth even when she shot blindly toward him. The bright day faded into darkness and from that darkness, she heard a gasping, moaning sound coupled with a curse. Then a strong arm was clasping hers, holding her upright, and Justin's cold voice brought reality back.

"He's dead in lawful combat. All of you heard the double challenge made in honor, something no gentlemen can refuse. He attacked without warning and paid the penalty. All of you saw it."

Tempest forced herself to look at the crumpled form on the grass. God knew he deserved his fate and she had been the willing instrument of it but part of her recoiled from that knowledge. Morna's tearful face came before hers. Would Morna's shade welcome this vengeance?

"Leave here and take him with you. All this is a matter for the magistrate and the law." Justin held control of the situation while the men stared unbelievingly at the body of the man who had spurred them on.

"He was guilty of everything he accused us of." Tempest lifted her head and found that her voice was just as icy as Justin's. Robert was dead, but this mob could be inflamed again with great ease.

"You're coming with us, the both of you!"

"Take 'em prisoner!"

"Burn his house! He's got to pay! Her, too!"

The cries swirled around them! Several men lifted leather flasks and drank greedily. Others slapped their sides, howling encouragement. In a few minutes they might try to storm Justin and Tempest. Two pistols could not hold back so many.

"You, Latimer, Horge, Bolton! What are you trying to accomplish? You used to be reasonable men. Dunston, you shouldn't be here either. Go home!"

Those mentioned by name shifted uneasily before Justin's roll call, but they did not back down. One man started purposefully toward Tempest and it took all her courage not to back away from the singed beard and red eyes. Had he sustained them in the fire of his own home? What if she had owned Cloud Ridge, that lovely house that existed no longer? The same fierce anger would have been hers.

Suddenly he was staring over her shoulder and the others were moving backward as if pushed. One cried, "He is in league with them! Look yonder! They've come!"

Tempest turned slightly and saw the blacks a few yards away. There must have been seventy or eighty of them, men and women, all armed with pistols, swords, and clubs. They might have risen up out of the earth, so silent had they been. She recognized the slender young woman who had a dagger in one hand and a cut on one cheek. It was Savora, and Jason stood beside her, very obviously the leader.

"You can die right now or live a little longer until we come to take you out of your homes. Take your pick. This man and woman stay with us." Jason gave absolutely no inflection to the words, but the white men fell back. "Take the Dornier carrion with you."

Tempest dared not speak, and Justin did not move. At least Savora was a friend if they were to be taken captive again. She had no illusions about their fate at the hands of the planters, who only wanted a scapegoat and would remember Robert's accusations. He had been one of their own, a leading man of the close community.

Robert's body was gathered up hurriedly, and the whites retreated. One man, bolder than the rest, called back, "We'll be back and then we'll get all of you! There'll be soldiers to teach you a lesson you won't forget!"

Jason sent a shot over their heads to send them on their way. "These two are our prisoners and will be examples. If you don't want to join them, you'd better run." His body shone with sweat and his black eyes blazed. Savora was very close to him, almost a part of his flesh.

Rescuers and prisoners alike stood silently until the invading white men vanished over the hill. Then Jason walked over to Justin and put out his hand. Savora came to Tempest with a rush, and they embraced as the years of mutual friendship bridged the recent gap. Tempest felt the tears come when she felt the sharp ridges of Savora's shoulders and saw what she had not seen before, the nearly imperceptible thrust of her abdomen. She was pregnant. Tempest pulled back and started to speak, but the other girl shook her head in warning. Jason did not know.

He spoke to Justin. "We're staying here if you don't mind. It's as good a place as any to trap them. We mean to have all Jamaica. You're a better man than a lot of them, Trevian, but you've supported slavery in your time. I'm afraid my people don't like the sight of a white skin much right now. Both of you have to go." He balled his huge fists together and eyed Justin.

Time seemed to mesh together for Tempest as she stood in what seemed to be another of the endless confrontations. Robert, Jason, Justin himself, blacks, and the white planters—she was sick of it all. The days apart with Justin seemed an idyllic dream, a thing beyond reality. The faint breeze lifted the tumbled red hair from her neck and carried a scent of flowering shrubs to her. Tall white clouds drifted across the brilliant sky to make shadows on the hillsides. Birds called to each other in the bushes and several spiraled high above. It was a day for loveliness, not disaster. She knew what was likely to happen to Meadowlands. Looting and burning were part of this rebellion. All Justin's past kindness to those who had served him would not save his home from either side. His love for it had been apparent, but now he was talking quietly with Jason, who was half nodding and half smiling.

"Tempest, come and talk. There's so little time and I may never see you again." Savora was pulling at her hand in an old, familiar gesture. Tempest followed her over to a flowering red bush, and they both sank down in the shade. Sunlight made dappled patterns on their skins, and Tempest found herself remembering all the times they had crouched so to share secrets.

"Don't talk that way. This'll be settled; it has to be." Tempest held up one hand to forestall the avowals she knew were coming. She simply could not bear more battles. The recollection of Robert's body would haunt her days and nights. "Have you been in the hills with Jason all along? It's really too bad you and he didn't settle down to live as freedmen—you with your dressmaking and he learning some sort of trade. And what about your child? What kind of life will it have?"

"A life of freedom! That's worth everything we have to suffer and you know it! Jason and I could never live under any form of slavery again, especially with the toleration of the whites. Our son will be born in freedom." Her lustrous eyes shone with determination. It was as if the word was holy to her. The skimpy brown dress she wore showed the curves of her too thin body when her hand lay protectively across her stomach. The angular, high cheek bones and arching brows might have belonged to a Nubian queen from the beginning of history. "I'll tell Jason soon. He'd send me away if he knew I was pregnant. He thinks about nothing but this struggle, you see."

Tempest glanced over at Justin, taking in the broad shoulders, tanned skin, and perfectly proportioned body. "You love him so much, Savora?"

Savora smiled. "More than anything. Before his cause, before our child, before any reason or thought. You love Trevian, don't you?"

"I desire him. That's different." Tempest stared past Savora, ignoring her friend's grin.

"Not too different. Not in the beginning."

Both girls rose as Justin and Jason approached. The hostility between the men was muted, and they seemed to have reached an agreement. Jason confirmed this as he said, "We're going to rest at Meadowlands tonight. Our people need food and relaxation. There'll be a feast, drinking, time for talk. Those planter's won't be back, but we'll post a watch. We'll forget our differences for this night. Tomorrow Trevian leaves with the girl."

Tempest felt unrest coil inside her. It seemed that she ought to protest this decision, but there was no valid reason for doing so. When Justin came to her side and took her hand in his warm one, she knew her senses were reeling. His gaze held both admiration and hunger; there was no sign of the rejection he had shown earlier. Blood rose to her cheeks, for she was aware that Jason and Savora watched with interest. She had to assert herself. She was not in love with him! She would not allow it! Had he not rejected her?

"Let's go and talk more, Savora. There's so much I have to ask you." Tempest pulled free and beckoned to her friend. Justin's brow went up, but he grinned and turned back to Jason.

All that long summer afternoon Tempest walked and talked with Savora in the glades of Meadowlands. They had never been so close, so open with their thoughts and feelings. All she held back was the intensity of her feeling for Justin. Savora scorned his position of neutrality for both sides, but when Tempest told her of how he had helped in her own rescue, she said thoughtfully, "Those who wear the boar's heads are the most savage. He took a great risk for you." Privately, Tempest thought her fate had been only part of Justin's being there, but she did not say it. She changed the subject to Jason and here the formerly independent Savora was eloquent as she talked of their love, the cause, their flight together, their passionate loving in the caves and hills, and all the life before was nothing compared to this. Tempest felt envious and was not sorry when Savora stretched and rose to go. Hunger for Justin hammered at her, inflamed by the conversation she and Savora had just had. She could not even think of the gulf that would now remain between her friend and herself.

"We'll be feasting tonight. Both of you will sit with Jason and me. Tempest, let yourself feel. There's nothing like it in all the world." Savora put her arms around Tempest and hugged her fiercely. "If I have a girl, I'll call her after you!" Then she was gone, running lightly down the path just as she had done so often in Savannah.

Tempest thought of the child she would never see. The gap between black and white was too great here. There was no room for simple friendship. It had never really been possible; she and Savora had taken the gift and made it live. A sense of last things permeated her as she walked slowly back up to the house.

An hour later she was sitting in a wooden tub on the veranda where Justin had first taken her. It had been a struggle to bring up enough water to fill two of them, but she achieved the task swiftly. The house rang with sounds, talk, laughter, plans of strategy, low-voiced mutters. No one offered to help her, but she did not expect it. She was as negligible to the blacks as their race had been to hers. It was a feeling she did not like, and she wondered if the dull anger she felt was anything akin to theirs.

Over and over she washed her skin and hair. Would she ever get the scent of blood, heat, and murder out of them? The purple flowers bloomed in the climbing vines like round stars and a green lizard curved among them. Sunlight lay across the old boards as dust motes spun in the rays. She had never been so alone. Fiercely, Tempest scrubbed her face once again.

"Personally, I think you look much better with your skin intact." The cool voice came from behind her. "Don't you think you'd better get out of that water? Cold baths are all very well, but you needn't over do."

"What are you doing here?" Tempest started to reach for the old sheet she used as a towel, but Justin grabbed it up and held it out of her reach. "Go away. You made yourself quite clear before."

"You talk too much." Justin's dark brows came together in a scowl and the amber eyes went nearly black. He wore only white breeches, his skin mahogany above them.

"I mean it." Tempest turned her back on him and tilted her head in what she hoped was a dismissing nod.

A second later he snatched her, dripping, from the tub and walked to the couch where they had first made love. His mouth fastened savagely on hers and his fingers clamped both her hands so she could not claw. His tongue battered against her teeth for entry and she was forced to yield. Her naked, wet body was held down by his hard one. It was impossible to get free. Her eyes opened to stare into the implacable face above her own. This was a contest, a battle. She would not be mastered! Her legs went around his while her breasts pushed against his broad chest. He only held her tighter, his mouth grinding down on hers. Everything else faded for Tempest but this most elemental of wars. The blood hammered in her veins; her brain forgot all conscious thought while she fought to be free.

There was no one certain moment when struggle became elemental passion. Her tongue twined with Justin's. Her pinned arms ceased to writhe and her whole flesh clamored with his. She could not free her mouth, but she did not care. Somehow he was naked and hard inside her. He did not seek her response, but hammered at her again and again until the flame rose high. She was captive and willing participant when the volcano he created began to erupt. She was going to explode. He penetrated her, drew partly away, and came in deeply until she arched high to meet his thrust. Now he released her hands and they moved over him in a rhythm of their own. When he entered her heat and moved there so powerfully that she felt she was about to split, Tempest felt the cries begin in her mouth. She could not endure the building of this unassuaged holocaust. Justin's fingers were on her breasts, his eyes bored into hers. She could not look away. The volcano, the fire everlasting, power forever, all flared to consummation and they fell together into its glory.

Afternoon went to twilight, which deepened into spangled night when the quarter moon rose, but Tempest and Justin had no sense of time or place. There was nothing but the longing of the flesh as their bodies twined in mutual pleasure. This was elemental; thought had no place. Tempest touched, caressed, held, and possessed Justin as he did her in his turn. Her mouth and hands covered every inch of his long, lean body. She held his manhood in her slim fingers and drank of it with her mouth. He drew on her woman's places until she cried for his entry. Each was master and yielder. The world of each was in the other.

Once Justin took his mouth from hers and whispered, "Enchantress, Morgana. Sorceress. Witch-woman." His hand trailed heat down her thigh while the other circled her rosy nipple.

"Justin, Justin." The name was incantation enough as they came together for the first time, the millionth, and forever.

The small cold thought came into Tempest's mind before the fire consumed her. The fate of enchantresses was death.

22

Power of the Beast

Tempest twisted her head back and forth to escape the light that was shining in her eyes. Why had Justin lit the lamp? She wanted to sleep as she had been, curled against his body, waking to the touch and smell of him. But it was hot, too hot, and who was making all that noise? She came awake in the next breath and dug her nails into Justin's arm so hard that he uttered a muffled curse and sat up. His gaze followed her horrified one.

A deep red glow shone through the vines on one side and lit up the depths of night. On another they heard crackling sounds, saw smoke curl up as flames rose high and close, and smelled an unfamiliar pungent odor. There were cries, oddly muted, almost strangled, and then a few shots. Tempest felt her eyes smart and water as it grew harder to breathe.

"My God! What an idiot I've been!" Justin was off the couch in one leap and rushing inside. His feet slammed on the boards and then he was rattling at the door knob.

Tempest pulled part of the sheet around her nudity and rose. The floor was warm to her feet, but she paid no attention as she padded over the edge of the veranda to look down. Her head felt fuzzy and she was dizzy; for the briefest span of time she could not comprehend what was going on below.

Bodies were everywhere, glowing black and white in the gutting fire. She was too far up to recognize any, but some battling was still going on. An enormous black man was in the act of choking a white, who held a smoking gun. Two whites were chopping at a woman who lay very quietly in a stream of blood not entirely her own. Others swayed back and forth in a fierce frieze of hatred. The fire was everything. It ate at the outbuildings, made red trails over the ground, rose in the trees, climbed in the house, and swept over the distant fields, where the cane grew.

A hand spun her around and she looked into Justin's hard face, which was twisted with rage. "I should have known they'd come back! Bastards! Bastards! The door's locked! Somebody meant for us to be burned alive! Put this on. We have to get out of here." He tossed a dark garment at her and stepped into brown breeches and shirt as he spoke.

"Do we jump or kick the door in? How could we sleep through all this carnage?" Tempest let the bitter words come. "Surely they could have posted a lookout!" She was not thinking of the danger they were both in; Savora's bright, eager face shone before her inner vision. Almost without conscious movement she felt the dark gown settle over her head and descend to her knees. The skirt had been savagely hacked, probably by the knife now thrust in Justin's belt. The loose sleeves could be rolled up, and she hurriedly fastened her spill of flaming hair with a piece of braid.

One corner of Justin's mouth went up in a caricature of amusement, which made his bitterness all the more apparent. "This room is part of the master's bedroom and study. It has various things for his comfort." He handed Tempest a length of cord to which an ornamental dagger with a long blade was attached. Except for his expression, they might have been in any peaceful place discussing the architecture of his house.

"The stairs!" Tempest fastened the weapon around her waist and let her gaze sweep over the interior of the bedroom to which they had come. It was more stifling here and her bare feet felt the hot boards more; the fire was not far away.

"Yes." Justin went to the far wall, touched a panel, and pushed it back. Darkness yawned at them. So did a blast of cool air. "Come on, Tempest. Those marauders won't hesitate to kill us. There's nothing to do but run."

"I understand that, Justin." Fear and rage filled her in equal parts. "Let's go." She knew him well enough by now to comprehend the emotions he kept rigidly controlled. He loved Meadowlands dearly, but what could one man and woman do? Tempest could do no more than he. She walked toward the stairs, wondering how long ago they had been used to bring a willing/unwilling slave to this or another master of Meadowlands in discretion so that his wife's sensibilities might not be offended. Anything was better than thinking about the horror outside.

The stair was long and winding, shaky in places, and it was very dark. Justin came around to go in front of her, but their pace was slow at best. She ached to hurry, but did not dare. It was highly likely that armed men waited at the end of this passage. If the earlier frenzy was upon them, Tempest knew rape was the least of what she might expect. Resolutely, she put everything from her mind except the next step.

It was almost anticlimax when Justin pushed on a door that creaked with age and was nearly bound down with vines. He worked cautiously with the bolts, then shoved, waited, and shoved again. The opening grew larger and they slipped through. Justin shut the door again, hoping their escape would not be evident. Tempest scattered the broken vines around. They could only hope the battle would take everyone's mind off the master of Meadowlands.

They were in an unused outside building a few paces from the back of the house. A glance out the window showed that the woods were very near. A short dash should take them there. The fire was eating at the house even more now, and they could feel the tremendous heat reaching out to engulf everything.

"Follow me when I go and don't look back." Justin whispered the words urgently in Tempest's ear.

"I will." Don't look back to all the things he had loved, at his home blazing up, at the death of his life in Jamaica. A pity she had never thought to feel for this bold man welled up in Tempest. "Ready when you are." She could control her emotions as he did.

"Now!" He had been looking out the tiny window on the far side where one wall had split boards set wide in it. They were about to tumble down, so it was the work of only a few seconds to pull them apart, look around again, and then run in the shelter of the overgrown bushes for the wooded area.

Once outside, the smoke was even more overpowering. The flames roared over distant shouts of those who had caused all this. There were crashing sounds behind them, and great waves of heat followed Justin and Tempest as they skimmed along the relatively flat ground.

Suddenly, Tempest heard a groan and anguished weeping very close. All the pain and hurt imagined seemed to be in those sounds; she could no more have turned away than she could have forsaken Justin. An echo of familiarity rang in the sounds also. She had heard them before. When Tempest looked to her left, just where a few flowering bushes grew thickly, she saw what appeared to be a clump of cloth attempting to move in the direction of the house. It was making one sound over and over between the groans and tears.

"Jason. Ja . . . son, Ja . . ."

Tempest forgot Justin's order, forgot everything else in the world as the horror swarmed over her. "Savora! Savora!"

This was certainly Savora, but how she lived and managed to move Tempest had no idea, for her body was livid with blood, her bare breasts torn and gouged, and her stomach torn. Tempest sat cross-legged holding Savora's head in her lap, and let the tears pour down on the once beautiful face.

It was not hard to guess what had happened. Tempest herself could face such a fate. Someone had tried to rape Savora, and she had fought and nearly been killed. Perhaps she should have died. Who could live with such injuries?

"He's dead. They shot him in the back. I went to him. There were a lot of them. They beat me. Kicked. Baby going." Savora broke the words off one at a time in a flat voice that took all her strength. Her nostrils flared with the effort, and her pupils dilated. Tempest wondered if her friend knew who held her. She felt the blood seeping over fingers and dripping into her lap.

"Darling, rest. It's Tempest, I'm here."

Savora pulled on Tempest's hand, a desperate urgency filling her. "He's dead. Nothing for me. Can't live. Kill me. Kill me."

"No!" Tempest cradled her closer, oblivious of the pain it must be causing. "No!"

Savora grabbed for the knife in Tempest's belt and pulled it hard, trying to pull the point toward her. She could not, and the tears dribbled slowly down her face as she whispered, "Please. Please."

There was a step beside her and Justin sank to his knees as he looked at Savora. His voice was unsteady as he said, "What can we do, Savora?"

What indeed, thought Tempest. The perpetrators of this evil might begin searching for them any minute now. The blacks themselves would want revenge. She and Justin were in more dreadful danger than earlier. But to give Savora what she wanted was unthinkable. Savora, her dear and only friend, companion of her young days, sharer of sorrows. Unthinkable!

Savora grabbed Tempest's arm again and now the deep-set eyes shone with rage and death. "Kill. Understand? All I want."

Tempest's eyes swam with tears. "I can't, Savora."

Justin leaned close to Savora and all the tenderness of a compassionate man was in his voice. "I used to be a doctor, Savora. I can help. Will you let me?"

She searched his face, then nodded. She seemed no longer capable of speech.

"You are sure? Very sure?" The low tone was reassuring. Calm in the very center of cataclysm.

Again the nod. The action brought blood rushing from her nose and the corner of her mouth. Tempest knew what Justin meant to do. She understood that he took her action upon himself. Savora was bound to her in love and friendship. It was her responsibility.

"Justin, I can't let you do this." Still, how could she do it?

"You can't? You have no choice." His face might have been carved in bronze. Far behind them more timbers fell into flame and there was a distant gunshot. Soon there must be pursuit.

"There is no choice." She repeated the words softly. It was true. She bent to Savora. "You'll have what you want. I promise it. Look at me, love." The pained eyes left Justin's face and fixed on hers. "Remember when we robbed the kitchen and how furious Aunt Hannah was? Remember how you pretended to be struck dumb with terror and got us both off?" Inane recollection after inane recollection. Surely she should be commending Savora's soul to God and making sure that she had forsaken the old deities of her girlhood. No. Any god who did not understand this deserved no worship. "And the plum thicket after we shook all the fruit down and gorged on it, then took the rest away? Bessie said ghosts had it. She worried so much." Tempest went on and on as she bent so close to Savora that she could feel the halting breath.

Tempest was aware when Justin's hand slipped toward Savora's neck, and she forced herself to continue in spite of the knowledge. She might have sworn her friend tried to smile, but that was wishful thinking, for Savora's head twisted sharply to the side, the resulting crack loud in Tempest's ears. Savora's tortured breath ceased. She, like her unborn child and warrior husband, was dead.

Tempest could not look at Justin as she said, "She loved flowers. Help me put her under the bush yonder."

"'Anoint her with beauty, for she was brave and fair.'" His voice was soft, with something behind she did not recognize. "It seems that I am cast well in the role of First Murderer."

Tempest found speech impossible. She had to endure from one minute till the next. That took all the power she had. The words of the Renaissance poet were not amiss in this holocaust, but if she thought about them, she would scream in anguish.

They covered Savora with branches, leaves, and lush flowers. Justin backed away, beckoning her to come, but Tempest had to say something over the hurriedly improvised grave. Then tender words of the Psalmist rose to her lips and for the first time it seemed that she knew what they really meant. She was half done when Justin began to speak along with her and their voices mingled.

"'They that sow in tears shall reap in joy. She that goeth forth and weepeth, bearing precious seed, shall doubtless come again with rejoicing bearing her sheaves.'"

So Tempest left the friend of her childhood, knowing that she herself could not really believe in the return of joy now, but praying that whatever implacable gods Savora served might understand and grant her surcease. For Tempest there was none. Blindly, she walked into the woods, a silent Justin at her side.

She did not know when they began to run. It must have been a mutual decision, for they disregarded possible snakes, thorns, rockfalls, and pursuit, and they fled from their own demons. The wanton destruction of Meadowlands, the burgeoning flames and blood of battle faded, as they went. The slim moon was long since gone and the bright morning was hot, lavish with the smell of flowers and summer. Clouds were piled high on the horizon while a breeze drifted in the patches of woods where Tempest and Justin raced in almost mindless exhaustion.

They finally stopped in a copse of trees that bordered a small meadow. A little stream trickled there and they gulped water greedily, then lifted their heads to stare at each other. Justin was first to speak.

"I think we're safe enough for a while. We can rest." His hair was wet from the stream and his eyes were curiously flat. That odd note was in his voice again. "When it's dark, we'll go on."

There was nothing to say. Tempest flung herself down on the leaves and let darkness overwhelm her. It was very welcome. Memories could destroy one's sanity. Was it eating at hers? Or Justin's? She understood his bitterness. Did he see alternative paths he could have taken just as she was doing?

She awoke in the cool breath of an afternoon breeze. Someone was sobbing, great racking gulps that brought back all the pain she had endured in Jamaica. Turning around, she saw Justin seated some distance away, his head in his arms, shoulders shaking as he fought to control himself. Justin the arrogant, the man of measured calm, the sardonic, was now suffering in his delayed pain.

Tempest ran to him and put both arms around his neck. His wet face grazed hers as his arms went up to break her hold. She held on, speaking as he had once done to her in an attempt to assuage hurt. "Let it come. It has to or you'll be more poisoned. You told me that, remember?" He struggled against her for another moment before clasping her to his chest as if he could never let her go. They sat together while the words erupted from him.

"I bought Meadowlands years ago. Always meant to really work and improve it, but never took the time. I was happy when I went there. The slaves stayed as freemen, the cane grew well, the atmosphere had peace. Now it's gone and I don't care if I never go back there again . . ." He went on and on talking of Jamaica and its promise, his lost home, the guilt he felt over bringing death, and once or twice he spoke of Cassandra, the bitter love and the dregs that had ruined him for more. Tempest murmured soothingly and when he was more in control, she shared her feelings with him. He did not comment, but his hand held hers and his amber eyes were washed clean when he looked into her gray ones.

"It is time for a new beginning." He spoke as if to himself, but Tempest felt a new warmth and honesty between them. Out of death, murder, and flame could come a new life for them both. She said as much and he smiled sadly but did not answer.

That night they slept under the sheltering branches of a great tree. They were clasped in each other's arms, with no sign of passion. Their sharing was beyond the flesh, for their minds had met and that was the true closeness. For the first time, no barriers existed between Tempest and Justin.

23

My Marks and Scars I Bear with Me

Tempest devoured another handful of purple berries and thought longingly of roasted meats, warm baked bread and succulent gravies, hot tea or coffee, and rich desserts. Her stomach gave a warning rumble as Justin turned to her.

"Will milady have more of the duck or just a touch of this delicately seasoned pork?" He held out more berries, giving her an obsequious grin and balancing an imaginary platter in the other.

"Perhaps a touch, but only that." She was languid, a bit bored.

"That's all the bush had." He divided the fruit between them. "You see, your desires have been anticipated."

"I'm ready for wine. Will you join me?" Tempest rose from the grass and brushed off her skirt, preparing to walk down to the stream.

"I have many pressing pursuits. I doubt that I have the time." He looked down his aristocratic nose and one corner of his mouth curled upward.

She eyed him up and down. "I can see that. A ragamuffin is well dressed beside you, sir. Do you go to attend to your wardrobe or your manners?"

He strode over and scooped her up, ignoring her simulated protests. A few quick strides brought them to the stream. He paused, then jumped in. It was shallow, barely up to their knees, but the splash was resounding and both were thoroughly wet. They looked at each other for an instant before Justin leaned over to kiss her mouth gently.

"Thank you, Tempest. For everything." His gaze was tender, but his touch was not an inflaming one. It was one of kinship.

"There is nothing to thank me for, Justin. You know that." Had he not taken her obligation to Savora upon himself? Could she ever have done what her friend begged?

"All the same." He gave a crooked grin and sent a shower of water toward the bank. "How are you at fishing?"

Her mouth watered. She welcomed the sudden change of mood. It helped conceal the fact that she wanted him to make love to her in the old demanding way. Old? He had done so not quite two days ago at Meadowlands, yet this seemed a virtual eternity ago. They had both changed, or so it seemed. She wanted to touch him, to stir his flesh with hers, but some inner warning restrained her. "Probably terrible. You don't think we've frightened away every fish around? If there were any."

"Maybe. We'll try downstream." He stood up, facing her in the sparkling light of early afternoon, his curls in disarray, upper body bare and smooth. There was laughter on his carved mouth, none in his eyes.

She took the hand he held out and smiled back, glad enough they could share this camaraderie. They still lived, might continue to do so, and a friendship was growing between them as it had not done in the time of their passion.

Earlier, Justin had suggested that they remain here today and rest. They would circle around toward Kingston tomorrow, keeping a watch for signs of pursuit, and try to reach the more rational element there. Sir Herbert Shurden, for all that he liked the ladies, had powerful friends. It might be well to seek his protection. As Justin had said, "All Jamaica cannot have gone mad. These men were only a scattered few, and they were inflamed with drink."

Tempest found that she did not want to think of the future. Ambition and safety alike faded in the closeness she shared with Justin. She had never thought she was one of those women who could submerge herself in a man, but the crucible through which they passed rendered some matters inconsequential.

A few minutes later they sat on the shady bank in the dappled light and dangled cloth lines with buttons for bait near a likely rock. The water purled along gently as it carried fallen leaves toward the distant sea. There was a heavy, spicy scent on the warm air that was made by pink flowers tumbling down a vine wrapped tree a few yards away. Tempest thought that whenever she remembered Jamaica in the future, she would remember flowers. Flowers and blood; the thought shook in her mind.

There was a jerk on her line, and she gave an excited squeal. Justin shook his head wisely. "You'll know if you have a fish. The line will have a special feel. We had a pond when I was a boy . . ."

The slow, almost contented voice drifted on about the various kinds of fish taken from that pond and how he, Justin, had caught the biggest fish ever. Tempest yawned slightly and shifted her position in the soft undergrowth. The top of her dress opened deeply with the motion, so that her breasts gleamed. She started to pull it back, then thought better of it. Justin's eyes were on her; the laziness of the boy was gone. She lifted her gaze to his and smiled. A shutter came down over his face, but a vein throbbed in one temple.

"I had nearly forgotten." The voice held a trace of that first arrogance, and the long brown fingers folded convulsively over his line.

"Forgotten? Did you want to?" Surely he referred to the times they had made love in the woods? That time of beginning for them both? She leaned forward a bit more. She was brazen and eager, she thought, but with all that had happened there must certainly be understanding between them.

"My memory is very sharp." He gave that odd quirking grin, put down the line, and stepped toward her as she rose to meet him.

Their clothes made a pallet for them when, locked in an embrace, they slipped to the ground. Patterns of light and shadow raced across their bodies, which moved in a hungry rhythm. Justin's fingers cupped Tempest's breasts so that their fullness spilled over. His mouth and tongue sought her nipples impartially, sending shudders of longing over her skin. She found his shaft and moved her hand softly over the tip. The moist warmth quivered as it pushed against her. She went down it and up the other side, arching to Justin's lips.

"Your breasts are beautiful. You know that, of course." He stretched out and extended one hand to pull her down beside him. He might have been a pagan deity lying bronzed and expectant while he awaited homage from a handmaiden. The flat stomach and lean hips gave onto long legs; his manhood was high and erect; the powerful chest and chiseled face excited Tempest all the more.

"You are beautiful." She had never been more serious. Another powerful emotion beat at her mind. Never had she been closer to loving this man, who had taken her whole being by storm and passion. "I'll come to you."

She swayed over him, teasing and tantalizing, red hair pushed back from her face. He reached up, but she avoided his grasp; bent to kiss his chin and bent to fit his tip into her heat. A spasm crossed his face, then he caught her hips. She could not pull away and did not really want to. He moved her rapidly up and down as their mutual burning began.

Tempest did not want him to take her completely. It was too soon. The stoked coals must have time to spring free. She rose slightly and held the hands he raised to hold her there. Her lower body undulated while his tip remained in her. Her breasts bounced with the force of their motions. A sheen of perspiration broke out on her chest and back. Justin's eyes were dark amber now. His strong white teeth were sunk in his lower lip. He let her lead for a few minutes, then he came to meet her, thrusting so hard and deep that she could not contain the cry.

"It belongs there and you know it." He grated out the words. "Don't you? Don't you?"

"Yes, if I want it!" Her mouth was dry. They poised, locked in love's essential conflict.

"Do you? Say it!"

This was a struggle of domination. She would not yield. Some perversity held her silent, but she kept up the long, slow motions while he quivered inside her. She could not control the contractions that began.

"Sorceress!" He grinned, undaunted.

"Pagan!" Tempest shifted a little and this time he pulled her flat on him so that they were locked once more.

She found his lips and thrust her tongue boldly inside. His joined it; at the same time their bodies throbbed together. Her hands were in his hair while he held her buttocks. She could not get enough of him. She wanted to drown him, to drown in him and have him drown in her. They were one body, one torch of passion.

Their storm built to a crescendo of power. Darkness hovered over them and lightning split their sky. Tempest's body was welded into Justin's. She felt his motions and they were her own. She wanted to cry out, but his mouth was engulfing hers. Her own lips set their seal upon him. One flesh.

Heaven and hell opened. They descended into the vortex and rose triumphant to drift into the morning that has no end. Tempest and Justin were fused in the flesh; their hands clung together and relaxed into peace. There was no struggle here, only the light everlasting.

"I love you." The soft words hung in the air. Tempest said them without thinking and knew that they were true. She had not the power to call them back. Nor would she in this time of truth.

Justin's hand detached hers and came down on her smooth back. "Yes, darling. I know. I wished so much for us." Tenderness laced his voice as he stroked her tangled hair. "Dear love."

It was enough. Tempest relaxed even more against him and felt his manhood stir inside her.

They made love again in the waning shadows of afternoon. This was a gentle, undemanding warmth that gave way to mutual tenderness. He sounded out her secret places and opened them to ecstasy. She responded to learn anew of his. Their kisses were slow, deep, and yielding. In their individual giving, they rose above the self into one whole. Tempest felt the slow tears against her lids. Such happiness as this could not last and yet it was all the sweeter for its transience. Justin, sensitive to her feelings beyond any imaginings, looked at her and she saw the same bittersweet sorrow in his face. They held each other while the glory came again.

Dawn light was faint in the sky when Tempest roused to Justin's shaking. The hawk profile was shadowed, his voice strained as he said, "We need to be on our way. There's a great deal of ground to cover in the next few days." He was buttoning his shirt and running his fingers through the crisp hair while he spoke. Impatience was in every line of his body.

Tempest thought she could spend many days the way they had yesterday. "So soon, Justin?" She tried to push sleep back, but she was still wrapped in the warmth and satisfaction of their passion. "Maybe we should wait a bit longer."

"We have to approach Sir Herbert while the full horror of what happened is still in his mind. Old men have short memories for the present. Don't you find it so?" His voice was polite and cool, faintly irritated.

Irritation overtook Tempest also. Was he regretting the time they had shared? Or was it simply a mood? "I'm sure you're right, but let's not exhaust ourselves in travel. We don't know how the rebellion went, if much of Jamaica was taken over, anything." And men thought women were strange!

"Better get dressed, Tempest." He turned away from her, ignoring the ripe curves of her slender body on the pallet where they had loved. They might have been acquaintances rather than passionate lovers who had faced death together.

Tempest felt her cheeks flame and was thankful for the gray morning. She said briskly, "Oh, I'm starving! Maybe we can find a berry bush on the way." The future was not to be considered, she thought. Concentrate on this time in the wilds of the country she had come to care about and the fact that she was with the man she loved. The rest would take care of itself.

She recalled that often during the next four days and nights as they tramped relentlessly in the direction of Kingston, foraging what food they could from the land—an abandoned stand of corn, a rabbit Justin killed with a rock, fish taken from a stream, where they were stabbed with peeled canes, the everlasting berries. They moved under concealment, skulking along the ridges of hills, scanning meadows before dashing across them, watching the horizon constantly, always alert for the sight or sound of danger. There were no more drums or fires at night. They might have been alone in these brilliant summer days and warm blowing nights except for the ghosts that walked between them. Never again did Justin seek Tempest's arms in the light of day. Word and feeling sharing was done; only the fierceness of their mutual passion remained. They took it at night on improvised beds of leaves, exhausting themselves until late and waking early.

Once Tempest tried to speak of the barrier so suddenly come up, but Justin brushed her aside almost savagely. Then he retreated into icy silence, and that night he sat long in the moonlight, not coming to her at all. She believed it was because she had told him of her love. He had spoken truthfully when he told her he was not capable of love, she thought angrily. He believed it and acted accordingly. She should never have spoken at all. After that, the former camaraderie dwindled and long stretches of time passed without speech of any sort.

Early on the morning of the fifth day they went through a narrow pass of rock and came out into blooming, carefully tended grounds. A tall white house gleamed in the distance, its facade untouched by rebellion. There was no sign of habitation. All was silence.

Justin said, "That is Salisbury, owned by Joseph Salisbury. A prig, and cruel to everyone, including his wife and children. If it remains, we have hope that this part of the country is all right. You will hide back in the woods and wait for me while I go to reconnoiter." His jaw was set, the golden eyes hard as he issued his commands.

"That I won't! Where you go, I go." Tempest could have wished she had thought to phrase her defiance another way. She sounded like the biblical Naomi, an idea unappealing to Justin in the extreme. Still, she meant every word. "If you go into danger, I mean to be with you." She tossed her hair back and looked firmly at him.

"I know the foreman here. We've shared drink, escapades, and other things. He's a friend. If I can find him, our troubles will be lessened considerably. But I don't want to have to worry about you while I look."

The injustice of it shook Tempest. "I can defend myself. I'm coming."

"No!" He caught her shoulders and shook her until her hair tumbled over her face. "Do as I tell you!"

"Who do you think you're talking to, Justin Trevian? I'm not a slave or a lacky or yet one of your little dalliances!" She freed herself in one jerk and lifted her hand as if to strike him.

The world narrowed down to their quarrel that had to be part frustration, she knew.

Justin pulled her to him in a hard embrace, then set her back. "I want you to be safe, Tempest. I want you to have your chance at life and happiness. There's so little I can give. You know that. I'll not be part of your future, but I intend for you to survive. For my sake, for my conscience's sake, let me do what I can to protect you." He had that inward-looking bitterness, the scars from his past experiences suddenly plain in his face.

It was then Tempest knew her love to be futile before his determination. She was Tempest Mallory and another world that was not his world awaited. For his sake and for that of her pride, which would not yield, she drew herself up and said calmly, "Very well, but if you are not back by the time the sun is overhead, I'll follow you. Is that understood?"

The old Justin flashed in his eyes briefly and for what might be the last time. "Understood, sorceress." Then he was gone and her heart, her passion, went with him.

24

Revelation and Reality

The closed carriage rattled and bumped along the road, tossing Tempest high one minute and depositing her on the floor the next. She did not care; it was heaven to touch a silk cloak, much less wear one, devour meat and cakes, feel the heady wine slip down her throat. She had applied salve to her feet, and the leather shoes, though too large, felt odd on them. Whatever fortune brought in the next few hours, she would at least have enjoyed these blessed comforts. Apparently she was not intended to be a wilderness girl. She took another long drink from the flask and considered again what had all the aspects of a melodrama. Perhaps she could use it one day in the creation of the roles she intended to have.

After Justin went down to the plantation of Salisbury, she had retreated to the edge of a small copse, where she watched. She had not allowed herself to think of anything but his return; her mind was purposely made blank to past and future. The heat of the morning was not fully come before she saw Justin returning with a very tall man in his early forties with whom he seemed to be on excellent terms. She ran to meet them on Justin's signal and was barely able to restrain herself from flinging herself into his arms. The foreman, introduced as

David Wyman, behaved as though he saw such bedraggled individuals every day. The laconic voice had relegated their nightmare to a very minor footnote in the history of this part of Jamaica.

"The way I heard it, only a few plantations were affected. Maybe five or six, and only one, Cloud Ridge, was wiped out all together. There's some sort of scandal about Dornier, but it's all being played down. Everybody's watching their slaves, I can tell you that. Sure aren't any moderates around." His sharp black eyes had assessed Tempest and flicked away. "The master's in Kingston with his family. As a matter of fact, I have to go and report in the next day or so. He'll be worried about some of his art, jewels, and the like. We'll take the carriage to hide your lady here, and you, Justin, can be an outrider. Little enough to do for a friend."

Justin had clapped him on the back and thanked him effusively, but Tempest felt the leashed curiosity in his manner. They could only hope he would not spread their story about before they could reach the dubious protection of Sir Herbert.

That had all been a few hours ago and soon they would arrive in Kingston. Tempest did not really know all that Justin had in mind, but she was determined to take charge of her fate. The hungry passion, the newly born love and tenderness she had for him, was not going to blind her to the fact that she had her own way to make. So she lectured herself; Tempest Mallory was not going to be love's dupe, pining after a man who did not want her love and who could never regard her as an equal. Had he not sought to send her away, suggested that she marry here in Jamaica, informed her that he wished only to have her body? Remember these things, she thought, banishing the memory of golden eyes and gentle hands, a man's bitter tears, and the agony he taken upon himself for her sake.

She had not taken into consideration the fact of food and wine and comparative safety after the turbulent days. The jouncing of the carriage and her thoughts could not keep her eyelids from drooping. Soon flames and cries mingled with Savora's face as Tempest fled from them all across the trackless sea.

Tempest roused to quiet and dark. Pushing her tumbled hair back from her forehead, she sat up. Where were they? Had they been ambushed? How could she have slept and for how long? She put her hand to the door and thrust at it just as the handle was jerked from the other side and a raised torch shone on her upturned face.

"By all your fellow Olympians, it is Athena!" Sir Herbert, gray hair blowing slightly in the breeze, was impeccable in a black suit, his old eyes snapping with what might have been amusement. Two slaves stood just behind him as if waiting for orders.

Tempest's memory snapped back to the night at Cloud Ridge when she had first met him. He had spoken disparagingly of Justin then, even wondering aloud why such a person had been invited to a proper household. And Justin warned her of his interest in the ladies. Yet he was powerful in Jamaica, certainly in Kingston, and now he was to be trusted with their lives. There was strangeness here and Tempest wondered she had not questioned before now.

"Where is Justin?" The words came out harshly. She could not dissemble or bend before another threat.

Sir Herbert grinned. "Having a brandy and a bath. He needed them in reverse order, I fear. Don't worry, Athena. Everything is all right."

Tempest straightened and looked him sharply in the eye. "Is it? Are we fugitives welcome in your house?" She was being rude, but the circumstances warranted it.

His face changed and he stretched out a hand to her; his eyes were sober now. "You were taken in by our little by-play that time, of course. Justin and I have been in league, you might say. Few people know that. Certainly not my friend the governor, nor yet the various magistrates. This is a lesser known house far from my home, and we are near the harbor. Will you get out of that carriage, Miss Mallory? Please?"

There was no mistaking his sincerity now. Tempest felt the waves of color wash over her face, and the flask she had been clutching dropped from her hand. It was a weapon of sorts if she had needed its bulk. Sir Herbert looked at it and grinned.

"You are as Justin said. A fighter." Something else lay behind his words and paid tribute to her.

"I thank you. For everything." She climbed down and stood in the bare area behind the house, which bulked large and dark in the night. Others were on both sides, but all was silent.

Curiosity hammered at her brain, but for the time being she would rein it in.

Sir Herbert seemed rather put out that she did not ask questions, but stood aside and waved her into the house, which was composed of tiny rooms and had a stale air. A middle-aged slave woman went before them as they walked through long halls devoid of furniture. The lamp she carried offered the only dim light.

Tempest's uneasiness grew, and her danger-haunted nerves tightened with each step. When the woman pulled open a heavy door to expose a flight of steps leading downward, she rebelled. Turning to Sir Herbert, she demanded, "What is all this? Where are you taking me? I want to see Justin!"

The timing was perfect. A brilliant light shone from the last step and illuminated the tawny hair, which looked faintly damp. It glinted off the smooth planes of his face and reflected from the sleeves of his loose green shirt as he lifted a glass toward them. Justin was freshly barbered as well and the faint scent of sandalwood drifted toward Tempest, who forced herself to calm after her outburst.

"My dear, you were sleeping so soundly when we arrived that I didn't want to disturb you until everything was prepared. Come, I think your bath is ready." Justin smiled, but this eyes were watchful.

Tempest said levelly, "Thank you. I am quite refreshed by my nap." She had no doubt he had heard her demand to see him, but she had no intention of giving away any more of her feelings.

His stiff pose relaxed a little. "Sir Herbert and I will await you at dinner." The formal manner came easily to him; it was both barrier and protection.

The world below stairs was a Sybarite's delight. There were carpets in jewel tones, clear colors of yellow, emerald, and turquoise. The furniture of inlaid woods was delicate, yet sturdy enough to hold a heavy man. There was a profusion of statuary, pictures, and art objects, along with tables filled by jade and ivory. Rooms stretched into each other and beckoned one on.

Tempest was taken into an ornate chamber of soft green. The wide bed was hung with paler shades and the carpet reflected the first brightness of spring grass. A tub was placed on some

spread cloth and water for rinsing stood near at hand. The
guide resisted Tempest's efforts at privacy and helped her
remove the grimy, torn gown she wore. Then Tempest simply
gave herself up to luxury while she was bathed, her hair
washed, and then her body swaddled in a long robe. The
woman did not speak; perhaps she could not, but Tempest
found that she was in a suspended state. This seemed a sort of
fairy land, unreality after nightmare.

Her hair was vigorously dried and brushed and pulled back
from her forehead to fall over her shoulders in a shimmering
cloud of flame. Undergarments of thin silk were followed by
an equally thin gown in such a strange hue of reddish pink that
Tempest expected it to ignite against her hair. She siad, "If
there's any other color available, I'd prefer it." The slave
shook her head emphatically, put both hands on Tempest's
shoulders, and sat her down, frowning so hard in her face that
Tempest wanted to giggle. She brought out several pots, not
unlike stage makeup, and touched her lids and cheeks with the
solutions there. Then she motioned for Tempest to look at
herself in the huge mirror rimmed with gold that occupied half
of one wall.

Nymph and wanton and innocent looked back. She was
more slender than she had been in a long time, but her breasts
seemed fuller, her waist curved in, and her slim legs outlined
by the near gossamer gown. It was the color of sunset and
flame, mingling so nearly with her hair that they were
interwoven. Against its shadings, her skin had a golden color
underlaid with pearl. The slave slipped two huge opal rings on
her thumbs and this light merged as well.

Tempest saw that her face was more elongated, the gray eyes
outlined with pale shadow, her high cheekbones prominent and
accentuated. It was a woman's face, not a girl's. Pride was
stamped there, and determination. Her appearance would serve
her greatly.

The slave handed her a sleeveless robe the same color as the
opals and hooked it over the silk so that she appeared more
clothed. She stood back to survey her handiwork and grinned
toothlessly. Tempest grinned back. How lovely it was to be
dressed this way, to know oneself fair! Live for the moment,
said her mind. Keep away from the thought of Savora dead.

Don't think about it. She kept the smile on her face and so swept in to dinner.

She had the satisfaction of seeing Justin's eyes widen before the admiration in them was shuttered and his face went blank. Sir Herbert approved loudly and openly as he escorted to her chair at one end of the long, gleaming table. They sat far apart, behaving as formally as though they were a party of twenty. Roasted meats, two soups, fresh bread, fruit, and four kinds of wine were served. Tempest applied herself heartily, noticing that Justin did likewise. Sir Herbert kept up a monologue about the weather and the possibilities of storms at sea, voyages he had been on, and the cargoes of the various ships. He expected no answer, but his shrewd eyes watched his guests. All Tempest's instincts warned her. Justin appeared lazy as a tiger and as conscious of danger. They played a game, Tempest felt, and she must be on her mettle lest she be the loser.

After dinner they sipped more brandy in one of the elegant rooms. The conversation was cautious and urbane, full of trivialities. It was more than Justin could bear. His patience gave way.

"Herbert, I don't want to press you, but what about the ship? You saw those letters from Dominic and you know the situation here. Are we going to prattle all night and act like dressed up dolls? What does all this prove?" He waved expressive fingers at the opulence around him.

Sir Herbert tensed in his chair, but his voice was silky. "There are always rumors and counter-rumors. I think you both need to tell me the absolute truth. Was Morna Dornier murdered? By whom? Did you and Miss Mallory have anything to do with it? I may indulge in smuggling, a bit of forbidden traffic here and there, supply things to people who— what shall I say?—need them, but I do object to murder. And, Justin, I'm not really sure that your political instincts are as sound as they used to be back in the days of our best bargaining." He poured out another drink of brandy and fixed cold eyes on Justin. "Lovely as she is, I do believe the lady is a complication. Your betrothed will hardly understand the presence of your mistress with you in New Orleans. Our cause needs her money. Perhaps Miss Mallory would like Canada."

Justin stared at him. His lithe body in the white breeches and green shirt was steady, but little points of fire gleamed in the amber gaze turned on the older man. Both ignored Tempest.

"Don't worry about her. She doesn't fit into this. Angelica will not be concerned." His manner was dismissing. For Tempest it was betrayal.

The cool words broke over Tempest and inflamed her. Justin started to speak again, but she broke in. Her hands lay loosely in her lap and her voice, carefully controlled, gave no hint of her fury.

"I wish only to leave Jamaica and return to the United States, Sir Herbert. Justin has his charms. Who could deny them? But I have other goals and ambitions. The New York stage, for one." She kept her unwavering look on both men. Justin showed no emotion, but Sir Herbert paused in lifting his glass to his lips. "As for Morna, she was deliberately poisoned by her husband. I can tell you all about it." Her lip curled. "I assure you there is nothing to interfere with your political games here or with Justin's pursuit of dalliance and wealth in New Orleans."

Sir Herbert's glass rang on the table as he put it down. He gave a short roar of laughter and then another. When he could speak, he said, "My dear young woman, do you not know or are you being simply clever to some end I haven't comprehended? Games indeed! I have the honor to represent one very strong faction of the actual government of Jamaica, and Justin Trevian is the representative of the southern states of America and of the Vice-President, the honorable John C. Calhoun."

"Damn fool!" Justin pounded the table so that the objects on it rattled.

Tempest felt the world tilt. It took all her skill to keep her face immobile under Sir Herbert's suddenly malevolent glare.

25

L'envoi

"Heavens, Sir Herbert, I don't care who's what. I just want to act. You knew that about me from the beginning. Politics are tiresome, and I've never wanted to discuss them. I'm afraid that includes now, if you don't mind." Tempest let irritation edge her voice. "I know Justin and I have to leave Jamaica quickly, but we can go our separate ways. I want out of all this. Violence is not one of the things I enjoy."

The men exchanged glances, but they seemed a frozen tableau. It was, Tempest thought grimly, one of her better performances and would fit right in with what Sir Herbert seemed to think about women in general. Justin had not thought of her feelings in this, but he cared little enough. They had given and taken in passion, shared memories, loss and thought, but they had not really come together in closeness that endured. So be it. She must think of herself.

"So you did tell her." Sir Herbert recovered his voice. "Women are so practical, aren't they?" He gave her a wolfish grin. "A purse of gold will be helpful in your ambition, my dear. You're right. Politics are wearying. Now about the Dorniers . . ."

"Herbert, this isn't the time." Justin began to protest, but was cut off by his comrade's slicing gesture. Obediently, he sank in a chair, his manner icy as Tempest began to speak, for what she hoped was the last time, of Morna and Robert Dornier.

For the most part the story was hers, supplemented at times by Justin, who said at one point, "He was giving her a very slow poison, maybe a mixture, that sometimes gave the victim the sense of spurious health. She had a delicate constitution anyway and might not have survived another childbirth. Dornier wanted a strong line and a wealthy wife; Tempest fascinated him, but marriage would have been another matter. The man didn't have a very savory reputation in early life. I think he must have been partially mad there at the end. Life really meant nothing to him. After the slaves rose up, he focused on us and tried to destroy both. The ones who followed him had grievances, real or imagined, and the drink didn't help." Tempest saw that he would not reveal his love for his lost plantation and warmth for him touched her briefly.

She did not think slaves were people to Sir Herbert, so she left Savora and Jason out of her tale, speaking slowly about the flight back to Kingston and the subterfuges they had used, stressing the fear she had felt. Sir Herbert must not imagine that she had enjoyed any of that journey. He must think her a bruised lady who had endured much; the exhibition of temper and a strong will would put him off from her if he had any interest in that way.

"I believe you. Both of you." Sir Herbert rose and brushed both hands together in a gesture that reminded Tempest vaguely of Pilate in the Bible. "An investigation will be conducted, and I doubt strongly that any blame will be attached to your names. Trouble is brewing here over slavery, and other matters will come up to occupy interest. But you have to leave for now. The only ship in port is something of a tub, the *Porfina*, and she goes to New Orleans tonight. We have talked into the early hours of this morning, have we not?"

"Strange that there's only one ship for New Orleans." Justin's voice was tinged with acid. "What about Tempest? She should go to the American North."

"Trade varies. And who knows what could be disturbed if news of your presence here got out? Both of you have to be on the *Porfina*, it's safer. Miss Mallory can embark on another vessel in New Orleans. Just don't keep her with you." Sir Herbert yawned. "We'll discuss our politics later today, Justin, and try to figure out what your feckless cousin Dominic is up to. Now take your lady and go off with you."

Tempest rose and shook out her skirts. "Would you summon the slave to show me back to my bedroom? I've forgotten the way." He thought she was actually going to spend what remained of the night with Justin!

Red suffused Justin's cheeks as Sir Herbert eyed him, grinning. He started to speak, but Tempest forestalled any comment by remarking, "I just know you won't mind her staying with me. Ever since all this happened, I've just been prone to all sorts of dreams." She wouldn't put it past Justin to come to her bed later. Excitement leaped in her veins, but she struggled against it. She must have her pride. Tempest Mallory could do no less. She would not, must not, think of the long barren years without Justin.

As he had done once in another beautiful place, Justin inclined his head and drawled, "Checkmate."

Tempest slept long and heavily despite tormenting visions of Savora's face in life and death. Justin and Sir Herbert surrounded her, asking questions she could not hear. Morna cried to her from the shades. A tall ship ran before the winds, her sails billowing out, and Tempest stood on the deck only to see that the water below was blood.

When she finally roused, the room was brilliant with lamplight and the slave woman was gone from the chair where she had spent the night. Several traveling cases stood in one corner and a pile of gowns lay over one of the chests. A covered pot, bread, and fruit were placed on the table near her wonderfully soft bed. A folded piece of paper lay close at hand. When she picked it up, she saw that the note was signed, "Herbert," in elegant writing.

The pot contained coffee, strong and dark. After several sips, Tempest felt able, if not to conquer this part of the world, to read and deal with whatever complications the note presented. It was addressed to "Pallas Athena."

"I think you will be a great actress. I express my homage. Justin has the most incredible luck. Morna Dornier had money of her own, and even though it belonged to her husband by law, she seems to have feared her death and left written wishes that it should come to you. If you lived. Another reason to believe your and Justin's story. The purse contains gold and more will be sent when you are settled in New York. It is not a great deal, but it will help. Take what clothes you can from here; don't be silly and girlish about accepting any of this. You will need it all. One word of warning. Justin's future is set. He will never change, and he is inflexible. Make your own way, Athena. May all the gods of Olympus be with you."

Tears filmed Tempest's eyes. She did not doubt the sincerity of what he had written, but she also did not doubt that Sir Herbert was not averse to dalliance if he could. He might have believed her words of the night; it was likely he did not. At any rate, she had won the toss. She gulped more coffee and debated whether to get up and try on gowns or sit here and be sentimental.

The decision was not hers to make. The door swung open and a tall dark woman entered, followed by two young girls who carried sewing materials. The woman stared at Tempest out of huge black eyes and spoke in a lilting accent that combined England and the islands of the sun. "Miss get up now. Boat go at good dark. Three hour. Lots to do."

Tempest forgot she was stark naked under the covers and kicked them off. It was the way she preferred to sleep, although the fashion was for long nightgowns with frills. The girls giggled, and the woman joined them. Tempest could not be stiff. She burst into laughter. Let this be an augury of her last hours in Jamaica.

The slaves had their orders and proceeded to follow them with all speed. Several of the gowns needed no alterations, others only minor ones. They packed these away, produced simple day dresses in shades of green, blue, and cream, fitted Tempest expertly, and then urged her to try on a variety of cloaks, hats, and shoes. Some were too small, some far too large. Tempest wondered again at all this variety, but she knew better than to ask questions of the slaves. At her first hint of curiosity, they rolled their eyes and retreated. She would learn nothing from them, and what did it matter? Best to play the game of ignorance until she was safely on board the *Porfina*.

"Miss wear this for boat. Best one." The older slave extended a gray gown, simply made but of good material, for Tempest's inspection. A dark cloak, lined with gray, and a matching bonnet lay ready. It was a costume many women might wear; no distinguishing features were observed.

Tempest's imagination jumped ahead as she recalled the stories she and Savora had often traded in their early years. There had been girls stolen away, immured in lonely houses, and held for the delectation of lovers not always desirable, maidens impregnated by gods and lured by them, some taken by old men and sold into sexual slavery. What if? Then she smiled to herself. After all that had happened in a few short months, how could she ever give way to the fantasy of old tales, deliciously thrilling as they had been under the grape arbor in Savannah?

There was a knock at the door, a muttered consultation, and then the woman said, "Carriage ready. Yo' man, he already gone. Hurry."

Justin hers? That arrogant, contradictory man would never belong to anyone but himself. She missed his arms, his kisses, his mercurial nature. Was it done between them? He would soon be married in New Orleans, and she would be put aboard the next ship north. Or so Justin and Sir Herbert thought. She had to make her own life, and thanks to Morna, she now had something of the the means to do so.

She scrambled quickly into the gray gown, which clung to her bosom and billowed around her ankles in graceful folds. The shade was nearly that of her eyes and made her skin seem luminous. Her flaming hair was swept back and confined at her neck, but wisps and tendrils escaped to curl at her ears. Not even the bonnet could make her look decorous and serious. Her eyes snapped with excitement, and her nerves were stretched with it.

Suddenly these slaves whose names she did not know, for they had volunteered nothing, were to her the last touch with this country. Tempest stretched out both hands as if to Savora, whose shade must linger here forever. "Thank you. Thank you for everything. God keep and aid you." Too much, too effusive. Her mind said one thing and her volatile emotions another.

"You too, miss. And the man." The slave stared at Tempest with Savora's eyes.

Was she never to be free of self-accusation, of the sense of having failed her friend? Tempest snatched up her reticule—Sir

Herbert had everything here—and one small bag, while the slaves followed with the others. It was time to leave, not time to brood.

She went through the strange opulence, into the barren section of the house, and was handed into the same carriage in which she had arrived. It was deep night; no moon or stars showed. The air held a scent of rain, a type of brooding heaviness that might mean storms. She hoped the *Porfina* was a sturdy vessel.

Tempest had a strong sense of anticlimax when, after what seemed hours of clattering through the streets of Kingston, the carriage stopped at the edge of some old buildings close to the wharf. This was a secret leavetaking, but a matter-of-fact one. A small ship stood ready but there were no other about, no sign of men or passengers. Yet her coachman and his helper piled her bags together, urged her forward, and started toward the ship.

A figure detached itself from the darkness and came at them in a swift movement. It was Justin. He was muffled in a dark cloak and hat, but Tempest could never have mistaken that walk, the tilt of his head, and the set of those muscular shoulders.

She gave a little breath of relief. Until that minute she had not known of her apprehension. Annoyed with herself, she began to twist the edges of her veil and had to make a conscious effort to stop. It was ridiculous, she told herself sternly, to be so affected by the mere glimpse of the man. Her heart told her otherwise.

"Keep your veil down and come on. They're ready." He whispered the words so that only she could hear. Then he handed out money, motioned for the bags to be carried along the wharf and up to the ship. "Hurry." Justin turned, walking rapidly, confident that she would dash after him.

The wind freshened now and there was a roll of thunder toward the south. Heat hung in the air. Heavy clouds were illuminated by a lightning flare. Tempest felt the forbidding atmosphere and hesitated. The *Porfina* seemed the merest scrap on the undulating water. Common sense came to her rescue. She had always found partings sad. Much of her past life and friends lay here in Jamaica. She was alone, but had she not always been?

Justin had paused and was looking back. She could feel the heat of his glare, although she could not see it. This was no time for introspection. She could do plenty of that on board in the days to come. Tempest hurried after him.

The bags were set in a corner on the deck. Money again exchanged hands and Justin led her down a short hall and into a tiny cabin furnished with one bunk, a stool, and a large bottle. The one porthole was covered in burlap. It was stifling and smelled of seawater, a not unpleasant odor when combined with Justin's male warmth and the violet water she had discovered in her bedroom at Sir Herbert's. A tiny lantern gave the only light.

Justin tossed his cloak aside and stood revealed in thin brown trousers and shirt, a costume that enhanced his build and highlighted the golden look of him. She could not read the expression in his eyes.

"How are you at subterfuge and trickery, my dear?" His tone was casual, but there was posed impatience behind it.

"Excellent, my dear Mr. Trevian, as you certainly have reason to know." She, too, could mock.

He yanked the cork from the bottle, took a quick drink, and offered it to Tempest, who declined. "Sorry there's no cup or glass. Maybe you'll join me later. We're traveling as husband and wife, you know."

"What?" Delight poured through her, potent as any wine, glorious as the heights they had attained. "You're not serious!"

"Oh, but I am. Mr. and Mrs. John Bulham, who are going to seek their fortunes in the American West. We have to stay out of sight as much as possible. Sir Herbert took a real chance getting us out of Jamaica, and I mustn't arrive in New Orleans with a woman. Gossip, you know. Bad for marriage. The *Porfina* goes on to Galveston, so it ought to work out. I know you're full of questions, but right now we have to settle some basics. Sure you won't have a drink?" He lifted the bottle and shook it invitingly.

Tempest felt the rage that only he could rouse in her. Perhaps it was passion's other face. At any rate she fairly spat the words at him. "Why would I have questions? You're involved in some sort of slave smuggling scheme with Sir Herbert, aren't you? You're representative only of yourself. I know that! You make love to one woman while planning a rich marriage and will likely be unfaithful to her also! I don't care about your schemes; just leave me out of them!" She jumped up and brushed past him. She had to get out and breathe.

His hard voice stopped her momentarily. "Judge yourself, Tempest! I don't doubt a second that you'd snap at a rich marriage, as you say, so as to further your ambitions! Women do it all the time and always have. Love is the exception. My wife will have no cause to reproach me; I shall be an impeccable husband according to society's lights. Men and women alike sell themselves, my dear, and well you know it! You have said that politics bore you and thus we'll not discuss it." The cork of the jug was loosened once again.

Tempest jerked the door open and headed down the passage. His words burned into her mind. They were true and she could not deny it. She wanted him to be different and he was not. She was not. They did not live in a fairy tale but in real life. Accept the truth and be done.

She came out on the deck, which was now filled with movement and quiet action. The huge sails billowed as the *Porfina* began to take the wind and move out from the wharf. The dark mass of Jamaica loomed up, mysterious and haunting. Tempest remembered it as she had first come, an emerald in the brilliant sea, a land of expectation and hope. Here she had known love and death, terror beyond nightmares, passion, and loss.

"Jamaica." She said the word softly as the sails spread before the gathering storm.

26

Love's Bargain

"I trust you are now in a more agreeable frame of mind. These quarters are much better, don't you think?" Justin removed his boots and gave Tempest a wolfish grin. "I never intended you to think that cabin, cramped as it was, could be ours. It was just a way to get out of sight until we sailed."

Tempest shook out her wet skirts and tried to ignore the *Porfina*'s roll. She had intended to watch Jamaica out of sight, but one of the sailors insisted on seeing her below. "Best to stay in your cabin, Mrs. Bulham. I'll take you there." Rather than protest and call more attention to herself, she had yielded. The rain had begun then and the force of it exploded at them, wetting her to the skin.

This cabin had a real bed instead of a bunk, several chests, a rather tattered chair, and two portholes. The furniture was nailed down, and shielded lanterns gave an intimate light. The air was fresh; Justin must have opened the porthole despite the pouring rain. This must clearly be the best cabin on the ship. Sir Herbert had spent lavishly on them. What had he claimed in return?

"I would have preferred my privacy." She spoke tartly. She had no wish to stir up their recent argument but still did not see

how she and Justin could share a bed with the unspent anger
between them.

"Husband and wife are one. Is it not so?" He unfastened his
shirt in a maddeningly slow way. One eyebrow went up as he
watched her.

"We have discussed that state quite enough for one night."
She longed to pull off the wet gown and settle into a
comfortable robe, but she was not going to undress in front of
him. Never mind that she had once gloried in her naked body
and his. "What did you mean about being good at trickery?"
Divert him from pulling at his belt, preparatory to pulling
down his trousers.

"Think up a good story as to why we're not often seen
abovedecks. We mustn't stir undue curiosity. That's a necessity.
Sir Herbert may not have all the power he thinks he has.
Warrants may be issued for us. Faster boats than this may bring
word to New Orleans, and it is one of the world's most
talkative cities." He rested his chin on his knee and his eyes
became contemplative.

"We've been married for some years and are used to each
other. I am to bear a child, am worried about our venture to the
West, and inclined to scold. You, alas, drink and shout. It is
clear what your problem is. I watch you, but it does not do any
good. You have taken me from our little town, where I had
many friends. A wife must follow her husband." She looked at
him with meek long-suffering eyes and let her voice rise.

"Nothing romantic about us." His voice was casual.

"Nothing," she agreed.

"It will suffice. If I think of anything better, I will let you
know." He stripped off his remaining clothes in one gesture,
stood tall and powerful in the wash of light for a moment
before blowing out the lantern on his side and climbing into the
bed, which dipped with his weight. "Coming to bed?"

She would have to sleep close up to him since the bed had
that tilt. Now she was angry enough to push him to the floor.
Her imagination and acting skill could protect them, but he
would change the story if he found one better, would he? It was
not to be borne! She did not intend to put up with such a
situation.

"Come on. The light bothers me and I need my rest." He

sounded fully as irritable as she intended to be in the course of their roles.

"Later." She wanted to think.

He muttered something she couldn't hear and pulled the pillow over his head. His back was partially covered with one sheet, which he was in the process of kicking off. As Tempest looked at him, he reached for the other pillow and burrowed more deeply into it.

"You'll suffocate." She spoke the words in a normal voice, but he didn't hear or chose to ignore the comment. Her fingers loosened the skirt of her gown and it fell to the floor. One of the wet petticoats followed before Justin gave another muffled groan.

Tempest jumped on the bed in one motion and pushed him as hard as she could. The bed tilted, dumping them both on the floor in a welter of covers. The mattress slipped over on them and they began to kick. Justin's curses were nearly silenced by the close quarters, but he was pushing at Tempest and she was shaking with laughter. How she wished she could have seen his face!

He tumbled free at last, perspiring, tawny hair curling riotously over his forehead, and yanked Tempest up by one shoulder. "Funny, is it?" He set both hands on her ribcage and began to tickle. She tried to twist away and could not. One hand went out toward his hair and jerked a tendril. He caught hers and they rolled about, scuffling as puppies might. Both were laughing at this shared insanity while they poked and tickled.

It changed in one breath. Tempest was lying on her side and giggling. He bent over her and ran his thumb down her back. Then he pulled at the top of her petticoat. Both breasts came into his hands. His eyes went dark with hunger. Tempest felt the hot moisture surge up between her legs. She reached out and put both arms around him, feeling the muscles tighten under her touch. His mouth moved against her cheek. She nodded her head, pulled back and let him see the longing in her own face. His shaft surged up strongly when she put her hand to it.

She put her head down to him so that her bright hair spilled over his legs. Her tongue touched him lightly, circled, withdrew, and settled. "Tempest! Tempest!" His voice was far away, past the roaring in her ears. His hands danced sensually on her bare back. She was as naked as he and had no recollection of how she had come to lose her clothes.

Now she took him fully into her mouth, allowing her tongue to play about his sensitive ridge and his very wellspring. He quivered and thrust convulsively in her but held back as his fingers went over her back and around her breasts. He circled and played with her nipples in almost the same motions she gave with her tongue. She opened her eyes to see the tender white skin of his crotch and the hair several shades paler than that on his head. Her hands grasped his hips and the speed of her mouth increased until she felt as though she drowned in him and he burned in her.

"Together, this time." His voice was hoarse and panting as he pulled back from her and they stood up. Leaning toward each other, they came together and apart as he thudded in, then she held him and they drew free simultaneously. He penetrated her, she hammered at him, they joined, clung, and exploded to the floor in perspiration and exhaustion and release.

The ship plowed before the gale, dropped from one wave to another, and swayed from side to side, but Tempest and Justin made a nest on the floor with the mattress and sheets, where they sipped brandy, nibbled on little cakes Sir Herbert had sent along, and made love until sleep came on them like a bludgeon.

"I suppose we'll have to go up and take some fresh air, see about food and all that." Tempest put her fist in front of her mouth as she yawned languidly and tickled Justin's foot, which rested, for the moment, in her lap. They had twined together, played and kissed for a while this morning as one or the other speculated about the hour. The bitterness and constraint between them was gone; they were able to be free and open in this time out of time.

"Guess so." Justin yawned in his turn, then reached over and wrapped a lock of her long hair around his hand so that the curls clung. "Tempest." His voice grew purposeful, and she was instantly alert. "There're some things that have to be said."

"I know it." She spoke softly, but her gaze held his without flinching.

"I can't alter anything about my future. It has to be the way it is. I told you about how my people were almost decimated in the wars of religion; it's bred in me to continue a line. I can understand Robert Dornier's need. The New Orleans match is long arranged. I have a plantation out from there, and it is managed by my cousin, the Dominic I talked about. I don't think he does a very good job, but it has potential. Prosperity in the South depends on slavery.'' He stopped and ran one hand through his hair. "I wish I could love you, Tempest, but you know all about that. I can only be honest with you.''

He believed what he was saying; Tempest understood well. There would be no shifting him from that position. She must not try. "I thank you for your honesty, Justin. Don't try to explain.''

He wrapped the sheet around his loins and crossed his legs. "Tempest, I am not totally the selfish individual you think. All this is not myself alone. Others are involved. Some of it comes down to slavery, but much of it is the right of the states as sovereign entities within the Union. How much power shall the federal government have in the affairs of the states? The questions are bitter ones and the angers they stir are deep. One thing is certain; there must be a balance of power and influence. The Vice-President, Mr. Calhoun, is a friend of mine. He believes strongly that the states can declare a federal law invalid in the individual states. A dangerous concept for the Union.'' His face grew brighter as he moved away from the personal emotions. "We have considered the various islands close to the United States, and Jamaica, anxious to preserve slavery and its economy, chafes at the English rule. It might be a great jewel for our country and many are willing to risk it. Sir Herbert is one of them. You see, England has not allowed slaves to be brought in and it is said that soon she will pronounce a ban on slavery itself.''

"That could mean war with England, couldn't it? Or a split in America if Jamaica did enter as a state, grateful to those who made it possible and upsetting the power balance. Another slave state.'' She had grown up with slavery and had thought little of it until she became friends with Savora and was thereafter altered.

"I have had, as they say, a foot in all the camps. But I am committed to my friend by honor and reason. The South must survive. If any breath of this Jamaica scheme touched

Calhoun, he could fall from power. I must see people in New Orleans, perhaps return to Jamaica again. I can't really expect you to understand." He sighed and stood up, looking about for his clothes. "I only hoped you would."

Tempest thought of Jason's determination to be free and Savora, who had not wanted to live without freedom. She knew Justin abhorred slavery in some ways but believed in its economic necessity. "You must do what you have to do, Justin." She only wanted to cry out that life was short; how many people experienced half as much as they had? Why throw passion and caring away for a nebulous goal that was probably all wrong? He would dream himself into exile or a traitor's destruction. She would be as devious as he thought her. You made your own future; Jamaica had shown her that. The scheme crystallized in her mind and she realized it had been there all along.

"Would you prefer I found somewhere else to sleep?" Justin stood up, shirt dangling from one hand, and studied her face warily. "Or if not, I can promise you nothing else will happen between us."

Let the patron saints of all actors be with her now! "I doubt that I will see you again after we dock. New York is far away and you'll have your own life as I will make mine. Justin, can we not take this time for our own and forget everything else? Ambition, parting, politics, unhappiness, and any talk of them must be banished! We will act our parts of Mr. and Mrs. Bulham, but in between we can do . . . other things. The one who becomes serious must pay a penalty. A penalty of kisses withheld! What do you say?" She made her voice light and shifted her body so that he might take in every curve. It was the coin in which she fought.

"Only if you will not regret what must be." He bent down to her, his eyes warm with tenderness.

"I will never regret knowing you, Justin. And I will not regret these days." She held out her arms to him.

He looked at the honey skin, the deep gray eyes, and the tumbling red hair. She saw the hesitation in him and honored him all the more for it. "For now, there is nothing but we two!"

As he spoke, he caught her to him and their mouths fused in a long, burning kiss that was the seal of their bargain.

In the next few days Tempest and Justin remained in the cabin in the daylight hours, making love and talking, playing word and quotation games, inventing jokes, and giving Mr. and Mrs. Bulham a reputation for disagreement. It was no effort to banish seriousness; this was their enchanted time and they took it freely. Justin told her stories of his childhood, a lonely one filled with the melancholy of his ancestors, a strain that ran in him now, though he did not often admit it. For Tempest there had been Savora, and in telling him of their gay times, much of her anguished loss in the present became bearable. She discovered that Justin was a practical idealist as well as a romantic. His dreams were grounded in reality, but he did not doubt that he could really change the world around him by his work with the southerners and the Jamaica faction. He wanted to make a difference and found an enduring line. She wanted him with all the power in her, but she wanted to act also. The two often merged, but when they came together in passion's molten embrace, Tempest knew that Justin was her great desire. There was always a price to be paid.

At night they came up on the decks and watched the dark waters split before the thrust of the *Porfina*. There had been no storms; the air was always fresh and balmy. They would watch the stars, name the constellations for each other, and recite the old myths, knowing their fundamental truth. The sails billowed out to send the ship skimming ever faster toward New Orleans and the end of something precious to them both. Now and then they would catch a glimpse of a dim island in the distance and see the massed trees bending down before the warm wind. At such times Tempest would say, "If only we had our own kingdom. A secret place. Would you like that, Mr. Bulham?"

"Careful, wife. You will give the impression we like each other and that will never do. What of our seasickness?" Justin was always innocent as he waited for her challenge.

The small rituals had come so easily. They had their own language. Then she said, "I know a cure for seasickness. A cure for dislike. A cure for most things."

He drawled, "How very fascinating. Let's go below and discuss it."

Once in their cabin they locked together, mouths fused, their fingers seeking out the places of the other in another more

powerful ritual, the eternal one. In the fire of their mutual
need, both could forget the nearness of the separate future.

One afternoon Justin went out for their food as he usually
did and returned without it. His face was set in the old mask as
he said, "We have entered the mouth of the Mississippi River."

His words came as a physical blow to Tempest, but she knew
she must not show the pain. He must suspect nothing. She
lifted her arms to him and made herself smile.

"I want you. Come and let me undress you." It was one of
their games. They loved to tantalize each other by removing
garments as slowly as possible and kissing all newly revealed
areas.

He came close and caught her to him. "And I want you. But
this way!" Then he was hammering into her as she opened
before his need that was her own. All thought vanished before
the consuming immolation.

27

Subterfuge

New Orleans, Louisiana
September 1831

Tempest stood on the wharf with Justin and waited for the carriage he had sent a boy to find. It was a hot day and she could feel the perspiration dripping between her petticoats and the sensible dark green gown she wore. The dark veil hid her face, and her gloves stuck to the palms of her hands. In a few minutes she would be saying goodbye to Justin.

He was walking up and down, scanning the activity around them, the picture of a man in a hurry. His traveling suit was black, as were his hat and boots, and their quality was ordinary, but he stood out by virtue of his height and bearing. The tanned face was hard and reserved; nothing in his manner reflected the intensity of the embrace he had given her little more than an hour ago in their cabin.

They had clung fiercely together in one last drowning, storm-evoking kiss that Tempest told herself might have to last forever. It was better to say farewell this way, they told themselves, than risk emotion in public and call attention to them. She did not really believe in such intrigue, but it was clear Justin did and he certainly had his reasons.

The fierce lion eyes had blazed into hers. "I'll see you in New York. You know that, don't you?"

"With your lady wife, years from now?" She could not resist the barb. All the love and caring were being squeezed out of her because of the cruelty they inflicted on each other.

"Ah, Tempest." He pulled her to him and held her close in that tenderness so much a part of his nature in these last days. "The pattern was set long ago."

As always, their bodies spoke for them. Once more the enveloping flame was there and bitterness was burned away.

Tempest knew she would remember such moments rather than the things that divided them. She would have to, for the way ahead left no room for anything else. Was she not a fighter? Let it take all her time and skill; she would welcome the struggle.

The sun hammered down relentlessly as they continued to wait. Justin began to mutter under his breath, and Tempest felt like adding a few of her own choice words. She forced herself to concentrate on the scene around her. Here she was in fabled, wicked New Orleans for the first time and there was much to see.

The great brown river, the Mississippi, carried all types of ships, barges, and flatboats. Masts of those at anchor were limned against the sky, the riggings standing out sharply as though inked there. Sailors and vendors called out, eddies of people on urgent business swarmed in one direction and seemed to return from another, others stood talking in different languages and using expressive gestures. It did not appear that any more ships could enter this particular crowded area but a small one, about the size of the *Porfina*, was even now swinging about the section to enter her tier. Tempest wondered where she had come from; one could only hope it was not Jamaica.

"Damnable boy, where can he be? We'll be conspicuous if we stay here much longer." Justin slapped one hand against the other and glowered in the direction of the dusty street.

They were well past the fashionable section of the levee, with its unbroken line of Pride of India trees, and into the more dangerous, brawling section. Justin had given out this information earlier and volunteered no more; she had not felt interest at that moment, but now the observer in her quickened. A bell clanged far off and the note was taken by another. Flocks of birds swirled overhead and a pack of dogs dashed by, a gang of boys in pursuit. A raffish one-eyed man in a red vest sauntered by, gave Tempest an impudent grin, and vanished before Justin could notice. A dark girl, bosom half bared, called out the virtues of her cakes in a tangle of French and English. The hot muddy river odor permeated everything and brought with it the distinct smell of fish.

"About time!" Justin caught her elbow, interrupting her reverie, and steered her along the planks laid down to protect skirts from mud, over sections of hard-packed ground, and around some construction, to the nondescript black carriage with a closed interior. Once inside, he gave the driver an incomprehensible address and turned to Tempest.

"I'll make arrangements for you to take the first ship north. You'll be a widow, going to your husband's people as quickly as possible; that's some reason for traveling alone. Or I can buy a slave for you." His voice was matter-of-fact and contained, that of a man in perfect control.

Tempest shook her head violently. "No!" All her feelings were in revulsion from the buying and selling of other human beings after what she had seen in Jamaica. Common sense told her Savora would have died early on if she had not been purchased by Aunt Hannah and befriended by Tempest. But now her emotions were raw from the coming parting. She could not trust herself to speak.

"I understand." Clutching his hands together in his lap, head turned slightly away from her, Justin launched into explanations calculated to bridge the awkwardness between them. "We're going into the French section of the city. I have a very old friend there—she admits to seventy, no more—whom I've known for many years. She'll be happy to have you with her and won't ask any questions. Everything will be fine, Tempest. I plan to appear in certain places as if I just arrived on one of the ships today or tomorrow, and then I'll be going out to my plantation. I grow cane there, and some cotton." He continued the virtues of the various crops, the weather required for them to flourish, and the necessity for skilled workers while the carriage moved rapidly on.

Tempest looked at his handsome profile, the arched nose, long lashes, and the bronzed skin. The familiar ache grew in her. "Justin, you really want things to be this way, don't you? You talk about causes and ideals and your own inability to love, but underneath you're doing what you want. Aren't you?" The words fell heavily around them.

He turned to her. Their eyes met as if across a chasm. In the silence they heard the scrape of the carriage wheels, the shouts of the driver as he traded insults with someone in his way, and the sounds of a loud argument conducted in the street. Sweat sprang out on Justin's lip as he pushed his shirt collar back.

"Yes, I am. There can never be any misunderstanding about that. I'm honest with you."

And I am not honest with you. Tempest's brain catalogued the words while she watched the inflexibility in his face. In that moment it seemed that she hated him as much as she cared about him. "You have not left any room for misunderstanding, Justin. It is better that way." She leaned back and pulled off her gloves. "Is it always so hot in New Orleans? I think I'll be glad to see the changing colors of the north country." Be cool, that was the way. He would be used to women weeping over him and making demands, begging him to do this and that. She was not such a one.

"I'll tell the driver to go faster." If Justin was discomfited, he did not show it. His mouth quirked down at her in the old gesture that stirred her heart, then he leaned out the window to roar at the man in a manner which caused their speed to increase twice over. When they were private again in the hot closeness of the interior, he spoke of the Americans and their rivalry with the Creoles in the differing parts of the city. It was a conversation two strangers might have had. And only a few hours ago, Tempest mused, she and Justin had been united in the dearness of the flesh, a surmounting longing to encompass all else. Yet it had not and could not. To that extent those who denounced the ephemeral flesh were right, but she would not turn against the sweetness.

The carriage stopped and Justin jumped out. "Wait. It will be only a few minutes." The door slammed, and she was left to her thoughts.

Tempest felt rage and amusement alternatingly. He was undoubtedly pleased at the way things appeared to be working out. Had he tended to other women this way? Made arrangements for them? Talked of what was inevitable? Been, as he said, honest in his own lights? Well, he would learn that

Tempest Mallory was no malleable lass, but a woman with a will and determination of her own.

"Come in, miss." The reviving air was sweeping in through the open doors of the carriage and two old black men, so alike as to be twins, were smiling at her. She smiled back and allowed herself to be assisted gently down.

The street must surely be a mire in bad weather, but now the dust was thick and the gray walls flanked with iron gates just ahead reminded her unpleasantly of a prison. There were several other dwellings, smaller and built of wood and clay, set diagonally from the one they approached. Several old trees swayed in the heat, their leaves turning up pale undersides toward the sky. Clouds built in the west, warning of rain in the evening.

"Come on, miss. You'll get all faint in this hot out here." One of the men urged her on while the other struggled with her bags.

Once past the forbidding entrance, Tempest felt impressions sweep upon her so rapidly that she was disconcerted. They went through a courtyard filled with statuary, flowering plants, and small trees placed so as to form a green barrier. She might have been in a bower in the forest. From there she was taken across a porch shaded with vines and into a dim, cool room done in touches of blue and cream. A very old lady, crinkled and folded with her years, sat in a velvet chair. A black maid, arms folded, stood beside her, eyes fixed firmly on Justin, who knelt beside the lady.

When Tempest entered, he rose and said smoothly, "Elizabeth, this is the widow of my friend Steven. Tempest Miranda Mallory." He gave her last name the French pronunciation and accented Miranda. "Mrs. Mallory, this is Madame LaBorgue, dearest of all the ladies in this city. She understands your need to take ship quickly and is kind enough to offer you shelter."

Madame LaBorgue smiled vaguely and extended one hand in Tempest's general direction. "Welcome, my dear. Stay as long as you like. Anything for you, Justin. He saved my son's life once. Took him away from a duel, he did. Saved him. Wonderful. Come with your wife. Come see me." Her voice trailed away and the papery lids closed over as she began to snore. The maid nodded at Tempest, then bent to her mistress.

Justin drew Tempest apart circumspectly, aware of the

slave's gaze. "She's like that. Vague one minute and sharp the next. You'll be fine, and I'll send word about the ship." He hesitated and added, "I must bid you farewell." His hand came out and clasped hers very correctly.

Tempest knew slaves gossiped and one must be discreet. She and Justin had agreed on how it must be at the last, but pain lanced through her all the same. Words surged in her mind as pride held sway. After all that had passed between them, finality was encompassed in one sentence.

"Goodbye, Mr. Trevian, and I wish you well."

Justin stared at her, his expression unreadable. She returned the look, veiling her feelings, determined he should not know that she was shaken beyond endurance. For an instant they stood paralyzed and silent, then he turned and walked from her, out into the bright day.

Tempest stood in the dimness with her snoring hostess and the watchful slave. Was this the way one's life ended? How could one person so encompass all existence so that nothing else appeared to matter? She had been right to want to avoid falling in love, yet she could not help that she had done so. If she had it all to do over again, she knew that she would still respond to Justin in exactly the same way.

"Come and rest." The flat gaze of the slave now rested on her face. "The madam'll sleep for hours and hours. You mustn't expect much. But Mr. Trevian will have told you that." Her language was precise, filled with the intonations of another land. "You be mournin', anyway."

Tempest supposed she must have murmured something to explain her lack of black garb, but she did not really care about anything except being alone. That was her great need and this house would provide the opportunity. "If I can be secluded a bit, pray and think?" She let the words trail off as if hesitant. "Mrs. LaBorgue wouldn't be offended?"

"She ain't in her mind much now. This's a favor for Mr. Justin." The woman led her through silent, high ceilinged halls and into a bedroom furnished in the heavy fashion of the turn of the century. The bed was curtained in white and several gray chairs were strewed about. A door led out into a section of the garden.

She indicated the bell pull. "I'm Esther, the housekeeper.

You'll have a girl to help. I tend the madam." After Tempest's nod, she stared another minute then rustled away.

Tempest was alone for the first time in days. She jerked off the hot dress, hose, and shoes, then threw her hat across the room. Her hair fell about her shoulders in a riot of flame. Tears burned behind her lids and now she could let them come. What more natural than that a widow should weep and want to be alone? She prepared herself for the anguish held back and banked for so long.

Nothing happened. Episodes with Justin moved back and forth across in her mind. He seemed so close that she could touch him, his profile clear in the Jamaica dawn as he laughed, leaned boldly over her, caressed her breasts, exchanged badinage, kissed, talked of his past. He came close and faded away, strode into darkness, entered the great hall at Cloud Ridge, walked onto the porch of Meadowlands with her in his arms. Justin walked in her heart and life and would do so forevermore. Her heart and her love were given to this one man who had foresworn it.

She lay dry-eyed on the soft bed and stared at the ceiling, where stray cobwebs were collected. It was not given to her that she should have the relief of tears. Something in her being recoiled from them even though she knew she would be temporarily eased. She would have gained nothing by clinging to Justin. Very well, go on from there. But where? The future seemed a blank wall at this moment, and her brave plans of the days in Jamaica, those she had considered on the *Porfina*, and which had been, in one way or another, centered for years in her mind were nebulous.

She rolled over so that she lay face down and stared into the white coverlet. The soft sound of a knock came, but she did not answer. She heard the door open, then close quickly. Let them think she slept. She dug her fingers into the pillows and kicked her feet hard, much as she had done when a rebellious child. The draining days and yearning nights loomed before her. Why had she not pressed Justin, shown her willingness to be his mistress? What else mattered but the sweet, immolating passion they had shared?

Tempest tossed long into the evening and night as she struggled with her personal demons. Her course had been set long ago. She did not really mean to deviate from it; loving

Justin had been unexpected, but nothing was actually altered. New Orleans was one of the theatrical centers of the United States and a city that loved all sorts of arts, music, and entertainment. What more natural than that an aspiring actress should come here? She had some money, clothes, and a natural ability for survival in addition to her talent. In past years she had intended to go to Charleston, maybe here, possibly New York. In addition to the ambition of her earlier life, Tempest realized anew the fact that she might see Justin again at any time and in a situation where she could establish control. He would ask for her favor and she might grant it. Perhaps.

She must think of practicalities tomorrow. For now she must try to rest and pray that she did not dream of a man with lion's eyes.

28

Pride's Coil

Tempest met Madame LaBorgue again over the noon meal the next day. They drank dark coffee and picked at the accumulation of soups and meats and fruits while maintaining a conversation generations apart. Esther sat at the old lady's side, sometimes helping spoon morsels into her mouth, and made encouraging sounds. Several other slaves circled about, watchful and correct.

"Feel perfectly free to shelter here as long as you like, my dear. It is awful, yes awful." The lids drooped several times and her cheeks drew in with the effort of memory. "Yes. Your husband and Justin are in the war, aren't they? We'll be all right against the British. Jackson'll see to that. Nothing to worry about. So uncivilized. War, I mean."

"I appreciate your kindness to me. This is my first visit to New Orleans and I know so little of the city." Tempest thought her hostess must be at least ninety and that was a charitable guess, for her mind and chatter moved across the years in a way impossible to follow and her sudden naps made continuity hopeless. Tempest could only respond to each remark casually and reiterate her thanks, for that always made Madame

LaBorgue smile as she embarked on another partially recollected memory.

Later, Tempest walked in the garden, which was carefully tended to give the appearance of disarray. She sat down under a palm tree and stared at the unopened volume of Chaucer in her lap. This house was an oasis in the desert; no one could want for more in the way of peace, fascinating old objects to look at, the well-stocked library, or the living history Madame La-Borgue represented. Tempest wanted this time apart, but she also wanted to begin the new and certainly hazardous life that awaited her. Resolutely, she fought back all memories of Justin and bent to the lively chatter of the Wife of Bath.

Three days inched by. Tempest had believed she craved peace, but the need for action hammered at her. She must have the ordering of her own life. Yet when the letter came and she opened it to read, the words danced in strange patterns before she could make out their sense. "*The Western Wind* leaves tomorrow for Boston and New York. She goes in the evening. All is arranged. You must not be late. This will keep you for a short time." It was unsigned and accompanied by a velvet purse with more money. The slave had extended both to her and rushed away, probably in accordance with his orders.

Tempest shredded the note and thrust the purse into her sleeve while she paced up and down. Why could Justin not have written something personal? A phrase or a comment? Even a good wish? He truly did wish to sever their connection as though it had never been.

She sought her hostess, who was tended, as always, by Esther as she sat in the dim parlor. Both were fanned by the two young slaves of the dining room. Hot air stirred Tempest's hair and she lifted both hands to right it as she said, "I am to go tomorrow."

Madame LaBorgue whispered, "Young ladies are so bold these days. That was not the way when the dear emperor ruled. As you wish. As you wish." Flecks of light pierced the drawn curtains and shone on her pink scalp under sparse hair. She raised palsied fingers to the starched lace of her cap and spoke in the arch voice of a young girl. "I flirted with the queen's lover. He liked me, too. He was so handsome." Her head tilted as Esther put a pillow under it and motioned Tempest away.

She went through the beaded curtains and stood in the hall,

mesmerized by what she had just experienced. The bands of history drawn together in that one old lady were astonishing. Marie Antoinette, queen of France; Napoleon, emperor of the French. Perhaps even Andrew Jackson, now President of the United States. It was likely she had known them all. What would Tempest Mallory know and remember if she lived to be so ancient? She was twenty. The driving years must be savored, ready for recall.

"I am ready." She murmured the words to herself, knowing them for total truth.

It was raining the next morning, blinding sheets from low dark clouds that obscured vision after a few yards. Madame LaBorgue was sleeping and Esther thought nothing of Tempest's desire to leave early, for her mind was full of her mistress. If she had been more alert, she might have considered it odd that the departing guest wore a sober brown outfit that had seen far better days and a cloak of the same vintage. Tempest had taken them from Sir Herbert's store of clothes, aware even then of what she intended to do. The rest of her baggage was thrust into two cases. Fortunately, they did not appear ostentatious. A close-fitting bonnet in a darker shade of brown hid her flaming hair.

When everything was ready, Esther came out. "The coachman will take you. God comfort you. I tell Madame you went and thanked her." Her face was masklike, unreadable. As she had often done, Tempest wondered what she knew and decided it did not matter. This house would not remember her.

The carriage was small and musty. Tempest felt it sway against the buffet of rain that was rapidly turning the streets to mire. Thunder hammered in the distance. She was grateful for the weather; it would hide much that she wished to accomplish.

The journey took hours. She knew it. Who would have thought they could have come so far? Back and forth in the drowning canyons, struggling through lakes of muck, feeling the dampness penetrating to every part of her body—all this went on for an eternity. When the horses finally stopped and the old coachman came to the carriage door, she could scarcely believe they had arrived.

He leaned in and said apologetically, "Missus, the wheel's 'bout off. Got to fix it and that'll take a while. You want I should see if there's some place around to wait? Some proper lady place?" The wind tore his hat off and sent it skimming. His gray hair was flattened by water, which poured down over his collar.

"I have to get to the ship! I'm afraid it will leave me! Get me another carriage! Go look for one!" Tempest gave her voice the type of hysteria she knew frightened many men. This was her chance given of the fates.

"Can't leave you here! No, sir. That's not right." He was prepared to be stubborn.

Tempest stared at the tightly shuttered houses along the road. There were no other people in sight. Lightning flared jaggedly across the sky, and she gave a shriek. "Go! I order it!" He gave a gasp and tottered away into the flood.

In good weather there might have been curiosity about a carriage tilting to the right, the stamping horses, and the black man who departed so reluctantly, but now not even the thieves of New Orleans ventured out. Tempest waited as best she might, thankful that a perfectly legitimate reason to get another conveyance had come up. It might have been dangerous to do from the wharf, but Tempest was confident of her ability for pretense. She meant to be an angry wife searching for her husband with whom she was to take ship tomorrow. The dowdy costume was a definite asset.

Soon a carriage struggled up and the driver, a bulky individual well covered with rain gear, bawled at Tempest's coachman to hurry. He did not offer help, but muttered under his breath as they transferred. She was now wet to the skin and her thin shoes squelched with mud. She put out her hand to her coachman and tried to smile. "Go on back. Thank you. I have to go." The thin edge of hysteria returned to her voice and she was glad to see him back nervously away.

"Yes'm. I understands. Yes'm." He took the coin she offered and turned back to his disabled carriage.

Tempest waited until her own carriage began a slow, steady progress in what she presumed to be the direction of the wharves. Then she tapped for the driver's attention and leaned out to speak to him. The bearded face with its red nose turned grudgingly in her direction and she caught the odor of wine.

"This weather is abominable! Take me to a boardinghouse immediately and make sure that it is respectable! My husband is arriving soon, and he is very demanding! Hurry up, my man, and do as I say." She forced power and authority into her voice, remembering as she did so that Aunt Hannah had often used that tone on people and that it often worked out of sheer surprise. Now he gaped at her so that trickles of rain ran into his mouth, and she had to stifle an impulse to giggle. Instinct told her that she had to be forceful. New Orleans, legendary city that it was, must be full of places to which young women were spirited away, never to be seen again. At this particular moment, Tempest did not think she would look as if she qualified for a possible inhabitant of the most minuscule bordello. "Well, are we to drown on this spot? Did you understand me?" Aunt Hannah's voice resounded sharply through Tempest's.

"I do. There's Mrs. Halvorsen's down on Chartres around Bienville, and then Mrs. Doran has a place down close to the convent. There are some others, but those . . ." He broke off and started to slap his pocket. The wind carried away his next words.

"Take me to Mrs. Halvorsen's. Immediately!" Tempest tensed her body and waited for argument, but there was none. Probably all he wanted to do was to get back to his shelter and the comforts of his bottle. Nonetheless, she kept a sharp eye out one of the tiny windows, not minding the chill and wet. She had examined some of the books in Madame LaBorgue's library and seen drawings of the city from early days. Chartres Street she recognized and knew it to be near the river. That, too, fitted in with her plans as she had formulated them, with many variations, during those past days with Justin. She knew she must be sensitive to the moment, make any opportunity she could, and be bold in the doing. As a power in her own right, she would have her ambition and possibly more chance to have Justin on an equal basis.

Tempest had dreaded attempting to find lodgings and offering explanations, for no respectable woman went about alone without risking reputation and virtue. She had decided on the absent but constantly expected husband, as well as letters written to her family in St. Louis that should bring them to New Orleans any day. Dowdy clothes and an abstracted air were to complete her role. She meant to look for work in any capacity of acting she could find—dresser, maid, general helper around the theaters, prompter, singer, or dancer. Her money would not last long, but she knew how to work, and surely New Orleans offered that. She remembered the various acting troupes that toured about and the one that had come to Savannah; probably there were some here, if so she must contact them all.

The matter of lodgings turned out to be more simple than she dared hope.

They rattled through dirt and stone streets at a rapid pace and stopped before a brick building. Her driver, mellowed by several coins and dips into the flask he must be carrying to judge from the smell of him, climbed down, hauled her bags inside and shouted for the landlady. An older man who might have been a relative came out to volunteer the information that Mrs. Halvorsen was out.

Tempest drew herself up and asked for a room, starting to go into her insistence on respectability and the demands of her husband, Mr. Williams, when he arrived. Her voice went high, and she was conscious of the fact that she dripped on the green rug on the sitting room, where lodgers were most customarily received.

The man eyed her up and down, evincing no interest, proof again that her disguise was good. "My niece can satisfy the most determined fault-finder with respect to her boarding-house, my dear woman. We have something available and you can discuss it with her on her return. Your husband will attend to the final matters, I assume?"

"Of course." Tempest allowed herself to shudder with chill, hoping she was playing the scene correctly.

A few minutes later she was standing in a long narrow room with pink walls, curtains, and dark carpet. The bed was high and looked comfortable; its cover was also pink. An armoire stood ready to receive her clothes, and the several chairs, the same shade as the carpet, looked comfortable. This was her first haven.

It continued to be so during the next several days. Tempest found Mrs. Halvorsen to be sternly practical and scatter-brained. She wanted her money and cared little about gossip; once she knew her latest guest was married, sober, possessed enough monies for immediate needs, and was interested in minding her own business, the landlady turned her attentions to those who were not. Tempest found that a request for a tray in her room was quickly granted, so she spared herself the scrutiny of others. When she went out in the day, she asked that one of the duller of the maids accompany her, and for a few coins, this was accomplished. Tempest thought her money well spent in these days of exploration. In the evenings she read the papers and periodicals, practiced various roles for her own amusement, and tried to decide when to begin her pursuit of ambition. The off-and-on-again rains coupled with spates of heat and cold hindered much actual getting about, but she knew that soon something must be set in motion.

Her brief acquaintance with the city made her want to know it better, for she was intrigued by the great river lined with ships, the many shops in buildings of French and Spanish construction filled with people of the same extraction, the open market where anything could be bought, lively cafés resounding with music and talk, iron-gated homes where a brilliance of flowers scented the air, and the great cathedral that loomed over the parade ground where President, then General, Jackson had once marshalled his troops. As the years went, New Orleans and Louisiana had not long been American and there was an intensity of feeling between Creoles and the newcomers. Tempest was drawn to the section to which she had come because it pulsated with life and vigor; temporarily she fit here, but she did not delude herself that it could continue for very long.

One cool rainy evening the maid, Molly, who went out with her often, brought the meal of roast chicken, macaroni, fresh cake, and white wine. When she placed it on the small table, she said, "The rain's quittin'. We'll be able to go round more. If you want to, of course." At Tempest's nod, she sighed. "Reckon your man'll be comin' long soon now the weather's better."

Tempest found herself liking the freckled little Irish girl more each day despite her obvious lack of common sense. Subterfuge was irksome, but she had her role to play. She thought hard about Justin and let her eyes fill.

"If no damage has come to his ship. I pray hourly for his safety." It would do no harm to let Molly return to the kitchens talking of the piety of the lady lodger.

"Yessum." Molly's eyes gazed a little in the beginnings of boredom. She put down a paper, one of those that circulated freely and was read by primarily by gentlemen. She often brought them to Tempest, knowing of her interest in what was going on in the city.

When she was gone, Tempest fingered the pages idly. Weather or not, she must soon go out and make the rounds of looking for employment in one capacity or another. The theatrical season in the great theaters did not start until very late in the year, but what hope could she have there in any event? The more she considered the matter, the more likely it seemed that her best possibilities lay in one of the family-owned cafés, where a good song and a bit of mime must always be welcome.

The name rose up from the inky page and slammed into her consciousness. "Mr. Justin Trevian, lately returned from abroad, adds his bounty and blessing to the charity benefit given at the Camp Street Theater on this Saturday night." Others followed in the long list, but Tempest sat staring at the page and felt the full cresting excitement in her.

29

Vision

"It will be something for every taste tonight. A very mixed program, one to whet the taste for the real drama to come." The wide-eyed young woman leaned close to her escort, who had just pronounced these words.

"Mr. Caldwell always has a good show." Her accent was piercing, and he drew back a little as he began to instruct her under his breath. Her gaze drifted, and she said, "Look at that gentleman, Edward. He's still wearing his hat. Some people . . ."

Tempest turned toward them very slowly. Her voice was level and hard. The faintest touch of French accent curved over the words. "Is something disturbing you, sir?" She let them see her stiffen as if affront had been taken. Others sitting and standing around them drew back slightly.

The young man kept his dignity, though his eyes flamed. Flat northern accents rang in his words. "Not at all, sir. I hope nothing has been misinterpreted . . ."

There was a stir far below as a gorgeously dressed lady and her equally resplendent escort swept to the front of their box. Tempest craned her neck with the rest, then settled back. He might not come; she doubted if she even wanted to see him.

What good would it do? She inwardly berated herself for being wildly foolish. Suppose that little exchange she had had led to a challenge for a duel? This far up in the public tier it was permissible, though perhaps odd, for a gentleman to come attired as he wished. The dark coat, gloves, and trousers, along with the muffling cloak and hat under which her flaming hair was piled, were proper enough. She had darkened her skin in a bit of color obtained on one of her explorations and the clothes had come from Sir Herbert's store of them. Once again she had cause to bless him. Creoles were touchy, she thought; let them think her one out for a night, viewing the doings at the American theater with condescension.

"Nothing has." She let the edge go out of her voice, pleased at the masculine sound of it. Her gaze swept over the theater again and she saw the young man relax while he whispered to the girl, who nodded and firmed her lips. Tempest relaxed. Possibly her bravado had been worth it. She shifted in her chair, noticing that those who had come close previously did not now do so.

When she looked out over the brilliant scene, Tempest felt an intensity of emotion that was almost sensual. The green curtain below seemed to hide a world of dreams. The ornate theater was a blaze of lights, crimson draperies, marble, a cut-glass chandelier, canopies of blue, golden paneling, and lavish gilding, and coloring of all types. The people varied from the richly dressed to the modest, according to which of the tiers they occupied. Tempest could see that the various boxes were ornamented with large mirror plates, which multiplied the audience over again. These in turn, were topped with blue material and huge eagles. The brilliance reflected appeared to be that of the rainbow.

Tempest squinted as hard as she could. Her sight was excellent, but it was impossible to recognize faces with all the shifting movement and light. It had been well worth the effort of muffling herself up, slipping down the side stairs, finding the random carriage, and coming out here in what she had already learned the French section called the "wilderness." She had come with many others into this rapidly growing American area and walked over the mud for a lengthy distance on plank walks made from old flatboats.

She heard a lady remark, "Charity for the homeless and

diseased is all very well, but that should be the province of the churches. I wouldn't have come except that everything has been so dull lately."

"Wait until the divine Jane begins the real season." Her companion, a portly man in his fifties, spoke so that the words carried.

"I say that is scandalous!" The lady gave a snort of disapproval.

Tempest heard the very real admiration in the man's voice and wondered what the enticing scandal might be. She had read enough to know that the Jane of whom they spoke was the foremost actress of this American theater on Camp Street.

"Look, it's starting!" Someone shifted behind her, and she drew closer to the edge of the tier so that she might see and still not block the view. Then the great green curtain lifted and she was catapulted into a different world.

There was a comic skit, a program of folk songs, several scenes from a work called *The Battle of New Orleans*, some rather lively American music, and a passionate version of Richard II as he abdicated his throne. Tempest thrilled to it all even as she wondered how she would feel playing *Medea* or some true tragedy in such a place. A young woman in elaborate makeup sang an aria from *Semiramide* and ended the first part of the presentations.

Tempest decided to move about, listen to comments, and keep an eye out for Justin. This venture must be worth the precious gold she had used! Who knew when a name dropped or a mention of a work in progress might be the door to an opportunity? She slipped out into one of the aisles, a young man intent on an assignation or a quick glass of wine before the rest of the evening began.

Throngs of people walked back and forth as they gesticulated and commented, saw and were seen. Tempest was pushed back against the wall several times before she gained the security of an outside area. The hot air of the theater was beginning to stifle her and she longed for some fresh air. She brushed her forehead with one gloved hand while she glanced in the direction of the side door. A familiar glimpse of tawny hair caught her gaze. She stood where she was, half in shadow, and watched Justin.

His suit was a shade of golden brown, the coat a shimmering

brocade that picked up the glints in his hair. Frills of lace tumbled over his hands, which shone with rings. His hawk face, dark brows, and elegant profile were the same. The broad shoulders graced the perfectly fitted clothes. The taut grace of his body showed to the same advantage as it had done on a veranda in Jamaica. Tempest felt her flesh go warm with longing.

Almost as if he felt her stare, he looked in her direction and his expression became grave. People swarmed in front of him, including a large woman in an improbable red-feathered gown. He spoke to her and then brought forward a girl who had been standing at his side. Tempest knew in an instant that this was his betrothed, the Creole girl Angelica. It could be no other. Her hair was raven black, her skin so pale that it shone, and her gown was white silk enhanced by white flowers. Diamonds gleamed on the hands she thrust out toward the lady. She carried long white gloves, which seemed to blend into the gown.

Her face fascinated Tempest. It held no expression at all, and the skin was so taut that her cheekbones stood out in high relief. Her mouth was palest pink and moved only a little when she spoke. She was well powdered to enhance the whiteness. When she drew back her hands, it was with a rush as she began to pull on the gloves. There was an air of strangeness about her that Tempest could not identify and it left her chilled.

An elderly lady in black and an older man were with them. Both watched the girl so sharply that Justin might have been on the periphery. A chaperon was expected; no lady could be seen without one if she was unwed, but this doting was odd.

Tempest felt the magnetic pull she had so often known with Justin and looked across the now clearing crowd to find him starting in her direction, a dark scowl on his features. How could he know her? It was impossible. Better to stand coolly and let him go by. Perhaps he had seen someone he knew.

He called, "One moment there! Could I speak . . ." His fists were clenched and he nearly collided with an aristocratic silk-hatted gentleman promenading with his lady. Exception was taken and he began to struggle with apologies.

Tempest wasted no time in moving back down the aisle as quickly as she could. She would look at the performance from some other vantage point, preferably as far from Justin as she could get. She had seen him, had branded his face again on her mind as he was forevermore branded on her body.

As she went down the nearest corridor, Tempest remembered what she had tried to remove from her perceptions earlier. Justin's look on his betrothed had been proprietary; it said that she was his, keep away. If there was no desire, neither was there arrogance. This was their world and they walked securely in it. For them, children, plantations, social life, the correct ordering of the future would be enough. Justin might think casually of his passion with Tempest, but what had that to do with real life?

"I've got to get out of here. I should never have come." She muttered the words through her teeth and quickened her pace. The corridor suddenly slanted downward and she went off balance. At the same time a door opened outward as a man charged out. He and Tempest collided and both went down. Her hat fell off from the force of the blow. The red braids cascaded over her shoulders to shine brilliantly in the cascade of light from the room her assailant had just quitted.

He was scrambling up now and dusting himself off as he extended one hand to pull her up. Tempest made no attempt to play-act as she had done earlier with the young man and his lady; she only wanted to get out of this situation. The man was surveying her leisurely from under bushy dark brows set in a lean face scored with lines. He was in his middle years, tall and rather spare, with a thin mouth. His appearance was rather forbidding and his grip on her arm tightened when she tried to pull away.

"I am sorry for this mishap, sir. I was looking for the door outside and became lost." She spoke in her normal voice. Let him think what he wished.

He took three steps and pulled her unwillingly into the light, observing the formation of her face, the now visible curve of her body under the loosened coat, and her tumbling hair. "Interesting." The tone was academic, his eyes assessing. "Do you often come to the theater dressed this way?"

Tempest heard footsteps in the distance, someone called out, and then music sounded. The performance had begun once more. "It was a dare. My sister said I wouldn't try this." She tried to pull free and found it impossible.

"Do you live in the city?" His brows were drawn together now.

She snapped, "That hardly matters. Let me go immediately. Immediately, do you hear?" Her arm tensed as she jerked it to the side and down in a sharp motion that freed her.

He folded his arms and grinned at her, a motion that transformed his face from severity into liveliness. "My dear, you do not have the sound of New Orleans and I know all of them. No gently brought up lady would come here as you have and certainly one couldn't get away as you just did or have the muscles in that arm. Moreover, you were running away. I find a mystery intriguing. If you are a thief, you'll find little enough here. Go up and try the rich patrons. I may not even give you away."

Tempest moved and he moved with her to cut off any attempt to get by. "This is not a thing that is easy to understand . . ." She sighed as if attempting to find words. Try helpless female in trouble; maybe that would help.

He shrugged impatiently. "I have to go. Some of these people may be good at what they do. I may want to hire them again. This has been amusing. Get your hat and I'll escort a young gentleman of my acquaintance to the door and put him in a carriage. Things get rowdy after performances, and this one will go late."

Tempest caught her breath in shock. "May I ask your name, sir?" Her tone was free of pretense for the first time.

"James Caldwell, manager of this theater." He spoke flatly, his mind already far from her. "Come on, I have to hurry."

Instinct came to Tempest's rescue. She wanted to blurt out her hopes and expectations, ask his pardon, his help, push her intrigue further. This one man could put her on his stage, give her opportunity beyond even her own early imaginings. Blind fate, coincidence, the will of the sardonic gods, her rashness— all had delivered her to this moment. A moment thrown away because he was already walking away, his interest centered firmly on what was happening onstage.

"I'm coming." Meekly, she followed, cramming her hat over the braids and setting her coat to rights. This was the stuff of fairy tales. By now she should be recognized for her talents and he ready to give her a starring role. But was it ever so in real life?

They went out into a wider aisle, around a corner, passed through the elegant vestibule, and approached a side door, where a young boy of perhaps twelve stood. Caldwell gestured and he came up.

"Get a carriage for this gentleman. Hurry." There was the faintest emphasis on *gentleman*. When he scurried away, Caldwell cocked his head, forgetting Tempest as the rich, fruity tones of a dramatic recitation on love emerged from the far interior of the theater. "I must have several words with that lady! Well, get on with you, whoever you are. Count yourself fortunate that I haven't called the gendarmes to you."

The boy appeared and beckoned. Tempest knew she had only an instant or two and that must count. Who knew what impressed such a man? In the end there was only herself and it had always been so. Caldwell was frowning, lips pursed and eyes going sharp.

"I suppose you can't afford the carriage? You can just thank God I'm a charitable man." He started to fumble in his pockets, but there was no mistaking the growing anger in him.

Tempest drew herself up, willing all the latent power she possessed into the words. Her voice came out round and full, underlining the declamatory phrases that still came out to their ears. The boy was holding the door open and the fresh air rushed in, bearing a strong odor of churned mud.

"Sir, I have reason to appreciate your kindness to me this night. Your patrons are safe from my ravages. My talents do not extend to those of a pickpocket. I, too, can be charitable!" She reached into her pocket and drew out the gold piece. Then she flipped it so that it flashed through the air and fell at Caldwell's feet. "In time to come, I would have you remember the name of Tempest Miranda Mallory, once of Savannah and Jamaica, now of New Orleans! Good night, Mr. Caldwell!"

It took all the will power she had to turn her back and march stiffly out the door. She was conscious of the glare of lamps from the theater and the various buildings close by, the waiting driver and gaping boy, of the man behind her and the closing sounds of the orotund phrases from the stage. Clearest of all the impressions was the rising laughter of James Caldwell behind her.

As she climbed into the carriage and gave the address of a café fairly close to Mrs. Halvorsen's boardinghouse, Tempest wondered what she would have said had the performance she imitated been other than it was. Martial music and opera were beyond her scope, but she could twist a dramatic phrase. The day would come when she claimed the gold piece and the memory it evoked. Now it was time to be herself, to have done with disguises, to be Tempest Miranda Mallory.

Justin's face rose in memory as she had seen him this night. Now she spoke to him as he had often done to her. "Check-mate!"

30

The Rose and the Briar

Tempest rubbed a concoction of rosewater and glycerin into her hands as she bent forward to examine her face in the streaked mirror. Her gray eyes were highlighted with dark liner, but her cheeks needed nothing to make them flush. Excitement did that. One braid of flaming hair was coiled in a crown over her head and the rest was in a chignon at her neck. Her white gown was a froth of ruffles from collarbone to toes. Imitation pearls gleamed on her fingers and in her ears. Her lips shone red and inviting. Once again she was ready.

When she stepped out into the flickering lights, there was an audible hush. Into it, a slow voice said, "La Entorcha." The liquid notes of a guitar rang out, trilled, and faded. Tempest stood very still, arms at her sides, chin lifted, eyes fixed on a far horizon. Her voice was not powerful, but at a certain range it was true and clear. The Spanish words came from her heart as they drifted into English.

"He is my torch, my light, my beacon. For him I came. I followed him to a strange shore. I sought him in the rain and in the wind. He is everywhere and nowhere. Who shall name love? Who shall call him? He is the chimera, the unknowable." So the poet had sung in eighth-century Spain; so did lovers sing today. Tempest held the last note to one of poignancy and spread her arms. There was no sound from her audience.

Her words rang out huskily. "And this is the dance of that chimera." The guitar pace quickened as she began to move in a stately measure first, then whirled faster, slowed and sped again—seeker and finder—until the wrath of the implacable gods halted and she sank to the floor, where, face down and flat, she began her song again. It rose to a crescendo of triumph when she came erect and ended where begun. "My torch, my light, my beacon."

Now the lamps were lit, swung high, and the applause poured over her. She did not bow or smile her thanks, simply inclined her head now and then waiting for it to subside. The calls were stronger than ever tonight. "La Entorcha!" "La Entorcha." "More, more!" She looked out over the bobbing heads and kept the enigmatic smile on her lips, but behind it her mind rang with delight. *I'm on my way!* Luck and a persuasive tongue had helped.

The Café Escorial was deep on Rampart Street, not far from Toulouse. It was a family enterprise and had a counterpart in Madrid, Señora Segures had told Tempest on that day six weeks ago when she had come looking for work "of a respectable nature." Washing dishes, sweeping floors, and help with the mending had been part of her duties. Serving coffee and wine as well as native Spanish dishes were the others. Exiles, homesick Spaniards, people living in the neighborhood, and the occasional wanderer from the livelier areas of the French section came here to drink and relax in the dark calm. Now and then someone would strum a guitar and everyone would enjoy the melancholy produced. Tempest had explained that she was a runaway from the Carolinas, avoiding an unpleasant marriage and determined to make her own way as best she could. Other cities might have ostracized such a person, but New Orleans, on this level at least, was not one of them. Tempest had sung a song now and then, been encouraged as trade picked up, and gradually became more forceful until La Entorcha was born. Old and young came to the Escorial, men and women mingled here and even brought their children. Tempest knew she had been fortunate to find such a place. How she had hated the dishwashing! Now she was beyond that and thankful.

She had never been more glad she knew a smattering of French, Spanish, and Italian and could give meaning to the phrases she sang. Now an old man called for "La Marseillaise"; she beckoned them all to sing and let her voice be the underpinning. Another French ballad followed. The patrons quenched their thirst eagerly. Tempest saw her employers grinning in the background and smiled in return. They were good for each other.

"Sing an American song! We're all Americans, after all!" The big man was ready to be belligerent for any imagined insult. The younger man with him whispered in his ear and both sank down in their seats.

Tempest dropped her hands again and spoke in the intimate tone she used to make them strain to hear. "We can hardly get more American than General Jackson, can we? I am told that after the battle of New Orleans many a young lady sang this song at receptions given in his honor. Legend, perhaps, but it is one of his favorites." Patriotism fired them up and cooled them down, she thought. Do an English song for an American sentiment.

"In Scarlet Town where I was born . . ." The age old words of lost love mourned on the air and resounded down to "and the rose grew round the briar." Tempest lifted her hands and let them fall with the last note. When she looked at the audience to give her customary faint smile—the accepting and discouraging one—she saw a tall, broad-shouldered figure leaning against the far wall.

The rose and the briar were met once more.

She could feel those golden, enigmatic eyes on her even through the dimming lamplight and swirls of smoke as she did her last song of the evening, "Wagons Go On," a mournful ballad of love and death in the western explorations. La Entorcha might appear once more if the whim struck her, but it was unlikely, as all the patrons of the Escorial knew; still, they stayed on the hope and continued to eat, talk, and drink.

Tempest was surprised that Justin had appeared. She had not expected that he would come to such a place as this; few fashionable gentlemen did. She might have seen him on a promenade at the levee, where many New Orleanians went to stroll on Sunday afternoons, or riding on Canal Street with his betrothed, but never here. Once more the blood sang in her veins and she felt fully alive with its power.

Now she ended and backed away toward the corridor leading to her tiny dressing room, once a rather large closet. The audience, knowing not to approach or ask after her—untouchability was part of the fascination she had deliberately fostered—turned back to the usual pursuits. Justin strode across the room, pushed several people out of the way, and came to face her. One of the sons of the house, a powerful man in his late thirties, came out, followed by his wife. Several other regulars rose and ambled closer.

Tempest saw only Justin. His tawny hair tumbled over his forehead and collar. The firm chin was set and she could feel the anger burning in him. He wore a white shirt with billowing sleeves and dark tight breeches thrust into high boots. His face was thinner, tauter. The dark brows were drawn together in a straight, hard line.

"La Entorcha, is it? And how much do you charge for a night, my little flame?" The harsh, evenly spaced words seemed to slam across the suddenly quiet room. He spread his legs and gave an unpleasant grin as he waited for her answer.

Her head went back in a swift motion. "You will not speak to me that way."

"I'll speak to you any damn way I please, madam!" He swayed back and forth, one corner of his mouth going up in a savage expression.

"You're drunk! Get away from me!" She started around him, but he jerked her back so that she nearly lost her balance.

Martin Segures said amiably, "The lady does not want to speak to you, sir. I advise you to leave. Now." His father, nearly as large as his son for all that he was in his late sixties, snapped out something in the Castilian Spanish of his youth and clenched his fists.

Justin's face did not change as he surveyed them. "Quite right. I've had a bit of the brandy. Guess I'll find a better place for a man to quench his thirst." He turned his back on them all and walked rapidly away. The outer door closed with an emphatic bang.

Martin Segures said, "That's all the excitement. Just one man with too much to drink." To Tempest he added, "Stay and rest for a while, then I'll have two of the servants take you home. I don't think you'll be bothered again." His dark eyes showed puzzlement, but he would never question her.

Tempest drew all her dignity up, gave a gracious smile and followed Elena, his wife, into the communal rooms, where she took a welcome glass of wine. In the chatter that went on Tempest tried to wonder what Justin's coming meant. There was no need for secrecy now. Was he wed and bored with his wife? Did he think to dally with her in the off moments? She thought of their passion and her flesh shivered with pleasure. Naturally he was angry at being deceived, but why had he found her if this were a barrier? He had insulted her in front of them all. Could drink excuse that? Then she thought of those fierce eyes and had her answer. He had done it for a reason. He had not been drunk.

Home was still Mrs. Halvorsen's boarding house. She had a singular lack of curiosity about Tempest, who paid the bill promptly and was circumspect in her late nights despite the fact she had confided that she had work at that hour. Several hours later Tempest went with the two older men Segures designated. They spoke only Spanish and hers was sketchy, but one sat on either side in the carriage as it rattled through the streets. Normally she came with the driver alone, but this night was different.

When it happened, Tempest was not in the least surprised. She had known confrontation must come again. The reins of the carriage horse were caught and the driver was curtly commanded to come down. Then the doors were wrenched open and Tempest's guardians ordered out by three ruffians, who stood with drawn pistols. The street was empty of any life; she saw that the very lateness of the hour militated against them. No one could argue with guns. She shook her head to forestall any dramatic gestures and spoke to her captors.

"What do you want? We carry no money."

"They speak no English. They are my men from the swamps and answer only to me. Come, La Entorcha. We have business to finish." Justin stepped from a sheltering doorway, his manner as calm as though they had parted only minutes ago in the best of moods. Only his eyes were savage. One hand rested on the pistol at his belt. "They will hurt Segures's men if I give the word. And I promise I will unless you put your hand on my

arm as you might a friend's, a very good friend's whom you
have not seen in a long time, and walk willingly away with me.
The choice, La Entorcha, is yours." The words were mocking,
but they were said caressingly so that the others must naturally
be fooled.

Tempest said, "What do you want, Justin? Why are you
doing this? I will meet you tomorrow if you like and we can
talk. You know they will go back to the Escorial and gossip if
you go on this way."

He grinned as he drew the pistol and aimed it at the men. "I
know. I planned well, don't you think? What's it to be?" He
took a step toward her. "Quite the liar, aren't you? Act it out."

She smiled through her teeth at him but obeyed; at this point
there was no choice. He caught her hand with his free one, held
her in a strong grip, and aimed a kiss at the side of her face.
Then he spoke to his men in a strange tangle of words she
could not understand. They laughed and responded.

"Come on." Justin jerked her arm, so she had no choice but
to follow him around the corner. "You're coming with me one
way or another if I have to carry you or summon help with my
erring wife who refuses to obey. I don't really care if you do
fight me. Tempest. La Entorcha. Whatever you choose to call
yourself." This time his voice was filled with bitterness
bordering on violence.

"I will come." Tempest wanted nothing more at this
moment in time than to be free and safe at the Café Escorial.
She doubted she would be welcome there again—their code
was rigid and unyielding. She had willingly gone with her
would-be savager. Spanish honor did not defend such. And yet
this side of Justin that she had never seen excited her greatly.

He did not release her but began to walk, forcing her to keep
his pace. "Wise of you." The words were grated out with no
lessening of tension.

They met few people; at this hour people were either drunk
or intent on their own business and Justin did not appear the
sort of man with whom one would meddle. Tempest was
surprised that his very forcefulness made her throb with new
life. She told herself she ought to be outraged at his behavior.
Was she not an independent woman, after all?

Justin went down a long alley, his hand ready on the pistol,
around several more curves, and up a narrow street, where he

paused before an iron gate, inserted a key, and drew Tempest into a dark garden. It was only then that she was released. He started up a staircase a few feet away but turned to her.

"Come, La Entorcha. We shall drink together." His voice had an undercurrent of savagery to it that vied with the bitterness of earlier.

Tempest hesitated, and then the action was not left to her. He came over, swung her up in his arms, his hands biting cruelly into her skin. "I gave you a command. You will obey me until I personally take you to the ship, the first one leaving, and put you on it."

She met his eyes. "I chose to pursue my own life here. You renounced any part in it. Remember? You told me farewell. You are not the master of the way I live. And stop calling me La Entorcha! I am Tempest!" She was suddenly shaking with fury.

He clasped her all the tighter in spite of her struggles. At the top of the stairs he aimed a kick at the door, which swung inward to reveal a spacious room dimly lit with lamps. Tempest had an impression of old dark furniture, gauzy curtains, and high ceilings before he tossed her down on a settee and leaned over her menacingly.

"Justin, you are acting foolishly! Are you trying to be a villain and terrify me? Explain yourself." She had seen him tender, passionate, and arrogant, but this was new. His inner anger seemed channeled toward her; she did not think him capable of hurting her and still her arms throbbed where he had held them. Tomorrow there would be bruises.

"I despise a liar! Cassandra was a consummate one! I thought you different, but you are alike. Lying tongues, hungry and bewitching bodies, a total lack of morals! I saw you at the theater that night. Your disguise didn't fool me at all. Later I heard that you made up to Caldwell; intrigued him, they said. With your eager little body, I imagine." Justin taunted her with words, then caught the neck of her gown and ripped it a little at a time, watching her face as he did so. "Do you begin to be just a slight bit afraid? You should." The golden eyes shone as they stared into hers; they were those of a jungle cat.

Tempest tried to sit up, but he pushed her back. When she slapped at his hands, he returned the blow with a restrained strength that made her realize his determination. She tried reason. "I am a free woman. There's no need to justify anything to you, but I have been discreet. Until tonight no one could have connected us. And what if they do? Who will be hurt? I intend to be an actress; this is one of the best cities to pursue it and I saw no reason to leave. You'll just have to accept that." She saw he was paying no attention to her words for all that his gaze did not leave her face. He continued to rip slowly at her gown, the deliberate action all the more infuriating. The indignity of it was too much. "Get back to your Creole lady with the wealth you ache for and let me alone. Damn you, damn you!" She kicked out at him and was instantly spread-eagled as he gripped her arms.

"We're to be married in November and she's gone to visit her aunt in the river country. Her father approached me and suggested that I had a few loose ends to take care of. A certain red-haired woman at Mrs. Halvorsen's was one of them. So you see, my dear, you're very inconvenient except for one thing."

Justin drawled out the words, his crooked smile matching their cruelty, and then lowered his mouth to Tempest's.

31

Storm Center

Tempest fought the plundering of her body, but it was no use. He stripped her naked, holding her hands so that she could not strike him, savaging her mouth with his so that she had to give way before the onslaught of his tongue, hammering deep into her moist warmth and demanding an answer that her traitor flesh gave all too readily. She thought of the tenderness and cherishing he had once shown and of her own glad response. Now passion came of bitterness and pain; she wanted to turn away from the mocking eyes that recorded her every move, but could not. He knew too well the touches that brought her to life. When she arched toward him he gave a satisfied laugh and they twined together in the hunger that always lay between them.

This was not the lovemaking of shared emotion; this was simply body to body that was fed with anger and stirred with force. Tempest found that her hands became as demanding as his, her mouth as bold. They strained in mutual battle, each attempting supremacy for subjection of the other. She saw that his eyes had gone flat, the pupils like pinpoints, and wondered if her own face reflected his. They turned to their sides and were opponents attempting to stir yet deeper sensations.

Justin set his mouth to her aching nipple, drawing hard there as he let his tongue move around the tender tip. His hands held her hips firmly while he rocked her toward him. She put her own to his manhood and felt the surge of power there. When she tried to stop the swelling eagerness, could not, and moaned aloud, Justin took his lips away and looked up at her.

"I see you like this. How many others have you used these talents on here in this city? How many of those at the café have you permitted to sample these delights? What about Caldwell? Did you distract him from his wife and his lover for the sake of your art? I believe it is an art?" The sarcastic, painful words were meant to devastate her completely.

Tempest could play this cruel game as well as he. "Why are you so concerned? You know you were the first. I have learned well, have I not? Is your betrothed appreciative of your talents?" She wanted to slap him, hurt him, cry in his arms for the pain they inflicted on themselves, they who had once loved so tenderly. How had they come to this? Yet she could not, did not, want to leave. She wanted him over and over; desire was not sated. She wanted to feel him hard and deep inside her, in her mouth and on her body. Her hands throbbed to the feel of his smoothness, the suppleness of his muscular body. Her skin tingled with the flames that were never quite put out.

"She is no part of this. Leave her out of it." He growled the words as he put both hands on her breasts and lifted their fullness.

"Then leave your thoughts of any lovers I may have taken. You said I was inconvenient except for one thing. Has it crossed your mind that I might say the same of you?" She tilted her head and allowed a slight smile to curve her lips.

Justin raised one hand as if to slap her silent. His eyes went opaque. "You're showing your true self, my dear." He caught her hair close to the scalp and pulled her toward him so that their faces were close together. "There's a bit of the harlot in you, isn't there?"

She laughed outright. "Because I enjoy what you have taught me?" She put her arms out and stretched so that the curves of her breasts showed to advantage. "Let me instruct you. We're talking too much." Her fingers drifted down and she began to massage his shaft delicately. If their bodies were the only way they could truly meet, then let it be so. She could not endure this flaying with words, although she held her own with him.

"Shameless!" Justin could not hide his reaction to her massaging fingers and their touch. Little goose prickles stood out on his arms. His hold on her hair eased as he sank his teeth into his lips.

Tempest felt her own pulse quicken. She longed to sink down with him into the sweet, wild delights of the flesh, but she was determined he was not going to treat her as if she were conquered territory, a woman of his whims, a thing to be used casually and discarded. Inconvenient, was she? Let him see his need plainly.

"Is pleasure shameless?" She shook free from his hand and lowered her mouth to his shaft, allowing her tongue to take up where her fingers stopped. Up and down, up and down; she drew each motion out as long as she could, taking pleasure in his hardness. She was wet with her own longing; she was one vast emptiness to be filled with this one man of her choice. "Shall I stop?" Tempest raised her head, the red hair falling about her face and spilling into his lap. Her skin shone honey-gold in the dim light. She knew she was fair to see. Why must she and Justin rend themselves apart? For what reason?

He was staring at her with a faraway look that made her know he saw both Tempest Mallory and the entrancing Cassandra. She thought now he hated and loved them both. No wonder he wanted the icy-seeming Angelica, who must bring peace and her fortune. He could spend himself in a cause and be content. For the first time Tempest began to believe Justin's statement that he was incapable of love. Shameless, he called her; possibly so, but she wanted him, love or not.

He, too, was golden in the light. The muscles of his superb body flowed into one another under the taut skin. His face might have been from a medieval painting or from a statue by the beauty-loving Greeks. His hair curled low on his nape and now he brushed it impatiently back from his forehead.

"What are you staring at?"

Caught off guard, Tempest could only say the truth. "How very beautiful you are."

Justin reached over and pulled her roughly to him, clamping her so she felt every inch of his body. Again his hands were in her hair so she could not move her head and his mouth took hers in a swift preliminary kiss that once again battered at her. Tempest went limp under the force. He relaxed slightly and thrust his knee up to part her legs. She twisted aside in one rapid motion and came astride him. Her hands were now on his shoulders, pushing him back as she fitted herself on to the great impaling length of him. She could nearly feel her female power absorbing him. When she leaned back she knew the involuntary sweetness of his counterthrust.

Justin's hands encircled her wrists and his loins rose with her as she rode him, man-woman in one fierce flesh, to seek the peaks that could not be found alone. They had dallied too long; the point had been too finely drawn. Tempest rose above him, allowing the tip of him to barely graze her. His body followed hers in a will of its own. She felt the convulsion begin and came down on him in that instant. He was deep inside her and she gloried in the delicious invasion. All conscious thought left her as the maelstrom overcame them. She heard Justin cry out her name, knew his fingernails dug into her back, and then they were swept out beyond the limits of return, into a primordial wilderness that outdistanced the mind.

Tempest thought later that this particular time with Justin when they were adversaries was, as it had been on the *Porfina* , a separate entity that bore little resemblance to reality. Outside the walls of this house in the French section of New Orleans ordinary life went on, but inside, she and Justin fought a duel of the flesh neither could win. They slept, woke to their hungers, satisfied them, and relaxed in near total exhaustion. Tempest had no concept of light or dark; there were only his mouth, his arms, and the shattering power of his manhood. If this were one-tenth the drugging passion he had shared with Cassandra, she did not wonder at the hold it had on him. She was forever marked by her affair with Justin Trevian.

He brought her wine in a plain earthen mug once and stood close, so close that the tips of her breasts touched his bare chest. She reached for it but he tipped the edge so that a trickle ran between them. He set his mouth to follow. The feathery contact went to the center of her ribcage, down her flat stomach, and approached the triangle of her womanhood, paused, lingered, and started up again. She leaned toward him and he pulled her down. Their lips met as they tested each other. The big bed sank beneath the weight.

"My turn now." She ran her fingers along his sides and caressed the hard buttocks, delighting in the responsiveness as they tightened. He shifted as if to avoid her touch, but she kissed him twice there and he tried to pull her around.

"I'm very thirsty. Would you bring us some wine, Tempest?" He had ceased to use La Entorcha in that deriding way. Now he stretched, his body long and lithe against the white sheets of the bed they had finally decided to use.

"Of course." She rose and made her way to a small table, where there were several bottles of wine. As always with Justin, any serious talk waited until they had spent the other emotions. It seemed natural to Tempest as she considered it. Was this the way with other lovers and adversaries?

His hands slipped over her breasts and began to rub her nipples, which were already slightly sore. She felt his shaft hard against her, started to straighten, and was prevented as he pushed at her back. He kissed her neck so that the little chills began to rush up and down. She relaxed and he entered, stroking swiftly so that the excitement began once more, bringing them both to the edge of the abyss.

Hours or years later, Tempest rose from the depths of sleep to crunching sounds that resembled someone chipping at a wall or breaking bones. She reached out to silence whatever it was and encountered warm flesh. When she sat up with a start of shock, she saw Justin sitting cross-legged at the end of the bed munching on a loaf of what appeared to be very hard bread. It was lavishly buttered, and a cup of steaming coffee rested on a stool close to hand. He was nude, but his face was freshly washed and his hair stood up in tendrils around his forehead.

"Let's go for a dip. I thought you'd sleep forever." His eyes were warm and clear; he might be the Justin of those tender times on the *Porfina*. "Aren't you hungry? I'm starving. How about an apple?" He produced a small red one and waved it triumphantly. "I've already had one, but I saved the best for you."

Tempest could not help it. She sat up and began to laugh. The soreness between her legs and the tenderness of her breasts reminded her anew of those fevered times of passion. He arched a quizzical eyebrow as he extended the cup of life-saving brew Tempest suddenly knew she could not live without.

" 'Comfort me with apples for I am sick of love?' " She took a deep gulp and then another. No nectar of the gods could ever equal this coffee of New Orleans!

"King Solomon had many ladies with whom to sport. And, of course, he didn't know Tempest Mallory, who enchants with a look." Justin grinned as a young boy might and bit deeply into his apple. "Eat. I'll be back in a minute." He set the food close to her and padded out, unselfconscious before her gaze.

Tempest rapidly found she was ravenous. The bread was surprisingly tasty, as was the apple. She decided to go in search of more coffee and looked about for something to wear. There was nothing in sight, so she pulled the sheet from the bed and wrapped it around her body. The idea of a bath sounded wonderful; it would probably be cold, but she was in need of refreshment. Then she and Justin must talk.

The door swung inward. "You don't need that. Come on." Justin plucked the sheet away and took her hand. "This is very private and we're the only ones here. There's an old slave who tidies up and leaves food out, but she came hours ago."

"What is this place, Justin?" Tempest could not resist the question, although she thought she knew the answer. Gentlemen were noted to have private places where they kept mistresses. Why should Justin be any different? What would she say if he asked her to be his in fact?

"Later, love, later." He grinned and pulled at her hand again. "Come on, I said. This is the best part of the day."

They went through the parlor and into the first light of a new day, although Tempest did not know which one it was. Time had turned back on itself in the long heat of their lovemaking. She felt purged and weary yet content to take the moment for what it was.

Justin led her down the staircase into a paved courtyard, which had high blank walls on all sides, and along a tiny aisle into a protected garden, which was drenched in exotic flowers and bushes of all types. The colors merged in an aureole of brilliance tempered with the softness of old gray walls and the splash of a fountain sheltered behind some delicate willow trees. She caught the scents of orange and lemon along with the headiness of late honeysuckle. It was very warm here and would possibly be so even in the chill of winter.

"It's beautiful." She breathed the words out, thinking the vision might fade if she spoke louder.

"And there's more coffee. I heated it for us and put it on the stone yonder." Justin headed for the fountain, beckoning her to come. He might have been a satyr from the very dawn of time as he stood there with the early light slipping over his long, lean body, white teeth flashing as he smiled at her pleasure.

Tempest looked down at her own nudity, partially covered by her flowing hair. Her nipples thrust outward through it and she saw the purpling mark on one, Justin's seal upon her. She began to follow him and stopped in surprise to stare at several statues nestled in the shrubs close by. Now that she was more fully into the garden, she saw that they were everywhere. When she peered more closely, the blood ran into her face and suffused it.

The statuary was composed of men in various stages of erection, their organs very large and high, women in strange positions of invitation, couplings of many types and variations, even animals. All were beautifully done, but faces were vague; only the sexual organs were explicit and highlighted.

Tempest did not want to appear shocked before Justin, who was clearly waiting for some reaction. "Grecian, I suppose?" She waved casually at the display, watching him out of the corner of one eye. His face did not change, though the long lashes rested on his cheeks to hide the expression in the golden eyes.

"Not totally." He walked ahead to part the willow fronds before the fountain and entered the bower with her.

Here water gushed out from another statue into a pink, marble-seeming declivity, where flowers, masses of white, floated. Just beyond the willow trees a curtain of morning glories in shimmering white, blue, and red hung. The breeze carried the scent of honeysuckle again. But this statue held her fascinated also. The face was vague, but she could make out details such as strong brows over a jutting nose, a forceful chin, and powerful shoulders. But the dominating factor was the huge phallus through which the water came. The stone eyes contemplated it with what could only be an expression of relish, and the mouth turned up. Every detail of the organ was perfect. It was done in pink marble, which was in contrast to the rough stone of the remainder of the figure.

Tempest giggled. This was too much; she exploded with laughter. "Priapus!" She pointed a shaking finger. "Priapus!"

Justin joined her in uncontrollable amusement. When it subsided for an instant, he said, "Not that Greek god, my dear, but my most honorable father-in-law to be, Aristide Louis de Foix, owner of this most estimable hideaway."

32

Choose You This Day

Justin must have known his words struck Tempest as a hammer blow, but he climbed, still laughing, into the pool and submerged his body. She came to the edge, reached over, and caught his chin, ignoring the jet of water he sent in her direction.

"Are you quite mad? What sort of game are you playing with me?"

"Tell you later. Come in." He wrenched free of her grip and pulled her forward all in one quick motion.

Tempest and Justin went over in water that was barely to their knees. They came under the spout of Priapus/de Foix, gurgled, and rose as their mock struggle began. Tempest stood under his flood, which sent her hair streaming over her honey skin. Justin dashed droplets at her and she returned them. Then he chased her among the floating pads. She lunged at his legs, caught him off balance, and he fell with a thump under Priapus. He twisted around, ducked her, and they came up together, arms entwined. The thunder began in Tempest's blood. She kissed his mouth, pushing with her tongue until it opened to take her for what might have been the first time.

They stood in the dappling early sunlight and caressed each

253

other with gentle hands. Justin touched her breasts softly, pressed feather kisses on them, trailed others up the sides of her neck and came again to her mouth, which he cherished with his. She melted into his warmth, glorying in the strong power of his body and the response it gave to hers. She wanted to surround him, to drink of the delights of their union and know the transporting joy once again. Who could tell when, if ever, it might come again?

In a few minutes they moved to a patch of soft grass near the morning glories and sank down. He cupped the back of her head as he tilted her face upward to kiss her still more tenderly. Tempest held him in her arms, love's captive, passion's giver, and they entered once more into that peculiarly special heaven that was theirs alone. He kissed her again and pulled her close so that their bodies might still have been joined. She put her hand on his broad chest, feeling again the hammering of his heart after pleasure.

A bird called from somewhere in the garden and the flowers drifted before the breeze. There was utter peace in this place of sensual delight and Tempest hated to break it, but she knew she must. They could not forever wrap themselves in passion and ignore the barriers to it. She raised up on one elbow and studied the chiseled face below her. She thought she understood much of what had just happened, but it must be clear in her mind.

"Why were you so angry with me for staying in New Orleans?"

Justin sighed as he opened his eyes and sat up. "Tempest, what if you had backing, money, a fine wardrobe, some credentials, all that sort of thing, and went to Charleston, Mobile, one of the southern cities, and established yourself there first? Sooner or later all actresses of any repute come to New Orleans, called here by the managers of the theaters. It might even be better for your chances in the future. Why don't you think about it?" He looked warily at her while he spoke.

She felt the familiar sinking in the pit of her stomach. Nothing had really changed between them. All they had in common was the glorious passion they shared, and probably, she was being foolish to expect anything else. Had she really thought she might win him away from the course he had mapped out for his life and into love for herself?

"And if I thought about it? What then?" She allowed her voice to sound soft and agreeable. The nails of both hands were clenched in her palms.

"I would travel to see you; we could meet in other cities. I have much business, as you are aware from our times in Jamaica. There would be few difficulties and in time to come you might be a great name in your own right."

Tempest said, "Let me tell you what you think to explain to me." The golden eyes met hers and did not falter. "You are to wed next month. The father of your betrothed is very rich, very powerful, and he knows of your little indiscretion with—how did you put it?—an inconvenient red-haired woman. Did he suggest this episode, the use of this place, to you, so that your interest might wane before the marriage to a woman you love for her money? Is he wise to take you for a son-in-law, this obvious man of the world?" She gestured toward Priapus, and what had seemed funny a short time ago now was ugly.

Justin's face went white, a literal bleaching of the skin under his tan. His eyes were flat and dangerous while his fingers twisted as though he longed to use a sword or a pistol. Tempest thought once more of the lion in the veldt as he waited for his prey.

"It's your story; you tell it." The words were rapped out harshly. One exchange, and they were enemies again.

She lifted her head so that the fast drying hair swirled back over her shoulders. Here she lay, nude in an exotic garden, with the lover of her heart and they battled over the realities of the world! A wise woman would take what was offered and use it. Her mind told her this, but her romantic, idealistic core never intended to accept. It would take so little for him to love her. Perhaps he did already. She meant to fight for her future and the one man who stirred her blood and spirit.

"You pursue your life; I'll pursue mine. Our paths need not cross at all and you can be a zealous, faithful husband. I thought you said Creole women knew their places. Surely the interest of your father-in-law does not deter you from handling your marriage in the way you always intended. I was doing well. Did I ask you to take me from the carriage?" Tempest thought she had tamped the fury down in her pleasure with their loving, but now it rose higher than ever. "Your kept mistress I will not be! I took some of your money, true, but it shall be repaid and with interest! I do not regret the lovemaking we shared, but that was of the body only! Our minds and hearts have never met and never will! My life is my own and remains so. Do you understand me?" She had half risen to her knees with the force of her anger and her voice had gone hard. For the first time she wished she had clothes on.

Justin rose and pulled her to her feet. The cords in his neck stood out. A pulse hammered in his temple as he fought to control himself. "I thought I was offering you something you could accept. You are not, as you have said, indifferent to my attentions. On the contrary. I did not force you to eagerness." He released her, then began to stride up and down. "I am contracted to Angelica de Foix; it is a matter of honor as well as being the best for us both. Her father is one of the most powerful men in this city and will tolerate no insults to his daughter. So long as I am discreet and the conventions are observed . . ."

She cut him off. "You are selling yourself! That's all it comes to in the end!"

His smile was bitter. "I take it that you refuse my offer."

"Yes! Yes! I refuse!"

"You cannot stay in New Orleans, Tempest. It will not be allowed."

She whirled on him and now the anger drummed so heavily in her brain that his features blurred. "Oh? You are to be obedient to this man in all things? What sort of person are you, Justin? You have told me much about yourself, but you did not reveal the decay underneath the handsome exterior." Tempest was shaking as if with the ague.

"I've had enough of this." He caught her shoulders and shook her so that her head bobbed. "My reasons for the union with Angelica are my own business and none of yours. Understand that once and for all. Aristide let me know he was aware of your existence and my involvement with you. You were observed at Mrs. Halvorsen's, that time at the theater, and later at the Café Escorial. There can be no success for you in this city. His money and influence are everywhere. If you will not see me in the future, then go and pursue your art where you can."

"If he is so powerful, why is he buying you as a husband for his daughter? Are you that much of a prize?" She broke away from his grip and started away. "I'm leaving here and I'll conduct my life. Just stay out of it." She struggled against the tears, but it was a losing battle. If only she might be alone to sob!

The deadly voice followed her. "It is, as I said, a matter of honor. If you were a man I'd call you out for one-tenth of what you've said to me this day."

"Pretty words will serve you well in bed, won't they!" She snapped the sentence out and ran for the house, feeling that she had lost this round with him. Nothing had been accomplished, and she had lost the shared warmth they always experienced together in their passion. Why not be his mistress? Was life so long that she should endure without him? There was no logical answer she could give herself. If he did what he did out of honor or some reason unfathomable to her, then she took her course out of pride and in the integrity of self. It was the core of Tempest Mallory who had walked alone before. For that Tempest, the world was not well lost for love or passion, however desirable at the moment.

She dashed into the cool parlor and looked for something to cover her body. Her gown had been torn from her and was unfit for the street. She had to put on some sort of clothing and get out of here; the rest of her life she would consider later.

A tall chiffonier stood against one wall. She snatched it open and fumbled among the garments there, drawing out several petticoats and some old gowns along with a dusty black cloak. Looks did not matter. In a few seconds she was adjusting a gray and black gown over the petticoats and scrambling into her shoes. The cloak was hooded and hid her tumbling hair. She was as ready as she would ever be.

The door banged back suddenly. "Just where do you think you're going?" Justin strode in and reached for his breeches, which had been tossed on the settee.

Tempest knew she could not endure another minute of this verbal agony. "I'm leaving. Surely that's obvious."

He gave her a lopsided, distinctly unpleasant grin. "No you're not. I have this house for another week. Now come here. You're right; words aren't always workable between us. I can think of any number of things I'd like for us to try. You won't miss the lack of conversation, I promise you that." He walked toward her at almost a stalking pace.

She backed away. The door was still open and the key to the gate lay on a shelf beside it. Would Justin pursue her into the street? Distract him while she edged nearer the door; say anything no matter how inane. Once he touched her, she would give in to the devastating fire between them. Even now awareness of him beat in her veins.

"How can you absent yourself from matters of business for so long, so important a man as you will be?"

He spread his hands wide and the golden eyes were devoid of anger for the moment. "My cousin is not a business manager, and he has some unfortunate habits. I'm more a pauper than I thought. But why am I going on like this? Tempest, I care for you as best I can. You must know that. Let's take the time we have and be grateful for it."

His mood changes were so mercurial that she was thrown off balance. What a strange mixture he was! How much of the real Justin had she ever known? All that was within her wanted to come closer, put her arms around him, and let the irksome questions go.

"Justin, I wish I could understand. We do have so very much." She hesitated, regretting the sharpness of her previous words but knowing their truth could not be denied.

Suddenly the loud clang of a bell was heard. It pealed three times and was silent, then started again. Justin looked at her quickly. "I have to answer that. Something has come up. Will you wait for me?"

"No." She lifted her head high and stood very still. "It will only be the same thing all over again."

"Would that be so bad?" One eyebrow went up.

"That's not the point and you know it."

"There's very little point to anything, Tempest. We must take what we can when we can."

"You try to sound the cynic. What a mass of contradictions you are!" He was nearer to her now and she felt the powerful pull of the emotions that lay between them. Lover, idealist, dealer in high politics and yet one who would give himself for the goods of this world—he was all these and more. The conflicting feelings showed on her face and Justin gave a slow smile. She swayed toward him.

The bell clanged more urgently. They jumped back with the

shock and Justin gave a low curse. "I'll be right back." He took her hand and raised it to his lips. "Wait."

His mouth seemed to burn through her skin and ignite the very bones. Was she insatiable? Probably it was just the sense of urgency that permeated their relationship, adding sparks to their quiet times and fueling the disparity between the two natures. "'Two halves forever set apart, never to find the other.'" She murmured the Platonism half under her breath, but Justin, nearly at the door and fastening his shirt, heard.

"That was the soul, my love. Our bodies are the reality." He gave her a small salute and was gone.

Tempest did not intend to remain here one minute longer. She was not going to be a slave to her senses. There had to be a way out of here besides the front staircase. She went through the back several rooms, each of which was furnished more ornately than the last, paused before one paneled entirely in mirrors, then hurried to a small door leading onto a rickety flight of wooden steps. This was probably the entry used by the slave who came to clean. The steps went up to stone wall and gave onto a gate set in the flowering vines. It was bolted from the inside. Did that mean the slave lived on the premises? Was it locked from the outside also? She started to pull at the iron lever, which gave easily but made a sharp scraping noise. When she began to work at it again, she heard voices so close they seemed almost at her elbow. A screen of bushes and flowers hid the speakers from view.

"What do you mean disappeared? How could she? It's incredible!" The surprise in Justin's words held Tempest rooted to the spot.

"Monsieur de Foix bids you come at once. The lady never reached the home of her relative and no one along the way saw her." The other voice was husky, the accent strange. "There was a garbled sort of message from your cousin Dominic to the effect that he knew something, but he wasn't at your plantation. I'm afraid Monsieur is very angry."

"I'll go find Dominic. What was the text of the message?" Justin was sharp. "What about Angelica's entourage?"

"She had a maid and two male slaves, in addition to the carriage driver and chaperon. All have disappeared. But you must come to Monsieur. He has given orders."

"The message, man, now!"

"I don't know. Hidden places, a scandal, revelations that could be stopped with gold. I've never seen Monsieur so enraged."

"Go back to him. Tell him that I go to find Dominic. Do as I command you!"

"I have my orders. You will come."

Tempest heard sounds of a scuffle, the crack of bone, and then the gate slammed. She heard the sound of running feet for an instant, but then there was only silence in the garden of sensual delight.

"I don't know. Maybe that... a carousel or whatever he hoped
could be inspected with gold. I've never seen Monsieur so
strong..."

33

Teeth of Lions

Tempest had only one thought—that Justin had been hurt.
There had been no mistaking the insolence in the voice of the
man who had come to summon him. But why? One would
expect a man to be disturbed over his betrothed's disappearance. That was natural, certainly. There had been a knowing
quality about the exchange that set her teeth on edge. Before
she stopped to think, Tempest was dashing through the bushes
and out into the little glade, where a man was in the act of
picking himself up from the ground and rubbing his jaw.

"Well, what have we here? Leaving early in the day from
your duties, aren't you?" He grinned and started toward her,
then gave a grimace of pain and sank down on the nearest seat,
a carved rock formation over which red flowers hung.

Tempest stared at him and was not reassured. He looked to
be in his late forties or early fifties, big and heavy, with a dark
beard and hair. His lips were abnormally red and he kept
running this tongue over them.

"Stay around and see to me. What do you say to that?"

She realized then that with the old gown and frayed cloak
that the wind molded against her body and with the concealing
hood framing her pale face, he took her for a servant who was

possibly taking advantage of an opportunity to have more time
away from her work. She bobbed a little curtsy and stayed
where she was. It was an opportunity, but not the kind he
thought.

"Master'll be back, maybe soon. I'll have to see to fine lady
sleepin' and clean and all. Got no time." She giggled and let
her accents grow broader. "Look at you! Was you fightin', you
and the master?" She looked beyond him and saw the wide
open gate plainly visible through the shrubs of the garden. This
house had many different exits, and she was grateful for that.
The owner was well prepared to escape in time of need. She
giggled again and let the cloak open more.

He guffawed. "He did what he was supposed to do, gone
haring off on one of them wild goose chases they call it. He
ain't exactly the kind of person you want in the family, but
these fancy folks'll let their women tell 'em what to do." He
reached inside his coat and pulled out a leather flask from
which he gulped heartily. From his manner this must have been
only one of many. "Drink?"

Tempest giggled again and edged nearer. "What're you
talkin' about? And, no, I don't want that stuff. Wine's better."

"Monsieur's mighty smart, but he ain't so smart. That high-
up girl's got the mark on her, the mark from way back, and she
knows if'n he don't. You come be friendly, why not?" He
lurched up and fell back, giving way to such a stream of curses
as Tempest had never heard. "M'damn ankle's broke, I think.
Got to go report." He cursed again and drank thirstily.

"I'll get somebody to help. You wait right there." Tempest
could not believe the fortune that had made him talk. He must
be far gone to do so. Her disguise helped, of course. "You
come back another time. All right?"

"Yeah. Yeah. Sure." He had lost interest as he began to
poke at his leg.

There was no question of what had to be done. Justin might
make sense of all he had told her, but one thing was clear. He
had walked into a trap of his father-in-law's making. It might or
might not be dangerous, but he must be warned.

She went out the gate and into the quiet street. She had some
few coins in a purse, which she had pinned in the bosom of her
gown that night at the Escorial and this morning thrust into the
pocket of the cloak. There was a rail at the front of the house

and a horse was tethered to it. Tempest did not stop to reflect on the penalties of thievery; she had intended to hire a horse if her few finances permitted, but this was better yet. The messenger would know where his mount was when he sobered up, but from the looks of him that was likely to be a while.

She was up on the horse in one smooth movement. He shied but she controlled any attempt to rear and sent him clattering down the streets and out into what eventually became plantation and sugar-cane land.

Tempest thought later that if she lived to be very old, she would never forget that wild ride in the heat of the autumn morning. Her mind seemed to have stored every remark Justin had made about his plantation managed by Dominic. It was small, rather rundown from lack of money, utilized only the necessary slaves, and counted for little by the opulent New Orleans standards. The Mississippi ran not far from it and the house was white-fronted, with a stand of oak trees in a circle by it, and the name, prosaically enough, was The Vines. As in his place in Jamaica, the principal crop was cane, and that could be a demanding mistress. "Follow the river and you will find it." Justin had been wry about the plantation, but she had not been deceived then nor was she now. His feelings about land went deep; contradictions again.

The horse was fresh and frisky; she gave him full rein once they were away from people and crowds. Those who paused to stare after them had little reason to wonder at a servant on a rather nondescript horse. There were many sights more interesting in this city, rousing itself now that the sun was full and high.

Tempest went past construction of all sorts, stores, tumbling houses, areas of sticky mud, roads being dug out of the wet land, the verdant growth of this land that rarely saw much winter, and out into the country proper. Tempest did not try to reason out her determination to overtake Justin. She only knew she had to do so. Every beat of the horse's hooves led her in the direction she had to go. She knew that as plantations went, this one was fairly close to the city, for it had been obtained in the days before too many people thought New Orleans would rise to the power among cities it now was.

She went now along the river road that was reasonably level except for mudholes from the recent rains and the constant battering of the river. Everything was still green; thick vines clung in the trees and birds fluttered in the branches, rose to wheel at her approach, and settled again. The smell of water and mud stung her nostrils. The sun beat on her head and caused sweat to come. She had long since loosened the cloak and rolled up the sleeves of the gown, but she continued to swelter despite the rush of wind. The air was moist and fecund; she felt the very ground growing underneath her gaze. It was approaching noon. Time was fading away.

She passed several isolated plantations, white and remote in their green settings, tall pillars rising against lines of trees, pavilions and statuary gleaming from the distance. Pulling on the reins, she slowed the pace to a near walk. How was she to know how to locate The Vines? A sense of urgency beat at her as she turned into one of the long-laned roads that led to a house set far back.

A humming sound reached her ears when she had gone a few yards. She started to ignore it and could not. When she looked around for the source, shading her eyes against the sun with one hand and lifting the heavy hair off her neck with the other, she saw a small black boy lying flat on his back in the shade of a bush. He was almost hidden by its spread, and his dark eyes were fixed full on her as he made the sound again.

"I'm looking for a plantation, The Vines. Can you tell me how to get there?"

He continued to hum. His gaze did not waver.

Was he simple? Deaf? Tempest phrased her question again, trying to keep the irritation out of her voice. "Do you know what I'm saying?"

"Yessum." The answer was interspersed by hummings.

"Then tell me how to get there!"

"Why you goin'? Bad place, that." She saw him roll his eyes and his thin body stiffened.

"Why is it bad?" She tried to get away from the question and answer, knowing that slaves often pretended ignorance when they did not want to give information. "Since you don't know, I'll go on up to the house and ask." She flipped the reins as if about to go.

"First fork down and left till you gets to a tumbly buildin'. Go right then till lots o' vines and one house. That it." He gabbled the words fast but she understood. "Bad things there, long time back." He began to hum again. "Gonna tole bees come spring. Steal right to us."

Tempest laughed at his earnestness and the idea of capturing bees in such a way. "Ghosts, you mean?"

He drew himself up and something in the gesture reminded Tempest of the young Savora long ago. She wanted to give him a coin, but knew she dared not spare anything. "Hants, maybe. Bad place." He jumped back as if in fear of her and then, turning his back, crashed away through the brush.

Tempest sat in the shade and felt a slight chill go down her spine. His fear was obvious and intelligence had been hidden by a deliberately foolish manner. She had no time to ponder meaning; again the urgency beat at her mind. Her hands were slippery on the reins as she guided the horse back to the road.

Hurry, hurry, said her alert senses and this was communicated to the horse. Once again they sped over the now rutted road on a mission she did not understand, nor was she aware of what she would say to Justin when she finally saw him.

The Vines could have been mistaken for no other place. Vines wrapped over the trees of the traditional drive, which now hardly permitted the entrance of a wide carriage. The ruts, moss-hung branches, and semi-light after the brilliance of the road gave her an eerie feeling. The undergrowth was so thick it would be difficult to penetrate. A bird gave a low, throaty call and she saw black wings spread as it lifted from its perch on a dead branch. There was rustling in the thickets which caused her to think of snakes.

When the drive opened out, she saw the house with its wide verandas and soaring lines flanked by the circle of trees Justin had described. It looked in need of paint. The lawns were overgrown and shaggy. She observed clusters of buildings far off to one side and assumed that these had to do with the process of sugar-making. At Cloud Ridge they had been in another section of the plantation, but apparently The Vines had no facilities for separation.

She reined the horse up near a tall magnolia tree and sat in silence for a moment. The atmosphere here was oppressive. The heat seemed to congeal in the air. The sense of menace was almost palpable and yet common sense told her that this was simply another working plantation where the owner was hard pressed and had no time to attend to it as others did. Then, too, it would have been entirely like Justin to free the slaves or, failing that, not order them to work hard enough to bring in a successful crop.

"Is anybody here?" She gave a soft call, not really expecting an answer. The sound rang back in the stillness. Her horse laid back his ears and gave a low whicker. She patted his neck and was surprised to find that her hand shook slightly. After all she had endured in Jamaica, this was foolishness in very truth! Tempest admonished herself, but found it was impossible to shake the eerie feelings she had.

She jerked around, suddenly aware of eyes on her back, boring into her, assessing her boldly. Her eyes swept the dense grass and bushy area, lifted to the trees, and returned to the facade of the house. Nothing. She determined not to be a victim of her emotions. Her heels urged the horse on until she reached the flat steps that led up to the portico of the building, where she dismounted. After tethering him to a convenient limb, she went to the door and knocked heavily.

It swung inward with a resounding creak. This was too much for Tempest. She had listened to stories of evil places, ghosts, and demons from Savora, who had had a wealth of them; they had enjoyed many an hour of pleasurable terror together. Now they all came back to Tempest in chilling detail and, with them, the horror of Savora's fate, which she had fought to put behind her.

"Is anyone at home?" She called as loudly as she could. An instinct older than time warned her not to enter The Vines. How could she continue to stand outside and call? She had come to find Justin and must do just that. It might be better to check the outbuildings. Entrance to the house was going to be a last resort.

The sense of being watched came at her again, far more powerfully than the last time. She turned slowly, hoping to catch the watcher off guard, but once more there was nothing. She called several more times, but only the pressing silence answered. The horse was stamping restlessly. It pulled back when she tried to soothe its nervousness and she communicated her own shakiness.

When Tempest lifted her eyes from the horse, she saw a flicker of movement in the bushes at the corner of the house. A familiar broad-shouldered figure became clearer as she stared at it. He seemed to be entangled in the branches and was engaged in freeing a sleeve, but she did not mistake the tawny hair lit by the sun as a ray pierced the growth around him.

"Justin! Didn't you hear me call? I have to talk to you . . ."

Her voice died away as the man pulled himself loose and walked rapidly toward her, mouth twisting downward and black gaze fixed on her face.

34

Silken Snare

"Who are you?" She rapped out the words as if they were an accusation and saw surprise cross the features in front of her. "Where is Mr. Trevian?"

The man who might have been a pale copy of Justin as far as build and hair went gave a half smile that stretched old scar tissue beside his mouth and said, "I might ask the same of you." He came closer and scrutinized her face intently.

It took all her will to remain firm and not retreat. "Forgive the rudeness of my manner, but I have urgent business with Mr. Trevian. Is he here? I knew he was on his way." She stopped before the glitter in his eyes.

"I am Dominic Cliffon, Justin's cousin, representative, manager, and general worker. You must be Tempest. With that hair you could be no other." He smiled openly this time and extended a hand to her. "Will you come in and refresh yourself? Yes, yes, Justin came a little while ago and then had to go off again on some urgent business. He'll be back by evening, I'm sure."

Her control was utterly shaken. "How do you know who I am?"

"My dear, Justin and I are very close in some ways. We have

talked, and your name figures a great deal in his speech. Come in and relax, won't you?"

What had Justin said to this man? Why had he never spoken of their presumed closeness? The chill crept up her back again and the blistering sun did nothing to dispel it. Yet she had no real choice but to stay; she was committed to this course.

"He's talked of you often, too." Might as well be brazen about it while she was at it. "And I'll accept your kind offer with pleasure, Mr. Cliffon."

"Do call me Dominic. I've been unmannerly and called you Tempest. Will you allow me to continue doing so?"

She had to take the extended hand that was reaching for hers. "Of course you may. Don't you think Justin might be back sooner? I really do need to talk to him."

"I'm sure it'll be soon. Tell you what, I'll just get one of the slave boys to try and locate him while you rest." He was leading her inside as he went on in his smooth, creamy voice. "Terribly hot after your ride, aren't you? I'll have a cold drink fetched to you."

Once inside, Tempest found that her feeling of foreboding faded. The rooms were sparsely furnished in old oak, obviously used for generations; chair seats, draperies, and carpets badly needed refurbishing and the floors needed a good scrubbing, but there was an air of gentility over the whole that was comforting.

She was conducted to a small sitting room, where an ancient slave woman brought tea and cakes. It was even more reassuring to see another presence, to know that she was not alone with Dominic. When she tried to talk to the woman, she tapped her ears and grimaced, exposing toothless gums before scurrying away. Several minutes later Dominic appeared, the likeness to Justin even more apparent as he stood in profile at the door.

"I wonder if you'll excuse me? I have to be working with the slaves; they need a lot of supervision. Just rest and try to feel at home. Old Hannah'll see to your needs. Just pantomime, she understands. I'll be back later in the afternoon." He grinned engagingly.

Tempest felt the tiredness slide through her very bones. Physical and emotional exhaustion were taking their toll. She felt almost like laughing at all her earlier fancies. The prospect of relaxation was very welcome, and still a certain wariness remained with her. "I suppose there's a great deal of work in the fields, cutting it and all, this time of year?"

"One of the busiest times." He watched her narrowly. "Justin and I will have something to look forward to, the presence of a beautiful lady at dinner tonight. Hannah will give you something to wear. Please do change; you'll be more comfortable." There was the barest edge of disdain in his voice. Then he gave her a small wave and was gone.

Tempest sipped her tea, which was strong and reviving. A release of tension came when she slipped off her shoes and lifted her feet to a convenient stool as she allowed herself to sink deeper in the chair. She felt as though she never wanted to move again. It took all her effort to set saucer and cup down on the floor. Her eyes closed and she drowsed.

She spun down into darkness, a darkness of no end. Her feet took her into blind alleys, convoluted paths, and spirals that turned back on themselves. She must go on forever, pursued by a thing with no name, something not to be faced or endured. Hopelessness pulled her down to destruction.

Then the scene changed to one of light. She lay naked on a long couch in an opulently furnished room. A strange odor pervaded it and her nose twitched in an attempt to avoid the tickling sensation. A man who was Justin and yet not Justin leaned over to touch the tips of her breasts with an oddly soft hand. The nipples seemed to reach up to him. Her whole body yearned for his touch, and her legs spread involuntarily as her back arched. She wanted him, had always wanted him, must have him. Why didn't he come to her? She heard herself moan and knew that she had been doing this for a long time. He put his fingers into the mound of her womanhood and smiled that quirking smile. She could not move. Something held her flat.

Then another man was in the room and he was grinning as he came close to the man who was not Justin and yet had to be. He touched her and then she wanted him. He was slim and blond, with large brown eyes and soft skin. He did not like her, she could tell, and that was very odd because she saw them plunging into each other right there. Two men? Twisting and turning in the same kind of contortions she wanted with them both. She had to join in. She had to; she was going mad with it.

Someone was pulling at her, forcing her to move, breaking

those peculiar bonds, and stopping the terrible ache in her lower body. She jerked, twisted, and came up with both hands over her mouth.

She was in the same room where she had fallen asleep. Her neck was bent over her shoulder, and the old woman was shaking the other one. Her legs were sprawled out just as they had been. Her mouth was dry and her head ached, but there was a new alertness about her now. In that instant of transition from one state to another, she remembered that Dominic's pupils had been pinpoints and the odd odor of her dream had been present on him at their meeting. His hands were soft, yet he had said he worked in the fields or had led her to that impression. She had come into danger of some kind. Pray God the dream had been just that, but she feared it was not.

The slave waved one hand at a large bowl of water, cosmetic materials, and several gowns, which were set off to one side. She indicated the windows from which the light of day had almost departed and made hurrying motions. Tempest stared at her, wondering if she could hear and speak. This might be some sort of game with herself as the pawn.

She stretched and yawned. Her voice was as near normal as she could make it. "I've slept the afternoon away and have a crick in my neck to show for it. Am I expected immediately? Is that what you're trying to tell me? Has Master Justin returned?" If only he had! Perhaps her imagination was running away with her again.

The slave pointed and jerked around, but Tempest could make nothing of what she meant. She motioned for the old woman to leave. The sooner she was dressed and out facing things, the better it would be.

It was a relief to strip off the old gown, wash, and slip into one of those provided, a long white tunic that gently emphasized her breasts and waist. A fringed stole of the same material covered her shoulders. The long, full sleeves belled out below the elbows to cover her fingertips. She was reminded of medieval times as she craned to see herself in the small mirror in one of the corners. Then she combed out her hair and bound it back from her face in a severe way that showed the jutting cheekbones and hollows. Her eyes glittered feverishly, and anticipation brought flags of color to her skin. Tempest thought she looked rather exotic and wondered, as she often did, how she could think of something so frivolous at a time when anything might happen.

When she came out, the slave led her down a hall and into a candle-lit dining room, where a polished table was set for two. Tempest felt her stomach growl and resisted the impulse to put one hand to it. How was she going to avoid eating or drinking? It was a near certainty she had been given something this afternoon, but perhaps the slave had wanted to make sure she rested and had exceeded Dominic's orders. She looked about for Justin and saw only his cousin, faultless in a suit of soft tan, coming through the side door.

"May I comment on your attractiveness? You might be a pagan priestess in those clothes. You must excuse the poor selection." Dominic came close to her and she could see the excitement in the heavy-lidded eyes.

"Justin. Where is he?" She had not been wrong. This was a predator at partial rest. All her instincts for survival came uppermost.

"He sent a message. He's been delayed. We're to sit down to dinner and he ought to be along before the third course. May I seat you?"

Dissemble. The word was emblazoned in her mind. Let him think what he wished so long as he did not suspect she was playing a part. She gave a little sigh. "Do you think I might have some wine first? I'm just so tired."

Dominic was the very essence of courtesy as he took her to a soft chair that was pushed back against the wall near a cabinet that bore several bottles. He turned to pour from one, but she stopped him, pointing to one far in the rear. "That one, please!" Surely he would not have doctored them all. The alacrity with which he acceded to her request made her think once more that her imagination was overheated.

She lifted the crystal goblet and smiled. "Do you think I'm rude if I say I don't really feel like eating just yet? May we just relax a little?"

He sat down in the chair opposite. "The wish of the guest is law; it is part of the hospitality of the South." He was completely at ease, but the alertness remained.

Tempest longed to demand an answer to the question of Justin's whereabouts or, failing that, simply to leave this sinister place. Even the darkness of the unfamiliar road would be better than this suave game. She launched another sort of attack.

"Do tell me about sugar cane growing. They raise it in Jamaica, but I wasn't there that long and I'm interested. Do you have a great many slaves here?" She rambled along without giving him a chance to answer. "I didn't see any in the house except the old one. I suppose they all go into the fields." On and on she went with inanities until she ran out of breath and set her lips to the glass.

Dominic sipped at his own white wine and spoke of flooding, levees, the omnipresent problems with slaves, the difficulty of maintaining a life of refinement without working capital, and the possibility of a colder winter than usual. All the while his eyes held her firmly. He was willing to play her out and was amused by it. He matched her sip for sip, raising his glass when she did and commenting on the fact that she seemed barely to touch the contents.

Tempest did not think there would be an open challenge between them; she still was not certain that he had anything definite in mind, and Justin must come soon. When a door opened and closed in the hall, she thought the waiting was ended. Footsteps rang in the silence and a hand was on the knocker of the dining room entrance. She jumped to her feet and cried out.

"Justin! I'm so glad you're here at last."

The newcomer entered and stared down at her. He was the slim, blond man of her afternoon dream that was no dream. Dominic jumped up, and there was no mistaking the eagerness in his face.

"Fabian, you're early! That wasn't wise, you know?" The question highlighted the words.

Fabian surveyed Tempest with the same bored dislike of the earlier time. He looked to be of an age with Dominic, in his late thirties, and was attired in a white suit, which set off his looks elegantly. His smile was a baring of teeth. "I was listening, prepared to wait for the next stage of all this, but I was so bored! This afternoon was more fun. I'm ready for more. Is the girl ready?"

Tempest exploded then. "What do you mean? What is going on? I think an explanation is called for, Dominic!"

Dominic looked at Fabian, who shrugged. It was easy

enough to tell who was the master of this relationship. Fabian said, "You swore this wasn't going to bore me, and it already has. You'll tell her, she'll shriek and howl, you'll have to force her, and we've done that with others."

Tempest spoke in the same tone. "Are men the only ones to be bored with things as they are arranged? How do you know I did not find this afternoon interesting? I remember it, you know." She did not mistake the languid air Fabian had; there was a thin edge of sanity behind those eyes. Robert Dornier had had it, and now it walked again before her. Dominic was besotted; that too was plain. Better to play this out and run when she could; the cleanliness of outside, whatever the dangers, was far safer.

"Do you, indeed?" Fabian came closer. "That is your misfortune. Acquiescence isn't quite our interest, either. You've picked the wrong gamble, lady. You think your attitude isn't obvious? I can feel you slipping toward the door, wanting to run out to where snakes and alligator and woman-hungry slaves are. Transparent, I believe, is a good word for you." He turned toward Dominic. "Where is her lover? Why don't you tell her, and let's get this over with. One of these days I'm going to be tired of this whole charade."

Dominic whitened before the implied threat. "There's not much civilization in you, do you know that?"

"Of course. It's one of my fascinations." The air between them was as sensually haunted to Tempest as it had ever been with herself and Justin.

"What about my lover?" Tempest's voice was so hard that she barely recognized it. "Tell me!"

"Now she's alive. The very mention of the dear one's name stirs her to the first real passion I've seen. Don't you think so, Dominic?" Fabian was very near Tempest, watching her as he played with the lace at his neck.

"Justin won't be coming, Tempest. You're better off not asking questions. I'm sure he told you to leave New Orleans. Why didn't you?" Dominic sank down into one of the dining room chairs. The candlelight turned his hair to a golden shade that was near the color of Justin's. He spoke directly to Fabian in a tone so intimate that they might have been alone. "I have the money, and another payment will be made next week. We'll leave, I promise. There's Paris, Vienna. We'll indulge ourselves."

"Tell her. I want to see her face." Fabian crossed both arms and lifted his chin arrogantly. He was in perfect control of the situation.

"What's the point? She's a nonentity and de Foix will take care of her in his own way."

Tempest felt the rage filling her throat. Her hand clenched on the heavy goblet. She could not have spoken if all the archangels stood before her. Let them goad each other and erode themselves.

Fabian bent over and smiled, his lips opening so she could see the small white teeth. "He's dead, your fine gentleman lover with his so-called sense of honor and his propensity for asking questions. Disgusting, he called us! He who's wallowed with you in many a place! Demanding to know where the girl was! I'd had enough, I tell you. Where is he, little bitch? Heaven or hell? I shot him, and we threw his body into the swamp."

Tempest brought the goblet down on the chair arm so hard it shattered into jagged edges. In the next breath she drove it into the smug white face with such force that crystal met bone.

35

Travail

Fabian screamed and fell back, stumbling across another chair and going to the floor, both hands clamped to his bleeding face. He writhed back and forth as he kept crying, "I can't see! I can't see!"

Dominic bent over him in a panic, then jumped up to snatch the cloth from the table and wet it with wine. "Be still for just one minute. Let me see how bad it is."

Tempest stayed where she was, the blood-stained shards remaining in her hand. Dead! Dead! The word lay like a slab in her mind. There was no room for anything but that. She wanted to kill Fabian, to drive the glass into his throat and feel the blood ooze over her hands. A life for a life, a death for a death! She heard inarticulate noises and realized she was making them. She rose and stood there, tasting the rage that was all she had left, the oldest hunger of all, that for revenge on the murderer, coming to dominate her in these moments of cataclysm.

Fabian was still speaking incoherently, the words Blind! Blind! coming out of bitten lips. Dominic put something in his lover's mouth and poured wine after it as he crooned soothingly. Then he turned a contorted face to Tempest.

"I'll get you! You can't escape! You'll pay for this!"

Suddenly Fabian kicked out and went limp. Dominic pressed the cloth over his eyes and roared for the slave woman. She appeared almost instantly. While she stared in fascination at the scene, he spat words at her in some sort of dialect and she answered in what must have been protest.

"Why did you let him do it?" Tempest croaked out the words, a pervading knowledge of loss making her uncaring to Dominic's menace. "Why? Why?"

"Wonder about that all the minutes that you have left!" He waved the slave out, and Tempest heard her feet thudding on the boards as she ran to do his bidding. "I gave Fabian something to ease the pain. I think he'll be all right, but the doctor will be able to tell me more." His voice was hoarse. He took a few steps and opened the drawer of a nearby cabinet. With one quick motion a long-barreled gun was raised to Tempest. "One or two shots now, placed properly so you won't be disposed to go anywhere, a lingering thing, and then the swamp will suck you down. Fabian will enjoy that!" He lifted the gun and sighted down the length of it.

Tempest threw the goblet at him with all the power of desperation. It hit him in the chest and bounced off. The gun went off, and she smelled powder burns on her torn sleeve. He plunged after her and she dashed around the table.

"Hannah'll be back with help in a minute. They're all loyal!"

Tempest did not waste her breath in reply. She ran for the nearest door and slammed it in his face. That bought her enough time to get through the hall and into the parlor, where she had been that afternoon. She did not want to think about what might have happened if she had not taken the right door. Once again Tempest had cause to thank the memory that recorded small details. She remembered the display of swords on one wall, held there in a cumbersome arrangement, seemingly ready to topple. Now she snatched at one and all fell at her feet. She swept them into a corner and then Dominic was upon her, a pistol raised.

It exploded and she went flat so that the shot went well over her head. The sword was long and supple. When she slashed at his arm, it went through the flesh easily and came out, drawing blood behind the blade. She moved well back; it was probably too much to hope that all his weapons had only one firing. There was one thought in her mind; safety was forgotten. All she wanted to do was kill these abominations who had slain her beloved. She lunged at him and this time it was he who dodged.

"Bitch! What kind of woman are you?" He was attempting to edge around to the fallen swords. She stayed where she was and relished the way he clutched his injured shoulder.

Her laughter was without amusement, drawn from hell itself. "Not one to sit by and let myself be murdered, if that's what you mean!"

He tossed the pistol to her side and she could not help but move even though she recognized it for the trick he meant. In that moment he whipped a cover from the back of a chair and whirled it about, aiming for the sword so that he might muffle the sharpness. Only her litheness saved Tempest as he charged her. Even then the folds of her skirt nearly tripped her as she twisted back and to the right. She brought the sword down in a hacking motion that just missed Dominic's free hand. He cursed and stalked her once again. She answered him in the profanity learned with Savora in their early days. The deadly struggle continued.

The cold, arrogant voice broke across their absorption. "Stay right there, Dominic. One move, one twitch, and I'll cut your throat just like I did to that swine friend of yours out there in the dining room." Justin walked into the light, two pistols ready in firm hands, booted legs wide apart, and an icy grin on his lips. The tawny hair fell over his forehead and the golden eyes glittered at the sight of his prey run to earth.

"Fabian! You didn't!"

"Justin!"

Their cries met and mingled in separate emotions.

"I'll explain later. Tempest, get that curtain cord and tie this bastard up. Don't spare the knots, either." He gestured toward his cousin with the weapon. "Not one more word out of you. I don't want to listen to your lying tongue."

"But Fabian? I have to . . ." The words were abruptly shut off as Justin strode up and slammed the pistol against his head so hard that the bone cracked. Dominic slumped to the floor.

Tempest jerked the dangling cord down and sliced it with the sword, then handed it to Justin, taking the pistols from him to stand watch while he bound Dominic so tightly the flow of blood was impeded. More of the curtain served as a gag. Justin pulled him behind the long couch and pushed it back into place. He turned and faced Tempest.

"You look as if you are the very goddess of war!"

"And you the very *deus ex machina*!" She spoke with his intonation and broke into nervous laughter at the realization.

Justin was at her side in one motion and they clung together in life's affirmation. His kiss was hard, savage, and she answered it in the same way. Warrior met warrior at the end of triumphant battle.

"Drink this down. Don't sip." Justin handed her a small silver cup filled with potent brandy. "It's from the dustiest bottle in the cupboard; I'm sure no one has touched it." His hand lingered on hers before withdrawing from the contact.

They moved to a side room away from the carnage. It held only several old chairs and a desk, but two entrance doors stood wide open and the fresh night air streamed in. Justin lifted his own cup to her. She returned the gesture and they drank as one.

"To life!" Tempest thought she had never meant anything more. When she had believed Justin dead, it was as if all life to come would be barren and empty. She knew she could have survived, but the darkness might have taken a long time to lift. A question struck her. "Fabian? What did you do to him?"

Justin burst into laughter. "I couldn't kill an unconscious man. He's out from a combination of opium and some other drug his dear friend gave him. I added a little brandy to the mixture. Not enough to kill him, but he'll be very sick when he wakes up. I wasn't able to tell about his vision, though. Did you do that?"

"I did. He said he'd killed you. Justin, tell me what all this means and what has been happening."

"Why did you come here, Tempest? We parted in anger, if you recall." His brows arched together and the brilliant eyes were sharp on her face.

"To warn you. What about the old slave woman? She went to get help as Dominic told her to do." The brandy was making her head spin, tingling her to excitement.

He laughed again and the sound was good to hear. "She

hears when she wants to and always has. Now she thinks the house has a new haunt—me. I was walking in and saw her face, knew what she thought, and made some grandiose motions toward the swamp. She's probably out doing some conjuring right now. I've never seen her move so fast. Answer my question, Tempest. Why did you come to warn me? Of what?"

His intensity was compelling. She had risked much for this man, although honesty forced her to admit it was as much for herself as for him. Like it or not, he was part of her life and, married or not, would continue to be so. Swiftly she told him what the man at the French Quarter hideaway had told her and mentioned Fabian's slurring remarks. "It sounded as if there is a plot involving your Monsieur and cousin against you. I wanted you to know." She had no intention of saying "father-in-law" before it was a fact. "The lady must have departed voluntarily, or so it appeared."

"Monsieur de Foix is afraid I won't marry his daughter now that you're on the scene. We have been long contracted, and as I explained, there is a principle of honor involved in addition to the considerations of which you and I have often spoken." Justin spread both hands in front of him and regarded them soberly. His thoughts seemed far away. "He believes in levers and additional sure procedures. Angelica may have found out and gone to a friend or distant relative. Maybe." He sounded doubtful.

Tempest said, "If you trusted Dominic as a plantation manager, I can see why you must marry for money." The bitterness had slipped out and she wished she could bite it back. He was alive and here. What else mattered? "I gather he and his lover indulged themselves in rather nasty, deadly ways among the slaves and in the surrounding countryside as well as using opium, I think you said."

Justin started to pace. She watched the coiled strength of him in the tight breeches and thin shirt. Did he feel the growing longing that she knew? She pushed back the emotion and waited for his next words.

"I didn't really know how things were. I came several times since my return from Jamaica and things seemed threadbare but acceptable. Dominic always had people working and the lack of money covered a lot. The weather's been bad, sickness among the slaves, crop rot. Excuses, all. The Vines has long been in our family's hands and I have often found it a refuge, but the course of my life has not been here. Dominic spent time in Germany; there were problems and he came home. This was the best way to kill the proverbial two birds. Or so it appeared. His letters to me painted a better view, I must say. Then I surprised him and Fabian one day in certain activities involving opium and other things. I sent Fabian away; we had a fight. Dominic swore all manner of things and I was fool enough to believe him. Later I discovered they'd debauched some young slaves of both sexes and some who were not ours. There were some deaths. I was coming to deal with him and then the message came about Angelica, hinting that he might have something to do with her. It would have been like him to take her and try to blackmail me into allowing things to continue."

"But how does Monsieur de Foix enter into this?" Tempest felt the uneasiness rising. She heard the beginning groans from the other room and knew Dominic was about to rouse. "Surely he would not trap you? And you haven't yet said how Fabian came to think he'd killed you."

"Monsieur thinks to rule completely those around him. He will learn. As for Fabian, he shot me as I was confronting Dominic. My head was barely creased, so they tied me up to deal with me later. I managed to get loose and came in on your battle."

He came to her and pulled her close. Her arms went around him and they held each other in wordless comfort. Both had come so close to death that it seemed a miracle they still lived. Tempest thought of the afternoon's sexual episode; would she ever know if it had really happened or not? There was still reticence between them, or she would ask Justin. She was herself, and the invasion, if that, could matter only if she allowed it to do so. She nestled her face in the hollow of his shoulder. His warm breath ruffled her hair. This was the briefest of communions, but passion pulsated in them.

"Tempest, if only I had met you years ago." Justin sighed the words out as he tightened his grip on her. "There's so much to be considered, and I am bound in so many ways. You're bold and forthright; I've never known a woman like you and I won't again."

She would not say all that she thought. It had all been said.

But knowing Justin as she now did, Tempest was aware that more than worldly greed and pure idealism held him to the course he had chosen. She loved him and meant to fight for him, but she could not tear him apart to do it. In that spirit she said, "We're together now and we've overcome a great deal. Surely we can take a few hours for ourselves." That was as close to invitation as she wanted to come.

He put her back and looked into her face. "I wish we could, but I have to find out what Dominic knows. He can be stubborn."

"I understand." She did not. She thought wildly of suggesting that they take whatever money and jewels they had and embarking on the next ship for the islands of the Bahamas or the Caribbean. Anywhere. Marriage, politics, ambition—let it all go for love. She and Justin could make their own way anywhere doing anything. Both had strength of will and determination. What was it Elizabeth of England had once said? "Were I cast out of this kingdom in my petticoat, I would survive anywhere." Tempest knew she had the same power. To wander the world with Justin, accountable only to themselves! It was an enchanting picture that had little of reality in it. She looked into the implacable face above hers, the set chin and hard golden eyes, and knew they had taken each other's measure long ago. They were as they were and loved despite it. At least she did; Justin might be close, but not admit his own knowledge.

"I want you to take the pistols and go watch the driveway. If there's any danger, it'll come from there. The slaves know better than to investigate anything in the big house. Dominic has much to answer for." His jaw set grimly.

"I will watch from the window and hold the pistol on Dominic. You will not be alone with him. Also, Fabian should be tied up."

"Then do that. This is not for a woman's eyes." Exasperation edged his tone.

"I am not just a woman. I am Tempest and I, too, have a score to settle with your cousin. Don't argue with me." She could be as implacable as he.

"If you faint, I will leave you there."

Challenge and challenge. Her head went high. "Do that."

Many times in the next hour Tempest wanted to faint or run

screaming out the door to vent her anguish in private. She forced herself to sit, both pistols in her hands, with watchfulness and no emotion while the questioning went on. Dominic's imploring eyes often went to her, and she returned the look with an icy stare. He believed Fabian was dead, but he said nothing about Angelica, only begged for his life, crying that he knew nothing of a message, was innocent, innocent, innocent. Justin said, over and over, "Tell me where she is and how she came to be there. I will not stop until you do." Fists, fire, and knife were his instruments.

Finally he screamed forth details, belching them out as if he might not hold them another second. "That's everything! Everything, do you hear? Don't kill me! Please!" He arched upward and fell back, struggling once more against the cords that held him. His mouth opened convulsively, and he collapsed.

Justin looked at Tempest and both understood that what he had had to do was utterly justified. That was to be their strength in time to come.

36

Shield And Buckler

"Does the fact that I don't want you to go make any difference to you? The swamp is a dangerous place, and the camp I will be looking for is cleverly hidden. Robbers and escaped slaves roam around there as well as wild animals. Go back to the city and wait there for me." Justin checked the pistols and hung them at his belt, where a long knife was already placed.

"No and no. I am going." Tempest had hunted ruthlessly through Dominic's clothes until she found breeches and a shirt that were close to fitting. A pair of worn boots were almost comfortable. She wondered what unfortunate woman guest had left them behind and then forced that thought from her mind.

"Why must you? Just tell me that. We may have to walk for miles, face a battle at the end of it, and if what I suspect is true, all the powers of New Orleans range against me at the end. De Foix will never believe the truth, if it is the truth." He scowled and rubbed his face. Dominic's words were nearly unbelievable. "Dominic always was a liar. I don't see any reason for him to change now."

"Whether you accept it or not, Justin, we're in this together. You can't dissuade me, so stop trying."

"Headstrong!"

"Always have been!" Tempest put both hands on his arm. "You can't really stop me, you know that, and we're wasting time arguing."

"All right. Have it your way, but you'll have to keep up! We leave in fifteen minutes." He strode away, leaving Tempest to wonder if her victory was a Pyrrhic one.

They rode out a little later, carrying cloaks, a change of clothes, food, water, and restorative brandy. The prisoners were securely locked in separate sections of the house, and two large slaves had been brought up, armed and set to guard them. If anyone approached the house for any reason, they were to be told cholera was suspected. Justin left written orders in case the issue was pressed, for slaveholders were constantly afraid of rebellion.

"I wish I could simply kill them, but it's impossible. Both will have to face trial in New Orleans. The law won't take into account the slaves, but attempted murder of a white man is something else again. So is blackmail."

Apart from these words just before they left, Justin said nothing else to Tempest. She had wondered why none of the slaves—his to command—were ordered to go with them if the peril was so great, but Dominic's cries made that plain enough. Those words and the pictures they conjured up were enough to bring nightmares.

"Angelica said she had the sickness and wanted to go out to Father Joaquin's camp. Offered gold and some jewelry to be guided there. A bracelet had her initials on it, and I remembered the old stories. Her looks were different, like she was about to crack open. I told her it wasn't enough for one of her family and that her father'd give more. She sent for more gold. We thought we'd work the game both ways and get money in addition to keeping quiet about the taint. Leprosy in the family."

There had been much more, all gasped out between sighs for breath and pleas for life. Dominic could no longer formulate sentences by the time he decided to speak; words ran together with little coherence. As she recalled them now, Tempest saw once more that moment at the American Theater. The beautiful and pale Angelica, with those who watched her carefully, had impressed her even then with a chill. Had it been the aura of that most fearful of diseases? She shuddered and suddenly remembered her aunt's comments when they read passages in the Bible about it. "I've seen people with it, tried to treat 'em, too, and don't see how it's catching. The horror is what destroys them." She had not understood human emotions, but she did not know much about disease.

Tempest shifted in the saddle and pulled off her wide-brimmed hat to let the cool wind touch her face. What would she, Tempest Mallory, have done in such circumstances? Young, beautiful, soon to be wed to a most desirable suitor, a protective family, and a good name—everything and nothing. Pity for Angelica de Foix burned in Tempest's heart, and she felt a pang of shame because she was so utterly glad that it was not she who was so afflicted. Perhaps there was another reason. Dominic could have lied. The girl might have been going to join her lover and chosen so strange a meeting place to ensure she was not pursued at once. Pray God that was it.

The road widened so they could now ride abreast. Dark walls of brush and vines rose on either side of them and trees laced their tips together high overhead. An owl hooted close by and the wind carried a mud scent. It was deep night, but near dawn. Justin's voice, oddly subdued, came as a shock, for he had been silent since they left the Vines.

"It'll be light soon and we'll have to leave the horses. The rest of the way we walk. I think we'd better relax while we can."

"Of course." Tempest had not really been surprised at the way Justin retreated into himself at the appalling news. It was not so strange that he had not wished to discuss the possible fate of Angelica with her, but he had shown no emotion except impatience and a determination to have her stay behind. Possibly, he dared not consider the consequences of finding the girl or not finding her. Surely he had had some idea this was in the offing?

They entered a small clearing, dismounted, tethered the horses, and spread their separate cloaks, and settled to try and sleep. Tempest found she could not in spite of the tiredness that buzzed in her ears. The horrors of the past hours and those sure to come marched in her brain and made her toss back and forth. Justin was faring no better. He appeared to move when she did.

He would not ask, but Tempest placed no such demands upon herself. She rose and went to his pallet. The words were simple, after all. "I need you." She sank down beside him and touched his shoulder. He went rigid, but she was not to be deterred. "Justin, shall I go away?"

He turned over and faced her, very pale in the darkness. If her fingers had not brushed over his eyelashes, she would not have felt the moisture there. For whom did he agonize, and why did he bear it alone?

"Stay. Please." He whispered the words and then caught her roughly, desperately, in his arms. "I need you, too."

Feverishly, they shed their clothes and lay fused in a kiss, born of mutual sharing, that went on and on. Their tongues probed and curved, touched and moved in darting motions. Tempest felt her will, her very self, opening outward to him in a rush. The familiar fire was coursing through her veins; she was moist, her very bones were melting. She did not try to halt the power of it. She could not have done so in any event.

Justin came to her in the same way. Nothing remained of their struggles for dominance. Now they anticipated each other's desires and delighted in the satisfaction of them. He took her nipple into his mouth and let his tongue lave the tip while she ran soft fingers over his shaft. When his mouth went lower and into the smooth inner core of her, she continued to tantalize his masculinity until he groaned with the hunger of it. In another instant she took him into her mouth and felt him shake with restraint. They pushed final consummation to the very edge and drew back.

Tempest could bear no more. Each nerve in her body was quivering and raw. She ached with need and saw this reflected on Justin's face. She slipped over onto her side and reached for him. "Now!" Her body arched to him, eager for the impalement, anguished for it. He thrust deeply several times and made to draw out, but her muscle clung. She set her hands on his hips and held him there. Their eyes met in the first gray light of dawn and it was as though it were the first time for them. Tempest cried out, "Hard, Justin! I can't wait anymore!"

"Nor I!" Then he was pounding home the final strokes that she must have, could not live without, and she was crying out for more. Their bodies were wet and clinging as they moved from one position to another and finally lay as they had begun, on their sides, welded together.

Tempest rose with the whirlwind and descended to quiet with it. Storm and fire were quenched and the broad avenues of peace lay ahead. Justin pulled her head onto his shoulder. "Sleep, dear love, sleep." She put her arm across his broad chest and obeyed.

Tempest opened her eyes and looked straight into large brown ones. Her sleep had been so deep and profound that she thought she was dreaming. This might be some fantasy from another time before the world began. Then there was a loud whicker and lips began to pull at a tendril of streaming red hair. She rolled away, slapped at the horse's muzzle gently, and began to laugh. The movement woke Justin, naked beside her, and he grappled for his pistol with one hand.

"What's going on?" He dashed the hair out of his face and looked wildly about.

"Invaded by the horse people! They were bored and came to look at us." She waved at the two horses, who had somehow loosed themselves and come to view the humans.

"Let's give them something to watch!" Justin jumped up and scooped her into his arms. Ignoring her laughing protests, he walked with her to the edge of a small freshwater stream through which they had passed the night before. He sat down with a plopping sound and lay back so that both were immersed in the shallow water. Tempest wriggled free and ducked him. He came up reaching for her, but she slipped out of his grasp and started up the bank on the other side.

"You'll not escape that way!" She heard him laughing as he caught her ankle and pulled her down flat so that she was half on the grass and in the water.

"Yes I will!" She made to get up, but he was pushing at her and in another minute his long, erect shaft slipped inside her and began to move. He lowered his body on her gently and his hands came around to cup her breasts, moving on the nipples while her flesh gave again to his.

The cold water swirled at her ankles and sand pricked her skin. A soft morning breeze stirred the overhanging branches above her head. A bird bounced several inches away as it poured out a paean of song to morning. The sun beat warm and heavy on them. It might have been the very dawn of time; just so might Adam and Eve have sported in the garden. Tempest was conscious of every detail; she seemed fine-tuned, keenly aware even as she responded to each thrust and pull Justin made. She held him inside her, tensing her muscles for the power of him, then slightly released only to pull him more strongly back. Then the hammering release took them and they sank bonelessly into the water.

Justin looked at her as he had not done since their days on the *Porfina*. "Witch woman. Sorceress." He had not used those words in that wondering intonation since, either.

"And you, of course, have been hopelessly seduced by this sorceress." Keep the tone light and bantering. This is not a time to be serious. Her mind could say one thing, but she longed to throw her arms around him and speak of her love.

Justin reached out and cupped her dripping chin in his tanned fingers. "Hopelessly." His mouth claimed hers, held and cherished it.

She held him in her arms, tears burning her eyes, and thought for this time and this minute her cup overflowed.

"When all this is over and if Angelica is well, then we will talk." Justin spoke into Tempest's hair, his hands grabbing her shoulders convulsively.

She realized that he could make no stronger commitment than this, for the past was always with him and the future had its own bonds, but some demon made her say, "And if she is not?"

He went stiff and released her. His face might have been hewn from granite. "Then there will be duty and my promise to keep." Then he was walking away, taking the morning brightness with him.

They were silent over hard rolls, water from the stream, and pieces of chocolate. Tempest regretted her question, but could not right it now. It was hard to understand Justin, strange mixture of cynic and idealist that he was; each time she considered this, she found it more peculiar. He had told her about much of his past; they had even discussed their relationship, but he would never admit to his feelings for her. What was the tie that bound him so closely to the De Foix family? Would she ever know?

It was not until they were walking along a narrow footpath between two marshy areas that Justin spoke to her and this only to tell her that the horses would return safely to The Vines of their own accord for they were very well trained. She responded agreeably, but silence fell heavily once more.

When he did speak an hour later, the words poured out in a torrent that wanted no reply. He walked well ahead of Tempest, but she saw his hands knot into fists, uncoil, and form them again. She wanted to go up and take them in hers but he did not need her sympathy, only her understanding.

"There are several camps of outcasts in the bayou and swamp areas. Some of them move around, living as best they can, scavenging, fishing, hunting, waiting for the time when the flesh peels from their bones and the disease goes inside to destroy them. Some are, so they say, places of debauch, others of prayer and treatment under the partial sanction of the Church. They're places of death where live skeletons walk, and no sick one who goes there ever returns. Sometimes those who travel to them are waylaid and robbed so they can contribute nothing to the community welfare; probably, they are better off. It is horror itself and must be faced. I should have come alone. I should have tied you up, Tempest, before I let you bend me to this. More on my conscience I cannot endure."

That statement flicked her to the raw. "Let it be on mine, then. I recall you had little say in the matter. Justin, you were once a physician, how could you have been so close to the girl and she your betrothed and not had some idea of what was supposed to be wrong? I suspect Dominic was lying. He wanted to stop the pain, as who would not?"

He remained with his broad back to her and ducked under a waving branch, passing one hand over his hair. "But I was not, you see. Always the chaperon, the slave, or an attendant of some sort. Very circumspect. Visually close, yes, but who would have thought? Who thinks of such things? A son, her father said, a son to unite the best strains of our blood. His heritage and that of those Huguenots of old France and America—he pointed out some of my relatives who were supposed to have been prize specimens, elaborated on his, vowed the children must be Catholic, not that I cared, and congratulated on a great match. Long ago it was set and my word was given. What did I care then? That was ten years ago and she was a gangly thing of eleven or so. No matter!" He plunged ahead as though all the demons were after him.

After that Justin withdrew into brooding and Tempest, in an effort to avoid thinking, concentrated on her surroundings and the possibilities of snakes in the dark water. They walked rapidly, their strides eating up the ground. The path grew narrower and vines hid the sun. With every step they took, their boots left prints in the soggy mud. Bird cries and rustlings stopped as they drew near and took on added fervor as they left. Once Tempest heard something crashing through the bushes and water; she did not want to imagine what it might be.

Then they came to the end of the path and were faced with a gleaming stretch of water dotted with green pads. Gnarled trees lifted great boles upward. Branches floated in the slime at the bank. It was land's end.

37

Sheol

"Where the blasted tree forks three times and the brush is thick at its base, you will find a pirogue, a native boat. Go to the south and take the left canal; walk inland a short way and you will find the camp where the girl was taken as she asked." Justin spoke the directions far more clearly than his cousin had gasped them out, but he was jerking at the undergrowth and judging the time all at once. "It cannot be far. We should make it tonight."

"I do not want to spend a night in such a place." Tempest's words were involuntary but heartfelt. She pulled a piece of brush aside and saw the tip of the boat, which was covered with heavy gray cloth against the ravages of weather.

"Do you think I do?" He was sharp. "You can remain on the outside, well away from danger of contagion. I will do what I must quickly and return."

"But your danger?"

The hawk profile lifted and the golden eyes had flecks in them from sunlight. "And hers?"

Tempest shrugged. They were at cross-purposes again; intimacy between them was no more than a shadow, a longing of the flesh. Suddenly she wished she were back in the pleasant routine of living at Mrs. Halvorsen's, singing at the Café Escorial, and thinking of a way to approach Mr. Campbell once more. Then she knew she must not try to fool herself. This was the way she had chosen; her passion for this one man was part of the high, hot core of her existence; it was not the whole, but she could not disavow it. *To the end.* So she must go, no matter what that end must be.

The pirogue was little more than a large hollowed-out log shaped to boat form, but it held them and some of their gear easily. Justin took up one of the crude paddles and passed the other to Tempest. She stroked the water as he did and soon they were skimming along at a fair speed. Justin gave himself up to the task as if trying to block out all thought in the performance of the physical.

Tempest lost herself in contemplation of this new world that surrounded them. It was good to think of something else besides her own tearing emotions and Justin's place in their center. Even the fierce pity she felt for Angelica was mitigated as she looked out at the shifting land and water. The soft ground stood in ridges here and there; the water seemed to pull at it so that it was hard to tell where one began and the other left off. Marsh grass swayed in the hot breeze. Gray moss hung from skeletal trees in the distance. White clouds lay on the horizon and reflected in the water. A great sense of peace rested over everything. As she perceived this, Tempest was eased.

"It's like the beginning of things. You know, 'in the beginning the spirit of God moved on the waters'?" She spoke half to herself, but Justin looked sharply at her.

"And we go into the world of the living dead, where He does not enter." The hoplessness in his voice was almost savage.

"But we will come out again." It was so in mythology. Why not in real life?

Justin's lips quirked up, but he said no more. The tension was erased between them in some indefinable way. He began to talk quite naturally of this wet country, the marshes and bayous, the animals and alligators that inhabited it. Tempest listened, paddled, and allowed herself to dream that Angelica de Foix was far away.

It was late afternoon when they slipped into the canal, guided the boat up a deep channel over which vines made a dark screen, and to a landing at the foot of a huge cypress. It was moss-hung; the feathery leaves seemed almost a decoration shimmering in the green water. The silence was complete, a mysterious entity of itself.

"The camp won't be far. I can go, ask, accomplish what I must, and be back to tell you what is happening very shortly. I'll leave a pistol with you." Justin had beached the craft and was now checking his weapons, avoiding Tempest's gaze.

"I am coming."

"You're the stubbornest woman in the world!"

"Probably."

Their eyes locked. Justin whirled and started along the narrow edge of dark ground that seemed to lead to a drier level. This was the last lap of their journey and Tempest's only chance for retreat.

They wove their way through marshy areas speckled with low brush and drowned trees, onto a densely wooded plane of earth that had possibly been placed here by a flood in not so distant times. She recognized sycamore and cottonwoods, but no others. Life bred hungrily here, she could feel it; but death was omnipresent as well.

Suddenly they stopped before the hundredth thicket and vine tangle. Tempest almost ran into Justin's back and had to clutch at him to keep from stumbling. A dark figure detached itself from the bole of a huge cypress half in and half out of the water and held up a white hand.

"Who are you? What do you want here?" The voice was clear and resonant, but the face and form were cowled so that no flesh showed.

"I am looking for a young woman who may have been brought here only a day or two ago. She is Angelica de Foix, and I am her betrothed. This is a friend who came to offer assistance."

"There is no such person here. There are no new arrivals. I know."

Justin scowled, his face hard in the shadows. Tempest interjected quickly, "She may have used another name. A young girl, early twenties, slender. We only wish to speak to her."

"We are outcasts of choice here. Go from this place and be

thankful you have no need for it." His voice was as a dirge in
the still air.

"Fetch the priest Father Joaquin. Immediately." Justin
snapped out the commands in what might have been rudeness
except for the desperation underneath.

"Wait here." The form vanished into the thicket.

Justin went back to the boat and brought their cloaks. They
swathed themselves in the folds and Tempest pulled her hood
up. The enveloping heat was uncomfortable but she did not
wish, any more than Justin, to stand out in such a community.
Her flesh crawled at the thought of actually seeing a leper. It
took little imagination to see what this place might be like.
Mortal fear shook her and she knew now what was stronger
than her passion for Justin.

They sat on an old log in the deep shade. By mutual consent
they were far apart. Justin gave her a strained smile once and
she tried to answer it, but her facial muscles would not move.
Time inched by. She felt numb; a prisoner in her own body.
There was a wild desire to inspect her skin, to make sure that it
remained firm and whole. All the dreadful stories she had ever
heard about this disease circulated in her brain to hold her
petrified.

"I am Father Joaquin. I have been informed of your
mission." The speaker materialized out of the undergrowth, a
short, rather squat man with a full beard and snapping brown
eyes. He wore a rumpled habit with the sleeves rolled high on
thick, tanned arms. His full mouth was drawn in a tight line.
"There is no more. Understand that. The name, the person,
has vanished. You have been paid in full. In the name of
Christ, leave this alone!"

"I have the right to see her." Justin's voice was low. "You
very nearly admit she is here."

The priest's hand went to his waist, where a very serviceable
cudgel was fastened to a cord. "People such as you prey on the
unfortunate and will be punished for it. I am bound to protect
these people and I will do so! You brought her here and then
seek to play games with me. Well, this time . . ."

Tempest's voice slashed across the heavy air. "He is not
Dominic! Father, look at him!"

Justin swept the cloak away and bared his face to the light.
He faced the angry priest without defense. Father Joaquin

stared, then moved closer. His face softened. He was careful to stay a few paces away.

"The other is a pale copy. I see. Tell me why you have come." He sat on the ground and waved a hand at them to follow suit. "There is no time here. Only eternity."

Justin did as he was told. The story followed only the bare outlines; he and Angelica betrothed long ago, the disappearance, the distraught family, Tempest presented as a friend, and his struggle with Dominic. "I have been away a long time and occupied with many matters. I did not realize all that my cousin has been doing or that he is ruthless when it comes to his own desires." He half rose and spoke sharply. "Is she here?"

"Yes, my son. She is. What do you want of her now?" Father Joaquin's eyes raked them both. "She has chosen what the rest of her life, such as it is, will be. Leave her in peace. Go and deal with your cousin instead. There are those here who are dead to that world of yours, gone on long journeys, visiting in far places, vanished, or assumed slain. So they have said in order that the unfortunate taint of this disease will not mark those left behind. Dominic learned of this and blackmailed them and some of the families in order to buy opium and indulge his tastes. He did so with Angelica. I, for my sins, threatened him after he brought her here. She did not know what sort of man she dealt with until his message arrived saying he wanted more money. She brought jewels with her and gave them into my keeping—they would ransom Solomon himself."

"I want to see her." Justin stood up, and the priest did likewise.

"It is not possible. Leave her to what she has chosen. There are other lives for you. For this woman here." He nodded toward Tempest.

Tempest resented his dismissing tone. "Ask Angelica to come. Tell her Justin is here. Let it be her decision." She came to stand beside Justin.

"No." Father Joaquin was obdurate.

Justin said, "I am a physician, trained in Edinburgh. I practiced in London and have done so on various ships in many parts of the world. I am familiar with all sorts of diseases and their manifestations. I will see her, without your permission or with it." He emphasized the word *without*.

"In Christian charity you should go and deal with your cousin, leaving Angelica to what has been willed for her by God himself. We are taught to accept what we must."

"You, perhaps. Not I." Justin put both hands on his hips and faced the priest. "What is it to be?"

As fiercely as he had resisted, it was a surprise when the other yielded. "You dare not come into our camp; it is dangerous and forbidden because of possible contagion. Come to the borders. There are several lean-to huts where no one ever goes except those who come seeking their loved ones as you have. You know the risk."

"I do." Justin walked ahead and the priest followed. It was as though command had been passed. After a moment's hesitation, Tempest went after them. She would stay apart, she told herself, even from Justin if she must.

They went deeper into the sheltering woods and came to several shacks pitched against tall old trees. A small canal ran close by. In the distance Tempest saw other such huts, the gleam of a campfire, and some robed figures walking about. Others lay on pallets and one was visible hobbling on two canes. She heard the sound of voices but could distinguish no words. A warm wind stirred the branches high above them and fanned the curtain of vines that helped to shield one area of this place from the other.

"Sheol." She spoke the word out loud and barely realized that she did so.

"Place of the undead. So some might call it, but God's mercy is extended to all." Father Joaquin's tone was reproving. He waved to one of the shacks. "Wait here. You, young man, take the one on the end. If she will come, you may speak with her yonder in the woods. If not . . ." He spread his hands and walked in the direction of the camp.

Tempest and Justin separated as bidden. He went inside his hut, but she could not face the flickering half light she saw inside or the past hopelessness that must have been its legacy. She clasped the cloak around her shoulders and went out behind it to walk there in the fading light. As she often did when disturbed, she shut her mind to everything but the reality of the moment. She concentrated on the strange shapes of the gnarled trees and cascading vines, on wondering what the rustlings in the bushes might be, and the strong water-mud scent which pervaded this place. This was possibly the low ground of a plantation of which she was mistress and she trying to decide what course to recommend to her manager. It was a wasteland and she the only survivor. This was too close to truth and she pulled herself back to imagination. Now she remembered Jamaica, the place where she and Justin had first made love, the mountainous land where they had walked and undergone danger, and the house that no longer existed in which more of their passion had come to fruition. How different her life was from the course she had planned when she left Savannah!

There was a sudden thrashing in the undergrowth and it was with a sharp sense of the cruelty that fate could sometimes bestow that she looked into Dominic's face. His eyes blazed with an unearthly anger in the greenish light of evening and his mouth was twisted. He held a pistol in one hand and it was pointed directly at her stomach. Another was in his belt. He was marked and bruised from the questioning Justin had done. An open cut ran from brow to jaw and blood was coagulated along the edges. His shirt hung open, but he was unheeding.

"Do you get the feeling we've done all this before, my dear Tempest? I think you know I'll shoot you if you call for help, don't you? Now you just go on back up to the shack and call for my cousin to come. I have a score or two to settle with him. You'll do as I say, won't you?" His voice was flat, with just the faintest touch of singsong.

Tempest knew he would do as he said and take joy in it. "I'm sick of all this, Dominic. I just wish I were back in New Orleans. You and Justin settle your problems. I'll get him, of course. Come on." She watched him out of the corner of her eye, hoping that the exasperated tone would cool the rage that threatened to boil over. She did not want to admit to herself the near truth of what she had just said.

"You're a good actress, my girl. Just think about what happens to people who're shot in the stomach. Or maybe I'll aim for that pretty face and do to you what you did to my poor Fabian." He gave a short laugh, which effectively underscored the savagery of his face. "Do as I said. I'm getting impatient."

She went ahead as he ordered, hating to turn her back but

knowing she had no choice. "What will you do to him? To us?"

"You'll see." He gave that laugh again. "You'll see."

So Tempest, her captor well behind her in concealment, came to the hut where she had left her weapons earlier. She thought now that her intuition had been well founded—it was a place of despair.

38

The Binding Words

"Call him! I know this place. He'll hear and come running. Put some urgency in your voice." Dominic spat the words out.

Tempest knew he was near his breaking point. He was close there in the back, intent on revenge at any cost. She recalled the near dementia of that laughter and understood that there was nothing she could do. She raised her voice as he commanded and heard the very real shreds of terror in it.

"I am here, Tempest. What is it?" Justin emerged from the hut on the far end. His head was turned back as though he spoke to someone and it appeared that he was not fully conscious of where she was. "Just a minute."

"Get him over here. Now." Dominic whispered the order, but Tempest heard every syllable and felt the gun brush very close to her.

In that instant Tempest understood he meant to kill Justin and herself as well. Long rivalry, the apparent loss or departure of Fabian, the drug he used, and being thwarted had all been too much. Murder was the final act of absolution. She did not stop to think or plan. When she saw Justin start toward her, there was no single thought; she simply did what had to be done.

"It's Dominic! Get back! He has a gun." She kicked backward, threw herself flat, and rolled to the side in one fluid motion.

"Damn you!"

She heard the curse, then her head was spinning and she was pulled upward against Dominic, who held her steady in a vise of pain. Her vision was very clear. Justin was standing to the far left, a large tree nearly shielding him from his cousin's gun. But the gun was not pointed at him. It was aimed at her chin.

"Get over here, Justin, or I swear I'll kill her now. You know what she'll look like if I shoot this off? Shall I describe it for you? Fabian's gone. Gone. He wandered off. He was fevered, out of his head from what had been done to him. I loved him. Loved him! You can't understand what that is, you arrogant pig. You're not capable of it. But you do lust after this woman—it shines all over you. Get out here or she dies!" The last sounds were nearly a scream.

"Let her go. I'm coming." Justin moved out into full view and lifted both hands slightly so that it was obvious he was unarmed. "This is between us."

Tempest could not move. Dominic was squeezing her more tightly all the time and yet he kept her so she did not miss a single motion Justin made. The pistol dug into her skin; his finger was firm on the trigger. She had no doubt he meant every word he said.

"Struggle. Please do. It would give me the greatest pleasure to settle you forever." He purred out the deadly invitation with such eagerness that Tempest dared not even breathe deeply. Then he was calling out to Justin, "I'm going to have my revenge on you, cousin. A slow, lingering revenge and one you'll live to regret every day of your life. You've always taken such delight in that body of yours. What if it's maimed? Torn? What if your beauty is spoiled the way I intend to do with this bitch here?"

When he paused, Justin broke in smoothly. "Let her alone. She is the interest of a few months, already palling. Come, Dominic, I'm not unreasonable; we can settle our differences with no need for this."

"In blood! That's how we'll settle them! And you needn't think to fool me about this woman, either. I can tell! Don't think anyone in this collection of diseased ones will come to help you. They have enough troubles. No, you're alone this time and it won't come out your way. Where shall I shoot you, I wonder? Face, groin, stomach? Kill her and mar you? Mar her so that you find her hideous? Pleasant choices. Wonderful." He began to laugh as he ground the pistol harder into Tempest's throat.

A sense of unreality came over her and the last vestiges of light in the grove merged into a more deepening gloom. She saw torches in the distance as those of the camp prepared for night. But the man who held her and spoke of a fearful fate appeared a monster from some nightmare. She knew dimly that he was close to choking her and she could do nothing.

It was part of this fantasy that a white figure should emerge from the trees to stand halfway between Justin and Dominic. Arms spread, dark hair tumbling, robes drifting in the evening wind, it was no more substantial than the beginning of a dream. Now it moved toward Dominic, into the line of fire between him and Justin.

"I knew you'd come back again and again, Dominic. There's no satisfying you, is there? You have to try to ferret out the real names of everyone here. You weren't satisfied with me, with what I paid you. Oh no. Greed never is. I should have gone further away, but I was desperate and marriage was so close. What does it take to get rid of you, Dominic?"

He peered ahead and his grip on Tempest lessened enough for her to get her breath so the world swung into focus once more. Now she recognized the features she had seen only once but that had been emblazoned on her brain. Angelica de Foix. She looked to be in good health and certainly had no lack of vitality as she blazed at Dominic.

"Get back, Angelica." He was shaken, but the venom remained in his voice.

"Why? What do the dead have to fear from such as you?" She came closer.

Tempest saw that all Dominic's attention was riveted on the approaching girl. Justin was moving, putting one cautious foot out at a time, and going to the side. It would not be enough; she had to take a chance with her own life.

"Ohhh." She sagged and went limp, a dead weight against the arm that gripped her. Any minute she expected the pistol to explode but did not dare open her eyes or do anything except stay as she was.

He was jerked off balance by the sudden burden and released Tempest as if by instinct. In another moment there was a rush and Angelica was upon him, arms around him as she rubbed herself against his skin. He screamed and tried to break free but could not. The pistol hung in his nerveless fingers.

"Take the disease! You'll get it, you know!" Her voice was as high and maniacal as his.

Tempest reached up and seized the gun, jumped to her feet, and sped back a few paces. Justin was with her, grabbing it and aiming for Dominic. It was too late. His cousin was staggering away as the blood poured from his chest, over his hands, and spattered his trousers. He tried to run and could not. An attempt to scream was abortive, for a prolonged rattle came out of his throat before he staggered and fell, face upward. His hands beat once on the ground; he arched once, and then was still.

"Don't come any closer." Angelica was as composed, as though she had not just done murder. "I don't want anyone else around me telling me what to do. I should not have come here, should never have asked Dominic to bring me. I asked him and he didn't believe me. He forced me to show him the marks on my skin. I wanted to kill him then."

Justin said softly, "Angelica, I do not think you have leprosy. I would have known. Let me examine you. Trust me. I can help. I swore to keep and protect you; I am your betrothed. My promise was given."

The dark head swung back and forth as the girl looked first at him and then at Tempest. "No. This happened to my mother. I tried to tell Papa it was happening to me, but he wouldn't believe me. Marry him, he told me, get a grandson. His blood is good and he is a man of honor. I'm sick of everything! Sick!"

Justin's cry mingled with Tempest's scream, but again it was too late. Angelica brought up the sharp knife she held in one hand, the knife with which she had slain Dominic, and pulled it across her throat in one quick gesture that severed the jugular vein.

When Father Joaquin ran up several minutes later, he found Justin cradling Angelica in his arms, her head lolling back at an unnatural angle, and her blood pouring over the ground.

Her lips were moving. Tempest sat out of her range of vision and tried to assimilate the various horrors of the last few minutes. Thankfulness for her own life pervaded her very being, but mixed with it was the recognition of how very close to death she had been and still was.

"I went looking for Angelica and could not find her. God forgive me that I stopped to talk with some others and did not keep on looking. This is in part my fault." He spoke sorrowfully as he bent over the dying girl. "Make your confession, my daughter."

The faint whisper reached Tempest's ears as the girl said, "No hell could be crueler than this life has been. Don't let anyone know what happened. Let them think I ran away. Don't let this be known. Justin, promise! Promise!" The words were gasped out one at a time but were all the more compelling for that.

"I promise, Angelica."

"Swear!" She was weaker as the bright blood swelled out.

"I swear it by all I have ever loved." The sincerity in his voice could not be mistaken.

She started to speak and was unable to do so. Angelica de Foix had gone to meet the death she had sought.

The priest bent over her, murmuring Latin words. Justin rose and went over to the nearest shack, brought out a lantern, and lit it. Tempest rose to meet him, but he waved her back. "Keep away. I have to know." She obeyed silently, her gaze never leaving the sad scene of death in front of her.

Justin bent over the girl with a detachment that might have been horrible but for all the agony that had preceded it. He touched her face, opened the shrouding gown, and examined the ends of her fingers. Then he felt about her ribcage and finally checked several of her joints. He sat back on his heels and stared into the distance.

"You desecrate her." Father Joaquin was glaring at him. "Cover her decently and pray with me, both of you, for her soul and the passing of the sin in which she died. And for your cousin, as well."

Tempest rasped out, "I can understand why she did what she did. If I, a mortal, can do this, why would not a compassionate God?"

Justin ignored the shocked hiss Father Joaquin gave and

spoke as if he were lecturing to students. The bright flame of the lantern attracted bugs, which coated the glass and fell away at the heat. The dark branches and empty huts in the surrounding blackness seemed to frame the carnage in which the remaining three were captured. Tempest was aware of shapes in the distance and knew that some from the camp had come to investigate the disturbance.

"Her face is very much like a mask; the skin is smooth and hard and shiny. Her joints are constricted, and there are sores on the ends of some of her fingers. Several go nearly to the bone. There are ulcers near some of the joints, and her chest expansion is very limited. It is a wonder she could have expended as much energy as she did tonight. Her breathing would have been very short, and I think her heart was beginning to fail. A clear case of sclerema adultorum and, as nearly as we can know, certainly hereditary."

Tempest remembered her first glimpse of Angelica and the strange stiffness she had wondered at as well as the watchfulness of those beside her. This explained it. Any diagnosis was better than leprosy. Pray God Justin was right. Tears prickled behind her lids and she knew later she would weep for the young girl caught in a horror with no solution. She, Tempest, had managed to vanquish much that had come against her in the relatively short time since she had left Savannah, but Angelica de Foix had been given no such opportunity.

"We will watch beside her body and that of Dominic. Both shall be buried at dawn. Will you remain here, Mr. Trevian, while I go to tend to those who need me more than these?" The priest withdrew part of his mantle and covered Angelica's face. "It does not matter what she had, you know. We can only pray."

"We will, Father. Go and do what you must." Tempest came to stand on the other side of Angelica's body.

He searched her face and that of Justin before turning away. There was nothing more to be said to these two and there was his flock waiting. She could almost read his mind as he lifted his hand in partial benediction. "I will return as soon as I can."

Justin did not speak for a long time after that, but simply sat staring into nothingness. Tempest did not know whether to go or stay, but it seemed reasonable to remain, a gesture of respect for the violently dead and a probable necessity for Justin, who must sooner or later release the iron control or shock that held him silent.

Tempest thought this would be the stuff of nightmares in later years, the swamp country, the dead and undead near at hand, the thought of the horrors through which she and Justin had passed fresh in her mind, and now, in the damp heat, the fear of something unknowable, unmentionable, waiting for a challenge. Superstition, she thought, and yet the sense of evil mounted.

"I was to marry her, and yet I knew nothing of what was happening to her. I escorted her, talked with her, and had no inkling of what she endured, of this thing that drove her to the likes of Dominic." Justin's voice was flat and accusatory. He ran his fingers through his hair, then began to beat one hand against the other in a gesture of which he seemed totally unaware. "I intended to use her. My interest and concerns were elsewhere. It was an easy thing to promise all those years ago. A man must wed and have sons. Love can be taken outside marriage; it has been so for generations and one does not expect otherwise. I would have honored her as my wife just as I promised Monsieur, who wanted me for the bloodlines of my family and a name old as his. But I did not see Angelica as a person or even as one soon to be my wife. My eye is supposed to be trained, and the symptoms were plain to see once I thought of them. My fault. Mine."

Tempest saw his agony and knew that he blamed her as well as himself. They had been so involved in each other that there had been little time for other considerations. *Mea culpa!* So man has always cried out and it was true enough in this case. But what could be done now? She was too much a person of life to contemplate any continuing self-abnegation. "Would the condition have been curable?" She kept her voice matter-of-fact. He would reject any touch of sympathy or commiseration.

"No, but there are periods of remission, some quite long. She was in one of them when this occurred. Mental pain carried its toll, of course. The date of the wedding was near, and she would have been unable to hide her condition. Her father would never have believed there was anything wrong with her; he knows this is in the family, but the secret is carefully kept. I understand some of his allusions now."

Tempest found this unbearable. "Justin, she is at peace. Try to let her remain there."

The golden eyes rested on hers in dawning awareness. "Not so. She is both murderess and suicide by the tenets of that faith she strongly believed in, by the Catholicism I would have entered so that our dynasty might rise in this land. I am guilty again of destruction. Just as I forgot my medical oath in England, so I have done here. All I can do for Angelica is keep my promise that none shall know what happened to her. None."

Tempest saw him fade from her again, and this time it was into a prison that could not be breached. By her death, even more than in life, Angelica de Foix had won the man who did not love her but whose sense of honor held him to her forevermore.

39

If I Forget Thee

Tempest soaped her body thoroughly and rinsed it repeatedly. She patted herself dry and stood before the full length mirror to view every inch of her skin as she had done on each of the twenty-two days since leaving the swamp. Once again all was unchanged. Her skin was smooth and faintly honey colored where the sun had touched it, white where it had not. Her stomach was flat, her breasts proud and high, the long legs rounded with a perfect shape. Her hair was red and flaming, filled with highlights from much brushing. The shadows under her gray eyes were gone and now the hollows under her cheekbones were merely interesting rather than indicating a gaunt state. She was fair, perhaps more than she had ever been, and she moved with a new confidence born of the perils through which she had passed. Fear was still with her, however, and it grew with each passing day.

She pulled a thin white robe on and sank down on the window seat, where she could see the street beyond. The whole sequence of events rolled over her again. She let them come; better to have memory this way than in the nightmares.

Angelica and Dominic had been buried far apart from each other at opposite sides of the leper camp. Father Joaquin did not distinguish between them in his prayers or at the services he conducted. The fall rains began and Tempest had stood, wet hair streaming, without tears as the sonorous Latin rolled out. Justin showed no emotion, but that was his way. His words to her afterward burned in her thoughts.

"You must leave now. There's no real danger of you catching anything; you didn't touch her or get around any of the places where the afflicted go. No one knows about that disease anyway. The father has friends in the swamp; they couldn't get along out here if they didn't. Several of them will take you over to the river, where you can catch a boat for Baton Rouge. I'll give you money for lodgings and come to you when I can, if I can."

"If?" She knew why. Possible contamination, the promise he had given to Angelica, the conscience that would permit him no rest.

He said, "I dare not attempt to return to New Orleans while the hue and cry for Angelica goes up—discreetly, of course, for her father would have no scandal; I will send word to him and must face him soon, but not until I can see if there is no disease process. Who can know about that?" He shrugged. "I find that I don't greatly care what happens. There are obligations to Monsieur, to the Vice-President, who has trusted me, to you. After that . . ."

Tempest wanted to put her arms around him and murmur reassurances, to invest some of her overwhelming feeling of life renewed in him, but she had the odd sensation that in many ways she no longer knew him. The arrogant, bold rover of their early days was now the man tempered by pain and loss, one who bore the consequences of his actions and endured the crucible.

"You will come to me in Baton Rouge?" She herself had changed, she thought. Once she would have demanded or gone on her way boldly. Love was the great alterer, it appeared. Yet in many ways she was as resolute as she had ever been. She had her own path to take; she did not fool herself that Justin intended to continue their affair. Baton Rouge would mean farewell.

"If I have not come within six weeks, take the boat north. Will you promise me that?" The golden eyes had impaled her and there had been no turning away.

She had promised and in the next hour went from the camp.

Two black freedmen and their wives had come with her to this city at the beginnings of the first hills she had seen in Louisiana, gone about with her in her guise of a respectable woman waiting for her husband to arrive, waited while she shopped for some necessities with the money she had reluctantly accepted from Justin, and finally gone downriver again with all her thanks. One of the women, Martha, had said only, "We free because of the father. Anything he ask, we do." They would accept nothing from her.

Now time dragged slowly by. The landlady, Mrs. Peters, and her husband were curious about her and did not hesitate to ask questions. When she went out to see the city in hopes of killing a few hours, she could not concentrate on the shops that dotted the side of the brown swath of the river or the graceful French and Spanish architecture of the houses set in their wide lanes. She could only wonder after Justin and watch her flesh in apprehension that something might appear and her own doom start.

Now it rained many afternoons and there was a chill in the air which presaged actual cold. She picked up the soft green shawl that had been a bargain and settled its warmth over her shoulders. Why had she not chosen a boardinghouse supplied with a few books? This one had only collections of sermons and boring ones at that. Still, the opinions of the Reverend Mr. Asbur on hell were better than thinking. Resolutely, she opened the heavy red volume to page ten and read, "Now the duties of the lesser demons are as follows . . ."

There was a hammering on the door, then someone fumbled with the lock and it sprang back. Tempest jumped to her feet, sending the worthy book flying. Justin was across the room in one instant and folding her in his arms. She hugged him fiercely, staring across his rain-wet shoulder at the round face of the landlady, who was frankly gaping. Her eyes met those of Tempest, and she retreated hastily.

"Let me look at you." She cupped his face in both hands, surveying the lean brown cheeks, firm chin, and tumble of hair. His eyes were eager on her, but somehow remote. His long, muscular body was taut and healthy. The breeches and coat of sober green fitted him perfectly and enhanced his litheness. "Is everything all right with you?"

"As well as it can be. I think there is no danger." He smiled at her and was suddenly Justin again, not a stranger with his face. "Can we talk later? Will you come to me, Tempest?" His hand touched her soft mouth and drifted through the long, loose hair. "The landlady seemed to doubt that I was your husband. Mr. Malone, I said, as we had agreed, but she wanted to bar my way. Do you think she'll be listening outside the door?"

"Undoubtedly," Tempest said. Her delight in him broke forth and there was nothing but this minute. "Ah, Justin, it has been so long!" She held out her arms and he came into them, clasping her so that she could barely catch her breath.

There would be time later for the serious matters that must be discussed, plans to be made, and the future laid out. For now it was enough for Tempest to feel the strength of his arms, to give and take his kisses and glory in the passion always present between them. The reckoning would come; it had to, but the bleak world of waiting had been transformed into one of light and warmth, one to be treasured.

Justin looked down at her. "I really do think there is nothing to fear. I was most careful about staying apart and trying all the remedies. How can I guess? There's more to fear from the cholera, yellow jack, smallpox, than from leprosy. It would be good to try to do something about these; I'd like to know so much more."

Tempest knew he was trying to reassure her and himself. It had taken more courage than she would ever possess to touch Angelica as he had done. The horror of that time must fade, but she did not want to talk about any of it. She wanted his body on hers. She wanted the thrust of his loins and the answer of her own. At this moment she needed the things he alone could give.

She shook her hair back so that it tumbled over her shoulders. One hand loosened the robe and her breasts shone provocatively through the parting folds. She looked down to see the growing swell of him against the tight material of his breeches. The hunger in his gaze was reflected in her own.

"I want you." His voice was a whisper in the room.

Tempest prolonged the moment, for it was something very akin to the deliberate postponement of the final motion before release when they lay in each other's arms. Rain drummed against the windows and the rising wind caused the oak branches to scratch back and forth. The spacious old room, shabbily and comfortably furnished in white and brown, provided a timeless haven. If only time could freeze in this moment!

Justin knew what she was doing and his mouth quirked upward. "Now, Tempest. A bolder lover would sweep you up and carry you to yonder bed. Shall I be bold?" He did not move, but his eyes challenged hers.

"I intend to be bold instead."

"What if I cannot wait?"

"But you will." She put both hands to the buttons on his shirt and unfastened the first three. He shrugged out of his coat and let it fall to the floor. Then Tempest touched his warm bare flesh, feeling the little prickles as it responded to her feathery motions. She pulled the shirt free and tossed it aside. His wide chest, covered with golden hairs, was deeply tanned. Muscles rippled as he moved slightly. When she set one hand on his lean waist, she felt it contract and thrilled to the latent power of him.

"I'll wait." The words had a ragged edge to them and his pulse beat in his temple. He reached for her but she shook her head, smiling and began to undo the wide leather belt of his breeches.

"Don't I make a good handmaiden?" She urged him to sit in the large stuffed chair where she had whiled away so many long hours.

"Tormentor, rather!" He held on to the chair arms and tried to maintain his composure.

"Names, names." She felt excitement peaking in her blood and resisted the urge to fling herself in his arms. "Be patient."

Tempest drew off the remainder of his clothes with a slowness she found hard to control. He gritted his teeth, determined to enjoy this game they played. His hands roamed over her now exposed bosom, touching and caressing the erect nipples, making little circles of heat on the white skin. She thought each must leave its mark, so strongly did his touch affect her.

When he sat naked before her, she knelt in front of him and put her fingers on the inner flesh of his thigh. His manhood was outthrust and powerful. His teeth were clamped in his lower lip and the brilliant eyes blazed. She tickled his skin and put her mouth there, tasting him delicately at first and then with more assurance as her tongue went back and forth.

"You're driving me mad!" The cry ripped out of him. He struggled against her soft mastery in vain.

Tempest lifted her head, well aware that she was only a short distance from his shaft. "Not yet." She caressed it with her lips for a second and lifted her eyes to his face. "Shall I stop?" Foolish question! Her heart was hammering triple time. The very core of her body was aching and filled with moisture. The need for him was a palpable, breathing thing. "Shall I, Justin?"

"No! Of course not!" He put his face down to hers and gave her a hard, hungry kiss, his tongue entwining with hers and doing battle for possession in a prelude of the dual conquest they were waging. When he relinquished her mouth, Tempest was shaking.

He trailed additional kisses down her neck before returning to her lips. "Sorceress." The familiar word, used at times of deepest lovemaking, sent shivers of delight over Tempest as she thought of the culmination that was close. He felt the response and began a sensual motion through her hair.

She started a pathway of kisses on his thighs, flicking her tongue to the skin and withdrawing it slowly. Every now and then she looked up at him to see his rigid desire. Then she came to take him in her mouth, softly at first and then more strongly until the repetitive movement took them both in its own rhythm.

There was no more tantalizing; this was elemental. He was rock-hard in her mouth in one instant and then he was filling her with the very stuff of life itself, the quintessence of his manhood. She drank of him, put her head against his heat, and felt her being encircle his. She went out from Tempest Mallory and entered into Justin in a union that was more of the spirit than of the flesh. He folded her again to him and she heard him calling her name as though it was a benediction and an incantation.

They remained quiet for a long time. The rain abated and the light grew clearer in the room. Tempest began to feel a faint chill, but she did not want to move from the comfort of Justin's body. He stirred and smiled at her as she tilted her head to look at him. His eyes were warm and the lines were smoothed from his face so that he appeared younger than when she first met him.

"Come up here. There's plenty of room for two and I'll warm you." He shifted lazily around in the cushioned chair and reached for her hand.

Awareness was like lighting between them. They probed each other, retreated, and grew closer. It was as though a war to remain separate were being waged. The curious merging sensation Tempest had had earlier was with her more strongly and she did not have the power to resist it. A puzzled expression remained far back in Justin's eyes; she understood that he was in the same sort of state and did not wish to yield. Did she?

Tempest rose and perched on the edge of the seat, suddenly stiff and faintly ill-at-ease despite all they had just shared. She felt a flush rising to her cheeks. Justin grinned and swept her to him, cradling her in his strong arms. His lips found her neck, traced the line of her jaw, rose to her eyelids, went down her nose, and came to rest on her mouth. They fused into a long, deep kiss which held them immobile as their passion rose. Her arms were around his neck and his hands were touching her nipples, slipping down into the aching wetness of her womanhood, caressing her smooth, full buttocks.

He turned her so that she faced him in the chair. Her legs were spread wide. Her head was thrown back so that the red hair fell nearly to the floor. He settled his mouth on her breasts, causing each in turn to crest and throb. His fingers continued to find the secret places of excitement and stir them still more. She moaned with the delay of culmination and saw that he took joy in it even as she had.

Then she was rising with his motion so that the long shaft fitted into her, penetrating so fully that she nearly cried out with the expansion. He shifted slightly and little prickles of sensation began. Her body answered his in the way all this was meant to be, a language all its own. Her legs locked; her hands were on his shoulders and they moved in quick, hard thrusts which lengthened as their fires grew hotter.

Tempest stood on the edge of the abyss, poised and ready for the great upheaval thundering toward her. There was no reality but Justin, nothing except the tearing, rending glory of life, of death. She met it, took it, delighted in it, was immolated, and rose again to lie spent in his arms. His head was on her shoulder and his heart hammered in accompaniment to her own. This was union beyond any she had known before, and in the small part of her that was still Tempest Mallory, she prayed it might be so for him.

40

The Reckoning

"Does it ever stop raining? This is the third day." Justin rolled over in bed, pulling most of the covers with him, and flipped the curtain partly open. "Harder than ever. Not a good day to go out."

"That's what you said before it started raining all day every day." Tempest pointed out as she snatched the nearest blanket and pulled it over her bare shoulders. "Why go out? We're fine in here."

He jerked at the cover. "I'm in bed with a cover snatcher."

"No you're not. She's been replaced by a wild woman." She caught him by the shoulder and pulled him toward her.

He drew her into his arms and kissed her forehead. "I'm terrified."

"You should be." She let her mouth linger on his.

There was a great hammering at the door. "Here's breakfast getting cold! You folks ready for it?" Mrs. Peters' interest in them had grown in the past week; she was determinedly jolly at every possible opportunity. No effort was too great for their comfort. Tempest could see her mind working as she pondered the strangeness of a married couple who spent all the time alone. Unnatural! She and Justin laughed over this and took turns playing out scenes that might shock the landlady if she should happen to see them. They always ended in each other's arms.

Justin grimaced now and, pulling on a robe, went to the door just wide enough to let in a laden tray and thanked her profusely. Her arch laughter resounded in the corridor as she moved away. Tempest put both hands over her mouth to keep from giggling.

"Six people couldn't eat all this." He put the breakfast down on the bed and went to pour coffee. "Ham, rice, bread, fruit, what else? Do you think she's fattening us?"

"Probably thinks we need nourishment." Tempest looked up at him and her amusement fled. "Oh, Justin, I wish this could go on forever. You and I apart from the world."

His face clouded. "We're both too much a part of that world to ever believe that. We've discussed it; you know what I have to do."

They had indeed discussed the course of action that would take him back to New Orleans, where he would try to explain to Monsieur de Foix all that had happened. "I doubt he will understand, but I owe him that much. Then I'll settle affairs at the Vines and go to Calhoun to report all that went on in Jamaica. I've done that by letter, but there were some things I preferred not to write down. After that, I don't really know." That remote look had come over him then and there was no penetrating beyond it.

He had repeated this at intervals during their time together. Tempest said once, "And what about us? You seem to think of everything but that." She hated the carping sound of the words but found it unbearable that he should think it so easy to throw away the relationship that meant so much to her—and to him, if only he would admit it.

"I do think of us. I often think only of us." His chiseled face bore the marks of inner pain; he was vulnerable as never before. "I cannot offer you anything except a scarred, cynical man who destroys all that matters to him. You are strong, Tempest, and you are ambitious. I think you can become an actress of note. The ordering of your life will be yours alone. Choose a city where the arts are loved and soon you'll have a place there. Perhaps you may allow me to see you now and then." He shrugged. "If not, I'll understand."

A world without Justin in close proximity seemed one devoid of light, but she could not press him anymore. She would retain her pride and take the moment for what it brought. As she recalled his words and her answers now, she saw him stiffen against her in preparation if the subject came up once more.

Her tone was light. "I know, of course. You're unmovable. Don't worry, Justin, I won't distract you. Come on, let's eat. Aren't you starving?" She reached for the crusty French bread and a pat of fresh butter. "Have some?"

"Tempest." Her name fell like a boulder in the sudden silence of the room. "Listen to me."

Her fingers clenched the bread so hard that it snapped. She forced herself to glance inquiringly at him. "Yes?" She had told herself that she was prepared for what he intended to say, but now it was upon her she was as unready as at the beginning.

"I have to go out and see about passage to New Orleans. I should have done so long ago, days ago. I have lingered here too long as it is. Monsieur deserved better from me. I can see about a boat north for you if you like. It isn't wise to think about returning to New Orleans now. He would blame you for his daughter's departure and pain more than I myself. He lives in that sort of world." He spread his hands imploringly. "I wish I could be different for your sake, Tempest. I wish I could marry you and love you and forget the past, but I cannot. If I only could!" The painful words were wrenched from him, but the golden eyes were steady and unyielding.

How very far they had come from the waterfall in Jamaica, from a bold challenge across a bright room, from a gay girl enchanted with a handsome man! Death and agony and blazing passion had shaped them into other beings. Intellectually, Tempest understood Justin's feelings and the savage emotions that drove him—he bore the Furies within him and from them there was no rest. He must first cleanse himself in his own sight before turning elsewhere. In her own heart she wanted to hold him to her and fight with him for the love that was certainly there. Yet if she did this, she would lose him utterly.

She was steady as she said, "Do what you have to do, Justin. Will you come and hold me now?" She must not allow her voice to tremble or reveal the shattering pain she felt. Only in the immolation of passion would there be momentary surcease.

Justin came to her and they embraced fiercely. He set his mouth on hers, their tongues entwined, and her body arched toward him in the delight that had never failed them.

Later, she lay in the crook of his arm and listened to the peaceful sounds of his breathing as he slept. She thought of him as he had revealed himself to her in these days of closeness that still held a barrier. He had spoken of his childhood and youth, a thing only barely mentioned before. He had been steeped in the tales of the family in France, the struggles of the Huguenots and their decimation, the remnants gradually dying out in America; old sorrows and new reality mingling in the mind of the boy until they became more than a possibility of truth. She heard Justin's soft, musing words again as he had said them several nights before, when they cuddled on cushions before the stove in the corner. "My grandfather always said I had a duty, the founding of a dynasty; that a man should see his sons growing up around him, marrying in their turn and replenishing. He said too many of us had died in futile battles of religion. Our blood was exhausted with it and the strain thinned. I must think of the future before there were no Trevians left. I didn't care about the future; I wanted now and I repudiated much of what he said. Then." The bitter smile curved his lips and faded. "But I allowed the betrothal and thought less of Angelica as a person than I did the de Foix name or power. We do not forget what we are, Tempest." It was as close to an explanation as he would ever come. She knew that. He still warred with himself and until that battle was ended there would be no real room for love. He was the only man she might ever love and she must take him as he was. Other men were shadows beside him. So she waged her own battle again and again as the minutes slipped away.

Now she turned onto her side, put an arm across his chest, and sighed. He pulled her closer in his sleep and they relaxed into comfort. Outside, the rain slowed and a chill wind began to blow. Tempest pulled the sheet up over them, willing herself not to think of the coming parting.

The call came across an infinity of loneliness, from a distance so far away that Tempest had to struggle up from reaches beyond her imaginings. It was a dream, she told herself, and decided to slide back. Why rouse when this was so comfortable?

"Get up! Quick!" Justin's voice had such an alarm in it that she was instantly awake and sitting up.

"What is it? I slept so deeply. What's going on?"

"I'm coming! Give a man time to get there!" Justin was fastening his breeches and pulling on his shirt as he called in the direction of the door.

"Open this door, Trevian or we break it down!" Then a great banging began and the knob rattled. "You've got one minute!"

Justin hissed, "I can't delay any longer, Tempest. Are you dressed?" He was crossing to the entrance as he spoke.

She shook out the petticoat she had snatched up and adjusted the skirt of her gray traveling gown, the closest one. "Yes, I'm ready."

He pulled the door open just as it shivered on its hinges. Four large men, bearded and in rough clothes, guns at their hips, stood ready. Another, smaller man with gray hair and clothes darted in front of them.

"Mrs. Malone? Mr. Malone? Otherwise known as Tempest Mallory and Justin Trevian?" His tone was tinged with distaste but his eyes were greedy on Tempest.

"What of it? Who are you to come banging on our door, disturbing us and calling out threats? Are you drunk?" Tempest snapped out the words aggressively. She was shaken at being pulled from sleep and forced to such a confrontation. Justin was standing silent; by rights he would have ordered them from the room. What was wrong with him? "Go away and leave us alone immediately!"

He gave her a pitying smile. "Are you the people I have named?"

"Yes." Justin put both hands on his hips and stared at the intruders without emotion.

"Then, Justin Trevian, I arrest you and this woman for conspiracy to murder Angelica de Foix, for causing her disappearance in the interests of same, and for the grievous mental pain you have caused her father, Monsieur Louis de Foix. You both are my prisoners and will return to New Orleans with me to face these charges."

"Who are you?" Tempest was amazed that her voice was steady.

"John Veris, a representative of the law in New Orleans." He stepped forward and the men came with him. "I will assume that you both know what this charge can mean and will conduct yourselves properly."

"De Foix sent you. You are in his pay and this is his revenge." Justin spoke tonelessly. "By all means take me with you; I am eager to go, but the girl should be allowed to go. He can have no concern with her."

"Both." Veris emphasized the word, apparently taking pleasure in so doing. "Those are my orders." He grinned savagely. "There is also the matter of a fortune of diamonds, emeralds, and sapphires that disappeared with Mademoiselle. You would know about those, of course?"

"No."

"Where is the girl? Alive or dead? Tell us, Mr. Trevian. You will sooner or later."

"I know nothing." Justin allowed his icy gaze to drift up and down the untidy figure of the lawman, and his disdain was obvious. "Nothing."

"Nothing that you will say." Veris flicked one hand at the closest of his men and he caught Tempest's arm roughly. "Your doxy is pretty. Do you want her to stay that way?"

Tempest slapped the hand away and raked the man with her sharp nails. Her eyes glittered with fury. He backed away even as he lifted one fist to strike her.

"Little bitch! I'll . . ."

"You'll do nothing!" Justin stepped up to the man, glaring at him. "Anything I have to say will be said only to Monsieur de Foix, and if you want any cooperation at all, you leave Miss Mallory alone." He stressed Tempest's name. "You'd best carry out your orders properly. Monsieur can take strong exception to those who disobey them."

Tempest said, "I go with you, Justin." She knew she had no choice in the matter, but she did not want to be separated from him and was glad beyond the telling that he tried to protect her. In the back of her mind she recalled the tonelessness of his voice, the look of near acceptance, and grew fearful. Justin was never a martyr and yet the way of blaming himself for much that happened appeared to tend in the direction of this.

"Let her go." Justin was looking at her with near entreaty as if to ask her not to protest any longer. "There is no need."

"She comes. None of us have any choice." Veris was weary of the game. He turned to Justin. "You will come and not attempt escape or struggle if she is treated with respect, will you not?"

"I will." Deliberately, he took his eyes from Tempest.

Veris said, "Agreed. You'll come outside with us while she gathers all your belongings up. Five minutes. The ship is waiting to take us back to New Orleans. He spoke with easy authority, and now Tempest found she could believe he was a policeman, although possibly not one designated as such by the city of New Orleans. The earlier attempt at bullying had been only a shield. He now had an air of subdued amusement about him that made him seem more dangerous. "We'll have to hurry. Monsieur is not a patient man, as you have reason to know, Mr. Trevian."

Tempest had the uneasy feeling she and Justin had laid themselves bare before this skimpy little man. Well, she could play the dissembler too! Let him think she had been brave once only. "You're not going to hurt us, are you?" Anger and fright mixed effectively in her voice.

"We're all civilized, Monsieur most of all. Now get busy. We've wasted enough time." Again that curious note of amusement, almost of satisfaction. He started for the door, his men moving up around Justin, who obediently went with them.

Left alone, Tempest pulled on her shoes, bound back her hair, and began to throw their belongings into separate cases without regard for order. Her head was whirling at this latest development. She had no doubt this was to be Monsieur's revenge on them both. If he knew Angelica dead for certain, would he seek to have them slain in return. From all Justin had said, it appeared to be a strong possibility.

She lifted Justin's shirt and heard something crackle in the inner pocket. When she looked down she saw it was a much creased letter of several pages, in a delicate, feminine handwriting. Almost instinctively, she thrust it into the bodice of her gown. In the next breath the door slammed back against the wall and John Veris stood grinning at her.

41

Slough of Despond

"Stand back from that case, Miss Mallory." Veris waved one of the men over to him and gestured toward it. His nostrils flared as he waited for Tempest to object.

She understood instantly that he wanted her to give him an excuse to make demands. The flare of his nostrils and the glittering eyes gave him away. "Of course. I was just trying to hurry." She sank down on the edge of the bed and sighed as if too weary or fearful to question him.

The man emptied the cases, shook out their clothes, felt in the linings, tossed everything aside, and stood back. Veris said mildly, "No jewels, eh? What about you, my dear? Do you know anything about them?"

"I do not! I suppose you think I have them somewhere." She knew the challenge might be taken up but the tone in which she delivered it, flat and enduring, rendered the duel unexciting. He would take pleasure in searching her if she fought or showed fright. Had she read him correctly?

She had. "It was worth a try. You've probably both hidden them somewhere accessible. You'll be glad to tell everything soon enough. Monsieur has his methods." Veris grinned, hoping for a reaction.

323

"You sound more interested in supposedly vanishing jewels than in the girl herself." It was not possible to resist the jab.

Veris sobered; a cloud seemed to come over him. "I have my duty. Monsieur worships her to the point of idolatry." He brushed his hands together. "I just thought a search was worthwhile. You've had your chance." He waited for her to reveal herself, and when no response was forthcoming, motioned for her to finish the packing and come with him.

Tempest pulled on the green cloak she had left out and drew up the hood. She hoped he could not hear the crackle of the letter as she moved. The man followed with the cases, and Veris brought up the rear. There was no sign of her landlady or anyone else as they went out to the side porch, where Justin and the others waited. A closed carriage stood in the driveway and two armed riders were beside it. The rain had begun again, a steady drumming for leaden skies which promised to go on forever. The air was chill and fresh. Her gaze met Justin's and he gave her a faint smile. One eyebrow went up in the old quizzical manner. They were still united.

It was late that night before Tempest had a chance to unfold the letter and attempt to read the closely written lines. She had a tiny cabin on the riverboat belonging to de Foix and it was bolted from the outside. There was a candle stub flickering in a glass container set above her reach, a narrow bunk with no pillow, one stool bolted to the floor, a piece of stale bread, and some indifferent wine. Poor amenities and yet the privacy was worth much. She was grateful for the hook on the door that would at least give some warning of attempted entrance.

Surprisingly enough, she found that she did not really fear the much-vaunted Monsieur. She and Justin must face him together and explain as best they could. The task was to be hard, but surely an understanding might be reached. Veris's talk of jewels was clearly an attempt to get a bribe. Justin's own sense of honor was driving him back to New Orleans, but any father as powerful as Angelica's could have acted this way. That was reasonable enough. It was bitter, certainly, but she was at peace now. So Tempest lulled her own uneasiness and bided her time until the sounds of stamping feet, rattling of locks and doors, and the calling back and forth of their captors ceased. She half hesitated at invading Justin's private being, but somehow she knew this course of action was necessary.

I have it as I have always known I would. I haven't been able to breathe properly for a long time. My heart hammers at the least little thing, and my skin is all hard on my face. My fingers are peeling. They hurt and it's hard to write this, but I have to. I've told Papa and tried to explain that I can't, I won't, marry. Not Mr. Trevian or anyone. I just want to go to the nuns and away from all this. The doctor says it isn't what I think, but how does he know? I saw him shudder away. Papa must be paying him a great deal of money so he'll say I can have a healthy child. I know differently; I just hate all this pretense.

Tempest stared at the pages, horror creeping through her. The desperate young voice of Angelica de Foix rang in her ears and shuddered in her mind. She realized now that what she read came from a diary and must have been snatched out in haste from the main book. But why? Had there been violence of some sort? The ragged edges seemed to indicate an unwilling interruption, but perhaps that was Angelica's own agony. Tempest's powers of understanding nearly stopped when she tried to think of the fearful situation the girl had faced with no help. She dropped her eyes and read again.

Another session with Papa. He is adamant. He cannot, will not, see the truth. Aunt Marthe, my mother, my second cousin I used to play with years ago, Grandfather in his last years, and who knows how many more? When I think back, I can recall others who had the symptoms I do now. And Papa is so anxious for health, for a son, for what he calls good blood to will out. I am a receptacle for him, one to be filled at all costs.

The boat swayed from side to side. The dim light flickered and heavy footsteps resounded near Tempest's door. She held the pages close, ready to thrust them back into the bodice of her gown. Sickness stuck in her throat and she reached out for some of the wine. Bad as it was, she was given comfort with the first swallows. There was little more to read, for the book in which Angelica had written was small. Her handwriting had deteriorated by this time. Some letters were large and sloping, others cramped and jumbled together. The purple ink was marred with tears and handling.

He will force me to marry Mr. Trevian. The betrothal was long ago, he said, and Mr. Trevian is a man of honor. I know that, and I know his heart is elsewhere. We have spoken briefly and always under supervision. I have no opportunity to explain anything, and he is Papa's man. I'll run away. I won't be forced! I won't!

Tears ran down Tempest's cheeks and she gave way to them unashamedly. Now, too, fear crept in. What manner of man was Monsieur that he could treat his daughter that way and she in mortal anguish? What would he do to the man who had flouted his wishes and the woman he preferred to Angelica and all that she could have brought him?

A new maidservant came today in place of old Jena, who's ill. She brought my morning chocolate and woke me up. I won't forget the shock on her face when she saw me without the powder and paint I use and how she stared at my fingers. I thought the swelling and ulcers were better. She's a slave for life, but I saw pity in those eyes. That's something I won't endure! I screamed at her, she dropped the cup and they took her away. To be whipped, I imagine. I can't be sorry for her; I've got to do something for myself and I can't wait any longer. Papa says he can make me do what he wants, and I know he's right. He'll drag me to the altar or give me some drug that'll make me "wild in my husband's bed." He said that to me! I am not his daughter; I am the means of a grandson to carry on the line. Mr. Trevian's blood is good, as is ours. There is the future to consider, he said. But there is none for me. If only I had the courage to end this! Mortal sin! But Our Lady would understand, wouldn't she?

The anguished words trailed off the page and were splotched at the bottom. From the bottom of her half-pagan soul, Tempest hoped that Angelica walked, beautiful and restored, in the purity of the Christian heaven. Surely hell suffered on this earth was enough. She said now, as she had stated to Father Joaquin, "If I understand, I a mortal, how much more so would our Lord understand?" And then, out of some strange compulsion, she made the sign of the cross over Angelica's last words.

The heavy sense of pain and foreboding eased a little when she folded the pages back into her gown and tried to settle down to sleep. She wondered if Justin knew what sort of man Monsieur was. Angelica had had one perception and that possibly distorted. What if they faced an even greater evil from him? Even a sort of madness? He could have made things so much easier for his daughter and still she had been driven out by his selfish demands. Such a man might want the ultimate revenge for those who flouted him. When exhaustion finally brought release, Tempest had set up many a possibility and won out over them all. If only fantasies could come true!

In the middle of the next day Tempest was allowed out of the room for a short walk on the deck. One of the nameless men pointed out the area where she could go and said tonelessly, "You have fifteen minutes." He went back inside and she was blessedly free to breathe deeply, lift her face to the damp wind, and move about briskly. It was intoxicating, and she felt her spirits lift from contemplation of the horror behind and before her.

The river stretched in a broad brown swath around their craft. There was no sign of any human habitation along its banks, which were hung with trees and vines of all types. Droplets of rain swirled into her eyes as she moved and thunder muttered in the distance. It was a wild scene and one that gave promise of the coming winter, for she saw touches of yellow in the remaining green as well as some bare branches.

"They've not hurt you in any way?" The beloved, familiar voice spoke almost in her ear and she whirled to see Justin regarding her seriously. "You're all right?"

"Yes." There was so much she wanted to say and could not. Her very heart welled up in her mouth. "And you?"

"Well enough." He leaned against her and whispered, "Do what they tell you. I don't think there's any danger for you. I can make Monsieur see reason. Apparently he doesn't know about Angelica and these men, who don't represent any law ever thought of in New Orleans, are just trying to get what they can out of us. Be innocent and agreeable. I know you can play a role. Just don't challenge anyone. Give me your promise!"

"I know what sort of man he has to be. I read Angelica's letter or diary, whichever it was intended for. He's ruthless, you said. He'll want revenge, will he not?" She kept her voice low with an effort.

"You shouldn't have read that." His brows drew down into a scowl.

"But I did, and it is much better to know." The wind whipped her hair loose from the knot she had fashioned and blew it into her face.

"Ignorance is best, Tempest. Do as I have bidden you."

Then he was gone, walking erectly away from her and not an instant too soon, for her watcher opened a nearby door and beckoned imperiously.

Veris stood just inside. His manner was silky. "I hope you had a nice chat. It'll be your last for a very long time. We dock in the morning. Be ready."

She swept him with a long stare, taking pleasure in making him wait. "I shall be; depend on it." The words were inoffensive enough, but the way they were delivered was not. His gray face twitched before he could mask the anger in it.

"Arrogant, aren't you? Just as he is. Excellent. Monsieur loves a challenge." He strode away, his laughter floating on the air.

Tempest knew she should have followed Justin's advice, but at this stage she could not regret what she had done. Veris was her enemy just as he was Justin's. She and the man of her heart stood together; that was solace enough for now.

Her sleep that night was dreamless, and she rose refreshed the next morning. Before they came for her, she was able to shake out one of the inexpensive gowns she had obtained in Baton Rouge, a creamy muslin, and slip into it. The green cloak set it off well and her hair was a coronet of braids at the back of her head. There was little water for washing, but she did as best she could and hoped she looked brave, for inside she was fearful.

She was escorted out onto a private dock and placed in a closed carriage by two of the men, who refused to acknowledge any of her questions as to Justin's whereabouts. There was no sign of Veris and she was thankful for that. The morning was dark and forbidding, faintly cool, and she pulled the cloak more closely over the thin gown. Angelica's pages were folded away in the bodice; she did not intend to let them out of her sight.

The carriage rolled on for what seemed to be a long time before stopping. Then the door was swung open and the smiling face of a middle-aged black woman shone at her. She could not help returning it as she climbed out. They were at the side door of a tall white house with many columns. Tempest was reminded of Cloud Ridge and thought of the doom that lovely place had held.

"Come in, missus. We'll get you on up to a nice quiet room

and find some breakfast. Bet you just starving!" The woman urged her inside. "I'm Polly and I'm to tend you."

"And the gentleman, Mr. Trevian? Is he here already?"

"Don't know 'bout no gentleman. I tend you." Polly set her chin stubbornly. "And that's what I do."

Tempest knew it would not be wise to antagonize her. She had expected to be hauled away to a confrontation with an angry autocrat. Jovial courtesy and hospitality were the least of the possibilities she had envisioned. She hurried to play her role. "Thank you, Polly. I'm hungry, after all."

Strangely enough, she was. Within minutes after being taken through elegant halls dominated with expensive art and hangings, up a marble staircase that was perfection itself, past several beautifully appointed rooms, and into one done in various shades of pale yellow, a meal of rolls, coffee, ham, and fruit was placed before her. She fell upon it while Polly watched approvingly.

"You want to bathe, miss?"

Tempest drank her third cup of coffee. It was ridiculous to feel so comfortable and at ease. She should be worrying about Justin's fate and her own problematical one. The man portrayed in Angelica's words and the one of Justin's dealings was not the sort to deal kindly with those who flouted his will. But what could she do until she saw the face of the enemy? "Be agreeable. Be innocent." So Justin had warned, and she would heed his words. Now she nodded eagerly and rose to follow Polly to where she assumed the bath would be set up.

To her amazement, they went through some filmy hangings and out into a flower garden in summer. A wide area was completely walled in by thick glass supported with carved poles. Lamps cast a diffused light against the outer grayness. It was warm and still; the many flowers and plants massed in tubs appeared to grow as she watched them. There were roses of all colors that perfumed the air, tall trees in lush shades of green, climbing morning glories, oleanders, others in gold, pink, red, and purple. The atmosphere was heavy and exotic, somehow frightening. Several benches were set close to some pansy beds and a weeping willow mourned near a small fountain. On the terrace to Tempest's left there was a secluded place resembling a gazebo, which was nearly drowned in open-faced red flowers with white centers. It was toward this that Polly was urging her.

Decadence. Beware. Tempest admired the opulence of this place even as she considered holding back and thought better of the action. It was with many misgivings that she approached the tubs of steaming water already set out. Cool water for rinsing waited, and robes hung close by. If she had to undress, what would she do with Angelica's letter? Why this strange treatment?

"You wash. I help you."

"No, Polly. I'd like to be alone. Will you just stay within call?" Tempest did not intend to act surprised or hesitant, nor did she mean to explain anything to the slave.

Oddly, Polly did not protest but nodded. "You call if'n you want anythin'."

When she was gone, Tempest touched the water in one tub, playing at the surface with her fingers. Once again she had the feeling she had had in the swamp. Evil was very close and it waited for her. It could take its time and savor matters, for she was a prisoner.

42

The Archfoe

Tempest moved about in the garden, bending over plants, exclaiming aloud at their beauty, staring up at the various vines, marveling at the fountain, breathing in the lovely rose smells. Under one particularly lush growth of well-controlled red honeysuckle, she contrived to slip Angelica's pages, which were folded compactly. She did not doubt that Polly was watching covertly, but it was highly unlikely the slave would investigate every move. This hiding place must serve.

Now she returned to the tubs, hung her clothes up before the concealing vines, and proceeded to enjoy her bath. Every reserve must be hoarded for the confrontation she knew was to come. She had always had the capacity to enjoy the moment; this was one of them.

The water was tepid but utterly delightful. She luxuriated in it as she scrubbed her skin to a shining pink and washed her hair until every strand squeaked. When she sluiced the rinse water over herself and used several of the soft cloths to dry off, she noticed that it had begun to rain outside and the drops clung to the glass. She had a sensation of incomparable luxury in this bower of brilliant flowers through which one might peer out

331

into a world approaching winter; she felt as if she were in the middle of June.

The sense of pervading evil did not totally leave her as she reveled in this place. There was nothing she could do but wait. Sooner or later the owner of all this must manifest himself. She longed to know about Justin, his safety, and how it was with him. Wait! The very word would drive her mad if she had to comtemplate it much longer.

"Miss? Missus Mallory? You ready to dress? You's been here an hour." Polly's hesitant voice penetrated her consciousness. "Miss?"

"Yes, coming." Tempest gathered the folds of a conveniently placed dressing gown around her nudity and was placidly drying her hair when Polly entered the bower.

She did not miss the black woman's quick glance about before gathering up Tempest's discarded clothes. How fortunate she had found a place to hide the pages! When Polly urged her back to the bedroom, she went docilely, although she was convinced the woman would search the area as well as her clothes, but she did not really understand why. Surely the tale about jewels was spurious and a few handwritten pages could not matter?

"Pick one." Polly had put out no fewer than ten gowns on the bed and chairs. There were accessories to match every one, soft shoes, gossamer stockings, shawls, fans, ornaments for the hair. Tempest saw that each was in a shade that complemented her coloring. Nothing was random. Her blood congealed, but she forced herself to cry out in delight as any young woman might when confronted with such largess.

She chose an ice-blue silk. The skirt belled out and the fitted bodice clung to her bosom. The sleeves were fitted to her arms, emphasizing their roundness. A band in darker blue showed her small waist to advantage. The slippers were a little large but comfortable; they were the same color as her waistband and showed under the edge of the gown when she moved.

Polly dried her hair and wanted to try to induce it to curl, but Tempest insisted that it be dressed once again in the high coronet of braids. They compromised on allowing a few tendrils to curve at her ears and the base of her neck. Then Polly said, "I get jewels. You need."

"No." Tempest shook her head emphatically. She would go

without more adornment; already she felt compromised by these surroundings and borrowed clothes. Polly shrugged and did not protest again but her annoyance was obvious.

When Tempest looked at herself in the full mirror she was surprised. She looked at ease and elegant in the fashionable gown, which set off her skin and hair. Her waist had never seemed so slim, the set of her head so precise. The red hair was a crown against the honeyed tone of her flesh. Her eyes were enormous pools of gray and the winged brows gave her an imperious look.

"You are beautiful." The soft words were almost breathed on the warm air.

For an instant Tempest thought Polly had spoken and she smiled at her reflection. She had matured, she thought. Her chin was high and proud; the girlish contours had vanished from her face. The stamp of love was upon her and it lent radiance.

Realization burst upon her suddenly and she whirled in a flutter of skirts. A man was standing just inside the door, viewing her with the look of a connoisseur. He was no taller than she, rather square of build, with very white skin and ink-dark hair. His eyes were black and hard. He might have been in his late fifties, perhaps early sixties, but there was a lithe look to him that belied such an age. The dark suit and ruffled shirt bore the stamp of quality. Two huge diamonds glittered on either hand and were the only jarring note. He leaned negligently on a long black cane with a head of what seemed to be ivory.

"You are indeed beautiful." He repeated his statement without moving.

Tempest considered any number of responses and discarded them all. There was an aura of danger about this man; the hunter can sense the fear of the prey. "I assume you are Monsieur de Foix. I must thank you for the hospitality and tell you that the beauty of your home is a delight."

He bowed, transferred the cane to his left hand, and extended his arm with a courtly gesture. "My compliments, Miss Mallory. Will you allow me to escort you to my library, where Justin waits? He has assured me that he has a long story to tell and that you are privy to everything that has gone on. Is this correct?"

"Yes." She moved to place her hand on his arm and instantly wanted to pull back. He smelled of some exotic perfume; the very softness of him was repellent. The feeling of danger and evil rose stronger than ever as the world swayed before her. She bit into her lower lip, fighting to control herself.

"Then come." He began to walk and she had no choice but to follow.

They went down another parquet and marble hall, past several sitting rooms, and entered an exquisitely carpeted room filled with books, comfortable chairs, a fireplace, and a table laden with bottles. Justin rose to greet them.

He was as elegant as Tempest herself, in coat and breeches of fawn with a shirt of pale beige. The tawny hair curled at his neck and around his ears. His golden eyes were watchful. She felt her heart go out to him with an intensity of feeling that was almost palpable.

Monsieur said smoothly, "I understand you have much to tell me. Let us dispense with formalities and begin. You must excuse the manner in which I had you brought here. My servants are sometimes too zealous."

"I must tell you about Angelica, sir." Justin's mouth was taut with strain. He pushed one hand through his hair and sought for words to convey tragedy.

"My daughter is dead, foully slain by her abductors, who overtook her as she drove out to visit an old relative. She lies buried with her ancestors in the St. Louis cemetery these five weeks and more. This household is in mourning and the culprits are being hunted down. They will pay with their lives for what they have done. I have sworn it." Monsieur spoke casually, as though he discussed the merits of a painting or a new wine.

Tempest burst out, "But that is not true! I saw her in the swamp!"

"Let Justin speak, my dear. We'll not interrupt." Monsieur waved his hand at Justin. Tell me."

Justin did not contradict him. He launched into the tale, giving the bare facts without interpretation of emotion. He said nothing of Tempest and their relationship, but reiterated his determination to marry Angelica and honor the betrothal that was very close to actual marriage. His voice was flat and controlled as he brought alive the struggle with Dominic and the episodes leading up to Angelica's death. "I regret so bitterly that she did not feel she could talk to me or to you. There can be no consolation for us, I know, but she did say so often that a son was necessary and you wanted one so much. She could not have borne a child. The disease had taken a severe toll. I pray she is at peace. I was coming back to tell you, sir, and you know me well enough to understand I speak truth. Having come from the leper camp, I could not enter the world again soon." He mentioned the disease and the fact that it was not leprosy. "But it is hereditary, as I think you have believed all along. There has been a great deal of intermarrying among people of your type in New Orleans and that is always a dangerous practice. The blood becomes too mixed. That was one reason you wished me to marry her." A flush came into his face and he spread both hands out in rueful gesture. "I hope I've not spoken too callously. I felt you must have the truth."

Monsieur's tone was very soft. Tempest's hair prickled on her neck. She had a swift image of the marsh grasses bending before the oncoming hurricane. "And this woman? She is fair, is she not? Healthy? Brave, too, since she went with you into that fearful place, was beside you in Jamaica, and later here in the French section of the city. She is your mistress? A wise choice, surely."

She blazed out. "I can speak for myself, Monsieur de Foix. I grieve for your loss, but you have no right to speak of the personal relationship between Justin and myself. We are separate individuals whose lives converged for a time. I have my own ambitions and he was betrothed. Nothing would have disturbed that balance."

"Forgive me." He seemed truly contrite. "My loss has upset me greatly. Please tell me again just what happened in your own words as Justin has. Indulge me in this, I ask you."

Justin sat immobile in his chair, arms folded, face impassive. Monsieur kept his gaze fastened on her as she recounted the story again, much as Justin had done. She tried to keep her feelings out of her voice but could not. The sorrow and pity for Angelica and her eventual fate nearly overwhelmed Tempest at times. She wondered how the father found it possible to sit calmly and listen to the tale twice.

"Your stories agree." Monsieur spoke mildly, without even the hint of a tremor in his voice.

"They should. They are the truth." Tempest forced herself to return that dark gaze without a shudder.

Justin rose. "We have brought the news to you and suffer with you, sir. If I may, I will remain with you in our mutual loss. Miss Mallory needs to continue upriver as she had planned."

Monsieur opened his coat and drew out a letter, which he handed to Justin. "This came for you some weeks ago. I regret that it was opened, but you must understand that we had no idea where you were and no messages ever arrived. I must say I had no comprehension of your value to the gentleman who wrote that." He emphasized *must* and *value* very slightly.

Long maroon drapes ran the length of one wall and it was into them that Monsieur stared while Justin read his letter. Tempest followed his look, judging it to be the fixed one of a person who does not want to watch another openly. There was an air of waiting about Monsieur, almost an eagerness that he found hard to suppress. Was it simply that he did not want to break down in front of them?

Justin glanced up and spoke directly to Tempest; it was as if Monsieur were not in the room. "I am bidden to Charleston and a meeting with the Vice-President on a matter vital to the interests of us all. It concerns, in part, my various travels. There is no need to answer, he says; just be there by December first."

"What do you think it means?" The cord of their intimacy was very strong now.

"We discussed the problem on the ship, if you remember." Plainly, he was reluctant to say more.

She understood. Slavery and the encroaching powers of the federal government. Jamaica's unhappiness over the British government's wish to end slavery and the limited possibility that she might try to join in the American union as a slave state. Justin's dislike for slavery and his recognition that it was the lifeblood of the South he loved. The time on the *Porfina* was fresh in her memory. If only they might be as free again without any sort of entanglements!

"Summoned by the Vice-President. How impressive."

Monsieur was smiling, but the black eyes were suddenly pools of hatred. "Pity you won't be going."

"But I can be there with no problem at all. That's weeks away." Justin was scowling down at the letter again and had not seen the change in Monsieur's appearance.

"But you will not." Again the silky tone.

Tempest cried, "What do you mean?"

"I mean that Justin Trevian shall pay the full penalty for the murder of my daughter, Angelica de Foix. Death! And you, my dear, shall entertain me for a brief period before I introduce you to those of my friends who have exotic tastes. After that, well, there are interesting sections of this city where a red-haired woman is a novelty. If you don't have some disease by then, of course."

They stared at him, unable to believe what he was saying. There was no possible mistaking the savagery in him now. Tempest's throat was frozen and Justin was rooted to the floor.

"My daughter was healthy in mind and body. Anyone who says otherwise is a liar! Anyone! I am still an excellent duelist with swords and pistols. I will not have our name defamed! It is obvious what happened. You became fascinated with this woman and intrigued with her to set up this scheme. You sent a letter to Angelica, asking her to bring her most expensive jewels and meet you in the swamp. Loving you and obedient to your will as her betrothed, she did so and there you killed her, leaving her body for the predators of the wild. Then you and your woman fled. You concocted this tale, hoping I would believe it. My daughter was perfect! Perfect in health. This story of a disease that pervades the family is nonsense!" He jerked a bag from his pocket, opened it, and tossed the contents on a table before them. "This was taken from your bag this morning, Justin; it was concealed by a false bottom. Not very smart for a friend of the Vice-President, was it?"

The great emeralds, rubies, diamonds, and glowing pearls caught the light and returned in prisms of all colors. They were the ransom of a rajah, the bride gift of a queen, the destruction of a pair of lovers.

"You lie! I never saw those before!" Justin's rage was choking him; the tanned skin was reddening.

Tempest screamed once and then again. "Liar! Liar!" Then she was screaming on another note, for the curtain was opening to show an alcove where five or six men sat listening to all that was said.

"How say you, gentlemen?" Monsieur ignored his captives.

"Guilty." The word went the rounds as the picked jury rose to render its set verdict.

43

Before the Gates of Hell

"This is impossible. This is no court of law, but cronies of yours who will do anything you say. I demand justice!" Justin faced them, arms wide, determined to try reasoning with them. "This is the United States of America, not some medieval castle! You're mad. Insane. You know we've told you the truth."

Monsieur said, "These gentlemen are respected in their communities just as I am. This is the justice of the family, and there is no higher. I will avenge my daughter. The evidence is clear. At times one must be one's own law. We understand that here in New Orleans, and you would have profited by that knowledge had you been the man I thought you were. Does your verdict hold, gentlemen?"

"It does." They spoke as one man and indeed they resembled each other, for all were full-fleshed, dark, and approximately the same age as Monsieur.

Tempest cried, "If anyone murdered Angelica de Foix, it was you, her father!" Caution took her before she blurted out anything more and she faced the men, using her charm and all the power of her voice. "I found part of her diary in the swamp and lost it there, but I remember most of what it said. Listen to what his daughter begged of him!" She spoke Angelica's words from memory and had the wit not to act out the dead girl's anguish. It dropped like bloodied stones into that room, which was filled with self-satisfaction.

"You made that up! She is an actress by profession." Monsieur's self-control was slipping and the freshness had faded a little from his skin as he listened to Tempest repeat pleas last heard from his daughter. "She will do anything, say anything, to protect herself and her lover!"

"It is true. I once studied medicine, as Monsieur knows. I recognized the diseases in her at the last. He wanted a grandson for the line; nothing else mattered. Now he wants revenge." Justin spoke heavily. "I don't know why she had part of the diary with her; I suppose she had no other outlet for her feelings."

"Monsieur, if any of this is truth . . ." One of the men who had judged them started to speak further, but one glance from his fellows silenced him effectively.

"The verdict holds." Monsieur did not ask it as a question. In the ensuing moment, he continued. "Very well, gentlemen. I thank you for your contribution to justice this day."

They filed out the door. Only once did the man who had tried to raise a question look back at Tempest, and then he was hurried along.

Monsieur crossed to Tempest and slapped her face in a backhanded blow that sent her to the floor. Justin grabbed him and returned the hit in full measure. Monsieur called a phrase and instantly six large slaves swarmed through the door and threw themselves upon Justin. Three held him while the others reduced him to unconsciousness in a matter of seconds. Their master held Tempest and his grip was like iron chains; all her struggles could not free her, and the cries she made were ignored.

"Take him away!"

Justin was hauled from the room, blood streaming from his mouth. Monsieur released Tempest, who wheeled on him, determined to render what damage she could if he beat her for it. He stepped back from her and hissed a command. One of the slaves returned and advanced toward them.

"If you make one move of which I do not approve, if you say one thing I do not permit, if you try to resist me or struggle in any way, double punishment shall be vented upon that carrion I thought to call my son-in-law. He dies; yes, he dies, but there are so many ways of death, some easy and some agonizing. I am a man of much knowledge in such matters. What happens to him before his death depends on you, my dear. I await your decision." He smiled. "George here will attend us so that he may leave at any time with my orders. I may even give him a taste of you when I am quite, quite done."

Tempest stared at him as though she could not believe what she saw. He was insane, of course, but it was the kind of madness that could go untrammeled in the world and be recognized only by his victims. She thought he must have had little feeling for his daughter beyond the fact that she was female and could produce the desired male heir. But why had he not remarried and begun anew? That was the logical course.

"You are considering my words, I believe?"

Tempest felt white-hot rage and fear run over her. He meant every word he had given. There seemed no way out of this trap for either Justin or herself. She must go along and watch for some possibility of escape. The game must be played out. She wondered if he really did think Angelica had not been ill. What did he intend as punishment? Coherent thought was not in her mind now. Survival was uppermost.

"I will do what you wish." She would have said more, but Monsieur held up one hand to check her.

His voice was full of amazement; his whole body was relaxed and it seemed as though he was prepared for a pleasant evening's entertainment. "That's enough and all I need to know for now. Just don't bore me with pleadings for your lover and yourself, and I suggest you not try any wiles. You will obey me."

Tempest would have done much more than indulge in words if she might buy a few minutes longer of life for them. *Perhaps I'm the ultimate survivor.* The wry words drifted through her mind as she nodded. "I understand."

"Good. I shall have a little test prepared for you. I'll see if you're in earnest. I know you both are excellent liars. That was really a well-planned tale about Angelica. You should have let her go without killing her. I would have paid, but you'd have been hunted down, taught a lesson, and released. But those

who touch what belongs to me must pay the ultimate price."
He clenched his fingers and the black eyes blazed.

"You can't really believe your own story!" Tempest spoke
before she could restrain herself and clapped her hands over
her mouth. Would he retaliate?

"Another comment of any sort and your lover will bear the
marks of the lash for it, and that is the very mildest form of
punishment he'll undergo. Do you doubt me? Do you? Do
you?" His composure gave way so that he nearly shrieked the
question.

"No. Of course not." Tempest forced herself to stand still,
arms at her sides.

His face was mottled red and brown; his breath came in
shallow gulps, and his lips were working as he fought for
control. Crossing to the array of bottles, he poured out a
generous drink. He took a few restorative sips and turned back
to Tempest.

"Remain here and don't even think of escape. George will
be just outside the door and there are no others. I'll see how
Justin is, tell of our agreement and that, later on, we'll let him
watch." He waved a hand toward the bottles. "Have a drink.
It'll relax you. I'll pay you the compliment of thinking you
have too much sense to mix up liquids in the bottles or try
hiding behind the door to hit me over the head. And no
weapons are around."

Tempest almost started, for she had been thinking along
those lines. She knew there was no overpowering him. He was
far too strong. It would be utter foolishness to risk bringing on
the fury of a few minutes ago, for he was capable of ordering
their deaths during it. While they lived, there was always hope.
She said nothing.

"Good. You will learn." Then he was gone and she was
blessedly alone.

Ten minutes later Tempest had discovered he spoke the truth
about the library. The windows were of heavy glass and wood,
with no openings on the inside. All desk drawers were locked.
The bottles he had mentioned stood in geometric order; the
absence of one would be instantly noticed. Her only recourse
must be her wits. She must accept that and go with the tide.

When Monsieur returned, he found her sitting in one of the
stuffed chairs, cup in hand, sipping wine. There was no hint

that she had taken several sustaining gulps before she heard him order George from the door. He was obviously pleased with himself.

"Women are resilient creatures. I don't see even one tear. Your lover was most upset. Struggled a bit, and we had to subdue him. I'm going to enjoy these next few hours." He looked straight into her eyes, watching for a reaction. When she gave none, he continued. "Ah yes, It is so seldom one can indulge fancies, get revenge, and relieve boredom all at the same time. Now, my dear, you're an actress. I'm in the mood for a bit of entertainment. Something from the classics, I think, then some music, some modern poetry, a light refreshment, and conversation. By that time I'll be feeling adventuresome and ready to see why Justin found you so alluring."

Tempest shuddered inwardly but dared give no hint of her feelings. Let him think he was winning over her; he might be in actual truth but there had to be some way out of this predicament. She murmured, "Yes, Monsieur."

"My name is Louis! You will address me by it."

"Yes, Louis."

"I know you're burning with anger. I can feel it. That will add all the more pleasure to our dealings because you're helpless." He burst into laughter that resounded like the trump of doom in Tempest's ears. "Begin! I do not like to be kept waiting."

He settled himself comfortably and watched her carefully. Tempest was reminded of Scherazade and all the tales of the *Arabian Nights*. Was it possible that this might be a way out? She rose and advanced to the center of the room, faced him, and began the same recitation from *The Furies* that she had done long ago in the drawing room of Cloud Ridge in Jamaica.

The face of her tormentor faded as she became the goddess Athena who struggled to reason with the recalcitrant Furies in order to turn them from blind destruction. All the fire and power latent in Tempest rose to the surface; it seemed to her that this one man represented evil in one of its worst manifestations. She stood in the brilliant light of the Greek land and for a time not only held it at bay, but won.

He brought his hands together in a series of short claps. For once, the smile was genuine. "Bravo. I do not miss the symbolism and I admire that you can express yourself so aptly through the medium of that play." He spoke a few sentences in the rolling, sonorous Greek she had once attempted to learn. "You see, I know the original. I'll not hold your display against you. But now the rest of your performance must be more decorous or I'm afraid your lover will suffer for it. Continue."

If he said "your lover" one more time in that deprecating tone of voice, Tempest thought she would scream. This was bad enough, but when he raped her, as he obviously intended to do—and with Justin present— how was that to be endured?

"Barbara Allen" and "Lord Randall" suited his fancy well, for he leaned back, eyes half-closed, and let one hand drift with the melody. Tempest recalled the times she had sung them in the Café Escorial. Would she live to see that place and the people who had given her a chance again?

"Now a bit of poetry. Really, this is most agreeable. Please, my dear, try to have a more pleasant expression on your face. I never did care for women who frowned a great deal. Smile."

She forced a half smile to her lips and kept it there as she recited as much as she could remember from "She Walks in Beauty." How she and Morna had delighted in the tormented, romantic poetry of, as they called him all in one roll of words, George Gordon Lord Byron, in their schoolgirl days of closeness! Now she had seen Morna die and possibly spoke her own epitaph.

There was a discreet knock on the door just then and Louis snapped out a command to enter. Two of the male slaves rolled in a cart and uncovered it so that he could examine the contents. The meal was for two; fish in a cream sauce, some vegetables cooked together in another sauce, fresh oranges, crusty bread, pecan pie, and some chocolates made a menu that might once have enticed Tempest but not at such a time.

"Eat before it grows cold. I'll take it amiss if you don't." He poured out wine for them, waved the slaves outside, and raised his fork. "The weather has not been good lately, has it? Most uncomfortable to get about." His eyebrows went up. "Have you no comment? Would you prefer to discuss the latest fashions? You have my permission to do so."

"I really have paid little attention to either." She loathed the sound of his name in her mouth and did not intend to utter it. "I have no comments to make on them."

"Pity. I find it hard to dine without conversation. I hate to be rude to a lady, especially one who very likely has a great deal to say on forbidden topics. I hope I don't bore you with talk of politics, but since you find yourself unable to chat, I'll indulge myself."

Tempest thought the rich food would choke her. She nodded at him and the corners of her mouth ached with the struggle to smile. "Please." Do anything other than torment Justin and herself!

"If I'd known the things in my youth that I know now, I would have been even more powerful. Did you know I can make my will known in any part of New Orleans and be obeyed? My influence reaches far, I can tell you. Much of this is based on slavery and an appreciation of how much the South lives by it. Those who seek to destroy that institution, as they do in Europe and England, will live to reap the losses, I can tell you." He went on and on until Tempest thought her very soul would sicken at his methods, selection, and work of those he considered to be lesser beings. "We'll rule our region down here and the government in Washington can keep its hands off. That's one thing Calhoun understands, although he has poor sense in choosing such people as your lover to work with. If you don't approve of a law, just nullify it within the state and give final powers to the states. Very sound doctrine."

Tempest nodded at times, but his self-important words passed over her. Soon enough the trial would arrive and she did not know how she would face it. This pretense was driving her mad, as he must have known it would. She was conscious of his sharp glances; he toyed with her and obtained the greatest pleasure from it. She ached to toss the contents of her plate in his face.

Abruptly, he rose and clapped his hands. The slaves came for the nearly untouched food and departed. He pointed to a wide couch in the far corner of the room. "Go over there and take off your clothes. Be slow about it."

The moment had come. Tempest tried to tell herself that he would not possess Tempest the woman, only the shell of her body, that her mind and heart were Justin's.

"You can't!" The protest burst from her involuntarily.

"Can't what? Say it!" He was goading, daring her to the

edge of the abyss. "Don't you know I'm capable of anything by now?"

Tempest did. The gates of hell were opening for her. The slaves entered with a bound and gagged man whose shirt was open at the back to show lash marks and whose face was caked with blood. Only his furious eyes were the same; they were those of a lion at bay.

"Put him where he can see everything, and bring the whip." Louis looked at Tempest. "What can't I do, Miss Mallory?"

As the slave hovered over Justin with the great black whip, Tempest opened the bodice of her gown.

44

Hand of Fire

Justin struggled against his bonds but could not budge them. The eyes of the man he had once trusted were savage on him and greedy on Tempest, who was now removing the skirt of her gown. The slave had been ordered to turn his back and await orders.

"Faster!" Louis was rubbing both hands together as he came close to Tempest. "You will handle me." He saw her revulsion, and the anger came over him again. In one rapid motion he ripped through camisole and petticoats so that she retained only the thin under one. His own clothes followed until he was naked before her. The only sound in the room was that of Justin's struggles.

"Take me in your hand or by God I'll have your lover beaten to a pulp!" As he spoke, Louis caught her by the arm and jerked her forward.

Tempest stared at the big, huskily built man whose shaft was small and limp. There was no sign of arousal. She put out her hand and withdrew it hastily.

"George!"

A muffled sound of pain went up and then Justin lay on the floor, blood oozing from a welt on his shoulder. The lash was

347

wet with it. The black man stood as he had before and Justin was placed so he could see all that went on.

Tempest took the flaccid member in her fingers and began enticing motions while Louis stood grinning before her. She dared not let him see the hate in her eyes or demeanor. She rubbed, tickled, pulled gently, but it remained as it was. He reached out and caught her wrist. "We'll lie down and you shall use that soft mouth to best advantage." He pulled her along and she had no choice but to go.

When they were near the couch, he touched a panel in the wall and drew out a black velvet box. He released her and opened it to show a long object made to the shape of a man's penis. "You'll like this, I promise you, and I expect you to show your delight."

"So that's why . . ." She gasped out the words, thinking that this nightmare of horror had no end. There were some instances in which death might truly be welcome.

"Yes. Impotent these many years. That's why I wanted that little bitch to get with child—the only hope of our line. Who cared what happened to her? Let her die in childbirth, only give me an heir. I couldn't remarry and risk anything becoming known. It was a miracle of persistence that I managed to get her mother pregnant and fortunate for her that she soon died. I do not take kindly to laughter. But I can feel pleasure and you shall give it to me. Do you know something else, Tempest Mallory? I have decided that the slaves may take their pleasure with you when I have finished. That will be a good joke on those who have you later, slave's leavings. Maybe a mulatto child! We can give you some fertility treatments; God knows I know enough about them!"

He lay down on the couch and motioned to her to come nearer. He pulled the rest of her clothes away in a savage gesture that appeared to give him as much excitement as the sudden nudity. "You are indeed lovely. It's a real pity such beauty must meet the end I've decreed." He gave a bark of laughter. "Get up here and take me in your mouth!"

Tempest did as he ordered, but suddenly the blind, unreasoning anger that had so often been her downfall took her. "Overbearing, murdering little swine! May the leprosy take you and devour flesh from the inside out! May you suffer the torments of the damned in the eternal reaches of hell for all you have done! May your soul wander in the outbacks of time! Curse you! Curse you forever!''

He rose up and slapped at her, but he was off balance and missed. "George! Hit him again and again and again!" The last word was repeated as though caught in his throat.

Tempest jumped up and back, meaning to run to Justin and shield him with her body, but before she could do so, he rolled at the legs of the black and sent him tumbling down. As George struggled to rise, the whip slipped out of his hand. Tempest dashed over and in an instant held it in her grip.

"Put that down, you little idiot! It'll be the worse for you!" Louis was moving toward her and urging George to take the other side. Justin was still fighting his bonds, the cords in his throat standing out as the sweat poured down his face.

"I curse your soul and so does Angelica! You may kill us here and now, but don't think you won't pay for it! Or don't you believe in retribution? Or the Furies themselves!" Anger and hate gave Tempest's arm superhuman strength as she lashed the whip toward Louis and split the side of his cheek to the bone. He clapped one hand against it and cursed as loudly as she had. She heard George coming up and whirled to lash at him. He backed away, but not before the tip came dangerously close to his eye and tore at the lid.

"Bitch! You'll die so slowly you'll be praying for the luxury of a death by beating!" Louis's eyes were standing out in the red suffusion of his face, and his lips were a thin lip of near purple.

Tempest moved nearer to Justin and kept slashing at them with the whip. It was strange that Louis did not summon assistance, she thought, but there was no time for speculation, only the battle for another few minutes of life. Her foot slipped, and she almost went down. In the second it took to recover herself, Louis was upon her and pulling at the only weapon she had.

His fingers were digging at her throat as they rolled on the floor. She heard tearing cloth and the sounds of a scuffle just beyond them and the steady flow of curses. The world spun before her eyes and she knew death was very close.

Then the pressure eased. Reality came into focus again and it was a dead weight on her body, a contorted, twisted face next to hers, and eyes rolled back so far that only the whites could be seen. She rolled over and pushed him from her.

"He is dead. Both of them are. And we still live." Justin, bloody and nearly naked, stood above her, hand extended.

She took it and rose. It was taking a few moments to understand just what had happened. One part was clear enough; Justin had broken his bonds and attacked the slave, who now lay crumpled, his head at an unnatural angle. But Louis? Monsieur?

"Apoplexy. Killed him instantly. Must have been prone to it. He had the look." Justin's words came in slow bursts. "God curse him."

"God curse him." She spoke the words, unable to believe the reality of their salvation.

Then she was in Justin's arms and they were clinging to each other in the midst of that place of carnage and death. Beyond the glory of life restored there hammered over and over in Tempest's head the memory of her curse, which might very well have begun the flame in Louis de Foix's head. And an older one came to her memory. "Mene, mene, tekel, upharsin." Belshazzar was dead, and his captives had a chance to live.

They kissed and there was nothing of passion in it for once in all their time together. This was thankfulness, renewal, and tenderness. Tempest knew that for her, he was life and strength, the core of her being. It was sufficient that she loved him with an all-encompassing love. For him she had come out of her being to enter into him, and for the rest of her life she would be the better for this. And she remained Tempest Mallory, inviolate as always. She wished Justin could know this feeling. Perhaps he might be less fearful of love.

"We have almost no chance of getting out of here. There're guards everywhere, along with Veris's group. I know the house a little. I was here twice. We're not all that far from the river road, although a rather good distance from New Orleans." Justin pulled up the remnants of his shirt and tucked it into his breeches. He saw her look of dismay and smiled. "The wounds are superficial. I just bled a lot."

She knew he was lying but could only applaud the effort that sought to save her worry. "We have to try, Justin. We simply cannot have come this far to lose at the end."

He took her hand and touched his lips to it. The golden eyes were tender with a warmth she had never seen before. "Yes, we must. If we can get to the garden room, we may have a slim chance. There are some glass panels that were put in unevenly and they have a tendency to pull away from the column. Of course that may have been remedied since I returned from Jamaica and came here to pay my respects, but I rather doubt it."

Tempest reached for the remains of the gown and drew it over her head. She tore part of the wide skirt loose and fastened it around her waist so that her feet would be free. She was as ready as she would ever be. "The slaves and guards must have known what he intended to do with us. They won't be mounting that much of a guard, do you think? He'll be having his pleasure, they believe, and won't want to be bothered, so they can have some relaxation."

"I imagine. He was very strict. We'll just have to slip out and hope." Justin began to pull off George's shirt and exclaimed with satisfaction as he held up a short dagger, then slipped it into his waistband. He rose and pulled the body over to the drapes. Monsieur's body was next. He closed them and pushed a chair close. Tempest brought a small table and placed a bottle within easy reach so that it might appear Monsieur had been sitting there contemplating the captives. Any small delaying tactic could save their lives. Tempest did the old trick of preparing the couch so that the casual glance would show a sleeper.

"If I am caught, you go on ahead."

Justin's quiet words stopped her where she stood. "You know I won't. Don't talk that way again. Together or not at all."

They stared into each other's eyes and the bond was formed all over again.

"Groan and toss about, Justin." Tempest went to listen at the door but could hear nothing. One eyebrow went up, but he did as he was bidden. She would remember Monsieur's laugh until she died; it was easy enough to release it now. Her throat shaped the sounds, and for a few dreadful moments it seemed that he lived again. "Maybe they'll be driven off by the idea of Monsieur enjoying himself."

Justin grimaced. Both listened at the door but it was so well made, nothing penetrated. There was no hope for any other course of action. Cautiously, he swung the door back a fraction of an inch and peered out. He watched for an eternity. Tempest felt her heart hammer and skip. Her hands and feet were cold. How could she move when the time came? Then Justin's hand beckoned; he opened the door wider, caught her fingers, and pulled. They slipped out into the hall and flattened themselves at one end of the huge old chest close to the library. The silence of the dead and mutilated hung over this once beautiful house.

Tempest knew if she lived she would never forget that agonizing journey back to the garden room; the fear of discovery was almost more than that of open battle. They had reason to be thankful that Monsieur's servants and slaves were trained to exact obedience, to come when called and otherwise remain out of sight. The twisted part of him had made his pleasure in cruelty a private one. It had also given them a faint possibility of survival.

They crouched behind furniture, slipped between wall hangings, moved into the open in short, desperate dashes, edged from one doorframe to another with the expectation of discovery at any instant. Once they heard far-off voices coupled with laughter and were forced to take shelter behind some filmy curtains lest those approaching should burst into this long, bare hallway. The curtains would not protect them if the guards stared directly into the folds. Fortunately, however, they went elsewhere and Tempest found her face wet with perspiration. Justin squeezed her hand hard, and she took comfort from the gesture.

At the entrance to the garden room, Tempest pantomimed to Justin that she would enter alone. She thought it reasonable for anyone there to think she had been released to rest and restore herself from the ravages of the master. He shook his head savagely, went ahead of her, and turned the knob, pushing the door open delicately.

Polly stood in front of them, an armload of bedclothes nearly obscuring her vision as she reached for the knob in her turn. Justin shoved her against the wall, his knife at her throat, making sure of her silence. Tempest ranged over the area to make sure no one was there, then returned to Polly, who was almost gray with terror as her eyes rolled from side to side.

"Be quiet and you might live another few minutes." Justin

snarled the words at her, and her legs began to buckle. "Who else is supposed to be coming in here? Is anyone expected?"

"No. Nobody. Please, don't. Don't hurt me." She was shivering more with each syllable. "Only Master come."

"Get some clothes for yourself, Tempest. I'll tie her up." Justin flicked one finger over the knife blade suggestively. It was too much for Polly. She collapsed in a faint.

Tempest giggled helplessly and Justin permitted himself a grin, which faded as he locked the door and began to rip the sheets apart to secure Polly. When she hunted in the depths of the closest chest for something simple to cover herself, Tempest felt more laughter beating inside her. She knew it could move into hysteria if she was not careful. Her fingers touched something hard and jerked away. That struck her as funny and she giggled again.

"What is it? Hang on, my love. One thing at a time." Justin spoke as calmly as though they were about to go strolling together.

"Money. Coins. Louis d'or." She swung the little cloth bag back and forth. Was she sounding like Polly? How funny! She shook with laughter.

Justin's hands bit into her shoulders and he pulled her into his embrace. The warm strength of him and his concern brought her back. She hugged him fiercely.

"I'm all right. It's just getting to be too much, and I'm afraid."

"So am I." He looked into her eyes and they drew courage from each other. "Now let's see about getting out of here."

He withdrew one of the coins and looked at the head imprinted on it and the freshness of the appearance. "Never used at all and probably issued about 1645. These'll help us if no one recognizes them for what they are. It's theft, of course."

Tempest wondered what theft mattered when you were in danger of being murdered and risked hanging for murder but all that was important was escape. She rummaged through the chests, chiffonier, and alcove, where some extra clothes hung, before finally scrambling into a rather skimpy brown gown and cloak that left her ankles bare.

"Come on!" Justin called to her from the garden, and after a hurried glance at the trussed Polly, who was still in her faint, she ran out. The glass had been set aside enough so they could struggle out. She smelled the rain-wet air and felt the welcome chill on her face. The forest of low trees and partial swamp loomed just beyond. "Hurry, Tempest, my God, hurry!"

"Wait!" Would she be able to recall where she had left Angelica's pages? She ran frantically from one plant to another, ignoring Justin's low calls. Every second was valuable. It could mean life or death. She had to go, but every instinct warned her to take them with her. Just when she was about to give up, her memory clicked and she went straight to the circular bush she now remembered clearly. Her fingers closed on the pages and she crammed them into her bodice.

In another minute she was through the glass and Justin was beside her, pushing it back as well as he could. When the inevitable pursuit began, it might take the form of a lengthy search through the house. Delay was life for them both.

He finished and turned to her. Their hands met, clung, and then they were running through the rain into the sweet air of freedom and life regained.

45

Alpha and Omega

The sun sparkled down through the moss-hung trees and glinted off the red mass of Tempest's hair. She breathed in the fresh morning air hungrily as she pulled the cloak more tightly about her shoulders. "Isn't it a real risk to hail the steamer? Especially since we don't have any luggage? Justin, I'd rather just go on the way we are. We'll get to a town or a place where we can buy some horses; that would be much safer. This is asking for trouble!"

He ignored her and continued to wave the long pole to which the pieces of his shirt were attached. The broad Mississippi rolled smoothly to the horizon and the oncoming white ship breasted it easily. She gave a short toot and began to slow as Justin waved all the more eagerly.

"This is insane! We can find a little town, stay there for a while until the hunt dies down. Justin, please."

"No, Tempest. This is the way it has to be. Please bear with me." He looked at her, an enigmatic gaze in the golden eyes. "This has to be played out. Follow my lead. Will you do that? You'll be on your own soon enough, I promise it."

Struck dumb by his implication, she could only stare at him. The beauty of the morning and the deliciousness of freedom were suddenly chilled. He meant to leave her, of course. How could she have doubted it? He had his summons to Calhoun and that would shield him if he wished it. Oh, he might see her to a northern city, but that was all. She had her pride and could bear anything. Now she wanted to retain freedom. Think about that; don't think about losing Justin and never seeing him again. Even the comradely way he had treated her during the afternoon and night of their flight from Monsieur's house was better than the alternative.

Her head went up and her look challenged him. "As you will have it."

"Good." He did not appear to notice her concern as he waved again at the steamer, which tooted again. "She's coming to. They're putting a boat off. Now let me do the talking."

"Gladly." Her tone was sharp.

After their departure from captivity, Tempest and Justin had nearly exhausted themselves in the pressing need to put as much distance as possible between pursuers and pursued. They had crashed through the swamp, gone over ground soggy with the recent rains, fought through dense undergrowth, run on half-cleared paths, and forded swollen streams, moving always upriver and away from New Orleans. They had managed a few hours of sleep and that had been sporadic at best. Tempest had expected tenderness, a closeness, some sharing due to all they had endured, and had been ready to pour out her own warmth, but Justin was preoccupied, though friendly enough in a brusque way. Once again, she knew she must be ready to walk alone and not give way before that understanding.

"We're lucky that this is a relatively accessible bend of the river." Justin waved at the wide spit of sand on which they stood and the wooded banks behind. "The smaller steamers will pick up a few people more than the larger ones, which only stop at certain places. I used to know this country very well. It's coming back to me."

"Better it hadn't." Tempest snapped the words out, and his face clouded momentarily before he returned the boatmen's hail.

Several minutes later, the small boat touched the bank and one of the men jumped out to help Tempest in. The other eyed them with a grin. "No luggage? Travelin' mighty light, wouldn't you say?" Tempest saw themselves through their gaze, unkempt and in old clothes, the stamp of haste clearly on them, and thought she might get her wish to remain on land. Surely steamers were selective of the passengers they picked up? She saw Justin set his jaw. The wind ruffled his tawny hair as he bent confidentially toward the man who had spoken. The steamer revolved her wheels against the strong river current and steam rushed noisily from the pipes. She shook her head. She had not heard what Justin said. He couldn't be doing this.

He said it again. "I have to speak to the captain on a matter of great urgency. You could say it is life or death. Take us on board." His fingers twitched on the knife at his belt. "It is urgent!"

The men grinned and shrugged. One said, "No telling what Cap'n will have to say, but come ahead!"

Justin scrambled in and sank down by Tempest. The look he gave her was inscrutable. She felt as though he were a stranger and, inexplicably, wanted to weep for very loss as she had not done even in the days of their worst perils. Then the boat lurched forward and was at the steamer before she could frame even one remark for Justin.

As soon as they touched the deck proper, a boatman dressed in casual white breeches and shirt came up to them. He gave Tempest a curious look as Justin repeated his request to see the captain and added, "The lady is weary, all our belongings have been lost, and we have only what we stand up in. Is there a vacant state-room she might use and a clean gown of any sort? Our circumstances are dire, as you can see." His manner was lordly.

"I don't want any special treatment. I am very well as I am." It was not true. She wanted to wash her face, weep, throw something at Justin for putting them in danger this way.

Justin said, "You see, she's exhausted."

The man looked as if he wished to ask for money and did not dare. Justin's eyebrow went up and his eyes were impaling. Better men than a boatman had gone down before that gaze. "Yes, sir. We are not very filled for this trip. We go only to Memphis, you know. There are several vacant state-rooms, and I am sure something in the way of a change can be found for the lady. A difficult bend of the river is coming up, but I will conduct you to the captain in a few moments."

"Attend to it, please." Justin strode toward the front of the steamer, ignoring the few gaping passengers, seemingly as at home here as he might have been on the promenade of New Orleans.

Tempest was taken below and shown into a velvet-hung room so well furnished she might have thought herself in an elegant house. Before she could recover from that surprise, a young black girl who might have been fourteen rushed in with warm water, soft towels, toilet articles, two gowns, and a shawl. She stared at Tempest in fascination and backed toward the door.

"The mister say hurry and come up! He look mad! These fit, maybe. We borrow. Hurry!" She dashed out.

She could not suppress a grin. Justin was being fierce, was he? He was going to tell her what was happening whether he wished to or not; she had no intention of allowing herself to be shunted into the background.

The water was heavenly, but Tempest was not disposed to linger. She was clean in minutes and her hair was combed to silkiness once more. One of the gowns was enormous and its petticoat would go around her twice. The other was too short, pale green, trimmed with several darker shades, and showed signs of wear. She silently thanked whatever generous passenger had loaned it as she wondered how she looked. The bodice was low and her breasts showed full. Her waist was slim; green was one of her better colors; it highlighted the honey shade of her skin. She pushed her hair back with a swift gesture. Their lives were in danger and here she loitered, thinking of her looks!

She went into the corridor and up on deck. Little clumps of passengers stood chatting; they paused to stare as she went by. Whose gown was she wearing? Why did they seem fascinated by her? She glimpsed Justin, now wearing white breeches and a shirt which looked suspiciously like those of the boatman who had greeted them, as he stood apart, obviously waiting for someone. The captain was taking his time.

"You wanted me to hurry?" She kept her tone cool. He must not know how lost she felt inside at the cool, preoccupied manner he had exhibited since their departure from Monsieur's plantation.

"Yes, I felt we should speak to the captain together. I have made some decisions." His voice was level, considerate, devoid of interest in her feelings or opinions. She kept her chin high as he spoke. "The louis d'or horde will buy safety for a time and can outfit us both. This boat stops at Natchez, where I have friends who can help me make overland arrangements to get to Charleston in ample time for my meeting with the Vice-President. Later, I know he will help settle matters in New Orleans quietly, so that it will not become public knowledge as to what Monsieur was and Angelica's name will be spared. I do not plan to go back there for some time, at any rate. I owe, and will owe, Calhoun much and have given him my allegiance, especially in the matter of Jamaica for the South as a slave state, but I will soon have to go my own way." His gaze locked on hers. "No longer the friend of the Vice-President or the holder of estates in various stages of disrepair, nor yet the hopeful stateman, but a man, perhaps a physician in or about Charleston. No prospects, just a man who has endured much." His voice rose to a curious intensity. "And a man for the union of this country, against whatever or whomsoever would try to break it apart. I have learned. Ah, I have learned."

Tempest noticed that his description of future plans did not include her. Very well, she intended to claim some of the gold as her fair share. Had she not fought for it as well as he? She said, "I only hope Monsieur's men don't catch us before we arrive in Natchez. Do you think your friends will be inclined to give me some assistance as well? I should prefer not to remain on this steamer; I still think it was unwise to catch it." She was justly proud of her voice, which matched his own for calm.

"Those men, certainly Veris, are a pack of brigands, for sale to the highest bidder. Monsieur planted those jewels in my clothes so he could have a motive for my death and blame us both for Angelica's. They'll be fighting over that horde until some are killed. I know the type. By the way, keep those pages from her diary safe. I'll consult attorneys in Charleston about the matter of clearing us. You need not worry." Justin looked past her at the broad river lined with heavy woods on either side. Its brown waves shimmered in the sun and the curves ahead seemed to fade into infinity. He grew reflective. "No, Tempest, in spite of everything, I believe the future to be bright. I must do what I have to do; you will understand that."

"Of course, Justin. Have I not always understood?" The familiar fury at his obduracy was near to strangling her. "And

perhaps you will try to understand me for a change! You have
wasted part of your life clinging to a vision of what was past—
that old passion and what it cost you, the dream of a great name
and wealth in this world, you think is now but it remains
simply another version of the past. Be what you want! Have
done with what others think! I shall! My name shall be
foremost in the theaters and my ambition will be satisfied. Be
well assured I have no idea of remembering the past! Any
past!" She halted for breath, aware that her eyes were flashing
and her bosom heaving. Her voice had risen so the few
passengers close to them could hear every word. During the
tirade, a tall white-haired man in late middle age had come to
stand close to Justin. He wore a dark suit and a white hat was
tilted back. There was an air of authority about him belied by
the amusement in his pale blue eyes.

"Will you both come with me?" He had no doubt about their
obedience as he led them forward into a simple whitewashed
room that had a certain elegance about it. A lady and
gentleman of his own age stood looking out one of the
windows as they entered. "I am, as you know, Captain
Abransom. Mr. and Mrs. Revels have kindly consented to be
witnesses. But I expect you will be wanting a few moments to
yourselves before we begin?" The question hung delicately in
the air while the couple nodded and turned back to contemplation of the river.

Justin stared at Tempest with such intensity that she felt the
blood rise to her cheeks. The pulse in his temple was pounding
as he twisted the fingers of one hand together. They might have
been alone, so powerfully did the pulse beat between them.
She suddenly saw need blaze naked in his eyes as all barriers
went down.

"Justin. What is this?" Her tongue was lead in her mouth.
She knew her heart, mind, flesh, and soul were giving way
with the intensity of emotion that was always theirs whether
they wished it or not.

"I was so confident. I made the plans, and now I fear your
answer." His voice shook.

She looked at him, the power of his body, the golden eyes
and tumbled tawny hair, saw through to the idealistic, half-
cynical, always honorable truth of him, and knew that she
would do anything, everything, so long as she might remain

with him. In the moment of that giving, she said, "Let me be with you, Justin, in whatever way you will have me." Proud Tempest Mallory let the world and ambition go for love and in so doing realized her own truth.

"Does that mean you'll have me?" He moved closer to her.

"Yes. In any way." Tears misted her eyes so that she did not see clearly the joy in his.

"There is no other way, my love. Tell me slowly. Tell me that you will marry here, this minute, before these witnesses."

She was stunned. She knew she dreamed. "I don't understand."

He caught her arms. "Will you marry me? Is that so hard to comprehend? I dared to think you would and so I made the arrangements with the captain, whom I have had the honor to meet in the past. He knows of our circumstances and will wed us by virtue of his authority. That is, if you will!"

"Is that why you were speaking with such finality out there just then? Justin, I thought . . ." She could not go on.

His control broke. "Infuriating woman! How long do you think it took me to get up the courage to ask you, and then you hold me off. I thought it might be better if I just presented you with the situation. Tempest, I love you and I think I have for a long time. Please answer me." He pulled her close and looked down into her face.

She put both arms around his neck and spoke with all the passion and love in her. "I will, Justin. I love you. There could be no other man for me, ever. I love you and will be proud to be your wife."

He kissed her then, and as the familiar sweetness rose, Tempest was conscious of a lady sobbing quietly in the corner. The men were clearing their throats and murmuring. She would not have cared if the entire passenger group watched. From bitter unhappiness, death, loss, and resignation as well as abnegation of self had come the glorious delight of this time. The man she loved and had loved for so long now loved her in return.

He said, "When we have come to Charleston, my love, and if it pleases you, we will marry again in the church of the Huguenots there. You are right about the past, but I would like to do that in its memory."

She smiled. "Anything, Justin."

"And the other? All that I said about the future? Can you know what I mean? Dare I ask you to live such a life?" The golden gaze seemed to burn her. "Be an actress, use the talent that is your gift of God. I will help you all I can, but I cannot serve a cause of division as I have in the past."

"I would not ask it." She, too, could be firm. It was no time for conversation. She pulled his face to hers and kissed him passionately. His arms tightened around her and the world faded in the beauty of love born anew.

A few minutes later Tempest Mallory and Justin Trevian were united in marriage by the captain, who spoke the sacred words while the sunlight gilded the lovers and the Mississippi flowed to the sea.

After a visit to Jamaica, **Anne Carsley** decided to combine her love of the tropical island with her knowledge of the South to produce the backdrop for TEMPEST, her sixth historical romance. Although a veteran traveler, Anne's favorite place to be is home in her native Jackson, Mississippi, with her big, fluffy dog, Isis.